Light and Darkness

Wendy Lawrance

First Published in 2013
by GWL Publishing
an imprint of Great War Literature Publishing LLP

Produced in United Kingdom

ISBN 978-1905378470 (1905378475) Paperback Edition

GWL Publishing
Forum House
Sterling Road
Chichester PO19 7DN
www.gwlpublishing.co.uk

Wendy was born and grew up in Surrey, attending school in Esher, where she developed an early interest in English Literature, especially that of the First World War. After twenty years running her own business in the graphic design industry, Wendy decided to fulfil her life's ambition and become a writer, she has now been doing professionally for over ten years, becoming a recognised academic authority on First World War Literature. Wendy lives near the beautiful West Sussex coast with her husband, grown-up daughter and teenage son.

For the men who came back damaged
and the friends they left behind.

Acknowledgements

Thank you to Dominic Ford for reading the first drafts, so many years ago and giving me honest feedback and encouragement.

A really big thank you to Claire Edge for reading through the final draft, giving me a "reader's" reaction and the most helpful comments I could have received. Claire - I owe you more than you'll know... and the 'honour' was mine entirely.

Thank you to The Script, who have provided the soundtrack to my story and my late nights.

A special thank you to my wonderful children, C & C, for their patience, and for putting up with my lengthy silences. I love you both.

My greatest and most heartfelt thanks go to my husband, Steve, without whom I would never have had the confidence to begin writing at all - in any capacity. He has accommodated me and my obsession with characteristic tolerance and understanding. He is my love, my inspiration and the light in my darkness.

Finally, I want to thank my dad simply for being my dad. He was a truly remarkable and very special man and it was losing him that motivated me to finally finish writing this story. I miss him and think of him every single day.

Prologue

New dead; old dead. What did it matter any more? Franz Werner swore under his breath, wading through the deep decaying mud, which bled through his tattered boots and thick socks. Either way, he thought, everyone dies. Either way, we just keep fighting over the same saturated ground, year in, year out. Forever.

Advancing across No Man's Land in the third wave of the advance, checking here and there for wounded men who could still be helped, there was no longer any need to duck into shell-holes, dodge bullets or avoid artillery. The British had retreated fast, at least for now. In this unusual safety, out of his gloomy worm hole, Franz was able to reflect upon his surroundings. Stakes that had once been trees, stood like signposts to hell. Earth pitted and cratered; wire like brambles caught with shredded cloth. Bodies scattered: some khaki, some grey, all muddy, bloody, dismembered, decomposing. Dead. Even the living were dead in this place.

A deep shell-hole lay ahead, a watery grave, stagnant with putrefying corpses. Skirting the outer lip of this gash in the earth, Franz glanced up to the sky, where the speck of an aeroplane slid across the clear blue. He stumbled. Two bodies lay at his feet; two more in this cauldron of death. Both were officers, their uniforms English; their fingers entwined. One, on his front; head turned to one side; blond hair caked, matted with blood, now beginning to dry and darken at the edges. A second wound in the centre of his back. Franz crouched: cold blue eyes stared vacantly back; beneath them, a hollow where the mouth should have been; a jaw torn open; teeth visible, a tongue protruding unnaturally through the side of the breach. The tear stretched down towards the man's throat, pulpy flesh and sinew mingled with wet brown sludge, where his body had fallen forward, untimely, into the mud.

His curiosity roused by these two dead friends, Franz turned his attention to the other man. Face up; much taller and older than his comrade. Dark hair, an angular jaw, a striking, undamaged face; his eyes closed. Beneath his legs, thick red fluid had seeped into the mud. Standing, moving around, Franz saw the shot through the side of his knee. A clean wound, if anything could be called "clean" in this disgusting place. The man's right arm rested by his side, his hand half buried in the dirt. Lifting it, Franz found a less clean wound, three fingers, now hanging on torn fibres like rent cloth. Franz sighed: loss of blood and shock must account for this wasted life.

Standing again, Franz sighed, unsure why the sight of these two bodies should affect him more than all the others; more than the dead of previous battles. He had seen many such injuries before and an abundance that were much worse. Perhaps it was the fingers enlaced in dying friendship: an image he knew would haunt him. He noticed that his men had moved on. Taking one last look at the two English officers, now just names on a casualty list, Franz stepped forward.

Part One

Chapter One

February 1912

It was dull and overcast. The grey sky hung heavy, a fine drizzle clouding the sombre graveyard. Heads bowed, the dark mourners gathered around the hollow as the black coffin was lowered. Earth was scattered; prayers said; tears dried. Slowly, they all withdrew, and Harry was left alone, staring down, unwilling to leave. Eventually, he too turned, retreating to the waiting carriage. Not even aware of the cold, he shivered, his blind stare freezing on the window pane, as he was driven home without her.

The fire was well alight in the sitting room where Susan, Harry's maid, had laid a light tea on the oak sideboard. With her help, Harry's mother, Margaret took charge, passing bone china cups and neatly sliced sandwiches to the subdued visitors. Knowing it was the right thing to do, Harry stood in a corner of the room, near to the window, speechless but nodding politely to kindly meant comments:

"Lovely girl, such a shame."

"She was so beautiful. And so young."

"Anything we can do, you only have to ask."

"I'm so sorry, dear boy."

As the afternoon progressed, they departed in a steady stream, until just Harry and his parents were left. They offered concern, assistance, comfort. Deaf to everything, Harry sat in his usual chair by the fireplace, elbows on his knees, chin resting on his upturned hands, staring into the bright orange flames.

"We'll come around tomorrow, shall we? Or would you like to come to us? Perhaps for lunch?" Margaret suggested.

"Fine." Harry's voice was distant, his mind elsewhere.

Richard looked at his wife, shaking his head and nodding towards the door. They both stood, crossing the room. Margaret bent, kissing the top of Harry's dark head, while Richard placed a hand on his son's shoulder. Harry didn't move, or acknowledge their departure.

A welcome peace finally descended and Harry left the sitting room, removed his black jacket and deposited it across a spindle-backed chair in the hallway. In his shirtsleeves and waistcoat, he climbed the steep wooden stairs. He walked to the third door on the left side of the landing, which stood ajar, revealing a narrow chink of yellow light. Pushing this open, Harry found Susan who was sitting in a rocking chair, cradling a bundled infant. He stood for a moment, watching them both, imagining the scene as it should have been.

Imagining Bella holding their baby in her arms; her bewitching face raised to his; their eyes locked in mutual happiness.

"She's just been fed, sir," Susan said, breaking his trance. "The nurse has gone to her room for a while. Would you like to take her?" Harry had barely held his daughter since her birth: since the instant of Bella's death. He looked down at the swaddled babe and nodded, knowing the time was right. Susan stood, so that Harry could sit in her place, his large frame filling the chair. She bent down and passed the infant to him, her tiny head rested gently in the crook of his elbow. Susan crossed the room, glanced back briefly and closed the door behind her.

Alone with his daughter, Harry gazed down at her. Her eyes were closed, her skin so perfect and unblemished. A tiny hand poked above the top of the blanket in which she'd been wrapped. He could discern nothing familiar in her face: no reflection of himself; no image of Bella, except the shock of auburn hair. He leant back into the chair, rocking, closed his eyes and pictured Bella's tawny curls glinting in the summer sun, just as they had that fine August morning only eighteen months ago.

****

Harry had been called upon to visit Downwillow Farm, home of the King family. Thomas King had recently died and his son, William, needed assistance with some complicated family papers. As the senior partner, Harry's father, Richard Belmont, should have attended, but at the time he had been too unwell, so had sent Harry in his place. It was on Harry's second visit, that warm August morning, that he had caught sight of two young women in the garden. One was cutting roses and handing the long thin stems to her companion, who was following behind. William was sorting through his massive and untidy desk, searching for some title deeds, so Harry had wandered over to the window. This was ostensibly to give William some privacy, but really he had wanted to get a better view of the women. The taller of the two, her back to Harry, wore a long pale blue, flowing dress, which clung to her trim waist, showing off her slender figure. Her rich chestnut hair, gathered at the back of her head, shone brightly in the summer sunshine. The other woman was much shorter with full, rounded hips, covered by a simple yellow skirt, which swayed as she twisted and turned, struggling to retain a hold on the long rose stems gathered in her arms. She didn't seem to have noticed, as Harry had done when she'd bent to retrieve a dropped bloom, that the second button on her pretty floral blouse had come undone, revealing a small diamond of white flesh.

The taller woman turned, moving towards the house. As she climbed the terrace steps, approaching the window where Harry was standing, he observed a pair of large emerald-green eyes framed in a long, pale and utterly exquisite face. Seeing her for the first time Harry was transfixed. Never before had he seen such beauty. For a moment, he felt as though nothing in the world existed except the two of them although, as yet, she hadn't even noticed him. She was looking for more blooms and talking animatedly to her companion, who scurried up the path behind her, waving eagerly in Harry's direction. He was about to wave back, when he realised that William was standing by his side.

"I do hope you've been admiring my sister, rather than my wife!" he joked, waving and blowing a kiss to Charlotte, his bride of two months.

In returning her husband's gesture, she only narrowly avoided tripping up the steps onto the terrace and spilled the blossoms onto the ground.

"Oh! Sorry. Yes, of course," blustered Harry, his angular face now suffused with a deep blush that reached to the very roots of his dark brown hair. "Your sister. She's so beautiful. I've never seen anyone so…" He stopped, embarrassed. Lowering his head and turning back into the room, Harry crossed to William's desk and began gathering his papers, attempting to restore some professionalism to the situation. He cleared his throat.

"I'll get all the paperwork drafted and sent back for your approval by the end of the week, Mr King." Harry tried to sound businesslike and efficient, fumbling with his briefcase.

"Call me William. There's no need to stand on ceremony with me."

"I'm not sure my father would approve."

"Yes, but your father's not here. And he's not doing all this work for me, or drafting my new will. You are. So call me William, or Bill, if you prefer. I insist."

"Very well." Harry was relieved that he'd finally fastened his unwilling briefcase and could leave. He towered over William, who stood by the open study door looking uncomfortable in a tweed jacket which stretched across his ample figure. As Harry passed through, William reached up, patting his shoulder.

"Annabelle," he said. "Her name's Annabelle."

The relationship between William and Harry had changed after that meeting. Any stiffness which might ordinarily have existed between a young solicitor and his client was now banished, and they quickly became friends. Almost the same age, they were nonetheless relative strangers. Harry had boarded at a school over a hundred and fifty miles away. A popular, sporting boy, he had then gone straight on to university at Oxford from where he had returned a quiet, thoughtful, frustrated young man of twenty-one, with a rather disappointing law degree. Six years of working in his father's practice had changed nothing, except his desire to leave the village and paint. William, in the meantime, had grown into a kind and level-headed farmer, who, even before his father's death, ran the estate almost single-handed, but was happiest out in the fields working with the men, rather than behind a desk, drowning in necessary paperwork.

Harry had been introduced to Annabelle at a family dinner, a few weeks after first seeing her. William also showed off his wife and Harry met his youngest sister, Katherine, but their presence was, in truth, an irrelevance to him. Annabelle had looked, quite simply, radiant. The candlelight in the large dining room had made her hair shine in rich tones of russet and caramel, like the leaves in Downley Woods at the height of autumn. Stray loose curls framed her well-defined face, with its high cheekbones, porcelain smooth skin and rosebud pink lips. Her eyes sparkled a brilliant bright green. From the moment William had introduced her, Harry had been entranced. At dinner as he and Annabelle sat together, she was reserved in her manner, speaking little, but listening intently. Occasionally, he managed to coax responses from her, but she kept her head lowered, her voice a mere whisper.

Over the coming weeks, as the long, warm summer turned to autumn, Harry had become a regular visitor at Downwillow Farm. He and Annabelle enjoyed each other's company. Six years his junior, she was initially diffident, but as the weeks progressed, her confidence grew in his company. She forgot her usual insecurities and became more involved in their conversations. She found Harry interesting to talk to and was fascinated by his plans for the future. He had explained to her that, when he turned thirty and inherited his grandfather's money, he intended to leave his father's practice and take up painting. Harry was pleased and relieved that, unlike many of the local girls, Annabelle didn't fawn over his good looks. His tall, broad figure, strong jaw-line, deep brown eyes and lop-sided grin were not wasted on her, of course, but she didn't sit and stare at him like the village girls. In his own mind, Harry had known that his heart belonged to her from the moment they'd met; he'd loved her so much and he'd wanted her more than he'd ever wanted anything in his life. By early December, he'd decided to propose marriage, but feeling unworthy of her beauty, and anticipating rejection, it had taken him until Christmas Eve to pluck up the courage to ask.

Despite his doubts, Annabelle had accepted him, delight bathing her beautiful face. As he'd departed later that evening, William's consent gained, he'd taken her hands in his and asked permission to kiss her. This embrace, although chaste and brief, had filled his already brimming heart.

They had married just over three months later, in late March 1911, on a warm, sunny spring morning, at the small village church. Annabelle, breathtaking in her white gown, had walked down the aisle with William by her side, her eyes lowered, looking up at Harry only at the last moment. Vows spoken, Harry had taken her arm. She was his. After a brief lunch, they had left together for the station. For their honeymoon, he had considered Paris or Rome, but eventually, had decided to take Bella – as he had come to call her – to his cottage, Watersmeet, on the South Cornish coast. Watersmeet had belonged to his parents for as long as Harry could remember, but they had gifted it to him on his twenty-fifth birthday and, over the last few years, he had made it his own, re-decorating the rooms in plain white, to show off his paintings which covered almost every inch of wall. It was here that he'd spent many a happy childhood holiday, drawing, painting and learning to swim under the guidance of his attentive father. Then, in recent years, the cottage, the coves and especially the cliff tops had become the only places where Harry really felt he could breathe properly, away from the confines of village life and office tedium. Arriving late on their wedding night, Harry and Bella had dined on a sumptuous picnic, including a bottle of champagne, all packed for them by Susan. Then, a little later, they had made love by candlelight. Although twenty-eight, Harry was still inexperienced and nervous; Bella was tense and fearful. She took some encouragement, but he was gentle in both actions and words. Bella had cried with pain, but he had held her in his arms comforting her, and afterwards, he had cradled her as they fell asleep together.

Bella had loved Watersmeet nearly as much as Harry, and was delighted by his ambition to make this a permanent home where they could live together and he could paint. They had spent two idyllic weeks there, walking on the beach and along the cliff tops, sitting by the fire in the evenings, talking about the future and all the things they would do together.

At the end of their honeymoon, they had been reluctant to return to Sussex, to their normal lives among friends and family, but return they did. Holly Cottage, the pretty thatched house which Harry had bought, stood on what passed for the main road through the village. Harry had spent months decorating it and enjoyed Bella's delight and surprise when he'd shown her around for the first time, two days before their wedding. They had lived there happily with Susan, a girl from the village, attending to their needs. Bella enjoyed the garden, growing flowers and herbs in the neat borders. It had to be said that theirs was not a passionate marriage, but they were both happy and Harry had felt more contented and comfortable in Bella's company than with any other person he'd known. Speech was often unnecessary between them. He enjoyed her very presence and longed to come home to her at the end of every day.

Nearly three months after their wedding, Harry had returned from the office early in the evening, the summer sun shining through into the sitting room. Bella had turned her radiant face to greet him as he entered, bidding him to sit by her side. Her news, when it came, brought him quickly back to his feet. He'd lifted her from the sofa and spun her around in his arms, kissing her.

"Careful!" Bella had admonished, laughing. "You'll knock everything flying."

"When?" he asked, returning her to the sofa and kneeling at her feet. "When will he be born?"

"After Christmas. Late January or early February, the doctor thinks. And he might be a she." How could such happiness be possible?

Bella's health had not been good during her pregnancy and she had spent much of it confined to bed. Harry took diligent care of her, returning from the office early every day to be with her, read to her and sit with her until she fell asleep. He had reluctantly moved into the spare bedroom during her fifth month. On the doctor's advice, a nurse was called in to help during the day and Harry was on hand at night, should the need arise.

Just over a week ago, on a bitter cold late January morning, with hoarfrost still settled on the hedgerows and grass, the nurse had summoned the doctor to the cottage. Harry, excited but apprehensive, had been instructed to wait downstairs, while the nurse and Doctor Price went upstairs. The bedroom door was closed to him. Hours passed. Harry sat in his chair at the fireside, his stomach churning, his mind racing. Susan brought him cups of tea and every so often, he would stride to the bottom of the stairs, thinking that perhaps he'd heard a noise; a whimper; a cry. Then all would go quiet again. It was late afternoon before he'd heard heavy footsteps on the landing. Harry had met Doctor Price on the stairs.

"Let's go down, son," the doctor said, motioning to the sitting room.

"But I want to see them," Harry pleaded.

"I need to talk to you first, Harry. Come and sit."

Reluctant, Harry did as he was told, and the doctor stood with his back to the fireplace, hands in his jacket pockets.

"Harry," he said quietly. "You have a lovely, healthy baby daughter."

"A girl!" Harry smiled, his voice little more than a whisper. "Bella always wanted a girl." He paused, sensing there was something that the doctor had left unsaid. "What is it?" he asked.

"It's Annabelle." The doctor's face was pale and serious. "I'm sorry," he continued. "We did everything we could. She just wasn't strong enough."

"What do you mean?"

"I'm sorry, Harry, truly I am. Annabelle is dead."

There was nothing. Nothing but blackness. There were other words, probably. There must have been. People arrived. Harry couldn't remember who. He heard different voices. He thought his parents must have been there; perhaps William and Charlotte as well, maybe Katherine? Someone gave him tea. He couldn't recall drinking it.

Outside darkness fell. Food was offered and rejected. Much later, his mother urged him to go to bed. He needed to rest, she said.

The next day, sleepless, he had gone into Bella's bedroom; their room until four months ago. It was empty. She'd gone. The room, decorated with pink and yellow roses, pink and white curtains and white embroidered bedding, had been cleaned and cleared. It looked so normal, so perfect. The whole place smelled of her. He had lain down on the bed and, burying his face in the pillow, he had wept. He'd stayed in the room all day. No-one had disturbed him. He'd heard voices downstairs, but no-one came into the bedroom. He'd sat at her dressing table, touching the brushes, the silver-backed hand-mirror, the pots of powder and creams. He'd smelled her perfume, breathing her in. Looking at his reflection in the mirror, he'd seen an older version of himself; unshaven, eyes red and swollen. He'd heard the baby cry. He'd felt nothing.

****

Opening his eyes, Harry looked down at the bundle, cradled in his arms. The baby was still asleep. Nearly three hours had passed and Susan had come back.

"Why don't you go to bed now, sir?" she asked. "The little one will want feeding again soon." Harry allowed his daughter to be taken from him. Standing, he left and returned to the sitting room. The fire had almost died out and it was starting to feel chilly. He sat for a while. The day had been too horrible to think about, and yet he couldn't help it. An image of the black coffin containing his young, beautiful wife filled his mind. He felt so helpless. He'd always supported her, comforted her, protected her. Now she was buried in the ground and there was nothing he could do for her. They'd had so little time. Harry got up and walked mechanically to the sideboard, on top of which stood a cut-glass decanter full of single malt whisky. He helped himself. After his second glass, he decided to take the decanter back to his chair, rather than to keep getting up. It was easier. The peaty, sweet-tasting liquid filled him with a familiar warmth, although with every mouthful, as his head became lighter, his heart turned more numb.

Early the next morning, when Susan came in to open the curtains and clean out the fireplace, she found her master slumped in the chair in his shirt sleeves, his waistcoat undone, tie nowhere to be seen. A glass was overturned on the floor, where it had fallen from his hand, which hung limp over the arm of the chair. The decanter by his side was now more than half empty, yet Susan was sure that she had filled it up only the day before the funeral. She wondered what she should do. Mr Belmont's mother had said she might call round this morning and if she found him like this, she would be bound to make a fuss. There was nothing else for it, she'd have to wake him, although she knew he wouldn't thank her.

"Sir?" she called, gently shaking his forearm. He didn't respond at all. She raised her voice and tried again. "Sir?" This time, she shook his arm with a little more vigour. He turned his head towards her and half opened one eye, before quickly closing it again. A few seconds passed before he tried again, with more success this time. Both eyes open, he licked his lips, which were sandy dry, as was his tongue, now feeling far too large to fit back into his mouth.

Susan left him for a few minutes, while she went to kitchen and made him a fresh, strong cup of coffee. By the time she came back, Harry was sitting up a little more, holding his head in his hands, his fingers spread through his dark hair.

"Here you are, sir," she said, handing him the steaming cup.

"Thank you, Susan."

"If you don't mind me saying so, sir. I think you'd best go and have a wash, and change into some fresh clothes. Your mother may be calling this morning."

"Oh. Did she say she might? I'd forgotten. I'll go upstairs." Harry stood, his head spinning. "Thank you."

Up in his room, Harry filled the basin with cold water and surrendered his face to it. Feeling the chill brought him back to his senses. He looked at himself in the mirror, drips of water falling from his nose and chin. Bloodshot eyes stared back and he knew that never again could he allow himself to give in like that. If he did, there would be no way back.

Once washed, shaved and changed, Harry returned to the now tidy sitting room and removed the decanter. In the kitchen, he stood and poured the contents down the sink, before leaving the empty decanter on the table. Susan, who had entered the room just as he was completing his task, watched him in silence.

"If you wouldn't mind washing that, and putting it away somewhere, please Susan?" Harry said, passing her on his way back to the hall.

It was late morning before Margaret Belmont arrived, alone.

"How are you, Harry?" she asked, removing her hat and coat.

"I'm fine, Mother." Harry lied. He kissed her soft cheek and showed her into the sitting room. They sat together in silence for a few minutes.

"Are you going to come to lunch today? Your father's at work, but I thought I could help get the baby ready and take you both back with me, if you like? We could spend the afternoon together."

"I don't know."

"It will do you good to get out. You haven't left the house since it happened, other than yesterday." Harry knew that if he agreed to go out, he'd only have to come back to the cottage afterwards and face the emptiness all over again.

"I don't feel much like going out at the moment," he said.

"I know, dear. Perhaps I could stay here for lunch, then?"

"If you like." His voice was non-committal. Margaret sighed, changing the subject.

"Have you thought about a name yet, Harry? We can't keep calling her 'the baby' for much longer. Perhaps we could sit together and come up with some ideas?"

"I've already decided," Harry replied. "I'm going to call her Rose."

"That's a lovely name, dear. Was that something Bella wanted?"

"No. We hadn't discussed names. Well, not really. I can't call her Bella, or Annabelle even, but roses have always been special. Bella was

gathering them the first time I saw her, you see. It just feels right."
Margaret nodded her approval, but neither spoke.

They drank coffee together and, again, Margaret suggested lunch.

"Would you mind if we left it for today, Mother?"

Margaret was disappointed, but hid it well.

As the weeks became months, everyone rallied round. Harry was rarely left alone during the day. His mother or father visited often; Charlotte and Katherine also called, sometimes trying to persuade him into a walk, or a visit to the farm. Some evenings, William would appear on the doorstep. The two men would sit over coffee and Harry would show an interest in the farm. As time progressed and he returned to work, he put on more and more of a brave face, pretending improvement, professing recovery. Only at night did the dark clouds descend. Only at night, when he lay awake in bed, would he reflect that he would happily and willingly give up everything he had, everything he owned, everything he ever hoped to be, if she would only come back to him.

Chapter Two

Christmas 1912

Christmas was always going to be difficult. Harry had known that for months. When autumn turned to winter and the frosts began to settle again, he started to dread the festive season. Rose's first Christmas should have been a joyful occasion, bringing the whole family together. Instead, it just reminded Harry of a happier time two years ago. Christmas Eve, his proposal to Bella, her smiled acceptance. The beginning of contentment and the beginning of the end.

Harry made no plans. Rose was not even eleven months old yet, he reasoned to himself. She would have no recollection of this time, so it made no difference what they did. Then, a week before Christmas, William called round to the cottage with an invitation from himself and Charlotte for Harry and Rose to share Christmas Day with them at the farm.

"I don't know," Harry replied. His immediate thought was that there would be too many memories of Bella.

"Come on, Harry," William pleaded. "We'd love to see you both and you can't stay here on your own."

"We may go to visit my parents for the day," Harry lied.

"No you won't. I've already been to see them, and they told me you're going there for lunch the day after. Your mother said that when she invited you for Christmas day, you told her that you were coming to us." Harry looked shamefaced.

"I can't do it, Bill," he said quietly.

"I know. It's going to be hard, but you have to face it sometime."

"There will be so many reminders of her."

"But there are reminders of her here. There are reminders of her everywhere you go. You can't escape that."

"Then what do I do?"

"Learn to deal with it, I suppose." The two men looked at each other for a short while. "Charlotte's not going to take 'no' for an answer, Harry. If I go back with a 'no', she's just going to send me back again, or else come round here herself. It's easier, all round, if you just say yes now really."

"Let me think about it, Bill," Harry replied. "I'll let you know by Sunday." William wasn't satisfied, but knew there was no point in arguing further.

By Friday, Harry had decided to decline William's offer, but on the Saturday night, just four days before Christmas, he realised that a family Christmas was what Bella would have wanted for Rose. He called round to the farm early the next morning and left a message, saying that he and Rose would be there on Christmas Day at noon.

On Christmas Eve, the day he had dreaded most of the whole festive season, Harry woke just after dawn to find a thick white blanket covering the ground. Snow had always excited Bella and he cherished the memory of the childish enjoyment it had given her. Standing at the window, a thought crossed his mind and without hesitating, he quickly got dressed in some old clothes. Downstairs, he added a warm overcoat and galoshes, a thick scarf, hat and gloves. Outside in the back garden, he began to build a large snowman, rolling up the sticky snow into one big ball for the body, and placing a smaller one on top for the head. Once this was completed, Harry took a knife from his studio at the end of the garden and began to carve, creating a polar bear with arms, hands, a face, ears and a snout. An hour or so later, standing back, he admired his work.

He went back into the house, removed his galoshes and climbed the stairs. Susan was just dressing Rose.

"Can you put Rose into some warm clothes, please Susan?" Harry asked. "I want to take her outside."

"In this weather, sir?"

"Yes, in this weather." He began opening drawers, searching for warmer clothing. "She'll need her coat and hat and a pair of mittens. It's freezing out there." Susan did as she was asked, shaking her head. A few minutes later, Harry descended the stairs, carrying his daughter, now wrapped as warmly as him. He stopped by the back door, putting his galoshes back on and then they went out into the garden together. Susan watched from the landing window as Harry carried Rose down the garden to the snow bear. Watched as he removed one glove from her tiny hand to let her touch the snow. Watched as she withdrew it, startled by the cold and then as he held her little hand in his to warm it again. She watched as their cheeks touched, red and chilly, while Harry pointed to the snow bear's hands and ears, his nose and his eyes. She watched Rose's smile broaden, her eyes sparkling and nose reddening. Then Susan remembered, a little under a year ago, when the master had built a snowman for the mistress and she, heavily pregnant and unable to leave the house, had stood at her bedroom window, her hands clasped together with excitement, while he had stood below, his arms spread wide, grinning up at her. Turning from the window, Susan sniffed, took a handkerchief from her sleeve, wiped her eyes and nose, and went downstairs to put the kettle on.

The next day, more snow had fallen. Harry, carrying Rose in his arms, trudged the two miles to the farm, not feeling the cold. A robin, perched on the snow-tipped fence, stared at them as they passed. The hedgerows had disappeared beneath a layer of fine white powder. The pine trees weighed heavy, their branches drooping down almost to the ground, and when the wind caught them, Harry and Rose were showered with droplets of snow.

Despite Harry's misgivings, the day itself was enjoyable and their welcome was warm. The Christmas tree, normally in the hall, had been located in the bay window of the large sitting room, and after a magnificent lunch, the whole family retired there. Charlotte and Katherine handed out colourfully wrapped parcels. Rose's face lit up at the sight of the tree, and as each present was handed to her, then to

Harry to be opened, she delighted - much to everyone's amusement - in the colourful paper, rather than the contents. Ribbons were especially fascinating and soon found their way into her mouth. Later in the afternoon, the curtains closed and candles lit, Charlotte played the piano, while the others gathered round, singing Christmas Carols.

When it was time to leave, William suggested driving Harry and Rose home, an offer which Harry gratefully accepted. There were presents to be transported and he was beginning to feel tired. William brought the cart round to the front of the house and, having sincerely and honestly thanked his hosts for a lovely day, Harry wrapped a yawning Rose tightly into his coat and they all set off. Rose was sound asleep within the first few hundred yards and Harry pulled her into him even closer, feeling her breathing against his chest. Never in all the time since Bella's death had he felt so in love with his daughter.

Back at the cottage that evening, with Rose sound asleep in her cot, Harry sat in his chair, his long legs stretched out to the fire. Bella would have loved a Christmas such as this, he thought to himself, would have relished her daughter's obvious enjoyment of the snow bear and the Christmas tree, the presents, and the wrapping paper. He looked around the room, sighing. Everything here was a constant reminder of the life they should have had. There was no escaping the recollections of their brief time together. The garden, now covered in snow, would come back to life in spring. The flowers would bloom again and he would imagine Bella picking daffodils to display in the dining room. In the autumn, the trees in Downley Woods would turn to brilliant shades of brown and russet, which would forever remind him of Bella's hair. The smell of apples would always bring to mind the tree in the back garden, where Bella had gathered the only crop they had harvested together, grimacing at the bitter taste, because she had picked them too early. In the summer, as the roses bloomed in the garden outside, Harry knew he would hardly be able to look. All of this had already happened in the months since her death. All of this would happen again as the seasons changed. On and on, forever. Everything he did; everything he thought and said, was done in the shadow of Bella.

Later that night, he went to bed: his bed, not theirs. That room had remained closed since the day after Bella's death, when he had gone there and wept for her; wept for himself and their baby and for everything they had lost. Now he lay under the sheets, looking out of the window, the skeletal tree tops waving in the breeze. He rarely closed the curtains anymore. Sleep came with difficulty, so there seemed little point. The night sky at least provided a diversion; an alternative to staring at the ceiling. He knew that if he was to begin to rebuild his life, to make a life for Rose, he couldn't remain here much longer. He needed freedom. He needed to put some distance between himself and this unhappy house. He needed to breathe again.

The next day, he and Rose were expected at his parents' house. A short snowy walk brought them to the large red-brick Victorian villa that dominated the village green. The long driveway had been cleared of snow, which decked the lawns, shrubs and naked cherry trees. Another warm welcome awaited them and they were shown into the sitting room. There were still reminders of Bella, even here, Harry thought. It wasn't the same as Downwillow Farm or Holly Cottage: they were places where Bella had lived, where she had made her own mark. This was Harry's home, where he had spent his childhood, but he and Bella had spent a lot of time here with Richard and Margaret. Just before lunch, Harry stood at the French windows, looking down the garden to the snow-covered swing, hanging from the branches of the enormous oak tree. He had played there as a child, but just weeks after their marriage, one hot Sunday, Harry had sat with Bella on his lap, her arms around his neck and head on his shoulder, as they swung back and forth. He closed his eyes, breathing deeply. There really was no escape.

Behind him, Margaret was playing with Rose. She enjoyed fussing over her granddaughter. Meanwhile Richard poured some drinks, although Harry declined the proffered whisky. It provided another unwelcome memory, even if he couldn't bring himself to explain.

After lunch, with Rose safely settled for her afternoon nap in the old nursery, Harry sat with his parents in the sitting room, drinking coffee.

Richard dozed, replete, in his chair, while Margaret sat on the sofa and took up her knitting. Harry watched them both, recalling earlier Christmases of childhood and adolescence. A train set, footballs, playing cards, oranges in the bottom of his stocking. Then, as he'd grown up, a chess set, books, paints and pencils; his first easel. The house unusually quiet as the servants were given the afternoon off.

"I need to talk to you both." His words were sudden, waking his father with a start.

"What? Sorry?" Richard spluttered, sitting up in his chair. Margaret raised her eyes, but carried on knitting.

"Yes, dear, what is it?"

There was no easy way of saying this, so it was best to just get it over with. "I've decided that Rose and I are going to move to Watersmeet." There, he'd said it. He waited.

"For how long?" Margaret replied eventually. She had lowered her knitting needles to her lap and was looking at him over the top of her spectacles.

"Permanently." Silence descended like a veil. Harry hesitated, knowing he should explain, but uncertain how to find the words. "I can't bear it here any longer," he began. "Everywhere I turn, I'm reminded of Bella."

"Don't you think it will be the same at Watersmeet? You spent your honeymoon there, after all. There will be memories there too," Margaret reasoned, putting her knitting down beside her on the sofa.

"Probably," Harry replied. "But at least there, we have a chance of starting again. Well, I think we do."

"And what if it doesn't work out?"

"Then I'll find somewhere else. Somewhere new. I have the inheritance now, so I can afford to."

"You couldn't just find somewhere else to live in the village, or nearby?"

"It wouldn't work, mother."

"Is it really so bad, Harry?" Richard asked.

"Yes."

"Will you sell the cottage?"

"I don't know. I haven't really thought about it yet."

Margaret stared at her husband. "You're both talking as though this were a foregone conclusion."

"That's because it is, Mother." Harry didn't look at her, his frustration rising. "I don't want to fall out with you, but the decision's made. We're going."

"Harry, dear, I really don't think that you've thought this through. You'll be miles away from all of us. What if you can't cope? And if it doesn't work out and you end up having to buy somewhere else, you'll start eating away at your inheritance. My father intended that it should last you a lifetime and be passed down to future generations. You've only had it a few weeks and already you're talking about spending a large sum. You should be thinking about Rose's future."

"Mother, really! Buying another house wouldn't even make a dent in the money. I could buy ten houses and still have enough to live in luxury for the rest of my life."

"Margaret." Richard stood and went to sit by his wife, moving her knitting to the coffee table. "I know this is difficult for you, but it's what Harry wants. More to the point, it's what Harry needs. And we really must accept that." He took her hands in his. "It's not as though we'll never see them again. We can go for visits, and I'm sure Harry will come back here regularly, won't you?" He looked across at his son.

"Of course we will. Please try to understand, Mother. I'm not doing this to deliberately hurt you. I'm not trying to separate you from Rose or myself. I just need a fresh start away from here." Margaret released her hands and got to her feet, crossing the room. As she opened the door, she stifled a sniff. Harry had never seen his mother cry and knew that she didn't intend him to now.

"I feel terrible, Father," Harry said once they were alone.

"Don't worry, Harry. Leave her for a while. She'll come round." Richard paused for a moment before returning to his own chair. "I'm assuming this means you'll be leaving the firm?"

"Yes. I'm sorry. I probably should have mentioned that. I got carried away with Mother's reaction."

"Don't worry. I've been expecting it. You haven't been yourself since Bella died. In any case, I've always known that when you came into your money, you'd be off. You've never really enjoyed law, have you?"

"No. I'm afraid not."

"Well, at the risk of sounding like a dull old fish, there are a few legal things we really ought to discuss." Richard sat upright, turning at once into the astute solicitor that Harry had always dreaded becoming. "You haven't made a new will yet, and you really should think about setting up a trust for Rose. I can draw up some papers for you, before you go, if you like."

"I'll give it some thought. Let us just get settled in at Watersmeet, then we can talk further."

"Don't leave it too long, Harry. These things are easily forgotten."

"I was thinking we'd come back for Rose's birthday – that's only just over a month away."

"Your mother will be pleased."

"I thought she might. We can stay at Holly Cottage, if you want."

"Not a bit of it, Harry. You'll stay here. Your mother wouldn't have it any other way."

"I was hoping you'd say that. I think I'd rather close up the cottage. At least until I've decided what to do with it."

"What about Susan?"

"I'm going to ask her to come with us. It's going to be a wrench for her to be so far away from her family, but I'm hoping she'll say yes. Rose is very attached to her, and she knows our ways. If she won't come, I'll just have to find someone else, I suppose." The two men sat together in silence for a while. It was starting to snow again and had turned overcast, when the door opened and Margaret re-appeared, carrying Rose in her arms.

"Look who I've found!" Her voice was brighter now.

"Let me have her for a while," Richard said, holding out his arms to take his granddaughter. Margaret sat back on the sofa, looking over to Harry, who went to sit beside her.

"I am sorry, Mother," he said, very quietly.

"It's alright, dear. I do understand. Really I do. I'm just so very sad."

"I know. But we'll be back, very often. I was just saying to Father that we'll be coming back for Rose's birthday and that's only a few weeks away now."

"Oh, Harry." She turned her head, looking directly into his eyes. "You don't understand at all, do you? Of course I'm going to miss you both terribly and I'm upset that you're leaving us. It's come as a bit of a shock. But that's not why I'm sad. I didn't realise that you were so desperately unhappy. I should have noticed. I just wish I could have done more."

"It's not your fault, Mother." Harry looked away. "It's nobody's fault." He swallowed hard, blinked a few times and excused himself from the room.

Chapter Three

The early dawn light shone through the large picture window, danced up his naked chest and across his face, kissing the sleep from his eyes. As Harry stretched his arms and legs to the four corners of the bed, straining every muscle and sinew, he groaned with satisfaction. Relaxing again, he ran his fingers through his hair and sat up on the edge of the bed, yawning.

The sun was starting to rise above the horizon by the time Harry closed the front door behind him. Watersmeet, despite its name, had been built on a cliff top, commanding a panoramic view of the rocky cove on one side and the harbour jetty on the other. In front of the single-storey cottage was a lane which, to the right, led past a few other isolated houses and eventually to the village with its shops, hotel and railway station. Harry, however, turned left and followed the lane for a few hundred yards until it bent to the right and became a narrow track, just wide enough for a horse and cart, leading steeply down to the tiny old fishing harbour. All the boats were out at the moment, as was the tide and there was a ghostly, deserted feeling to the place, which Harry preferred to the hustle and bustle that would prevail in a few hours' time. Half-way down the harbour wall, Harry descended the slippery steps and jumped down onto the soft, wet sand, which squelched up over the soles of his boots. He set off at a pace, walking in between the rocks, his hands plunged deep into his pockets. He barely looked up as he strode away from the harbour and around the headland. He enjoyed the feeling of the wind catching in his hair, the slight autumn chill prickling on his cheeks and chin.

Once away from the harbour and beyond the possibility of any early morning prying eyes, Harry stood on the shoreline, the waves gently lapping up to his boots. He looked out to sea, breathing deeply, his lungs filling with fresh air. Turning, he walked back up the beach, above the tide line of dried seaweed and laid down on the soft sand. There was now a cloudless pale blue sky above his head. Harry placed his hands behind his head and stared at the rising sun, hovering suspended above the distant horizon.

Even now he could still see her, still smell her, still hear her, still feel her. Her shy smile and lowered eyes; her powder pink soft cheek next to his. Her floral perfume; the tunes she used to hum to herself in the garden, when she thought no-one was listening. The feeling of her fingers entwined in his, her slim waist cradled in his arms, her soft flesh yielding to him. Here, on the beach, on the cliff tops, he no longer sought freedom from his memories. Here, he remembered her living, rather than dead. He recalled their honeymoon and their happiness, rather than her funeral and his sadness.

As the sun began to warm his face, Harry got up and set off again, shoulders hunched and head bowed. Around the curve of the tiny cove were more rocks and, at the foot of many of these were little rock pools. This had always been one of his favourite haunts ever since childhood. He smiled as he recalled his holidays from university when he would visit the beach at low tide, sculpting intricate sand animals for the local children, who would gather around, waiting for him to finish each creature. They would clamour for his attention, hoping that they might be the one to name his next creation. Then, as the tide came in, swallowing his works of art, one or two of the younger children would cry. Harry would pick them up, hold them and explain that he would return the next day and they could begin all over again. Year in, year out, it was the same. The children might change, or grow up, but they still came back every summer to watch.

Harry had to clamber over slippery rocks to reach the next cove, where there were very steep steps which wound up, zig-zagging through the trees, to the top of the cliff above. He started the long climb, his stomach beginning to relish the prospect of bacon and eggs and a cup of tea. The sun was really quite warm now and he was hot and weary by the time he emerged from the shelter of the trees, into the sunshine. Not far from the cottage, on the grassy cliff top, he stopped, looking down to the blue carpet beneath him, stretching to the skyline in the distance. The wind at this height was gratifyingly cool and he breathed deeply, sighing and whispering her name to the waves below him, before turning back to the cottage.

Susan was already hard at work in the kitchen, preparing breakfast and chattering to Rose, who was sitting in her high-chair, finishing her toast and playing with a spoon. Harry's appearance, flush-cheeked and wind-swept, didn't surprise Susan. He left the house early in the morning on most days, even in the cold, rough weather when they had first arrived last January. Susan had been pleased to be invited to join Harry and Rose in this new adventure. She missed her mother, her two sisters and her older brother, but then her sisters were younger and still kept her mother busy, and Albert was a Corporal now, and wasn't at home much anyway. She still managed to visit quite often and, indeed, they'd only just returned from a month in Sussex. She placed a plate of bacon and eggs in front of Harry.

"That looks lovely. Thank you, Susan." Harry poured himself a cup of tea from the brown betty teapot that sat underneath a striped woollen tea-cosy. He enjoyed the daily breakfast ritual in the kitchen. "I don't suppose that you could pack a little picnic for Rosie and me, could you? It's still quite warm out there today. I thought we might go down to the beach, before the weather starts to turn cold again."

"Certainly, sir."

"I really do wish you'd stop calling me 'Sir', Susan."

Susan smiled, turning back to the sink. The problem was that if she didn't call him 'Sir', neither of them really knew what she should call him.

"I'll make you some sandwiches, shall I? And there's some cake, and fruit. Will that do, Mr Belmont?"

"That all sounds marvellous," Harry answered, and smiled across at her before turning his attention from his almost empty plate, to his daughter. "How about a few hours down on the beach, Rosie?" She nodded her approval, grinning. "Would you like Daddy to draw you something?" Again she nodded. Finishing his breakfast, Harry got up and, taking Rose from her chair, carried her to his studio at the back of the cottage, where he put her down for a few minutes while he packed a small satchel with sketch pads and pencils.

An hour later, Harry and Rose were settled on the beach, a tartan blanket beneath them, the picnic basket placed to one side. Harry had brought a couple of Rose's favourite toys to keep her occupied, but for now, she was happy to play with the sand and watch him sketch the harbour, which was now alive with activity. The fishing boats had returned and were unloading their catch; the local women were busy in the few shops that serviced the harbour, chatting and gossiping as they queued for their goods. Once his drawing was complete, Harry offered to make Rose a sand creature. She clapped her hands in glee.

"What would you like today?" he asked.

"Dog!" she shouted.

"A dog? Again?" He thought for a minute. "What about a fish? When the tide comes in, the fish will be going home – back to the sea."

"Fish!"

"Right, a fish it is, then." Harry took Rose's hand and they both went further down the beach, where he began to build up a long mound of damp sand, shaping and moulding it with his hands and fingers. As he moved around, Rose followed him, watching his every move. He drew his hands along the body of the fish, giving it sleek, graceful lines, a long snout and dorsal fin. When it was complete, Rose jumped up and down, her hands clasped together.

"Fish!" she cried.

"Well, it's a dolphin, actually, but fish is close enough." Harry pulled her to him in an enormous hug. "Shall we have some lunch now?"

"Yes please!" Harry carried Rose back up the beach and they sat together on the rug, eating ham sandwiches, sliced into crustless fingers for Rose, followed by apples, which Harry cut up into small pieces and then cake, which was delicious. Afterwards, Harry suggested a paddle, but had barely finished his sentence before Rose had begun trying to undo her shoes. He helped her and then removed his own. They pulled off their socks and soon they were both yelling and screaming as their feet touched the freezing water for the first time, waves washing over their toes. Rose jumped up and down in the shallow water, splashing both of them and giggling when Harry pretended it was too cold for him, chattering his teeth. As Rose's legs began to turn red with cold, they returned to the rug and dried their feet on the small towel that Susan had provided. Rose was yawning now. Her shoes and socks replaced, she patted the dolphin goodbye while Harry packed up the basket and folded the blanket. Then she put her tiny hand in his and they walked together, back to the harbour wall. When they reached the steps, Harry gathered Rose into his arms and climbed up carefully, the basket hanging from his elbow. She nestled into him, her head on his shoulder and arms around his neck. A few of the local women looked on; some with admiration, others with pity. Oblivious to their glances, Harry carried Rose back to the cottage, and laid her on his bed to finish her sleep.

In the still-bright afternoon light, Harry went into his studio at the back of the cottage. There was a sheet of watercolour paper already taped to his board and he quickly applied a wash. Without really thinking, he found himself applying soft, muted flesh-coloured tones to the dampened surface. The layers of colour developed into smooth, pale pink cheeks; rich auburn hair; a delicate neck and milky-white bare shoulders. He worked quickly, not stopping to reflect on the subject, just painting what he felt. He barely seemed to breathe as his brush flowed across the surface of the paper. Once dry he sketched in the intricate detail with a pen and ink: the shape of her chin; a few strands of loose hair; fine eyebrows and wide enchanting eyes. Harry finally breathed in deeply, stretched, stood and looked at the portrait. Bella had sat for him several times during their marriage and two or three times during their honeymoon but he hadn't tried to paint her at all since her death, until now. Turning, he shook his head and walked away.

The next morning, Harry left the house early again, despite the threatening rain. Susan, when she rose, left the kettle boiling on the stove, while she went into the studio to clear up from the previous evening. The master had taken his coffee in there after dinner and had remained there until well after midnight. Opening the door, she found scraps of torn paper on the floor and, bending to pick them up, noticed subtle tones of pale pink and russet, a solitary green eye, a wispy ringlet, the vague outline of a naked shoulder. She collected the pieces together and placed them in the waste paper basket, then picked up the master's empty coffee cup and left, closing the door behind her.

Chapter Four

Summer 1914

Rose clambered down the terrace steps and ran up to her grandfather, who was lazing in a deckchair on the perfectly manicured lawn. His legs were crossed in front of him, arms behind his head and a wide-brimmed straw hat tilted downwards, almost covering his face. Without warning, she flung herself onto his lap.

"Goodness gracious me, Rose!" he cried, sitting up and pushing his hat back on his head. "I didn't hear you coming. Where's daddy?"

Rose pointed to the open French doors, where Harry stood, leaning against the doorframe, with his arms folded, proudly watching his daughter. His eyes were lit up by his wide smile, his skin bronzed by the warm summer sunshine of many hours spent walking and playing with Rose on the beach.

"I hope you don't mind, Father," Harry said, strolling across the terrace and down the steps. "Polly let us in. We left our cases in the hall. Rosie was desperate to surprise you."

"Well, she certainly did that!"

"Where's Mother?" Harry asked, looking around the garden.

"She's pottering in the greenhouse, as usual. I say, Rosie, why don't you go and find grandmama? See if you can surprise her too!" Rose jumped from her grandfather's lap and ran down the garden, towards the large greenhouse which was partially hidden by a laurel bush, in which Margaret kept her most prized blooms.

"You're looking well, son." Richard got to his feet, shaking Harry warmly by the hand and patting him on the shoulder. "The Cornish air seems to be agreeing with you both. Your mother and I weren't sure if you'd still come – what with all this talk of war. We wondered if you'd stay out of the way, down at Watersmeet."

"Well, I did think about it, but we both really wanted to see you, and it seemed like a good idea to take advantage of the bank holiday weekend, before you go back to the office on Tuesday."

"How long do you think you'll stay this time?"

"Probably the whole month, as usual, if you'll have us."

"Of course we'll have you!" Richard sat down again and lowered his voice. "By the way, Harry," he said. "Your mother's accepted an invitation to lunch at Downwillow on Monday."

"Oh." Harry was dismayed. He had managed to avoid visiting Downwillow since leaving the village. Every time he'd returned, it had always been arranged that Charlotte, William and Katherine would lunch or dine with the Belmonts, so that they could see Rose.

"Charlotte wouldn't take no for an answer, Harry. It was all rather awkward for your mother. You mustn't blame her."

Before Harry could say anything, Rose and her grandmother appeared from the greenhouse, hand in hand.

"Harry!" Margaret called, waving as they walked together up the garden. "What on earth have you been feeding this child? She's grown at least an inch and a half since Easter."

"Just Susan's home cooking and plenty of fresh sea air," Harry called, watching Rose drag his mother towards the house. He kissed Margaret on the cheek as she removed her gardening gloves, while Rose clambered back up into Richard's welcoming arms, settling comfortably on his lap. "I hope it's alright," Harry said, "but we dropped Susan at her mother's house on the way here. She's going to stay there for a week or so. I thought we could manage without her for that long. There's evidently a chance that her brother, Albert, will be allowed some leave and she wants to see him, if she can. He was away at Easter, so she hasn't seen him since Christmas. Mind you, from what I read in the newspaper on the train, I'm not sure he'll be here for that long. Did I tell you, he's been promoted again? He's a Sergeant now. Susan was so proud, when her mother wrote with the news…" Harry let the sentence die, noticing the expression on his mother's face.

"Let's go and see what's happened to the tea, shall we, Rosie?" she said, lifting her granddaughter down from Richard's lap and turning away. Margaret helped Rose up the terrace steps and into the house. Harry was confused.

"What did I say?" he asked his father, once they were safely inside.

"I think your mother is getting worried by all the headlines." Richard looked up at his son, shielding his eyes from the sun. "The war is the only thing anyone talks about these days and she seems rather nervous about it all."

"Well, it's difficult to avoid it, Father, the newspapers are simply full of stories." Harry sat down on the steps, running his fingers through a lavender bush and releasing its sweet, delicate scent. His father turned his deckchair around so they could face each other.

"It's probably best to say as little as possible in front of your mother, Harry," Richard said. "There's no need to go upsetting her unnecessarily. It may all come to nothing yet."

"I don't know." Harry was doubtful. He leant back on his elbows, and looked up thoughtfully at the clear blue sky, the colour contrasting with the green leaves of the enormous oak tree that dominated the long garden, shading it from the bright summer sunshine. The old rope swing still hung from its branches, although the seat had recently been repainted. The borders of hollyhocks, foxgloves and poppies were in full bloom and, glancing to his left Harry saw his mother's tea roses. His breath caught in his throat, but then roses still affected him, even now. He took a moment to compose himself. "I wouldn't be surprised if something happened in the next few days, Father," he said. "The Russians have mobilised already, according to *The Times*. I was reading about it on the train. If you ask me, we'll all be in it within a week."

"Well don't say that in front of your mother, for heaven's sake." Richard cleared his throat, as Margaret and Rose appeared again, through the French doors.

"We'll have tea on the terrace, shall we?" Margaret asked, of nobody in particular. "Mrs Cox has baked a lovely cake and made some fresh scones too." She helped Rose sit up in a chair as Harry and his father walked over to join them. "Harry, dear, pop down to your studio and fetch Rose a cushion would you? She can't reach the table properly."

"Yes, mother," said Harry. He turned and strolled down the garden, beyond the greenhouse to the small brick studio that had been built just before he'd left for university. Pulling the door open, Harry looked around. Everything was tidy; the paints on the bench were arranged neatly. Water jars were stacked by the sink and canvasses propped up against the wall. How it contrasted with his studio at Watersmeet, which was disordered and messy to the untrained eye: not that it mattered to him – he knew where everything was and at least it was used. He picked up a cushion from the wicker chair in the corner and closed the door. As he climbed up the steps again, Polly was wheeling a tea trolley onto the terrace. It was laden with freshly cut ham and cucumber sandwiches, scones with butter, jam and cream in separate pots, and a splendid seed cake, which was one of Harry's particular favourites.

He put the cushion under Rose, sat her up properly and took a seat next to her. Looking at the magnificent tea, he leant across towards his daughter.

"We'd better not tell Susan about this, had we?" he whispered. "She'll be jealous!" Rose giggled, taking an enormous bite from her sandwich.

Later that evening, after dinner, with Rose safely tucked up in bed in the old nursery, Harry and his parents sat in the drawing room.

"I understand from father that we're going out to lunch on Monday," Harry said to his mother, who was concentrating on her knitting.

"Yes, dear. Charlotte came round yesterday. She caught me unawares, I'm afraid. I hope it's alright with you, but I had to accept. You don't mind, do you?"

"Do I have a choice?" Harry's voice was resigned. Margaret looked up, losing count of her stitches. He saw the troubled look on her face. "Don't worry, mother, it's fine," he said, trying to sound more cheerful than he felt. "I can't avoid it forever, can I?"

"I know. But I wanted to wait until you got here, to ask whether you were happy with the arrangements. It was very difficult. Charlotte was pressing me for an answer."

"I imagine she thought if she waited for me to arrive and gave me the choice, I'd say no."

"Would you have said no, Harry, if it had been left up to you?" Margaret asked.

"Yes, I would." Harry got up. He bent to kiss his mother, wished his father goodnight and left the room.

Up in his bedroom, Harry lay on the bed, staring at the ceiling. He'd opened the windows as wide as they would go, but still there wasn't enough air. As pleased as he was to see his parents, he already longed to hear the waves lapping on the shore beneath Watersmeet, and feel the warm sea breeze teasing across his skin as he lay naked on top of the covers. He'd only been back for a few hours and already he was yearning to be able to breathe properly again.

At twelve-thirty sharp on Bank Holiday Monday, Harry, Rose, Richard and Margaret were ushered into the sitting room at Downwillow. William, who had been standing by the empty fireplace, came forward to shake Harry enthusiastically by the hand. Charlotte leapt from her chair and ran over to Harry, kissing him briefly on the cheek. She knelt down in front of Rose, squeezing her tightly in her arms, then led her back to the sofa, where a collection of dolls and teddy bears awaited them. Richard and Margaret were greeted warmly, if a little more formally, and sherry was passed around.

"Where's Katherine?" Harry asked, declining a drink.

"Ah, well. There we've got a bit of news," William exclaimed. "She's become engaged to be married. To an architect, named Philip Lowell, and she's spending the day with his family."

"I had no idea!" Harry was genuinely pleased. "When did this happen?"

"She met him at a party last Christmas. They've been walking out ever since and he proposed two weeks ago," William said.

"I hope he knows how lucky he is," Harry remarked.

"I think he does. They're both deliriously happy." William said, smiling. "She won't stop talking to us about him, actually! It's quite sickening!"

"Well, tell her to come over and see us one day soon," Harry laughed. "I won't mind hearing all about it!"

William looked across at Charlotte, whose nod was almost imperceptible.

"That's not our only bit of news actually," he said, looking around the room, his eyes settling on Harry. "One of the main reasons we asked you over here today, was because we've got an announcement of our own to make." Harry raised his eyebrows, but had already guessed what was coming. "Charlotte and I are expecting a baby," William announced. There was a brief, awkward moment of silence.

"Congratulations!" Richard stepped forward and shook William's hand. Margaret, who was sitting on the sofa next to Rose, leant across and patted Charlotte's hand.

"How lovely, my dear," she said. "When is the baby due?"

"At the end of January." Charlotte looked towards Harry.

"Oh," Margaret's gaze followed Charlotte's. "About the same time as Rose's birthday?"

"Yes." Both women fell silent and Harry realised that everyone was waiting for him to say something. He walked across the room.

"Congratulations, Bill." He shook William's hand and patted him on the arm. "I'm really pleased for you." Then he turned and crossed to Charlotte, bending and kissing her on both cheeks.

"I'm so happy for both of you," he said. She looked up at him.

"Really?" she asked.

"Yes, really."

After lunch, they all sat outside on the terrace. Rose had been taken for her afternoon nap, clutching a large brown bear, known as Toby. The sun had passed over the top of the house and the welcome shade it provided made the early August afternoon heat a little more tolerable. Everyone was in full conversation, talking mainly of

Charlotte's condition or Katherine's engagement and whenever anyone mentioned the war, Richard adeptly changed the subject. They had all noticed that Harry had moved his chair a little way off from the others and was sitting with his elbows on his knees, gazing into the distance. After a short while, William went to sit on the low wall alongside Harry's chair.

"I do understand, Harry," he whispered.

"Sorry?" Harry replied, speaking quite normally.

"I said, I do understand," William repeated, his voice a little louder.

"Understand what?"

"Why you don't like coming here."

"Oh. Do you?"

"There are too many reminders, aren't there? Especially at this time of year."

"Yes." Harry wondered, if William understood so well, why he and Charlotte had been so insistent on him coming.

William seemed to have read his mind. "We only asked you here because we wanted to give you our news and…" he paused, "And we thought it was about time you started to enjoy Bella's home. She loved Downwillow in the summer, you know. She was so happy here. I've always hated the thought that you'd never know. That you'd hide yourself down in Cornwall, away from us and never enjoy the farm in the way she did, and never let Rose learn to love it too."

"And did it ever occur to you that I'm just not ready yet?" Harry asked, unable to hide his displeasure.

"Yes," William replied honestly. "Charlotte and I discussed it."

"Then why be so insistent about us coming today? You could have told us your news at my parents' house."

"Because she's gone, Harry," William persisted. "And you have to move on at some point."

Harry turned his face towards William, genuinely angry now and raising his voice. "I know perfectly well she's gone. But what if I don't want to move on?" Everyone turned to look at them.

"You can't live your life like that. It's not fair on Rose."

"Don't tell me what's fair on Rose and what isn't."

"I'm not trying to, Harry." William's voice remained calm and soothing. "It's just that you need to accept it and start again for Rose's sake. Do you actually think that Bella would have wanted you to be alone for the rest of your life? Do you think she would have wanted you to be unhappy? She was my sister, Harry. I knew her."

"So did I, Bill."

"Then you know that she always wanted other people to be happy. And you're not."

"I'm alright." Harry looked away.

"You're coping, Harry. But you're not happy."

Harry turned back, raising his voice again. "And you thought that bringing me back here and reminding me of our first meeting was going to cheer me up, did you?"

"Of course not!" William's tone was louder now as well. "For heaven's sake, Harry. I'm just trying to get you to realise that the Bella I knew – my sister – was not the sort of person who would have wanted you to be miserable. She wouldn't have wanted you to grieve forever. She would have wanted you to find happiness."

"With someone else, I suppose you mean?"

"However you want. Wherever you can."

Harry stood, his chair scraping across the stone paved terrace and walked off down the garden, his hands in his pockets. William glanced at Charlotte, who shook her head reproachfully. He wondered if he'd done the right thing, speaking his mind. Harry, meanwhile, was wondering who the hell William thought he was, telling him how to live his life. Harry didn't want someone else. He wanted Bella, and if he couldn't have her, then he didn't want anyone. Rose was enough for him and he was happy. Well, he was happy when he was with Rose and that was all he needed. Rose seemed contented; she didn't seem to miss having a mother and he certainly wasn't going to marry someone just to give Rose a mother in her life. They were fine by themselves, he reasoned.

He walked away from the house, towards the fields beyond the garden. After a while, he stopped and glanced back towards the terrace. He could see them all still sitting there and knew that they were probably watching him, maybe talking about him. He realised that Rose would be waking up soon and might need him, so with his head bowed, he began walking back. William was still perched on the wall, evidently waiting for him to return.

"Sorry, Harry," William began after a short pause. "It's none of my business. I shouldn't have said anything."

"It doesn't matter." Harry's voice was calm now.

"I can't imagine what you've been through. And I don't know how I'd react if it happened to Charlotte."

"Well, let's hope you never have to find out." Harry didn't raise his eyes. He just stared at the paved terrace, keen to avoid prying eyes and blooming roses.

When Richard came home from work the next evening, he walked straight into the sitting room, still carrying his briefcase, which he set down on the chair by the door. He didn't say anything, but went straight to the sideboard and poured himself a large whisky. Margaret raised her eyebrows in Harry's direction but neither of them said anything. They watched Richard drink most of the contents of his glass and waited for him to speak.

"I'm sorry Margaret, my dear," he said, finally. "I know we agreed not to talk about it, but I'm afraid we're going to have to."

"Talk about what Richard?" Margaret asked, putting her cross-stitch to one side and looking at her husband.

"The war," he answered simply. "It's all over the town. Everyone's saying that we'll be in it by tonight."

"Really?" It was Harry's turn to look up at his father.

"Yes, son. The barracks are simply alive with soldiers. They're coming in on trains from all over the place."

"Oh, Richard." Margaret's voice was quite calm, but her anxiety was obvious.

"Now, don't you fret, my dear." Richard crossed the room and sat next to his wife, taking her hands in his. Harry watched them for a moment. They seemed absorbed in their own thoughts and fears and, feeling like an intruder, he left the room. "It'll soon be over and done with and a good thing too, if you ask me," Richard continued. "Nothing for you to worry about though, Margaret. You can trust the good old British Army to sort 'em out."

"Oh do be quiet, dear." Margaret's voice was stronger now. She got to her feet, straightening her skirt. "I must go and see Polly. Her fiancé is in the army, if you remember. She might want some time off before he goes away. I'll go and find her now."

"That's right, dear. You do that," Richard soothed, sitting back into the sofa and taking another sip of his whisky as his wife hurried from the room.

Just as Richard had predicted, war was declared later that evening. The mobilisation was ordered the next day, so Polly snatched a little time off to say goodbye to her Walter. He was a man of whom Margaret had never really approved. Nonetheless, even she had to admit, he had settled down since joining the army, nearly a year ago. In most other ways, daily life was unaffected by the declaration of war. Richard continued to go into the office, although the crowds of people and vehicles in the town made his journey more laborious than ever. Margaret and Richard both noticed that Harry had become rather preoccupied. Margaret occasionally caught him staring out of the window, or watching Rose playing in the garden, and he was even more quiet and thoughtful than usual, but they both put this down to his unfortunate argument with William. He'd refused to talk about it since they'd returned from lunch on Monday and neither of them wanted to press him for information.

A few days later, Harry rose early and left the house before breakfast. He had a long walk ahead of him, and wanted to go while the roads were quiet and before anyone else got up. It was a warm day, and the fields were heavy with corn, ripe for harvesting. Alongside the dusty road, a few poppies grew between the grasses and the hedgerows were weighed down with plump blackberries. Harry picked a few as he walked along, enjoying their sweet juiciness bursting inside his mouth. As he approached the town centre, the hedgerows thinned and the streets became busier and finally, near the barracks, he joined a thronging crowd of young men, massed in front of the large red-brick Victorian building. No-one seemed to know what to do and, although there was a general atmosphere of excitement, everyone was looking rather baffled. Then, the doors opened and two sergeants came out. In the blink of an eye – or so it seemed to Harry – they'd formed the men into an orderly queue, which slowly ebbed as men passed through the wide doors and into the dim interior. The mid-morning August sunshine beat down as Harry waited his turn, and he began chatting to the other men around him, some of whom had travelled for miles, just because they wanted the opportunity to serve with the Royal Sussex Regiment. Harry realised that he hadn't even thought about who he might be serving with. He hadn't really even thought about the reality of enlisting at all. Suddenly, now, in front of the barracks, with all these others, so keen and excited, he found himself wondering about Rose and whether he was really doing the right thing. The man in front of him was a butcher's assistant who, by rights ought to have been at work. Harry wondered if the lad was really old enough to be there in the first place, but he was certainly enthusiastic. His older brother had already joined up, he told Harry, and he was keen not to miss out himself.

After nearly two hours, Harry found himself inside the cool, dark interior of the barracks. The process of enlistment was quick and painless. Harry watched the young butcher's assistant being questioned by the recruiting sergeant, who eyed him up and down suspiciously, but handed him his papers anyway. They walked outside together and Harry wished the youngster good luck, before turning to begin the long walk home again.

By the time Harry let himself into the house, it was early afternoon and his mother was none too pleased that he'd missed lunch, without letting anyone know.

"Really, Harry!" she said. "You might show a little more consideration. We waited over half an hour, before finally giving up and starting without you." Her voice was tired.

"I'm sorry, Mother," Harry leant down to kiss her forehead.

"Where have you been anyway?" she asked, glancing up at him.

"Nowhere important. Just out for a walk. I lost track of time." He looked out of the window as he spoke, changing the subject quickly. "Where's Rosie?"

"Oh!" Margaret exclaimed. "Susan called in just after lunch. She's taken her out for a walk."

"Susan?" Harry was surprised. "What was she doing here?"

"She said that her brother's gone off with his regiment now and, if it's alright with you, she'll be resuming her duties. I said that would be perfectly alright. I hope I did the right thing?"

"Yes, Mother. That's absolutely fine. Couldn't be better actually," he smiled. "Now, I'm going to have a bath and change my clothes. I'm horribly dusty." He paused by the door. "What time is Father due home tonight?"

"Five-thirty, as usual, dear. Why?"

"Oh," Harry hesitated. "No particular reason, I was just wondering." And with that, he quickly left the room.

"I want to speak to you both," Harry announced abruptly, as he walked into the sitting room before dinner. His parents were standing by the window, admiring the front garden.

"Why?" his father looked up nervously, and Harry wondered if he'd already guessed the truth. There was really nothing else to do, but tell them the whole story, as soon as possible. Harry took a deep breath.

"I went out this morning, into town." He cleared his throat, surprised by his own nerves.

"Oh, no!" his father interjected.

"What, Richard? What's the matter?" Margaret looked uncertainly between the two men.

"I've joined up." Harry wanted the words to come from him, rather than his father, so he ended up blurting them out rather quickly.

"Harry!" Margaret's hand moved to her mouth.

"I thought as much," said Richard.

"But what about Rose, Harry? You can't just abandon her." Tears filled Margaret's eyes.

"Come and sit down, both of you." Harry motioned to the sofa, and his parents reluctantly sat. "It's Rose I'm doing it for," he explained, standing in front of them. He pushed his fingers through his hair, took a breath, and crouched down before his mother, taking her soft, small hands in his and looking into her tearful eyes. "Please try to understand. Rose has both of you. She has Susan, and Bill and Charlotte. She's surrounded by people who care for her and love her nearly as much as I do. Any of you could raise her just as well as I could. But, you see mother, the difference is that I'm the only one who'd die for her. I'd do it in the blink of an eye, without even thinking about it." Margaret gulped back her tears. Releasing one of her hands from his grasp, she placed it gently on his cheek.

"I'm very proud of you, Harry," she managed to say, her voice stronger than Harry or his father would have thought possible. "Very proud indeed." Harry took her hand and kissed the palm gently, before standing.

"So." Richard's voice wavered more than he'd expected and he cleared his throat. "You'll be with the Royal Sussex, then?"

"Yes." Harry crossed to the sideboard and poured a glass of whisky for his father, and a larger than average sherry for his mother. "You'll never guess what, though," He said, turning and handing out the drinks. "They've only suggested that I become an officer!"

"An officer?" his mother asked. "But why? I mean, how?" Everyone stopped for a moment, then they all laughed. "I'm sorry Harry, dear," Margaret said. "I didn't mean that to sound the way it did, but, let's be honest, you know nothing about the army, or fighting wars. I mean, is it wise for you to be in charge?" Again they laughed.

"Well, Mother, I don't think I'll be in charge of the whole army – not yet anyway! I'm reliably informed that they'll train me. There was an officer there, and while the sergeant was filling in my form, he came over and talked to me. It's evidently got something to do with me being a bit older than most of the others, and having gone to the right schools, or something."

"So what happens now?" Margaret asked.

"I wait, evidently. My orders will come through."

"When?"

"I've got absolutely no idea. A few days, I think."

"And then you'll be leaving?" Margaret's voice was anxious.

"Yes, Mother. But only for training."

"For now," Richard added, under his breath.

Over the next few days, as nothing further happened, Harry began to wonder whether his papers had been lost, or whether they'd just forgotten about him. It was very difficult for him to make plans, when he had no idea what was going on, or what to expect. It was Rose that concerned him most and he wondered over and over, in his mind, whether she would be best staying with his parents and whether they could cope with her. Would his mother find it too much, having a child running around all the time? Having them stay for a few weeks was one thing, but Harry was always there, and having Rose in the house all the time without him to help, was something else altogether. He was mulling this over in his mind for the umpteenth time during breakfast on Friday morning, when Polly brought in a tray of envelopes. Richard sorted through them quickly, stopping only when he came upon a thin brown envelope, addressed to 'Mr H Belmont'. He glanced up at Margaret, before handing the letter to Harry.

"I'm to report tomorrow afternoon, to the barracks." He said, placing the letter beside his plate. He felt relieved that at last he knew what was happening, but was surprised by how little time he would have to prepare everything. Attached to the letter was a list of uniform and equipment which Harry was expected to purchase and bring with him the following afternoon. He silently passed this list to his mother, whose eyes widened considerably.

"Well!" she exclaimed, replacing her teacup in its saucer. "We're going to have our work cut out here, aren't we?" She got up from the table. "You'll have to go into town straight away, this morning, to buy most of this – at least the things we don't already have. I'll go up to your room with Polly, if you don't mind, and start sorting out everything else." Harry got up, walked around the table and bent to kiss his mother on the forehead.

"You're wonderful!" he announced, receiving a pat on the arm for his compliment. Margaret went calmly from the room, clutching the list and muttering to herself. Harry caught a couple of words, sounding like 'typical' and 'men', which brought a wry smile to his face. He turned to face his father and sat down again. "Before I go," he said, "I need to talk to you about Rose, Father."

"Yes, son. What do you want to do?"

"I don't know, really. Part of me thinks she's better off here with you and mother. It's more familiar for her and she's used to staying here. But then part of me wonders whether that's too much to ask of you both. She can be quite a handful."

"Yes. And we're not getting any younger." Richard stared at his breakfast plate.

"That's not what I meant, Father," Harry responded. "I just want an arrangement that everyone feels happy with." Richard thought for a moment.

"I can't imagine you'll be gone for that long, Harry, and your mother will definitely want Rose to stay here, but we could perhaps ask William and Charlotte to step in if things get too much. How would you feel about that?"

"It might work, I suppose." Harry sounded doubtful.

"Are you still angry with William, Harry?" Richard asked.

"No, Father. That's not important anymore. But, they're having their own baby in January. It might be too much for them as well."

"Well it probably won't come to that anyway. The war won't last more than a few months. I very much doubt you'll even be sent overseas. Why don't we invite William and Charlotte for tea this afternoon. We can discuss any arrangements you want to make and see how they feel about it."

"Very well, Father."

Richard got up from the table, walked round to his son and placed a firm hand on his shoulder. "Leave it with me, Harry. I'll take the day off and see to things. Now, you go and get yourself kitted out."

Harry was delayed in town. It would seem that he wasn't the only local man with 'officer potential' who was required to buy a uniform that morning and the queues in the outfitters were lengthy and tedious. It was mid-afternoon before he opened the front door, to be greeted by Rose, running through the hallway.

"Daddy!" she cried, as Harry dropped his parcels, fell to his knees and swept her up into his arms.

"Darling!" Harry held her head close to him, breathing in the smell of her, squeezing her tiny body in his arms. He looked up to see Susan, standing a little way away, tears in her eyes. "Rosie," Harry said, putting her down on the floor. "Can you do something for me?" She nodded. "Can you run along and find grandmama? Can you tell her that daddy's back?" He held onto her hands just a little longer. "Then, once I've unpacked all these parcels, can we have a play in the garden?" Rose nodded her head again, then freed her hands and ran headlong into the sitting room, which was the shortest route to the garden, where she knew Margaret was dead-heading the roses.

Harry got to his feet again. "Susan," he said, once Rose had gone. "I need to have a word with you."

"Yes, sir." Her tears threatened to overflow.

"Come into the sitting room for a moment. I have an awful lot to do, but we need to talk." Leaving his parcels scattered on the floor, Harry led the way into the cool sitting room. Once inside, he wandered over to the French doors and closed them. "I'm sure you've heard that I'll be leaving tomorrow," he said, calmly, turning back to Susan.

"Yes, sir."

"Well, I want you to know that Rose will almost certainly be staying here for the time being, unless it becomes too much for my parents, in which case she'll probably go to William and Charlotte King at Downwillow, or they may just help out with things here. We're all getting together later to discuss the arrangements and I want you to join us. I want everyone to understand that, whatever happens, wherever she lives, you and Rose must be together. You're part of her life and I won't have you separated under any circumstances."

Susan gulped, now incapable of speaking, as tears rolled down her cheeks. She just about managed to nod her head. Harry stepped forward, standing in front of her.

"Please don't cry, Susan," he said. "Everything will be alright. I'll see to it that you're taken care of. I promise." As he turned to leave, she wondered how it was that he had completely failed to understand that it wasn't Rose, or herself, that she was crying for.

Chapter Five

Moore Barracks, Shorncliffe, Kent
Monday, October 26th, 1914

Dear Mother and Father,

I hope this letter finds you well. We are now quite settled in here. I'm sharing a room with my friend Edward, who I think I mentioned in my last letter. There are two other men with us, Timmings and Bishop, both from the Brighton area. We all get along quite well, although all three of them are much younger than me. Our mornings are still spent drilling the men, or rather trying to, but the afternoons are filled with lectures on all manner of different topics, which I'm probably not supposed to mention. I don't find the physical work as hard as some of the others. Many of them have only done office work - or no work at all, in some cases. Exercise of any sort seems quite foreign to them! Some of the men, like Edward, have come out of university, or have only just finished school and are really little more than boys. They're organising a concert later in the week. These are normally good fun, so I think I'll go along - even if only to support Edward. He's the only man we've got who can play the piano, which he does very well.

I'm due a weekend leave, which I hope I can take this Saturday and Sunday coming. I will only be able to find out on Friday afternoon or evening, so I'll send you a telegram and let you know. If not, it will almost certainly be the following weekend. Please don't go to any trouble or arrange anything special. I just want some peace and quiet and a few hours with Rose. I received her drawings and have pinned them to the wall next to my bed.

I don't feel like I have anything of interest to tell you, so I apologise if this letter is a little dull. However, I have my fingers crossed for the weekend and, in the meantime, please give Rosie a big cuddle from me.

With fondest regards, your loving son, Harry.

****

Harry looked up as he finished his letter. Edward was in the bunk opposite, still writing. His fair head turned from side to side as he wrote, and occasionally he would put his pencil into his mouth, staring into space. He smiled to himself, seemingly unaware of Harry's presence. He sat cross-legged, balancing his writing pad on one knee, his pencil moving quickly across the page. Even in the dimly-lit room, Harry was acutely aware of Edward's youth; the innocence of his expression coupled with the purity of his complexion could not escape Harry's artistic eye and he sometimes used these quiet moments to sketch his young friend, secretly capturing his carefree, boyish features.

"Another long letter then?" Harry asked, interrupting Edward's train of thought. "Honestly, poor Isabel. I don't know how she finds the time to do anything else in the day, by the time she's finished reading them."

"She likes my letters, so be quiet! Anyway, I've nearly finished." Edward blushed, resuming his writing.

"I don't know what you find to write about!"

"Well that's for me to know, isn't it?"

"Are you up for leave this weekend?" Harry asked, putting his own pencil and writing paper away.

"Yes, hopefully. Well, I've been told I should, anyway. That's what I've been writing to Isabel about. It's ever so difficult, you know, with her father not approving of me. It sort of spoils my leave."

"The vicar clearly has very poor taste. What's not to approve of?" Harry laughed.

"Oh, I think he had hopes of someone more like you. Well educated, tall, handsome, eloquent… oh yes, and rich!" Edward smiled, looking up from his letter. "What about you?"

"What about me?" Harry asked, grinning. "Weren't we just talking about me?"

"I meant are you getting any leave this weekend?"

"Hopefully."

"So, you'll be able to snatch a few hours with Rose then?"

"With any luck, yes. And I can't wait. It's been weeks since I last saw her and I'll bet she's grown so much."

"Well, look on the bright side. At least you don't have any obstacles in seeing your beloved. It might be easier if my parents were still alive. My mother was always very good at listening. She would have understood and I think she would have liked Isabel. Also, I'd at least have somewhere to stay. There's an inn near to where Isabel lives – actually it's more of a hotel really, but it's quite expensive – well it is for me."

"There's no chance of staying at the vicarage then?"

"Stay at the vicarage? You are joking, aren't you? I'm lucky if they let me in the house, let alone allow me to stay!"

"Can't you at least try talking to her father?"

"I have!" Edward finally finished his letter with a flourish. "He's made his feelings very plain. Goodness only knows what he'd say if I asked Isabel to marry me."

"Are you thinking about asking her to marry you, then?" Harry asked.

"I think of little else. The problem is that we're both still only nineteen, so we'd need her father's permission."

"And you don't think that will be forthcoming?"

"It's not very likely." Edward looked dreamily out of the grimy window. "It must be lovely, being married, not having all these things to worry about. Not having other people interfering..." He stopped suddenly, glancing over at Harry. "Oh, sorry Harry. I didn't mean to remind you..."

"It's alright. Don't worry about it. I'm sure you and Isabel will be very happy together, one day. In spite of her father. And in the meantime, you'll both just have to be patient, won't you?"

"I suppose so."

The door burst opened, admitting not only the smell of stale cabbage, which seemed to pervade the entire barracks, but also Timmings and Bishop, both of whom had been playing football. "I don't care what they say, that was never a goal!" Bishop announced in his customary thunderous tone, before he'd even crossed the threshold.

"Keep it down!" Harry urged.

"Sorry. Didn't mean to interrupt," Bishop replied, closing the door. "What are you two up to then?"

"Oh, nothing much." It was Edward who replied. "Just writing letters."

"Not to the lovely Isabel? Again?" Timmings walked over to Edward's bed, sat down and nudged him, knowingly.

"Yes, to the lovely Isabel," Edward retorted. Timmings looked up.

"What about you then, Harry? Writing to the famous mystery woman in your life?"

"Timmings, will you stop fishing. There is no mystery woman – famous or otherwise."

"You can't fool us, Harry. At your age, there must be someone waiting for you at home. Someone looking after that daughter of yours." Harry looked up, suddenly uncertain what to say.

"I'm going to turn in." Edward announced, getting up.

"To dream of the lovely Isabel, I'll bet?" Bishop leered from his bunk, where he was now sitting, picking at his fingernails and biting them avidly, which was just one of his many unpleasant habits.

"Wouldn't you dream of her, if she was yours?" Timmings laughed.

"Too right!" Bishop laid down.

"That's not a likely circumstance for either of you, with your appalling manners," Edward said, lying down on his bunk, and winking across at Harry, who smiled back gratefully.

At three o'clock on Friday afternoons, the list was always posted outside the adjutant's office, detailing who had been granted weekend leave, but the men were kept in lectures until five. They would sit, unhearing, watching the hands on the clock tick slowly round, waiting to be released. As soon as they were free, they all scrambled to see whose name was listed, and whose wasn't. Edward ran along the corridor to the noticeboard, craning to see past the swarming men. Harry drifted along behind, trying to look unconcerned, his fingers crossed behind his back. If it was good news, there would be plenty of time to celebrate afterwards and if it was bad, then he'd rather delay the inevitable disappointment for as long as possible. Being so tall, Harry could see over the heads of most of the other men. His own name, he knew would be near the top of the list and sure enough it was there. Edward was still struggling to see through the other faces, but Harry stood on his tiptoes, used his height and looked further down the page. *Thank goodness*. He heaved a sigh of relief, reading the last name on the list: *Edward Wilson*.

Edward felt a hand on his shoulder.

"You're there, Edward," Harry said.

"Am I? I can't see." They both moved away to give the others more space. "What do they feed you in the country to make you so impossibly tall?"

"I've got absolutely no idea."

"Was your name there too?" Edward asked. "I couldn't see the top of the list either."

"Yes. So aren't we both the lucky ones?"

"Yes, aren't we!" Harry and Edward knew, without having to say a word, that both of them would have felt terrible if only one had been granted leave. "I feel like a school boy at the end of term, which, when you think about it is a bit ridiculous, isn't it? We're only getting two days' leave, after all!" He slapped Harry across the back and ran through the doors and onto the parade ground, whooping for joy.

****

"Army food isn't bad, really," Harry announced, wiping his mouth with his napkin and sitting back, satisfied, in his chair. "But nothing beats Mrs Cox's roast beef." He'd only arrived home half an hour before dinner and hadn't had time to change out of his uniform. He couldn't help feeling slightly self-conscious as he looked around the table. His mother's idea of not doing anything special had been to invite

William, Charlotte and Katherine King to dine. At Harry's request, Rose had been allowed to join the adults in the dining room.

"Did I tell you that Philip's enlisted too, Harry?" Katherine asked, her voice shaking a little.

"No, you didn't," Harry replied.

"I'm terribly worried about him," she continued. "I really don't think he's cut out for army life."

"Oh, don't you fret, Katherine. He'll be fine! The army's not so bad, you know," Harry said, trying to sound reassuring.

"He's not like you, though Harry," Katherine went on. "He's very quiet. More of an indoors type of man, if you know what I mean." William rolled his eyes, sighing loudly and Harry wondered whether Katherine ever talked of anything else.

"The army takes all sorts, Katherine. One of my room-mates in the barracks is just the same," Harry lied. "A very quiet, unassuming chap. He was really shy at the beginning, but we all rallied round and he's getting along just fine now. You'll see. Your young man will probably thrive."

"Now, young Rose," Margaret said, changing the subject. "What about a little slice of treacle tart? And then I think you should be off to bed. It's getting late."

"Treacle tart!" Harry exclaimed. "My favourite! Just like being back in the nursery. Watch out, Rosie, or Daddy will eat it all up first!"

Harry sat with Rose through two stories and then stayed at her bedside, gently caressing her auburn ringlets, as she began to doze, her eyes opening every so often, just to check he was still there. He watched her breathing; his own breath matching hers. Once he was certain she was sound asleep he reluctantly left her lying in bed and closed her door. At the bottom of the stairs, he paused, straightened his tunic and took a breath before rejoining the others in the sitting room.

"Sorry I've been so long everyone," he announced cheerfully, as he entered. "Rose insisted on two stories tonight." Margaret poured Harry a cup of coffee.

"So, Charlotte. How are you?" Harry looked across to where Charlotte was sitting on the sofa next to Katherine, her hand resting on her swollen stomach.

"I'm absolutely fine, thank you, Harry."

"You're certainly looking well. And how's everything going on the farm, Bill?" he asked, turning to William.

"Oh," William replied, "I suppose things are a bit harder, really. I only have a few farmhands now, and most of them are either boys or are getting on in years. But who am I to complain, when I'm safe at home?"

"Don't be ridiculous, Bill," Harry responded quickly. "No-one expects you to fight when you've got a farm to run. The work that you're doing is just as important as anything we're doing in the army."

"I suppose so. It just feels wrong, not to be doing my bit, that's all."

"But you are, Bill, you are." Harry smiled at William, draining his coffee cup and missing the glance that was exchanged between Charlotte and Margaret, both of whom wondered how it was that Harry always seemed to manage to say the right thing.

Later, when the Kings had gone home, Margaret and Richard studied Harry for a short while, Margaret looking at him over the top of her glasses, while she pretended to be engrossed in her cross stitch.

"How are you really, son?" Richard asked, putting down the newspaper which he hadn't been reading.

"I'm fine, honestly, Father. The army's not as bad as many people would have you believe. And there's Edward. He's great company. I don't know what I'd do without him."

"This is the young man from Lewes, isn't it? The one you wrote about?" Margaret enquired.

"Yes, Mother. We met on the first day and, luckily enough, we've been together ever since. I suppose I rather took him under my wing. He was ever so nervous, even though he was in the O.T.C. at University. He'd just finished his first year and interrupted his studies to enlist. He's only nineteen, you see, and he doesn't really have anyone else. His parents died when he was in his last year at school."

"Oh, how awful," Margaret said. "He must have been terribly lonely."

"I think he was, but he's been seeing a young lady, named Isabel for over a year now." Harry smiled. "We're never allowed to forget it! He talks of nothing else, but his beloved Isabel, and writes to her constantly."

"What about the other men?" Margaret asked. "What are they like?"

"Oh. They're nice enough, but some of them are a bit loud for me. They're all about Edward's age, so I do feel a bit old sometimes. They seem to be mainly concerned with football and food. It's a fine life, really, all things considered. It's a bit boring, perhaps, but that's not much to complain about." He paused for a moment. "I just miss Rose. I miss her terribly – and you, of course!" he added quickly, smiling.

"We know son," Richard replied. "She misses you too."

"I'm worried she'll forget me if I'm sent overseas. I won't be able to get so much leave then."

"Do you think you will be – sent overseas, I mean?" Margaret asked.

"Oh. Not yet. We're nowhere near ready. I think it will be next year at least before we get to go."

"But, it'll all be over by then, surely?" Margaret said, hopefully.

"I don't know, Mother. None of us do really. No-one tells us anything." Harry desperately wanted to change the subject now. He was fed up with talking about the war. It was all that anyone spoke about in the barracks, except they knew nothing either, so their stories became more and more far-fetched every day. "Rosie seems very happy here. She's certainly grown a lot!" Harry said.

"Yes, hasn't she?" Margaret replied. "I'm going to take her into town next week to get a new coat for the winter."

"I wish I could come. She always loved trying on clothes."

"Susan is going to come with us. Rose is insisting."

"Somehow I thought she might."

The next morning, while Margaret and Rose attended church, Harry sat in his father's study. He'd wanted to go to church too, desperate not to be parted from Rose, even for a moment, but he also knew that this might be his only chance to talk to his father alone.

"Are you sure about this, Harry?" Richard asked from behind his desk.

"Yes, Father. I've been giving it a lot of thought and I think it's for the best." Harry's words were final and Richard knew from his tone that there was no point in arguing with him. "The trust is already set up for Rose; my will is made, so that won't change and Rose won't be affected. I'm only suggesting that while I'm away, you will take control of my money, that's all. I can't do anything from a trench in Belgium or France, so it makes sense for you to manage my affairs."

"Just until you get back."

"Yes, Father." Neither of them would admit the possibility of the alternative. "Of course, I may need some funds occasionally, but I'll let you know."

"And I'll write to you if I'm going to spend anything."

"No, Father." Harry leant forward, looking across the desk. "That's not how I want it to work. I trust you implicitly. You don't need my permission to touch the money, nor do you have to account to me for every penny. If Rose wants something, or you and mother need some money – just take it."

"I'm not sure I feel entirely happy about that, Harry."

"Well I do. If I end up going out there, I'm going to have other things on my mind. I want to know that you're all taken care of."

Richard cleared his throat. "We'll need to clear it with the bank. There's going to be some paperwork involved."

"If I can ask you to arrange things, and send me through the documents, or I might get a weekend leave again soon. I'll let you know. As long as we arrange it all before I go overseas."

"I'm sure it can all be dealt with in plenty of time. I'll go into the bank tomorrow."

"I think it's best if we don't tell Mother," Harry suggested. "She'll probably misunderstand and it might make her worry, when there's no need."

Richard nodded his agreement, hiding his feelings of discomfort about the arrangement.

Sunday lunch was very subdued, everyone being well aware that Harry had only a few hours left before his wrenching departure. Rose was the only member of the family who was oblivious, and she chattered her way through the meal. Harry tried to join in with his daughter's conversation, but even he found it increasingly difficult as the meal progressed. Later, as dusk began to settle over the garden and Margaret closed the curtains, Harry went to his bedroom, put on his uniform and packed his small valise. Coming back down the stairs, he was greeted by the sight of everyone standing in the hallway. He took a breath and braced himself for the ordeal of saying goodbye. Polly stood at the bottom of the stairs, holding his cap and greatcoat. Putting these on, he asked after Walter, apologising for not having done so before.

"He's quite well, thank you, sir." Polly smiled. "He writes all the time. I don't know where he is, of course. Somewhere in Belgium, but I don't know exactly where."

"I see. Well, next time you write, tell him from me to take care of himself."

"I will, sir. Thank you, sir," she beamed.

Harry turned to be faced with Margaret and Susan, who was holding Rose, and then Richard, who was waiting by the sitting room door.

"Well, goodbye, everyone." Harry tried to sound cheerful. Margaret moved forward first, kissing Harry on both cheeks.

"I'll be home again soon," he said to her. She just nodded, smiling. Next came his father, who shook his hand.

"Take care of yourself son."

"Of course, Father," Harry replied. "Look after everyone."

"That goes without saying, Harry."

Taking a deep breath, Harry turned to Susan. Rose was hoisted in her arms, tired after a long day. Harry took his daughter and she rested her head on his shoulder. He pulled her close to him, feeling her breath on his neck, the softness of her skin on his. He wanted to fill his senses with her, to treasure every touch and smell. After a few minutes, Harry glanced up at the grandfather clock in the corner of the hallway. He gave a small nod to Susan, who stepped forward and eased Rose away from Harry and back into her own arms. She was so sleepy that she barely noticed.

"Goodbye, my darling," he whispered, then turned, picked up his case and walked away.

****

As he lay in his bunk that night, wide awake, listening to the stentorian snores coming from Bishop's gaping mouth, Harry buried his face in the rough pillow case. Weekend leave was an ecstasy of pleasure and pain, so closely mingled that it was becoming impossible to discern one from the other. He had looked forward to it so much, but parting from Rose was getting harder and harder to bear.

Edward too, had been quiet and distant upon his return. Harry knew that Isabel would have gone to the station with him; she always did, despite her father's protests. She would have stood on the platform, with countless other girlfriends, wives and lovers. They would all have waved as the train departed, handkerchiefs in hand, or held to weeping eyes. Then they would have turned to walk solemnly home, leaving their men, alone in the company of strangers, all of them sharing the same silent thoughts.

It was lunchtime the next day before Edward and Harry had a chance to sit quietly together, away from the other men.

"How was it?" Edward asked first, his face a little paler than usual, his generous mouth attempting a smile which went nowhere near touching his light blue eyes.

"Oh, you know. The same as last time."

"Yes," Edward hesitated. "I wonder if it will ever get any easier – saying goodbye, I mean."

"No. I think it will probably get much harder."

"Oh, don't." Edward lowered his eyes.

"How was Isabel?" Harry wanted to lighten the mood. It didn't work.

"Upset," Edward replied. "A friend of hers, Connie, had heard that her fiancé has been wounded; in the leg, I think. He's on his way back to England, so it must be fairly bad. Isabel's talking about going with her friend to visit him in the hospital. I rather wish that she wouldn't." Edward paused, looking at the ceiling. "It's odd, you know. I'm really not afraid of going out there. I'm not even afraid of dying, not really. Well, as long as it's quick, anyway. As long as I don't really know anything about it. But, what really frightens me is being wounded – scarred or maimed in some way. And then coming back home to see that look on Isabel's face. That look of pity. She had something of that look on her face when she was talking to her friend. I never want her to think that about me. I'd rather be dead than see that look."

"I don't think it would be pity on Rose's face, Edward. The look on her face would be fear. And all in all, I think I'd rather have pity. That, or nothing at all."

The next few weeks continued, pretty much as before. The training intensified a little, and they were given additional responsibilities. The dread of parting from loved ones was soon forgotten, replaced once again by the earnest desire for further leave. Edward's letters to Isabel remained long and constant. He sat most evenings, pushing his fingers through his hair, his head bent over his writing pad. Two weeks before Christmas, both he and Harry began to hope that they might be the lucky ones, chosen to spend a few precious days at home. Then came the news. The battalion was to be moved, and all leave was cancelled.

"Folkestone?" Bishop cried. "But that's only up the road. Surely we can still have some leave before we go!"

"It's bloody unfair, if you ask me." Timmings agreed with his friend.

"And I've heard it's a God-awful barracks – old wooden shacks and sodding freezing," Bishop said. He wasn't wrong.

Harry was disappointed that there were eight of them sharing a large wooden barrack room, with a single brazier in the centre, its flue rising up through the high roof. But their dismay was short-lived. Within a few weeks, they were on the move again.

"What on earth are they doing?" Edward protested while they packed.

"I'm not sure they know," Harry replied. "But they seem to be slowly moving us around the country. Perhaps this is the army's idea of sightseeing. Still, at least it's Aldershot this time. That might mean we're not going abroad yet. I'd have thought they'd have kept us near the coast if they were going to send us out anytime soon. So, more training, I suppose, although what else they think we need to be taught, goodness only knows."

Harry's hopes seemed well founded to begin with. Ramilies Barracks was certainly an improvement on Folkestone, and instead of being trained themselves, they were now being put in charge of their own platoons of men. Harry was also made responsible for provisions and pay: a mundane duty, which meant less weekend leave, as pay was always given out on Saturdays, making it difficult for him to get away from the barracks himself. Edward resented this greatly, on Harry's behalf, but Harry himself was less aggrieved. He managed to arrange for his parents and Rose to visit for tea on occasional Sundays, when he could get time off. They would meet at a little tea shop in the town, where Harry would treat Rose to whatever she wanted, which was usually sandwiches and an enormous cream cake. Harry reached the conclusion that actually this arrangement was easier for Rose than him going home. She didn't have time to get used to him being there before it was time for him to leave again. Harry would wave them off at the station and return to the barracks with a heavy heart. On a couple of occasions, Edward offered to take over Harry's Saturday pay duties so that Harry could go home.

"It's very kind, Edward," Harry replied, after one such offer. "But I think it's best this way. It's easier for Rose."

"And what about you, Harry? You're bloody miserable."

"It's alright. At least I still get to see her."

"For a couple of hours every few weeks. It's not the same."

"A few hours is better than nothing. And I think we're just going to have to get used to it. We can't stay in training forever. They're going to send us out eventually and then I'll be grateful for whatever I can get."

Chapter Six

Spring 1915

Ramilies Barracks, Aldershot, Hampshire
Saturday, May 15th 1915

Dear Mother and Father

We're moving to a new barracks tomorrow and then I've been granted ten days' leave, starting the day after, so this is just a quick note to let you know, and to ask if it would be possible for all of us to go down to Watersmeet, at least for part of my leave, if father can be spared from the office, and if it can be arranged in time. Sorry for the short notice, but we have only just been told ourselves.

I will see you on Monday afternoon, and remain, your loving son, Harry.

p.s. Love and cuddles to Rosie.

****

Stopping at the end of the driveway, Harry studied the front garden, which looked neat and tidy, as ever, although the pink cherry blossom, a little late this year, still garnished the grass to either side of the wide driveway. Harry stood still for a moment, taking in all the details of the garden and the house. He wanted to remember as much as possible. Looking at the front door, he wished that he could just run inside and gather Rose into his arms, but knew at the same time, that to do so would mean the beginning of the end: the start of the countdown to departure. He took the final few paces to the front door and knocked. He waited for a few moments, then the door opened, to reveal Polly, her white shiny face, contrasting starkly with a pair of red, swollen eyes.

Harry knew at once. "Oh no, Polly. Not Walter?"

The young girl snivelled, nodding her head. Then she let out a great sob and covered her face with her hands, turning to run away. Harry caught her arm and pulled her back to him. Still standing in the doorway, he held her tightly in his arms, as she shook and sobbed onto the rough fibres of his tunic. After a few minutes she drew back from him, her cheeks now red and wet. She dabbed at her face with a soaking handkerchief and blew her nose.

"When?" Harry asked, his hands resting on her shoulders, his voice little more than a whisper. She couldn't respond. He turned away for a moment and kicked his suitcase to one side, closing the front door behind him. Then he took Polly's hand and led her to the chair by the staircase. She hesitated before allowing him to lower her gently down onto the seat. "When was it?" He repeated, crouching in front of her.

"His mother found out this morning, sir," she whimpered, in between sniffs. "They didn't write to me, what with us not being married yet. It just says 'killed in action', that's all." She wiped her nose again. "Mr Belmont – your father, sir – said he'd try to find out something more from the barracks."

"I'm sure he will." Harry's voice was reassuring. Hearing footsteps on the stairs behind her Polly shot to her feet.

"Polly." Harry heard his mother's voice. "I told you to go and lie down. What are you doing down here?"

"Mr Harry's home, ma'am." Polly sniffed and nodded in Harry's direction. "I thought you'd be wanting me to help with the dinner."

"I can see that Harry's home, Polly. But right now what I'd like is for you to go up to your room and lie down. We can manage dinner perfectly well. Now run along. I'll bring you up a cup of tea in a minute." Margaret Belmont led the girl towards the staircase as she was talking, then she turned back and reached up to kiss her son on the cheek. "I'm so sorry, Harry, dear. I didn't mean to ignore you. It's been absolute chaos here today! You simply wouldn't believe it. Leave your case there for now, if you want. Rose is upstairs in the nursery."

"Is Polly alright?" Harry asked, looking at the maid as she climbed up the stairs, her head bowed.

"No, dear. But she will be, in time. It's been an awful shock for her. She's got no family, since her mother died. She has nowhere else to go, otherwise I'd have sent her home."

"This is her home, Mother – and we're her family."

"Yes, I suppose you're right, Harry."

"It might be better if she kept herself busy," he suggested.

"We'll see how she is a bit later on. Now, you go and see Rose, while I arrange this tea for Polly. We'll have dinner a bit early, shall we? Then Rose can join us."

Harry marvelled, as he watched his mother disappear into the kitchen, how she always seemed to take everything in her stride. He smiled and shook his head, remembering his own and his father's worries about her at the beginning of the war. In reality, she was turning out to be the strongest and most practical of all of them.

After an early dinner, Rose was taken upstairs by Susan and changed into her nightdress. Then, as a special treat, she was allowed to come back downstairs for a little while. She sat on Harry's lap, her arms clasped around his neck. He held onto her tightly.

"Not too long now, Rosie," Margaret said. "We've got a busy day tomorrow." She turned to her husband. "Did you manage to find out anything about Polly's young man, dear?"

"Not very much. I went up to see her when I got in. The Colonel wasn't very forthcoming, I'm afraid, but said Walter's unit had been fighting near somewhere called Ypres. He doesn't know any details as yet. He said he'd see what he could do, though. I'll go and see him again when we get back from Cornwall." Richard got up and walked to the sideboard. He offered Harry a glass of whisky, which was declined, then poured one for himself.

"I must say, son." He said, replacing the glass stopper into the decanter and turning back to Harry. "It's splendid to have you home for a bit longer than a couple of days – it makes a pleasant change." Harry pulled Rose even closer to him.

"It's called embarkation leave," he said. No-one uttered a word. "I can't tell you exactly when we're leaving, or where I'll end up – I don't actually know that bit myself yet, but they try to let us have a bit longer at home before we go."

"I see," Richard said, returning slowly to sit next to his wife.

"What time are we leaving tomorrow?" Harry asked, trying to brighten the atmosphere.

"We're catching the ten o'clock train," Margaret replied, her face remaining pale, her eyes fixed on Harry.

"I'd better get Rosie up to bed, then." Harry stood, gathering Rose in his arms. "I'm sure we'll have a lovely few days. I'm really looking forward to it." When he reached the door, he glanced back. His parents were sitting close together on the sofa, holding hands and looking at each other. He quietly left the room, shutting door behind him.

****

Harry sat on the cliff top, breathing deeply. The breeze teased through his hair and the early morning sun shone down onto his upturned face. He'd left everyone else sleeping and knew that, after their long journey the previous day, provided he wasn't too much longer, no-one would ever know that he'd stolen out of the cottage in the early hours of the morning, to watch the sun rise over the bay. He wanted to soak up the sights, sounds and smells, to take with him to France. Beneath him, the waves lapped gently over the seaweed-coated rocks. Harry lay down, the grass soft and damp below his broad back. Closing his eyes, he saw Bella, walking across a flat green lawn, a red rose in her hand, her pale blue dress clinging to her slim waist, its skirts flowing around her ankles. "Bella…" he whispered. "Oh, God! Make it stop!" he cried aloud, his eyes snapping open. He pushed his fingers through his hair, feeling the familiar numbness creeping over him.

As dawn turned into day, Harry came sharply back to his senses. He jumped to his feet and glanced at his watch. He didn't want to have to make any explanations for his absence, so he turned his back on the sea and walked towards to the cottage, the soft leather of his worn boots soaking up the dew which still coated the thick grass.

The cottage was bathed in silence as Harry let himself in, creeping down the hallway to the kitchen, where he found his mother sitting alone at the table, turning a teaspoon between her fingers.

"Hello, dear," she said in a half-whisper.

"Good morning, Mother," Harry replied, disguising his surprise very well. "You're up early."

"Yes. I couldn't sleep either. Shall I make some tea?"

Harry offered to make it himself and walked over to the range. Margaret joined him, laying her hand on his arm. "It's alright, you know, Harry," she said, looking up into his face.

"What is?" he asked.

"To still be mourning. I wish you weren't so unhappy, but it's alright to still grieve for her." Harry moved to the sink, filling the kettle.

"You know?" he asked.

"Of course I know, Harry. You don't actually think that you could keep anything from me, do you?" Margaret gathered cups and saucers and put the teapot on the table.

"Oh." Harry's voice betrayed his disappointment. "I thought I was hiding it quite well."

"You are, dear. But you can't hide much from me. You never could. Even when you were little I always knew when something was wrong."

"I'm sure everyone thinks I should be over it by now. It's been more than three years, after all."

"It doesn't matter what everyone thinks. You can't put a time on these things, Harry. It will take as long as it takes." The kettle began to whistle. Harry took it from the heat, warmed the pot and added three teaspoons of dusty black leaves before filling it with steaming water. He sat, staring out of the window to the small kitchen garden.

"You must think I'm terribly weak, Mother."

"Oh, don't be ridiculous, Harry," Margaret replied, sitting opposite him. "You're the strongest, bravest man I know." She paused, "And I'm immeasurably proud of you." Harry felt the prick of tears in his eyes, as his mother reached forward and took his hands in hers. "You'll get over this one day and, who knows, maybe you'll find someone else."

"Maybe," Harry replied. "But I'm still not sure that I want to."

Margaret released Harry's hands, smiling at him. "You will, Harry. You can't live your whole life by yourself. You're too nice to be alone."

"You would say that, you're my mother!"

"You wait and see. One day it will just happen, probably when you're least expecting it." Margaret poured the tea. "Fetch me another cup, Harry. I'll take one into your father." Harry did as he was told. "I'm glad we had this little chat," his mother said, taking the cup from him. "I'd have hated you to go away without us having spoken."

"We haven't spoken about me going away though, have we, Mother? Not really." Margaret picked up two of the steaming cups, her hands shaking slightly.

"I'm not up to discussing that with you yet, Harry. I may never be able to talk about it. I only keep myself going by not thinking about it too much." She turned towards the door, averting her gaze from his. "Once you've gone; when you write, please don't tell me anything. No details, if you don't mind. I'm sorry. I know you might want to tell us, but I can't bear to know anything about it all."

"Of course, Mother. If that's what you want." Margaret glanced back at him and smiled, her eyes glistening, before she turned and left him alone.

After a few days of good weather, plenty of fresh air and exercise, Harry felt as though he'd got the army out of his system, even if only for a brief time. Life in the harbour seemed to have carried on just as before and it really was quite hard at times to remember that there was a war on. Harry got up early on a couple of very fine mornings and went out to sketch. The view from the cliff top was a particular favourite and he took a sketch pad with him each day, capturing a different view from the cliffs, or the harbour wall, to take to France with him as reminders of exactly what he was missing; what he was fighting for. The view out to sea, the cliff top, the grass under his feet, the sand, the waves, the tiny harbour. All of them were his. He also made a couple of pencil sketches of Rose in the same pad, wanting to show her off to Edward. It was hard to get her to sit still, but Harry didn't really need her to. He knew every contour of her face, every curl of auburn hair, the blue-green glint in her sparkling eyes, her perfect grinning lips and the way the tip of her tiny nose turned up, just a little. They spent the warmest part of the day on the beach, just Harry and Rose. Susan supplied them with a picnic lunch and Harry passed the time playing, drawing and making sand sculptures for his enchanted daughter. They paddled together, but the water was still too cold for swimming properly. Harry so wanted to teach Rose to swim and to dive, just as his father had taught him and occasionally, when he let his mind wander from those brief moments of perfection, he worried that he might not get the chance.

The evenings were spent telling stories to Rose, playing cards with his father and reading by himself: a luxury that army life did not afford. Harry slept soundly after the first night and took no more solitary, early morning walks. All too soon, though, the week was over and they were on the homeward-bound train again. Harry sat by the window, with Rose nestling up against him, sucking her thumb. He wondered, as he stared out at the passing countryside, why he couldn't just freeze time and why this happiness couldn't go on forever.

Saying goodbye after that delicious week, was the hardest thing that Harry had ever done. Knowing where he was going when he left, not even his stoic mother had dry eyes and, for the first time in his life, Harry saw her cry openly. He held her in his arms for a long time until Richard came and comforted her, giving Harry a meaningful nod. Then, after Harry had finished saying goodbye to a tearful Rose and had just reached the door, she cried out and started to run after him. Susan held her back, her arms thrashing wildly, her screams piercing his heart. Eventually Harry just had to leave, not even closing the door behind him. He could still hear Rose sobbing behind him, as he walked quickly down the driveway. He didn't dare look back, even for a second. He knew that if he did, he would have to go back, run to her, take her in his arms, comfort her and never, ever let her go again.

At the barracks in Dover, the others joined him one by one, and he could tell from the look on their faces that he wasn't alone. They had all had difficult goodbyes to make. Edward was one of the last to return and, when he did, he simply walked over to his bunk, dropped his bag on the floor and sat down heavily, staring into space, eyes unseeing. Harry knew that neither of them could speak, but after a while, when Edward glanced over in his direction, their eyes briefly met.

The following evening, while some of the others were playing cards, Harry and Edward sat on their bunks in the furthest corner of the barrack room.

"That really was the toughest thing I've ever done," Edward began. "I don't think anything we'll have to do out there will ever match that."

"No," Harry agreed. "How was Isabel?"

"Well, it was lovely to start with."

"Despite the vicar?"

"Yes, despite the vicar," Edward smiled. "He was busy for most of the week and then we were able to spend a little time alone, on the Sunday, while her parents were at church."

"They left you on your own? Knowing your disreputable character?"

"Yes, alright! It was just for an hour or so." Edward paused, turned red and mumbled, "I asked her to marry me."

"You did what?"

"I asked her to marry me." Edward's voice was clearer this time.

"And what did the vicar say to that?"

"He doesn't know. We haven't told anyone yet. It's just between us."

"Oh, I see."

"Well, Isabel's still only twenty."

"And so are you."

"Yes, obviously. So without her father's permission, there's nothing doing." Edward kicked his heels along the floor. "I just wanted to ask her before leaving. You understand, don't you?"

"Of course I do." Harry hesitated. "So what went wrong?"

"Sorry?"

"Well, you said it was good to start with. What happened? Isabel didn't change her mind, did she?"

"No, she bloody well didn't!"

"Oh, well. That's alright then."

"Her father's just been very difficult during this last few days. It was almost as though he'd guessed, or sensed something. He did everything he could to keep us apart. He was just unbearable. We'd had such a lovely day on Sunday and he was spoiling the whole thing. Then, yesterday, there was a terrible row between Isabel and her father and he said she couldn't come to see me off."

"Oh, Edward. So Isabel didn't come to the station?"

"No. We said our goodbyes at her parents' house, in front of her mother and father. Isabel was crying. It was bloody awful. I just wanted to hold her, Harry, you know. Just to comfort her and say goodbye properly. I tried to and he stopped me. He pulled me away from her, and turned on me. As if it wasn't bad enough that I was leaving, he had to go and create this terrible scene." Edward dropped his head. "He pushed me out onto the garden path. Then he slammed the door on me. I could happily have punched him." Tears were welling in Edward's eyes. "I could still hear her through the door. She was crying and he was shouting at her. I should have gone back." Aware of the other men across the barrack room, Harry went and sat next to Edward, shielding him from their view.

"There was nothing you could have done, Eddie," he said.

"I should have tried."

"What would you have done, if you'd gone back, Eddie?"

"I'd have taken her away from there."

"And then what?"

"I don't know. I'd have found her somewhere else to live, I suppose."

"And how would you have done that? You were due to catch a train back here. You didn't have time to organise anywhere for Isabel to stay and even if you could have arranged it, she'd have been left on her own, without either you or her family. Living with them may not be what you want for her. It may not even be what she wants, but right now, Eddie, it's about all she's got. She has a roof over her head and with you going out to France, she's better off with her family." Edward sat still and silent for a while.

"I know you're right, Harry," he said eventually. "I couldn't have done anything. That's what makes it worse really. I feel so useless."

"Oh do be quiet, Eddie. You're not useless. It's just an awful situation that you can't control. If we weren't about to go to France, things would be very different, but there's nothing you can do about that either."

"It could be months before we get home again."

"You can still write. You'll be able to make sure she's alright."

"What if he stops my letters, Harry? He could keep them back from her, couldn't he?"

"Isabel will still be able to write to you. She can get out of the house to post a letter, can't she?"

"Yes."

"Then she'll write and tell you if your letters aren't getting through. She's used to getting at least one a day, after all."

"And if they aren't? What will I do?"

"You'll stop panicking for a start. There are other ways of sending letters, Eddie. You said she had a friend, remember? The one with the injured fiancé? You could write to Isabel at her friend's address."

"Nice idea Harry, except that I don't know her friend's address. I only know her first name is Connie, or Constance."

"Do you know her surname?" Harry asked.

"No."

"Any idea at all of where she lives?"

"Well, Isabel and I met her once, outside her parents' house. I could take you there, but I can't remember the address. It's not far from Isabel's house."

"Then you've nothing to worry about," Harry said.

"How do you work that out?"

"Eddie, if the need arises, you just give me whatever details you have and I'll get my father to track her down. He'll get somebody from the office onto it. It won't be that difficult."

"Can you really find someone, just like that?" Edward asked, his face brightening.

"Well, not personally: not from France. But I can arrange it, if we need to." Harry leant in towards Edward. "But we probably won't need to. The vicar might calm down with you out of the way and everything may be absolutely fine. Wait and see... and stop worrying."

Edward paused for a minute or two. "Thanks, Harry." He looked at his friend, pausing for a moment or two. "I'm sorry," he said. "I haven't asked about your leave. How was it?"

"Oh, you know. The usual."

"The usual what? Give me some details, it will help take my mind off Isabel."

"Alright," Harry agreed, taking a deep breath. "Most of the time we were at Watersmeet. It was beautiful. Rose and I spent almost every day at the beach. I did some sketches." He reached under his bed, pulled out his case and brought out his sketch pad. "Have a look, if you want," he offered. Edward turned the pages.

"It looks like a lovely place, Harry."

"I'll take you there one day." He looked across at Edward, smiling. "You and Isabel." Edward had reached the pictures of Rose.

"She's gorgeous," he said.

"I know. I did those so you could see what she looks like."

"Does she..." Edward hesitated. "I hope you don't mind me asking, but does she look like your wife?"

"Like Bella? Yes, she does a bit. Rose is getting more and more like Bella as she grows up. Their hair is exactly the same shade." Harry was looking into the distance.

"I've never seen a picture of your wife," Edward said, flicking through the pages. "Have you got one of her?"

"No, not here. There are some at home from... from before, but since she died, I haven't been able to draw her. I've tried a couple of times, but it just doesn't work anymore. I can't get it right. It's not that I've forgotten what she looks like. I don't think I'll ever do that. I just can't put it down on paper."

"I'm sorry, you probably don't want to talk about this." Edward closed the sketch book.

"I don't mind. Not with you." Harry coughed.

"Tell me about the rest of your leave," Edward said.

"There's not much more to tell, really." Harry took back the sketch book, moved to his own bunk and began taking off his boots. "We got back from Cornwall a couple of days ago, I visited Bella's family, then packed up and came back here."

"How was it? Leaving I mean."

"The worst ever. I don't care if I never have to do that again." The card game was breaking up and the men were returning to their bunks. As the lights were switched off, Edward leant over.

"Thanks, Harry," he whispered.

The next few days were extremely busy as the men prepared to embark for France. There was a great deal to pack up and organise. Then on the night of the 31st, Harry found himself back in Folkestone, overseeing the boarding of his men onto the SS Victoria. He'd heard of, and anticipated, throngs of waving crowds and a military band, but found that, as the gangplank was raised, the only sounds that could be heard were the sniffs of the men around him, coupled with sighs and the occasional striking of a match as the ship moved away and the men gazed out onto the deserted dockside below.

Chapter Seven

Spring 1916

7th Battalion, Royal Sussex Regiment, BEF
Tuesday, April 25th 1916

Dearest Mother and Father,

I hope you are keeping well. The weather here has been terrible and it is hard to believe that it is spring. The nights are still like winter and during the day it isn't much better, although the sun is now trying to make an appearance. The men are fed up: they thought the cold weather would be over with by now.

We're in a quiet sector at present, which Edward hates. He loathes the boredom - it gives him too much time to think, he says. Personally, I don't mind so much.

I'm hoping that we'll be sent back for a rest soon. We've been in the lines for several weeks now and the men could do with a bit of respite. The countryside around here is rather like England, really, so it would be nice to get out and see some of it.

I'm afraid to say that my spell of leave has been cancelled, but I'm not allowed to say why.

Please give Rose a hug from me and tell her that I love her.

I'd better close now. It will soon be my turn to go on duty.

Your affectionate son, Harry.

****

"It's bloody freezing out there!" Edward exclaimed, almost falling down the steps into the dugout. He coughed several times, the warm, stuffy, smoke-laden air catching in his throat. Captain Johnstone looked up from the table, raising his eyebrows.

"Thank you for that, Wilson," he said. Johnstone's voice was weary. He put down his pencil and leant back casually in his chair, stretching his legs underneath the table. "Is there much going on up there?"

"No," Edward replied. "Is there ever?" He hooked his coat on the rusty nail above his bunk before going over to the brazier and rubbing his hands vigorously. "There's a biting wind, though. There should be apple blossom, or at least daffodils by now. Instead of which it feels like it's going to snow again. Honestly, has no-one at H.Q. told the weather that it's nearly the end of April now and it's supposed to be warming up?"

"Clearly not, Wilson. Still, look on the bright side," Johnstone said, extinguishing his cigarette and running his thumb and forefinger along the length of his unkempt moustache, "The cold seems to be keeping the Bosch quiet. Who's out there now – just Hamilton, I suppose?"

"Yes," Edward answered. Johnstone got up, straightening his back and yawning.

"Oh well. I'd better get along and keep an eye on him. He always seems to make the men a bit twitchy."

"He's only nineteen, sir. He'll get used to it." Harry spoke for the first time, not looking up from his book. "We all do, in the end. Would you rather I went up instead?"

"No, Belmont," Johnstone replied. "What I want is for you to get some sleep for once – even if it's just for an hour or two." Johnstone was doing up his coat, pulling the collar up around his neck. "Come and relieve Hamilton at ten, though, would you?" he called behind him, as he slowly climbed the steps.

Once Johnstone was out of earshot, Edward sat down in his place at the small square table. He looked around him. The dugout was dark and dingy. There were four bunks, one against each wall and various nails and hooks had been hammered into the wooden supports above each bed to hold helmets, caps and coats. In the centre was the small table where he and Harry were both sitting. An empty wine bottle stood between them, a half used, guttering candle stuck in the top. Next to Harry was a bottle of whisky and two metal cups. Even by this dim candlelight, Harry had already noticed the dark circles that had formed under Edward's blue eyes, which didn't seem to shine quite so brightly anymore. He'd just got back from a week's leave, but he looked more tired than ever.

"It's very cramped in here, isn't it?," Edward said at last, his eyes settling back on Harry.

"Yes," Harry replied. "But at least we've got a proper table and some chairs here, and there's only four of us at the moment, otherwise it would be even more crowded."

"So now I suppose you want us to be grateful to Mitchell for getting himself killed, do you?"

"That's not what I meant, Eddie." Harry said patiently. He glanced across at Edward, who now looked a little shame-faced. "Is everything alright?" Harry asked. He knew that Edward felt responsible for Mitchell's death and wanted to get him to talk, to understand that none of it was his fault, that there was nothing he could have done.

"Yes Harry, everything's fine." Edward was keen to change the subject for now. "I never got the chance earlier to tell you about my leave, did I?"

Harry put down his book. "No you didn't." He sat upright, pushing the bottle of whisky across the table. Edward poured a generous amount into one of the cups. "So, how was it?" Harry asked, while Edward took a gulp of his drink.

"Leaving Isabel behind was harder than ever. That bit doesn't get any easier."

"No, I suppose it doesn't," Harry replied. "What about the leave itself?"

"It was good and bad, really," Edward said, taking another swig from the cup. "I spent the Sunday at her parents' house. Her father wouldn't leave us alone, of course, and spent the day asking me all sorts of questions about the war and what I've been doing. There were lots of things I couldn't tell him and other things I didn't feel like telling him, so I fobbed him off with indirect answers. He just made me angry. He seemed to be under the impression that he knew more about it than me. Do you know? Sometimes he was even answering his own questions! It would have been quite funny really, if he hadn't been so infuriatingly stupid. Then later on, when I was alone with Isabel just for a few minutes, while he went to lock up the church, I did desperately want to tell her what it's been like. I needed to tell someone about what happened, you know? But when I started to, she asked me to stop. She said she didn't want to know, which is fair enough, I suppose. It just makes it bloody difficult for me."

"I know." Harry's voice was soothing, but he sensed that Edward wasn't ready to talk to him just yet. "So, it sounds as though Isabel's father was a bit better this time. Is he coming round to you yet, do you think?"

"No, but Isabel stands up to him tremendously. She's been marvellous. Every time he's tried to stop her writing to me, she's still stuck up for me and stood her ground," Edward replied. "She even persuaded him to let us spend a couple of days in London."

"What? Just you and Isabel?"

"No, of course not. Her parents came too, worse luck. It took us ages to convince Isabel's father that it was a decent idea. He thought it was an outrageous waste of time and money. But Isabel spoke to her mother and she stepped in and pointed out that I don't get much leave and all that. He prevaricated for a while, but Isabel persevered and eventually he gave in. I don't really know what he's got against me, but I'm definitely not his idea of decent son-in-law material."

"Well you could certainly do with a shave!" Harry smiled. Edward ignored him.

"There was a new show on called *The Bing Boys Are Here*," he continued. "You should go, if you get a chance during your leave. George Robey sang a duet with Violet Lorraine – *If You Were The Only Girl In The World*, it was called. It was wonderful stuff! It had all the girls in the audience falling into the arms of their loved ones! Luckily it was quite dark in the theatre. It certainly worked wonders on Isabel!"

"Perhaps the vicar has a point then?"

"Hey!" Edward threw a pencil across the table at Harry, who batted it aside. "I've been more than patient, Harry. In all the years we've been walking out, we've never done anything we couldn't tell the grandchildren about."

Harry grinned across the table. "If you don't get a move on, Eddie, you might not have any grandchildren to tell!"

"Don't remind me!" Edward leaned back in his chair. "You must be off home any day now, surely?" he asked.

Harry looked down at the table, fiddling with the frayed corner of his book. "My leave's been cancelled," he said. "I think we're going to be on the move at last."

"Oh, Harry!" Edward seemed much more distressed than his friend. "But you haven't been home since, what was it, December?"

"Late November." Harry picked up his book, stood and crossed to his bunk, keeping his back to Edward. "I don't mind," he said.

"You bloody well do. I can tell."

"Yes, alright, I do. But it's like you said. It gets harder every time. Rosie's so upset when I have to come back. Mother said it took weeks for her to really get over it last time. And she's getting older now. She's starting to understand where I'm going when I leave. I wonder if perhaps it's better not to go home at all, you know?" Harry put the book down and turned round.

"Possibly," Edward said, gulping down the last of his drink. "Let's face it, none of them really have a clue, anyway."

Harry walked back to the table and sat down again. He decided to take the plunge. "So," he said, "You haven't been able to talk to anyone about what happened to Mitchell?".

"No. It might have been different, easier maybe, if I'd been staying on here, if I hadn't been going on leave so soon afterwards. I could have talked to you. You'd have understood. I thought about telling Isabel's father, when we were in London, you know? He'd batted on at me all through the previous Sunday and I'd really had enough of it. Then, when we were having dinner at the hotel, there were some soldiers there on leave, larking about a bit, and he was running them down, saying how they should have more respect for other people. They weren't really doing anything wrong. I thought I could shock him: tell him the truth about what it's really like. But I wasn't sure he'd even believe me. I mean, how do you say to someone whose life revolves around writing sermons and tending to his prize begonias, that less than a week ago you'd spent six hours sitting in a freezing shell hole full of blood and shit, in the middle of No Man's Land, next to a man with a hole the size of a football in his stomach, his guts spilling out all over the place? How the hell was I supposed to tell him that for most of those six hours, the poor bastard was still alive, pleading with me to kill him? Honestly, Harry, do you really think anyone at home would understand that one? Do you think they're ready for that? How could I explain that what I'd really wanted to do, what I really should have done, if I was any kind of man, was to shoot the poor bugger? Except I'm just not brave enough."

"Who is?"

"You are, Harry."

"No, I'm not, Eddie," Harry reasoned quietly. "In your shoes, I'd have done exactly the same thing."

"Oh yes, Harry, of course you'd have done what I did. You'd have crouched as far away as possible and pretended not to hear his screams. You'd have covered your ears, looked away, buried your face in your hands and made believe you couldn't understand a word he said, even though you knew he was begging you to put him out of his misery. You'd have just sat there and listened to that? You'd have managed to ignore his pleading, would you? You'd have done nothing? Just like I did?"

"Yes!"

"Liar!" Neither man spoke. They just stared at each other for a while, both knowing that Edward was right: Harry would have shot Mitchell.

Edward broke the silence. "I was leading that stupid, bloody, pointless raid, Harry, and all I managed to achieve was two men dead and three badly wounded. We only picked up one prisoner and he couldn't give us anything useful."

"You got the wounded back, Eddie." Harry tried to reassure him.

Edward looked away. He reached over and poured more whisky into his cup, drinking most of it in one swallow. Harry picked up the bottle, moving it to the floor beside him. Edward didn't seem to notice.

He sat back, looking at the dugout roof for a few minutes, then leant forward again.

"Any word on where we're going then?" he asked. His voice was brighter, but his eyes remained dull and fixed.

"Nothing official. Johnstone says he thinks a bit further south. He's got to report to H.Q. in the morning, so we should know more then. Mind you, they said we were going last week, and nothing happened."

"Well. I shan't be sorry to say goodbye to this dump, that's for sure. We need to see a bit of proper action for once. All this sitting around, night raids and waiting for the next attack is enough to put the wind up anyone. We've all had enough!"

"I'm just hoping we get a bit of a rest, before they throw us in again."

"Don't you get bored, though Harry? With all the waiting, I mean."

"No. Frustrated maybe. But not bored. Oh, I almost forgot. I sent that picture home to Rose – you know – the one I did of you. I got a reply a couple of days ago, with Susan's help of course. Rose says she thinks you're lovely – especially your sparkling blue eyes evidently! So, if Isabel gives up on you, or the Vicar finally gets his way, you'll only have to wait another fifteen years or so, and I might consider allowing you to walk out with Rosie – under my strict supervision, of course!" Both men laughed and Edward's eyes brightened just a little. Harry glanced at his watch.

"Time to go," he said, getting up and pulling on his coat.

"But it's not ten o'clock yet."

"I know it isn't. I also know that Hamilton's nervous chatter drives Johnstone insane."

"Oh thanks. So you're going to send him back down here to me instead, are you?"

"That's what friends are for! Why not pretend to be asleep? It shouldn't be too hard." Harry took the dugout steps two at a time, managing to avoid the empty cup that Edward had thrown in his direction.

"I'd be quiet on the way down, if I was you, Hamilton," Harry said. "Wilson was just saying he's going to get some shut-eye. He's probably asleep already, if I know him." Hamilton nodded, glancing nervously around the trench, before ducking his head and descending the steps. Even in the shrouding darkness, his eyes glinted, darting from one side to another, like a terrified rabbit hiding from the farmer's gun.

Johnstone looked over at Harry once they were alone.

"Thank you," he said. "I was just starting to contemplate whether I could legitimately send him away on another course. I know that would only leave the three of us here, but even that would be a relief. Does he ever shut up do you think?"

"He means well, sir," Harry replied, while he clapped his hands together against the cold, his breath hanging in front of his face. "He's just nervous." Johnstone gave Harry a sideways glance.

"Well, he makes me nervous too. Speaking of shut-eye, did you manage to get any?"

"No, sir."

"At least you're honest, I suppose. Do you actually intend to sleep at all this year?"

"I do sleep sir, sometimes."

"I'd just like to actually see it happen once in a while. Look, Harry," Johnstone said, "you're the best man I've got and I need you on top form."

"I'm fine sir, really." Harry hesitated for a moment, looking along the trench to his left. "I think I'll take a wander. Sergeant Warner posted two of the new men down here. I'll go and see how they're getting along – have a chat with them, you know?" Harry turned, relieved to be alone, even if only for a few moments. He looked up at the strip of sky above his head: a cloak of deepest blue, dusted with stars. There were no clouds tonight, and a nearly full moon: just like home. Harry smiled, surprised that H.Q. hadn't ordered a raid. They normally chose the nights when visibility was good just for the fun of it. There was much more likelihood that at least a few men would be picked off by snipers. Still, he told himself, perhaps that was a sign that a move was imminent, after all.

Harry walked around two or three traverses, occasionally stopping to talk to the sentries on duty. Finally he came across Jones and Warren, standing close together by a fire step. "Good evening gentlemen," he said. "Anything going on down here?"

"No, sir!" They both jumped up sharply, turned away from the loophole and stood to attention. Jones instinctively dropped his cigarette.

"Are you managing to keep warm?" Harry asked. In the bright moonlight he could easily make out their wary, nervous expressions.

"Yes, sir."

Harry glanced at his watch. "Only an hour or so to go and then you'll be relieved. You don't have to stand to attention, by the way." He smiled at them and they relaxed just a little. "Just one word of advice. You need to space yourselves out a bit more. Jones, perhaps you should move along to your left." Harry kept smiling, reassuringly. "We're a bit short of men, you see. It's a game that they like to play with us up at H.Q. It's called 'see how many yards of trench you can hold with as few men as possible'. It gives them hours of entertainment! Normally we might be able to double-up, but we don't have enough men at the moment. And we can't leave the far end of our trench exposed. The chaps next door don't like it, although I can't imagine why!" The two men looked nervously at each other and nodded simultaneously. "So, when I go, it's probably best if you move along to the next post, Jones, alright?"

"Yes, sir!" The young man seemed unsure whether or not to salute, so he adjusted his helmet instead. Harry looked them up and down. He'd only seen them briefly when they'd arrived that afternoon, accompanied on the last leg of their journey by Edward, returning from his leave. He had commented to Harry, at the time, that these two barely seemed old enough to have begun shaving and Harry had smiled at this comment, coming from an "old man" of twenty-one, like Edward. Now, he was starting to see Edward's point.

"So, how are you finding it?" Harry asked.

"Oh, alright sir," Jones replied. Warren looked down at his feet, shuffling anxiously from one to the other.

"That's it, Warren," Harry said. The boy looked up abruptly, startled at the mention of his own name. "That's an excellent way to keep warm, stamping your feet."

"Yes, sir. Th… thank you, sir," Warren stammered. Harry wondered, now that Warren had finally spoken, whether his voice had broken much more than a few months ago.

"Remember to keep your ears open, won't you?" They both turned bemused faces towards him.

"I thought we were supposed to be on look-out, sir." Jones seemed to be the spokesman.

"You are. But when it's quiet like this, your ears are sometimes just as valuable as your eyes."

"What are we listening for though, sir?"

"Anything that doesn't belong really. You might hear voices, or something metallic. Anything that doesn't feel right."

"Do you think they'll attack then, sir?" It was Warren again, only now Harry wasn't sure his voice had broken at all.

"No." Harry smiled broadly at them both. "It's too damned cold! Besides, this is a quiet sector. We've been here, on and off, for months now and nothing's happened. I can't for the life of me imagine why they'd want to start a show now. Anyway, you'll be relieved soon, so you can get a hot cup of tea and try to get a few hours' sleep, alright?" They nodded. Harry turned and walked back the way he had come, shaking his head.

It was the next afternoon before Harry had the chance to speak to Johnstone alone. He had just returned from H.Q.

"Have you seen the two new men yet, sir?" Harry asked, looking over the top of a hot cup, containing a liquid that purported to be coffee.

"Not since they arrived yesterday. Why? Is there something wrong?" Johnstone didn't look up from his notebook in which he was scribbling, occasionally checking references on the map which was spread out on the table in front of him.

"One of them," Harry said, "Warren's his name, I'm not sure he's much over fifteen or sixteen years old."

"And what would you like me to do about it, Harry?" Johnstone asked, finally looking up. "I brought this up last time, you know? That young kid who was killed in the same raid as Mitchell, what was his name?"

"Dunlop," Harry supplied.

"Yes. Dunlop, that's it…" Johnstone looked back at the map, turning the page of his notebook. "I told them at H.Q., when Dunlop first arrived that he was too young to be here. They reassured me that underage enlisting doesn't happen anymore. It can't evidently. I said that sending boys out here to do a man's work is stupid, they can't keep up, they don't have the strength or the stamina, and it proves costly to the whole unit in the end. I made all the usual points. I even lost my temper and shouted at the Major. Needless to say, he sent me away with a flea in my ear for my trouble. Sure enough, Dunlop was dead within a fortnight."

"And was he old enough?"

"What? Oh, I've got no idea. His paperwork said he was, and that's all that matters, evidently. They don't care that these boys are my responsibility while they're out here, or that I'm the one who has to write to their mothers when they die, which they do – every bloody time. That's got nothing to do with it."

Harry looked at Johnstone. He was a few years younger than Harry, but was beginning to look much older. His moustache was greying and the lines around his light brown eyes were deepening.

"Well," Harry persevered, "I just wanted to let you know that this one's definitely on the young side of youthful, and if we're moving to a hotter sector soon, I don't think he'll be up to it."

"Unfortunately, he might be about to get the chance to find out."

"Really?" Harry said.

"Yes." Johnstone pointed to the map. "That's where we're going for the moment. Lapugnoy. It's a village about five miles south-west of Bethune."

"Then what do we do?"

"A few days' rest and then they'll move us on again, I expect. But we won't be sent to a quiet sector like this again. There's something big going on soon and I think we're going be dumped right in the middle of it. In the meantime, we need to get the men ready, Harry. We're being relieved this evening by the Cameron Highlanders."

****

The road to Bethune was cluttered with men, horses, wagons, ammunition and supplies. The men of A Company, marched at a regular pace, taking frequent breaks to rest their tired feet and take on food or water. Harry walked alongside his platoon, occasionally offering words of encouragement or advice to some of the younger men who'd never before undertaken a long fully-laden route-march. During this time, he saw less of Edward, who was doing the same job a few hundred yards ahead. Hamilton, however, walked behind his men, not talking to them at all. Every so often someone would fall out of line, exhausted and Harry noticed that Hamilton would just shout at the man to fall back in again. Johnstone had told Harry that they'd been promised two new officers upon their arrival in Bethune and he sensed that Hamilton's platoon would be more grateful than anyone to find him relieved of his duties.

When they arrived at Bethune, Harry was surprised to find that, if you ignored the hoards of soldiers, the place seemed just like any other French town. The shops, the cafés, the bank and the post-office were all open for business. The weather had warmed up a little since the previous day, and tables spilled out onto the pavements. The officers sitting at them filled themselves with coffee, wine or beer. Johnstone corralled his men into one corner of the town square and left Harry in charge while he went to get further instructions from Colonel Watts, who had set up his brigade headquarters in the hotel on the far side of the square. The men sat down gratefully on the cobbled ground, many of them removing their tight boots, ignoring Harry's advice that it would be almost impossible to get them back on again. Edward joined Harry, and they moved a few yards away, watching the men.

"I do wish we could stay here tonight," Edward said after a while, removing his hat and pushing his hand back through his thick blond hair. "The men are exhausted – and so am I!"

"It looks like a nice place," Harry agreed, studying a group of Sutherland Highlanders gathered at the base of the tall Belfry in the middle of the square.

"At the moment, I'd settle for anywhere that had a bed and four solid walls," Edward said.

Harry stood up straight as he noticed Johnstone returning from the hotel.

"No change, I'm afraid," Johnstone muttered, as he approached, his face showing the tiredness of a two-day march and little sleep. "I'd hoped we might be able to stop here, but we're to move on to Lapugnoy as planned, although we can't stay there either, it would seem. There's a small farmhouse on the other side of the village. The family still lives on the farm, but they take in waifs and strays like us, I'm reliably informed. We're to stay there until we get our orders. We're not to get too settled in though. We have to be ready to move off at three hours' notice. How's your French, Harry?"

"Still passable, thank you sir." Harry smiled.

"Good," Johnstone replied. "I can't imagine the people at the farm will speak much English."

The new officers, Sinclair and Brown, arrived just before the company was due to leave, having been delayed en-route. They barely had time to make their introductions before the company set off on the final leg of their journey.

****

The farm was unmissable, even though the light was beginning to fade by the time they arrived. The fields were fallow, although the farmhouse itself seemed quite tidy. Behind the house, there was a small, neat vegetable plot, and beyond this was a wall, with an archway leading to a large orchard. The whitewashed house, which sat side-on to the road, faced onto a courtyard, flanked on two sides by large barns, one slightly bigger than the other. At the far end of the courtyard was a cowshed and a small stable and beyond these were fields and pastures as far as they eye could see. On the opposite side of the road stood an enormous willow tree, nestling beside a stream which ran down through the fields and into the valley below, where it was bordered by woods.

Johnstone fell back slightly and walked alongside Harry as they approached the farm.

"I'll get Wilson to fall the men out on the roadside under that willow tree over there. Perhaps it would be best if you and I went in alone to start with, don't you think? Just because H.Q. have said it's alright for us to stay here doesn't mean we should make assumptions, does it? It's only polite to ask, rather than all of us just barging in." Harry agreed and Johnstone went to speak to Edward.

With the men resting under and around the large draping willow tree, Harry and Johnstone entered the courtyard. Harry was about to knock on the door of the farmhouse, when he heard footsteps behind him. He and Johnstone turned to see a young girl, possibly twenty years old, carrying a large bucket full of milk.

"Bonjour mademoiselle," Harry said, removing his hat. The captain followed suit.

"Monsieur?" she said, putting down her pail. Harry couldn't help but notice, despite the impending dusk, that she had deep brown eyes and that a couple of strands of nearly black hair had slipped from the ribbon that was tied loosely behind her head.

"We need somewhere to stay," he said in perfect French. "We were told that you could provide accommodation for us."

"Very well," she sighed. "How many of you?"

"Around two hundred men and six officers. Have you space for that many?"

"Your men may sleep in the barns." She sounded resigned. "There is fresh straw and they will be quite warm. The officers may sleep in the house. We have three rooms upstairs which you can use." She bent, wearily, to pick up her bucket, but Harry stepped forward quickly, lifting it from the ground.

"Allow me, mademoiselle. Where do you want this?" he asked.

"I can manage, monsieur." She tried to take the pail from him, evidently insulted by his offer of help, but he smiled resolutely at her, so she shrugged her shoulders and opened the door.

The three of them stepped inside, to be greeted by the smell of fresh coffee. The door had opened directly onto a large kitchen, in the centre of which there stood a table, surrounded by six unmatched chairs. The girl pointed to the table and Harry deposited the bucket. One wall of the kitchen was almost filled with an enormous black range and, directly in front of this stood an older woman, dressed entirely in black. The girl went over to the woman and whispered something, before turning back to Harry and Johnstone.

"This is my mother, Madame Martin," she said. Harry stepped forward.

"Bonjour Madame," he said. "We are very grateful for your kindness."

The older woman nodded. "It is nothing," she said. Her voice was monotone and Harry glanced over at the young girl, whose eyes were fixed intently on her mother.

"I hope they told you at Bethune that we cannot feed all of your men here," she said. Her voice seemed softer to Harry, now that they were inside. "But if the officers are hungry, I can prepare some supper for them."

"That would be most kind." Harry replied, explaining that other arrangements had already been made for the men. He translated this for Johnstone, who said, "Merci" as though he were begging for his life, rather than showing his gratitude. The girl stifled a smile at Johnstone's appalling accent and her eyes briefly met Harry's in a shared moment of amusement, before she turned away.

An hour later, the men were settled into the barns, under the watchful eye of the platoon sergeants, who had occupied one corner of the cavernous space. The barns were warm and weatherproof, so they were all happy. A few of the men began writing letters, as Harry knew Edward would do later; others played cards and one man had a mouth-organ and soon had several of his comrades singing along to popular tunes. The men had changed the words of the songs and Harry smiled to himself, as he and Sinclair walked back to the farmhouse, grateful that the girl and her mother didn't seem to understand English.

The six officers were soon seated around the large table enjoying an impromptu supper of eggs, fried potatoes and home-made bread, followed by strong coffee, which Edward for one, seemed to find almost undrinkable, although Harry thoroughly enjoyed the fact that it actually tasted of coffee. Sinclair and Brown fitted in well. Brown had been transferred from the 9th Battalion and had been in France since September of the previous year. For Sinclair, this was his first tour of duty, but he seemed to have acclimatised well to his new surroundings. Hamilton ate his food quickly, before excusing himself and wandering outside into the courtyard for a cigarette. Even though the door was closed, they could still hear him muttering to himself as he paced up and down. Madame Martin had retired to bed as soon as the meal was served and when everyone had finished eating, much to the embarrassment of the young girl, Harry rose from the table and began to clear away the plates before starting the washing up. Edward and Sinclair joined in, leaving Brown and Johnstone to watch on and make the odd unhelpful comment. The girl stood with her back to the range, watching these three grown men, whose words made little sense to her, clearing up her kitchen.

Eventually, when everything was tidied away, the girl took a lamp from the window sill and explained to Harry that she would show the officers to their bedrooms, if they would like to go with her. Harry quickly translated to the others, holding open a door that led to a steep stairway. Johnstone took the first, smallest room at the top of the stairs. The largest room, further along the corridor with three beds, was shared between Sinclair, Brown and Hamilton, who had now rejoined them. With everyone else settled, Harry and Edward were shown to the next room along.

"I don't mean to pry, mademoiselle." Harry hesitated outside the bedroom door, a little embarrassed. "But, where do you and your mother sleep?"

"My mother's room is downstairs, beyond the kitchen. Mine is the next one along from yours." She pointed to the end of the landing where a large door stood ajar. "Why do you ask?" There was just a hint of suspicion in her voice.

"Because I'll tell the others to stay away from that end of the corridor, that's all. You're entitled to your privacy, mademoiselle, even if we have trespassed on your kindness." The girl smiled up at Harry and once again he noticed her eyes, which in this light seemed so dark that they were almost black. It was not an unpleasant, sinister colour, as they shone with a sparkling intensity, brown flecks highlighted by the flickering lamplight. As he looked down at her, he felt as though we was being pulled into her and then when she turned away, he became aware of an inconvenient lurch, a longing, in the pit of his stomach.

Later, as Edward finished another long letter to Isabel, Harry got out his sketch pad and began a drawing. Without even realising it, he found himself sketching the girl. She had worn an embroidered white blouse open at the neck, revealing a triangle of sun-browned flesh. Her lips, he recalled, were full and deep pink in colour, and her skin was clear and soft. Her wild, dark hair was held in place by only a thin white ribbon. When he'd finished drawing, Harry looked up to find Edward gazing at him from the narrow bed on the opposite side of the room.

"What are you smiling at?" Edward asked. Harry had not been aware that he was smiling and closed his sketch pad before replying.

"Oh, nothing in particular." He put his pad away.

"Well, something's put a smile on your face," Edward persisted.

"Just a good meal and a comfortable bed," Harry answered.

"I believe you, Harry," Edward smiled. "If you say so."

"Goodnight, Eddie," Harry said, lying down and staring up at the ceiling. Edward sighed. He knew Harry too well to push him. Harry would tell him, when he was ready. A small lamp lit the tiny room which contained nothing more than two beds and a wash-stand. Not that Harry or Edward wanted for anything more. They had certainly slept in far less comfortable places than this since joining the army and were glad of beds with sheets and blankets. The next morning, they were equally pleased to have clean, hot water in which to wash and shave.

The next day was much warmer, just how it should be in late April, and the mood among the men was cheerful. They spent the morning checking their kit, some of which had been lost or left behind. This was a long and laborious job which none of the men or officers enjoyed and they were all relieved to return to their billets once the task was complete. Later in the afternoon some of the men started a game of football, in one of the fields beyond the farm, with Sergeant Warner acting as referee, his strict decisions unquestioned by those who knew that the punishment for disputing his authority would be meted out when they got back into the trenches. Edward wandered away from the farmhouse and went to sleep down by the stream; Johnstone was busy writing reports, and later, went back into Lapugnoy, joining the other officers, who had gone there to visit the estaminet earlier in the afternoon. Harry, meanwhile, went up to his room and collected his sketch pad and pencils. He settled himself on an old, uneven bench at the side of the house, overlooking the road and, beyond it, the willow tree, the stream and the open fields and pastures stretching into the distance. For a long while, he just sat, taking in the scene and then as shades of palest pink and orange shimmered across the sky, he began to draw.

He'd done little more than trace the outline of the willow tree, when the girl came around the corner of the house from the kitchen garden, carrying a basket loaded with freshly picked vegetables. Harry put his pad down on the bench, leapt to his feet and once again offered to help her.

"Really, monsieur," she said, with obvious impatience. "You don't have to keep doing this."

"I know," Harry said, smiling and taking the basket from her, regardless. "But I want to."

"I managed perfectly well before you arrived," the girl said, folding her arms. "And I'll manage perfectly well when you've gone."

"I'm sure you will, mademoiselle, but you don't have to manage perfectly well while I'm here." Harry stooped to pick up his pad and pencils, placing them on top of the vegetables. The girl turned, walking around the corner of the farmhouse and in through the open door. Harry followed her.

"Shall I put these on the table?" he asked.

"Yes, thank you." Her voice was a little softer again. Harry deposited the basket, then took his sketch pad and went to leave.

"What have you been drawing?" the girl asked.

"Oh, nothing much, I was just about to sketch the view from the bench. I think I'll go and finish it."

An hour or so later, with the light now beginning to fade, the girl appeared before him, blocking his view.

"I brought you a cup of coffee," she said, offering it to him. Harry put his sketch pad down and took the cup from her.

"That's very kind of you," he said. "Thank you." She picked up the pad and sat next to him, idly flicking through its pages.

"These are very good, monsieur," she commented. Harry sipped his coffee. Suddenly she stopped. "Is this me?" she asked, holding the pad out in front of him.

"Oh. Yes." He went to take it from her.

"Do I really look like that?" she asked

"Yes," Harry replied, his face reddening. "Well, you do to me."

"But, you've made me look pretty."

"That's because you are pretty." Harry found he'd said the words, before even thinking about it. The girl turned a deep red, handing Harry his sketch pad as she got up.

"Sorry, mademoiselle. I didn't mean…" Harry faltered.

"Dinner will be ready at seven o'clock, monsieur." She said quietly, her blushes still not fading, as she walked away.

After supper that night, which Johnstone missed, having not returned from the village, Edward announced that he was going upstairs to write a letter, explaining himself to the girl with hand gestures, motioning make-believe writing on make-believe paper. Sinclair, Brown and Hamilton decided to take a stroll back to the estaminet. Harry suggested, as they were going, that they try to find

Johnstone and bring him back in one piece. Sitting at the table, he watched the girl putting away the dishes.

"I'm sorry if I offended you earlier," he said.

"You didn't offend me," she said. "I was surprised by your words, but not offended."

"Good."

"Do you really think I'm pretty?" she asked, after a short pause, without stopping her work, or looking at him

"Yes." Harry felt the colour rising to his cheeks. "I think you're very pretty." He hesitated. "If you don't mind, may I ask your name? I can't keep calling you 'mademoiselle'."

The girl turned to him. "Elise, Monsieur. My name is Elise."

"And I'm Harry," he said.

"'Arry?" Elise found Harry's name difficult to pronounce.

"Something like that." Harry smiled across at her and she came to sit down opposite him. "Do you and your mother live here alone?" he asked, relaxing a little.

"Yes." Elise replied. "My father died the year before the war started. That left me, my brother, Henri and our mother. Henri has gone to fight in the war and my mother worries about him." She stopped for a moment. "So do I, of course," she added. "But with my mother, it has become an obsession. She is convinced that Henri won't return and that we will not be able to keep the farm going by ourselves; that we will be destitute. She worries a lot, my mother." A dim smile crossed her face.

"Does all this land around here belong to you?"

"Yes. When my father was alive and Henri was here, we used to farm the fields as far as you can see. My mother and I cannot manage it alone, so we just grow what we need to live. We used to have more cows too, but now we only have a few. Just enough to give us the milk we need and I sell the apples and pears from the orchard to make enough money to buy what we can't grow." Harry was watching her intently as she spoke. "It is hard work," she concluded.

"I'm sure it is," Harry said.

"And you are an artist, Monsieur? I mean was that your job before the war, or is it just a hobby?"

"Well, I suppose you could say it was my job." Harry replied, not wanting to tell her that he didn't really have an occupation, especially as she and her mother were clearly struggling to make ends meet. "I have a house by the sea and my daughter, Rose used to come down to the beach with me. She'd carry my paints and watch while I sketched. I would make her sand sculptures of animals and for some reason, it used to keep her happy for hours." He smiled, remembering.

"You have a daughter?" Elise asked.

"Yes."

"And now she lives in England with your wife?"

"No," Harry hesitated. "My wife died." He hadn't said it to a stranger before. The words hung in the air for a moment and he felt uncomfortable leaving them there. He got up from the table. "I think I'll go to bed now," he said. "Thank you for a lovely dinner, Elise." He turned and walked towards the door.

"I'm sorry, monsieur. I didn't mean to pry." Her voice was suddenly very quiet and she sounded hurt. Harry turned back towards her.

"You didn't," he said and retraced his steps. Crouching down next to her, he placed a hand on the back of her chair. "I'm sorry too," he continued. "It's not your fault." Elise looked at him. "How old are you?" Harry asked.

"Nineteen," Elise answered.

He took a deep breath, noting the confusion in her eyes. "Well, Elise. Goodnight."

"Goodnight, monsieur."

Edward was sitting up on his bed, finishing his letter.

"You've been ages." he said, as Harry entered the room.

"Have I?"

"Yes, you have. What on earth have you been doing – or shouldn't I ask?" Edward grinned.

"Don't be ridiculous." Harry turned his back, hoping that Edward wouldn't notice the blush which he felt sure was creeping across his face.

"What's ridiculous?"

"Well, I hardly know her for a start."

"Then get to know her, Harry."

"We'll be gone before I get the opportunity."

"Then don't waste so much time thinking about it."

"It's not that simple, Eddie. She's only nineteen years old."

"So what?" Edward replied, putting away his notepaper and pencil.

"I'm rapidly approaching thirty-five, that's what!"

"Harry, you foolish old bugger. What has that got to do with anything? None of that matters if you like her. And you do like her, don't you?" Harry turned and sat down on the edge of his bed.

"Something like that, yes." He looked across at Edward.

"I thought so."

"Am I that bloody transparent?"

"Only to me," Edward smiled.

Harry sighed and, sensing that he no longer wished to talk, Edward settled down into bed. Before long, his breathing altered, becoming deeper and more even, and Harry knew that he was asleep. Harry walked across to the window, looking out across the moonlit fields. He wondered if perhaps the time might finally be right. He remembered his mother's words: 'One day it will just happen, probably when you're least expecting it,' she'd said. Breathing in deeply, he knew he had no choice anyway. Like it, or not, it had happened and there was nothing whatsoever he could do about it.

For two days, the Company enjoyed a rest at the farm. Harry spent as much time as he could with Elise, helping in the garden or sitting in the kitchen watching her work. He talked to her and listened to her; they laughed together and, in the evenings as the light faded, he walked with her across the fields, watching her animated face, her wide smile and shining eyes. She talked mostly about her brother and the love she felt for him was obvious. Her face lit up and her voice became warm when she spoke of him, and Harry felt a completely unreasonable sense of jealousy, willing her to think and speak of him in the same way.

At noon on the fifth day, Johnstone called all the officers together in the courtyard. "We're leaving this afternoon," he announced.

"Where for?" asked Harry.

"We're relieving the 9th Essex at Bully-Grenay," Johnstone said, before pausing for a moment. "Get everything packed up and have the men ready to leave by 16.00 hours. Any questions?"

"No sir." Harry answered for the rest.

Before going to his men, Harry walked quickly around the back of the house, where he found Elise hanging out some washing. Without saying a word, he took her hand and led her through the archway into the privacy of the orchard. He stood her against the trunk of a large apple tree, its blossom now dying beneath her feet.

"We're leaving," he said, standing in front of her.

"I thought so," she replied.

"I wish we weren't. I'd hoped we'd have a bit longer."

"Yes," she said. "I'm sure you're in need of the rest."

"No, Elise. I meant a bit longer for us to be together."

"Why?"

"Don't you know?"

"Know what?"

"That I'm in love with you." He didn't really know why he'd said it – he certainly hadn't meant to, but once the words had left his lips, he was pleased they had. It was true, after all. Elise turned her head away.

"Yes, monsieur, of course you are." She gazed down the orchard. "Just like every other soldier that comes here."

"Elise," Harry pleaded. "Don't say that."

"You don't really know me, monsieur, but I suppose you're going to tell me that it doesn't matter; that this is different," she continued. "You'll say that you've never felt this way before. That you fell madly in love with me the moment you saw me. Well, do you know what? I've heard it all before, dozens of times. And at the next farm or village that you stay in, there will be another girl, and another and another. And you'll tell all of them the exact same thing."

"No I won't, Elise, because it wouldn't be true." He stood back a little. "Of course I've felt this way before. I was married. My wife died, and I grieved for her and I missed her every single day. I never thought I would be lucky enough to feel this way again, but I do." Turning away, he could hear someone calling his name in the distance. He sighed. "Oh, just forget it, Elise," he said, looking back at her. "I stupidly thought you might feel the same way as I do. Obviously I was wrong." She looked up, went to reach out to him, went to speak, but he'd already turned and walked away.

The next four hours passed quickly and, before Harry knew it, the men were lined up in the courtyard outside the farmhouse, ready to leave. He was talking to Sergeant Warner, when Elise appeared in the doorway, the skirt of her floral dress catching in the breeze.

"Monsieur?" she called in his direction. "You have left something behind in your room." She turned and went back into the house.

"What's she saying?" Johnstone called.

"I've evidently left something behind upstairs."

"Can't she bring it out to you?"

"It would seem not."

"You'd better go and fetch it then. Don't be long. We're moving off in a few minutes."

"Yes, sir." Harry walked towards the farmhouse. He knew he'd packed all his belongings and wondered what she wanted. Having managed to avoid seeing Elise all afternoon, he didn't relish the idea of talking to her now.

Passing through the door, Harry's eyes adjusted quickly to the dim kitchen, where she stood, leaning against the table.

"What do you want, Elise?" he asked abruptly.

"I owe you an apology," she said, her eyes fixed on the floor between them.

"What for?"

"I was very rude to you earlier, monsieur."

"It doesn't matter," Harry said. "Is that it? Was that all you wanted?" He turned to go.

"No," she said. Harry stopped and waited. "So many men pass through here, you see."

"And they all tell you they love you, do they?" Harry knew he sounded bitter, but he couldn't help it.

"Well, not all of them, no. But some of them do and I know they don't really mean it."

"And what if they do?" he said, turning back to her.

"But they don't," she replied.

"I did," Harry said, his voice softening.

"And you don't anymore?"

"What does it matter if I do, Elise? You don't feel the same way, do you?"

"I can't afford to feel the same, monsieur. You might walk out of here and get killed tomorrow, and then where would I be?"

"You'd be grieving, just like I was when my wife died. But I wouldn't have given up the time I had with her for anything."

"Then maybe you're stronger than I am."

"Or maybe I just care more." Harry looked at her. She lowered her head, staring at her feet. "I'm sorry," he said. "That wasn't fair." He looked out of the window. The men were beginning to move off. He heard Edward calling his name. "I have to go," he said.

"Will you be coming back?" Elise asked, moving towards him as he turned to go.

"I have no idea. It depends where they send us. But does it matter?"

Elise looked at the floor again, hesitating and embarrassed. "Yes it matters, monsieur. I've enjoyed our time together these last few days and... I'd like... I'd like us to be... friends."

"Would you?" Harry asked, glancing anxiously out of the window again. "Then, to start with, can I suggest that you stop calling me 'monsieur'. My name is Harry, remember?"

"Yes," she replied, with a smile that lit up her eyes. Edward called again, a little louder this time.

"Oh God, I really do have to go." He moved towards the front door. "Can I write to you, Elise?" he asked, looking back.

"Yes," she replied. "Yes, please. I'd like that."

Chapter Eight

Summer 1916

7th Battalion, Royal Sussex Regiment, BEF
Friday, June 23rd 1916

Dearest Mother and Father

This is just a quick line to let you know that I am well. I believe there's due to be big show soon quite near to where I am, and you will doubtless read about it in the newspapers. I don't want you to worry, however, as my Company is unlikely to be involved.

We've been busy lately working behind the lines, although I can't tell you what we've been doing. I'm not sure when I'm going to get any leave again, probably not for some time.

I did enjoy hearing about the picnic that you had with William and Charlotte. I can well imagine that young George must be getting quite a handful now, but I'm sure that Charlotte manages him very well.

Sorry this is such a short letter, but we're getting ready to move again at present. I will write as soon as I am able.

Please give my love and a big kiss to Rosie and,
I remain as ever, your loving son, Harry

****

My dear Elise,

We have had a busy time these last two days, and this is the first chance I have had to write. I cannot tell you where I am, but you may soon hear about it anyway. As we have been so well occupied, we have had very little time out of the lines, only a couple of days in a rest camp, but that was hardly a 'rest' as even there we still had to work quite hard.

I hope that everything is running smoothly on the farm. The weather has been good, so hopefully the apples and pears are ripening well. I picture you all the time, working in the garden and hope that you are not getting too tired. Unfortunately, I also picture the soldiers visiting the farm, and declaring their love for you, but I hope you fend them off, as you did with me and I try not to dwell on those thoughts.

I must go now.

With love,

Your affectionate friend, (Monsieur) Harry.

****

Sergeant Warner looked at Harry from underneath his helmet.

"Do we know why the hell they decided to stick us out in the middle of No Man's Land, sir?" he asked, ducking as another shell landed just behind the assembly trench.

"Target practice!" Harry shouted back, glancing at his watch. "Only about half an hour to go before the off."

"If there's any of us left to go off, sir! Six men have been killed already and another four wounded. I can't even send them back yet, so the worst of those have probably had it too. This is hopeless."

"I know." Harry shifted his position slightly, trying to look along the trench to where he knew Edward was cowering, sheltering from the fierce bombardment.

"It's bad enough being shelled by the Germans, sir. But I'm sure half of these are our own," Warner continued. Harry turned back.

"Don't let the men hear you saying that, Warner."

"Why not, sir? Do you think they don't know it for themselves?"

Harry didn't reply. He was getting tired of shouting above the thunderous artillery fire. Suddenly he heard a sharp cry from over his left shoulder. He spun around to find Jones lying on the floor of the trench, his helmet lying behind his head which was bleeding from the right temple. The boy was twitching, screaming and clutching at his head. Fearing the worst, Harry knelt down and removed his own helmet.

"Calm down!" he shouted, reaching inside the boy's tunic for his field dressing, before struggling with his flailing arms. "Warner!" Harry shouted. "Get down here and hold his arms will you?" The sergeant did as he was told, which enabled Harry to take a proper look at the wound and place the field dressing over the spurting gash. "Jones!" Harry struggled to gain the boy's attention. "Listen to me!" He took Jones's head and held it in his hands, forcing him to make eye contact. "It's only a minor wound. You're going to be fine. Once we've gone, the stretcher bearers can come in and they'll help you back." Jones's eyes were livid with panic. "Do you understand me?" Harry shouted slowly, sounding each syllable. Jones gave an almost imperceptible nod of his head, saliva dripping from his taut, quivering lips. "Good lad." Harry turned. "Warner, see to him, will you?" Harry replaced his own helmet and got back to his feet, ducking down once again beneath the parapet as another shell landed just in front, showering him and his men with great clods of mud. Despite his best efforts, as he looked around to check that no-one else had been hurt, Harry still couldn't see Edward. What he saw was a sea of backs, topped by rounded tin helmets, all crouched together like a long, khaki caterpillar.

As Warner returned to his place next to Harry, the lieutenant felt a tap on his shoulder and turned to see Captain Johnstone standing behind him, swaying slightly, blood trickling down the left side of his face.

"Sir!" Harry shouted. "You're wounded."

"Yes, Belmont. I'd noticed." Johnstone's words were slurred, the overall impression being that he'd had too much to drink.

"Sit down then, sir." Harry went to take Johnstone by the arm.

"No!" Johnstone pulled back from his concerned lieutenant. "I don't want anyone to see me sitting down." He motioned to Harry to step away from the other men, pulling him to the back wall of the trench. "We're due off at 08.30. You're to make for the trenches directly opposite, take them and hold on until reserves come up. Those are our orders. Is that clear?"

"Yes, sir. I know. You told us earlier this morning," Harry shouted. "Why are you telling me again now?"

"Because, Harry, I don't think I'll make it. You're my most senior man. I'm putting you in charge for now." Johnstone licked his lips, taking a deep breath. "The Colonel will follow with the second wave just behind and you can hand over directly to him when he catches you up. Understood?" Johnstone was looking deeply into Harry's eyes. His own were somewhat misty now and he was finding it difficult to focus.

"Yes, sir." Harry felt a lump in his throat, but swallowed hard.

"Good man." Johnstone swayed again slightly, grasping Harry's arm. "All the best, Harry," he said. He didn't wait for a response but continued along the trench, staggering slightly. Harry turned back to see Sergeant Warner shaking his lowered head.

Standing silently now, Harry checked his watch. There were less than two minutes to go. The bombardment had died down slightly, although the German artillery was still firing with a degree of accuracy. The British guns had lifted to allow the men to move forward as zero hour approached. Harry took the whistle from its pouch on his belt and held it between his bone-dry lips. Not wanting to be the first to blow, he pulled his Webley revolver from its holster and waited until he heard other whistles sounding from further along the trench, before blasting as hard as he could on his own. To either side of him, men climbed up unquestioningly, over the top of the parapet. Two fell straight back at Harry's feet.

"Warner!" Harry cried. "Take care of those men." He didn't wait to see what Warner did, but clambered up himself to join the others.

Bullets seemed to be flying all around him, but Harry kept his head down and ran headlong, shouting out to the men on either side of him to keep up. He glanced around him, looking to the left and then to the right. At first, there didn't seem to be anyone else with him. Some had fallen, injured or killed. Others, weighed down by their packs, simply couldn't run as fast as Harry. Then, a little further over to his right, perhaps twenty yards away, Harry noticed Warren. He seemed to stand still for a split second, as a bullet struck his chest, his arms falling to his sides. Then he fell to his knees, where he remained, quite still, until another bullet struck him moments later, in the side of the head. Slowly he fell forward, already dead before his bleeding face hit the ground beneath him. Harry had stopped to watch this one spectacle among many, which had somehow caught his attention but, feeling the bullets whistle past his head, he turned and ran forward once more.

It took Harry less than five minutes to cross No Man's Land, although it felt more like twenty. When he reached the German wire, he found a gap, with surprising ease and, without thinking and assuming, wrongly, that his men were right behind him, Harry jumped down into the trench. He looked left and right, realising quickly and with an immediate sense of panic, that he was quite alone. There was no-one in sight, either British or German. Harry hesitated for a moment and then decided to head to his right. Just as he did, another of his men dropped down into the trench, right where Harry had been standing. Harry turned just in time to see this man, Private Spencer, fire off his rifle directly into the chest of a German trooper who had appeared from a dugout in the back wall of the trench. Another followed and Harry fired off a shot from his revolver, catching the next German in the side of the head. He fell on top of his comrade and further shots rang out from the dark mouth of the dugout, all of which were returned by Spencer and Harry, who had emptied the chamber of his revolver before realising that he was the only one still firing.

Harry and Spencer looked at each other, both breathing hard. Then, while Harry quickly reloaded his revolver, Spencer checked carefully to see if any more Germans were hiding in the dugout. The trench was now silent. A few minutes passed before three more of

Harry's platoon jumped down into the trench, followed by some other men, who Harry recognised as belonging to Number 4 Platoon – Edward's men.

"Where's Lieutenant Wilson?" he shouted at them.

"No idea, sir," one of the men replied. "He was at the opposite end from me – he's probably gone into the trench further up." He pointed to the right. They now numbered nine men in total.

Harry looked around him, knowing that he should distribute these men to hold both ends of the traverse, but there were only seven privates, three of whom he didn't know, plus a corporal, and himself. At that moment, just above Harry's head, he heard a voice.

"Hey!" it cried. "Make room down there!" Without waiting for the men to move, Colonel Watts dropped down into the trench. "Right!" he called out. "What are we all doing standing around? Lieutenant Belmont, isn't it?" He looked at Harry. "Sort your men out and send some to each end of the traverse, block it and hold it. I'm going to set up my H.Q. in this dugout. You there!" The colonel pointed to Spencer. "Help me move these men out of the doorway, would you?"

"Yes, sir!" Spencer moved forward, obeying the Colonel.

"Alright, you heard the Colonel," Harry shouted, pointing at the four men nearest to him, one of whom was a corporal. "You four, move along to the left there and block that end of the traverse. We'll head the other way and do the same. Spencer, when you've finished helping the Colonel, you remain here. Any others who arrive, send them to reinforce either end. Got it?" Spencer nodded his head, dragging one of the German bodies towards the front wall of the trench.

Harry turned away and took his three men, heading for the right hand end of the trench. No sooner had they arrived at the corner of the traverse, than a terrible noise of incoherent screaming and shouting broke out behind them. German troops had approached from the left, bayonetting the four men that Harry had just sent there and throwing stick bombs further down the trench, one of which exploded by the dugout entrance. Suddenly several more men from Edward's platoon jumped down into the trench, followed by Edward himself, who landed just in front of Harry. One of Edward's men was killed immediately, a bullet ripping through his chest and into the earth wall behind him. Edward cried out to the others to follow him, and began to charge along the trench, towards the five Germans, who had become isolated from the rest of their group, but were determined to hold their ground, despite being outnumbered. Harry and his men followed and they kept firing even after the men had all fallen.

Harry took a moment to realise that the German soldiers were all dead, before he dropped to his knees beside the prone figure of Spencer, who was lying at the dugout entrance. He was clutching his stomach, thick dark blood seeping from between his fingers. Reaching inside his own tunic, Harry pulled out his field dressing and, removing Spencer's shaking, sticky hands, held it tightly over the wound in the man's belly. Edward, standing beside him, did the same, handing his own dressing down to Harry to staunch the blood flow. Spencer's face had gone a sickly white and even his lips had lost their colour.

"It doesn't hurt, sir," Spencer said, his voice so quiet that Harry had to lower his head in order to hear the words.

"Just keep still," Harry said, while above him, he heard the familiar cry for stretcher bearers. "They'll come and pick you up soon, Spencer. Just lay there quietly now." Harry turned. "Smedley!" he called to one of his own men. "Stay with him. Keep calling for a stretcher bearer so they know where to find you. Alright?" The private nodded, kneeling down beside Spencer and averting his eyes from the oozing bloody dressings.

Harry turned back towards the shattered dugout entrance. "Oh Christ!" he uttered, his heart sinking. "The Colonel was down there." He and Edward peered down the steps, where they were greeted by the sight of two legs lying prostrate on the floor.

"Oh God!" Edward cried out. "They've got Colonel Watts."

"Oh no they damned well haven't!" came a voice from the depths, as Colonel Watts stuck his head around the corner, looking up at them. "Belmont!" he cried. Edward stood up, allowing Harry a better view into the dugout.

"Yes, sir," Harry said.

"Make sure you've got both ends of the traverse covered, will you? Try to find a few sergeants to help out, if there are any left, and then come down here with whatever officers you've got."

"Very good, sir," Harry shouted. "Edward?" he said, turning round, "Do we have any sergeants around here?"

"I'm not sure," Edward called back. "I don't have a bloody clue what's going on, actually."

"We need to leave some men in charge up here before we go down to see the Colonel."

"There's a corporal over there, and one of my men – Dawson – came over with me. He's only a private, but he's a good man." He glanced around trying to locate the man in question.

"That will have to do. Let them know what to do and then join me in the dugout. Alright?"

"Fine." Edward went to move off, but stopped abruptly. "I'm glad you made it," he smiled, clapping Harry on the shoulder.

Harry smiled back, disappearing down the steps.

****

The village of Lapugnoy looked the same as it had on their last visit. Harry had led the bedraggled remnants of A Company into the square, and noticed that the faces of most of the men of the battalion, who were lying or sitting on the cobbles, now bore a lifeless expression. Their uniforms were covered in dust and, in some cases, dried blood – presumably not their own. Their eyes had a distant, lost look and even the cigarettes hung limp from their dry mouths. There was very little noise; no-one seemed to speak or move at all.

"Why on earth are we back here?" Edward whispered, reluctant to break the silence.

"Because this is where Colonel Watts told me to bring the men," Harry answered. "Fall them out, will you? Find them some water and I'll be back in a minute."

"Where are you going?" Edward asked.

Harry pointed towards a group of senior officers. "Orders."

When he came back again, the late morning sunshine had warmed into a sweltering noon. The men of A Company were lying in various positions in front of a cobbler's shop, which had long since closed its doors. Edward walked slowly towards Harry, whose face was blank.

"Well?" Edward asked. Other men around him raised their heads for a moment, before lowering them and staring back into oblivion.

Harry glanced at Edward. "We're too depleted to be sent back into the line," he said. "We've lost more than half the men in the battalion – there's only about a third of us left."

"Out of over six hundred?" Edward looked at Harry who simply nodded his head. "How long will we get?"

"I have no idea. It all depends on the reinforcements. In the meantime, our company's been billeted back at the farmhouse, together with the remains of a company of Royal Fusiliers. They went through it as well, it seems. The rest of the battalion is staying on here for now."

"Is Elise still there?" Edward asked.

"I don't know. I didn't ask. I suppose so." Harry's face fell. "It's not quite the same though is it? Not now."

"No…" Edward looked down at the cobbles beneath his dusty boots.

The farm looked different as they approached it, mainly because other men in similar uniforms were already there, some standing in the courtyard, others sitting in the field beyond the house, a few were down by the stream. The apples and pears in the orchard had started to ripen and the kitchen garden was abundant with vegetables. Harry, who was leading his drained men, could see Elise, working among the crops, weeding. He momentarily toyed with the idea of calling out to her, but thought better of it.

They were almost at the farm gates before Elise stood up and turned to see the approaching soldiers. Initially, her face wore the same tired, worn expression that Harry recalled from their first meeting, but then she saw him and her eyes brightened, a smile coming to her lips.

"Mademoiselle?" Harry called before she could say anything.

"Yes, monsieur?" Elise approached the fence which stood between herself and Harry.

"We need somewhere to stay." Harry stared down at her. She looked exactly the same.

"Are you alright?" she whispered.

"I'll tell you inside."

"Come with me into the house, monsieur," she said, raising her voice again. "I will see what can be done. There are some men staying here already, but I'm sure we can find space." Harry turned towards Edward.

"Lieutenant Wilson?" he called. Edward jogged forward. "Fall the men out at the roadside. They can rest under the tree, while I speak to the young lady."

"Will do." Edward turned back to the men and issued their instructions, which they received gratefully. Some sat or lay down under the enormous willow tree, shading them from the still strong mid-afternoon sun; others removed their boots and socks, bathing their feet in the cool waters of the gently flowing stream.

The inside of the farmhouse was dark, cool and familiar but Harry didn't care, or even notice. He sat down at the kitchen table, his head in his hands. Elise sat opposite him.

"Where are the rest of your men, and your captain?" she asked. "Are they staying in the village?"

"No," Harry replied. "They're dead. Or they're wounded, but mostly they're dead. The captain is, anyway. Edward and I are the only officers left from our company. Sinclair and Brown were wounded. Hamilton was killed." He swallowed. His mouth was dry and dusty. Elise said nothing. "Can we stay?" Harry asked.

"Of course," Elise replied. There was a softness to her voice. "There are other men here already, but only a few. There is enough room for all of you."

"How many officers are here?" Harry asked. "I mean, how many men are staying in the house?"

"Two. Like you and your friend. They have a room each," Elise replied. "There will be space enough for all of you," she continued.

"I'd better get the men settled into their billets," Harry said, standing up again.

"Can I see you later?" Elise asked.

"Do you want to?" Harry looked at her uncertainly.

"Yes, I want to."

Outside, Harry noticed that some of the men had already fallen asleep where they lay. Edward got up and stepped away from the main group as Harry approached and the two men decided to leave Warner in charge while they went in search of the officers from the Royal Fusiliers to discuss the sleeping arrangements for the men.

"It won't do to step on their toes," Harry pointed out. "They were here first."

As they departed, Edward nudged Harry with his elbow. "So?" he asked.

"So what?"

"How's Elise?"

"Elise is fine." Harry looked away, so Edward didn't push the point. They wandered through the courtyard and out into the pasture beyond. Two men, clearly officers, were walking towards them.

"Hello!" Harry called.

"Hello there. I'm Lieutenant Quinnell," announced the older of the two, holding out his hand, as they neared each other. He was much shorter than Harry, with a shiny, round, rather knowing face and very small eyes beneath an untidy mop of dark hair, probably in his mid-twenties, Harry guessed. His voice sounded as though he had come directly from the Home Counties.

"Belmont." Harry replied. "And this is Lieutenant Wilson."

"I'm Second Lieutenant Ferguson. How do you do?" said the other man. Ferguson was younger, probably not yet twenty, rather thin, with protruding cheekbones and a small, neat moustache. Harry guessed that this young man had arrived in France directly from school and, judging by the dark shadows around his eyes, had already seen too much.

Once the formalities were completed, Harry explained the situation and that they would now need to share the accommodation.

"Absolutely, old man. No problem," Quinnell said, with the air of a man who enjoyed being in charge. At his suggestion, they all turned and walked back towards the farmhouse. "My men are only using one of the barns anyway, so the other one is completely at your disposal. Ferguson and I are staying in the farmhouse of course, but there's another room going spare, if you two don't mind sharing?"

"No, that'll be fine," Harry replied.

"When did you get here?" Edward asked of Ferguson, who was either shy, or perhaps used to letting Quinnell do the talking.

"Yesterday morning," Ferguson replied.

"Yes," Quinnell interrupted. "The girl cooked us a smashing dinner last night. The best I've had since arriving in France, I must say. She's a most obliging young girl – and quite a looker too!" Harry clenched his fists, instinctively.

"Well," Edward said abruptly, "there's no need for us to disturb you any further." He turned to Harry. "We'd better get the men settled down for the night, don't you think?"

"See you at dinner," Quinnell called to their retreating figures. "I'll introduce you to the girl, if you like. But remember, I saw her first!"

At dinner that night, Quinnell held court, introducing Harry and Edward to Elise, even though Edward had explained before the meal that they had already met.

"You have to admire these French girls, don't you?" Quinnell commented, filling his mouth with fried egg, the grease dripping onto his chin. "All this going on around them, and they still manage to look ravishing. She's just my type, you know. Quiet and demure on the outside, but I'll bet you a month's wages there's something a bit more primitive hiding underneath." Edward glanced across the table, noticing the tense furrows on Harry's forehead, the anger brewing in his eyes.

"Have you been into the village much?" he asked of Ferguson, trying to deflect the conversation.

"No, not yet. I thought I might go later. The men say you can get a decent glass of wine and quite reasonable beer at the estaminet."

"Yes, I believe so," Edward said.

As they all finished eating, Elise began to clear away the plates.

"She doesn't understand a word of English, you know?" Quinnell continued with his own train of thought, even though no-one else was joining in. Edward glanced over at Harry, who was now leaning on his elbows. His hands were clasped under his chin, the knuckles whitening, his dark eyes fixed on Quinnell. Ferguson didn't look up from the table at all. "I thought I might try my luck later on," Quinnell chuckled. "See if I can find out what's hidden under that skirt, heh?" Two chairs scraped sharply across the floor, as both Edward and Harry got up, but before either of them could do anything, Elise had crossed the room herself and was standing next to Quinnell.

"Monsieur!" she cried in broken English. "I comprehend what you say. You behave like a pig!" Harry and Edward remained standing.

"I say!" Quinnell blustered. "No harm done. Just joking around, you know." He leant back in his chair and patted Elise on the bottom. She turned and caught his hand with one of hers, while the other slapped his shiny face, hard across the cheek. A stream of words left her lips. She no longer spoke in English, reverting instead to her native language.

"Sorry, I didn't get a word of that," Quinnell announced, rubbing his cheek and grinning round at the others, evidently proud of his own ignorance.

"She said," Harry translated, leaning over the table, his face only inches from Quinnell's oily features, "that you need to learn some manners and, if you don't she will report you to the authorities in Bethune – as she was told to when she and her mother agreed to take in our men – or words to that effect." He paused before leaning in a little further, adding, "And if she doesn't, I will deal with you myself. And now, Lieutenant, I think it would be best for everyone if you left."

"I don't see why I should," Quinnell said, getting up and looking at Harry.

"One bloody good reason," said Harry, standing up straight and staring down at Quinnell, "would be because I said so." Quinnell wasn't stupid and knew when to back down.

"I'm off into the village," he announced. "The girls are less trouble there." Before anyone could comment, he'd left the room.

It was Ferguson who broke the silence. "I'm terribly sorry," he said. "I know he's my senior officer and everything, but he's an awful boor."

"We noticed," Edward agreed, looking up briefly at Harry, who was still standing next to the table, staring at Elise. "I say, Ferguson," Edward continued, "why don't you and I take a walk around the grounds? I think you'd best avoid the village tonight and I could do with some fresh air after that little scene." He got to his feet. "Thank you, Elise, for a lovely meal." He spoke in English, but very slowly so that she could understand. Ferguson merely nodded his head and smiled his appreciation, his hands clasped diffidently behind his back.

"You are welcome, messieurs," Elise replied, bowing her head.

"I'm so sorry, Elise," Harry said once they were alone. He still spoke in French – it seemed more natural to him, when he was with her. "I should have spoken up sooner."

"Don't worry. I'm used to dealing with men like him."

"Are they all like that?"

"No. Most of them are quieter now. They've seen too much fighting to behave like him. They mainly just walk around the farm or sit in the fields."

"And declare their undying love for you?" He smiled at her but she looked away. "I'm only teasing, Elise," he said. "Shall we go outside for a while? I could do with some fresh air too." Harry took her hand and led her out of the door, past the kitchen garden, through the archway and into the orchard. In the farthest corner, away from the house and the road, he sat down under a tree. It was almost dark, but there was a full moon and Harry could see her well enough. Elise sat next to him, her knees pulled up to her chest and her chin resting on the folds of her skirt.

"When did you learn to speak English?" Harry asked.

"My brother taught me a little, before he left. I find it very difficult to follow, so I prefer French."

A short silence followed. Harry looked up. In the dimming light, the tops of the trees no longer seemed green, but had a blue-grey hue about them. The apples and pears had begun to hang heavy on their branches.

"What happened to your captain?" Elise asked. "He seemed like such a nice man."

"Would you mind if we didn't talk about it?" Harry said.

"If you prefer." She turned her face away from him.

"I'm sorry," Harry said. "I'm just not in the mood for talking about all of that at the moment." He watched her, longing to reach across and touch her, caress her, pull her to him.

"Tell me about your wife," Elise said, suddenly, turning back to him. "Do you mind?"

"No. What do you want to know?" Harry asked, taking a breath. He leant back on his elbows and stretched out his legs.

"What was her name?" Elise asked.

"Annabelle. But I called her Bella."

"How did you meet her?"

"I had to visit her family's home. She was in the garden, picking roses. I took one look at her and fell in love, I suppose."

"Was she pretty?"

"Yes, she was."

"How long did you know her?"

"About eighteen months."

"And how long were you married?" Elise turned over, laying down on her side and resting on one elbow.

"A little under a year," he answered.

"That's not a very long time."

"No, it's not."

"When did she die?" Elise asked.

"Just over four years ago. When our daughter was born."

"Oh. I'm sorry. I hadn't realised."

"Why should you have realised, Elise?"

"That must have been very hard for you."

"It was." Harry looked up at her.

"Did you love her very much?" Elise asked.

"Yes." He didn't take his eyes from hers, scanning her face for a reaction.

"Do you still love her?"

"Yes, in a way." He waited to see if she would respond at all, but she didn't. "You don't stop loving someone just because they're not there anymore," he explained. "I still love you, even when I'm not here. I'd still love you, even if I never saw you again." He waited again, but still she said nothing. Harry sighed and stood up. Taking Elise's hand, he pulled her to her feet. "We should go inside, before any of the others get back," he said. He went to walk away, but she kept hold of his hand, stopping him. He let her pull him back.

"I'm sorry," she said, looking up at him.

"What are you sorry for?" he asked, still holding her hand.

"I know what you want me to say," she paused. "I just can't say it."

"Don't worry about it." He let go of her hand and walked slowly back towards the house.

Upstairs, Harry leant against the window frame, gazing at the willow tree waving in the breeze. He didn't turn around when Edward came back in from his walk.

"Ferguson's quite a nice chap, you know," he said, sitting down on his bed. He looked up. "Harry? What's wrong?" he asked.

"Oh, nothing." Harry turned and sat down opposite his friend.

"Really? Well you could have fooled me."

"Oh, I don't know, Eddie. I just thought that if we came back here, things would…" he hesitated.

"What?" Edward said. "You thought things would be different?"

"Yes."

"You thought Elise would take one look at you and fall into your arms?"

"No, of course not, Eddie."

"Harry, that was never going to happen, was it? She said she wanted to be friends. You knew that when we left."

"I know, I know. But there was something in the way she said it… it gave me something to hope for. I've thought of little else since we left. But whatever I might of wished for, I certainly didn't think I'd spend my first evening back here talking to her about Bella."

"Oh. That must have been bloody difficult."

"It was alright to start with. She just wanted a few details, you know? What did she look like; how did we meet, things like that. Then she asked me if I still loved Bella."

"Don't tell me? You said 'yes'," Edward said.

"Of course I did."

"It didn't occur to you that this might be one of those occasions when a white lie would be a good idea?"

"Eddie, I couldn't lie to her."

"No, I suppose you couldn't. I could, in the right circumstances. But you couldn't. How did she take it?" Edward asked.

"She didn't react at all. That's the point. I thought she might have been hurt, or jealous perhaps, or just have shown some sort of emotion. But there was nothing. No reaction at all. I've been deluding myself, haven't I?"

"I don't know. Maybe you're just going to have to accept that she really does just want to be friends, Harry."

"I'm not sure I can do that, Eddie."

"Then you'll have to keep yourself to yourself until we leave and hope to God that we don't get sent back here again." Edward started taking off his boots.

"I hope we get our orders soon, then. I'd rather be in the front lines and face everything the Germans can throw at us, than have to stay here for another day."

The men were still shaken from their experiences. They sat in small groups talking quietly, or alone staring into the distance, or walking around the farm. Harry and Edward discussed the situation with Sergeant Warner the next day and they decided to give the men a complete rest, without any training or lectures. Harry had no idea whether this was the right thing to do: he'd never been in charge before, but he'd been given no orders to follow and in any case, he didn't really care. The men were exhausted and needed to rest and recover. Reinforcements would soon arrive and then, they'd be sent back into the trenches again. He didn't know how long they would be at the farm, but he didn't see why the men shouldn't take advantage of a complete break from the fighting.

Harry deliberately avoided Elise. He and Edward went into the village where they had lunch at the estaminet. Quinnell was there, flirting with one of the waitresses, who didn't seem to object to his attentions. At dinner that night in the farmhouse kitchen, Quinnell was absent. Fortunately, he'd stayed on in the village. Edward worked hard to keep the conversation going, but in between his efforts, there were awkward silences. Afterwards, Harry excused himself and went outside to sit on the bench, taking his sketch pad and pencils with him. He wasn't really very interested in drawing anything; he just didn't want to be inside with Elise. He sat, looking at the sunset streaming across the sky, pale yellows and pinks mingling gently with the light blue of the fading day. He was unaware that Elise had rounded the corner of the farmhouse and was leaning against the wall with her arms folded, watching him.

"I thought you were coming out here to draw," she said. Harry was startled.

"I was," he lied. "I got distracted."

"Do you mind if I sit with you?" she asked.

"No," he lied again.

"It's a lovely sunset," Elise said, following the direction of Harry's gaze.

"Yes, isn't it." Harry hated this. They were making polite conversation, but all he wanted to do was hold her in his arms and kiss her. She was close enough for him to feel the warmth of her body, her leg almost touching his.

"Have you been avoiding me, 'Arry?" she asked.

"No." He was getting better at lying.

"Good, because there's something I want to tell you." From her tone, he had a feeling he wasn't going to like what he was about to hear. He said nothing. Elise paused, turning her face away from him and looking across the field, so he had to strain to hear her words. "When I was younger," she began, "there was a boy that I used to know, from the village. Jean-Claude was his name. He loved me. At least he said he did." She paused.

"Did you love him?" Harry asked. He couldn't help himself.

"Not in the same way that he loved me," she replied. "He was a friend. He was kind and funny. I'd known him all my life. He was a friend of my brother's, you see. We all grew up together. They looked after me, him and Henri. They always made sure I was alright." She swallowed hard, before continuing, "He was killed in March at Verdun."

"I'm so sorry, Elise. I didn't realise." Harry reached across and took her hand in his. "You should have told me."

She turned back, looking at the sunset again. "You don't understand 'Arry," she said. "I haven't told you because I want your sympathy. This is not the same as you and your wife. I cared about him, but Jean-Claude and I were friends, nothing more. We were not lovers. I've never had a lover." Harry was surprised by her honesty. She sighed.

"What's your point, Elise?" Harry asked.

"Jean-Claude was a friend, 'Arry, and I lost him, and it was horrible. It hurt so much knowing that he was gone and I'd never see him again," she said, lowering her voice to a whisper. "That's why I can't… It would be too…"

She stifled a sob, pulled herself free of him, got up and ran through the farm gate, and across the road. Harry watched her as she disappeared under the hanging branches of the willow tree. Leaning forward, he rested his elbows on his knees and stared at the ground. He sat for a while, then he shook his head and got up, walking at a slow pace, his hands in his pockets, not really sure why he was following her. Entering the dark canopy of the tree, he found her leaning against its rough bark. Tears were rolling down her cheeks and he pulled her to him, resting her head against his chest.

"Don't cry," he said, stroking her hair. "It's alright. I know you don't love me – or can't love me – or something like that. Whichever it is, it doesn't matter."

"You don't understand," she whispered.

"Then tell me."

"I can't tell you." She turned and tried to pull herself away from him.

"Don't!" Harry said, dragging her back and looking down into her eyes. "Are you saying you don't even want us to be friends anymore? Is that it?"

"You don't understand, 'Arry," she repeated

"Then explain it to me, for crying out loud."

"I can't."

"You have to, Elise, if you expect me to understand." He held on to her arms. "Listen, I'm not going to play games with you any more. I don't have the time for all this. You're not making sense. First you said you didn't care about me, then that you just wanted us to be friends and – if I understood what you just said correctly – you're saying that you're scared of losing me, and that it would be easier if we weren't even friends anymore. I'm bloody confused, Elise. What the hell do you want?"

"I've never said I don't care," she said, lowering her head. "How stupid can you be, 'Arry? I'm scared of losing you because I *do* care." Her voice was a whisper.

"So you do want us to be friends?"

"No."

"What the...?" Harry's exasperation was more than obvious. He released his grip on her and stepped away. "Elise! For Christ's sake! Tell me what it is you want," he shouted.

"You." Her voice was little more than a whisper.

Harry turned back. "What did you say?" he asked.

"I said that I want you," she said.

"As a friend?"

"No. More than a friend." She began to blush and looked down at her feet. "That day in the orchard," she continued quietly as he walked back and stood before her again. "The day you left. When you first said you loved me… It shocked me. It was so sudden and I wasn't expecting it. We'd only just met and I didn't know what to say to you, or how to react. But the moment you walked away from me, I knew then that I wanted you; that I loved you."

"You did?" He lifted her face to his, trying to make contact with her eyes. She evaded his look, turning her head away. "Then why didn't you tell me, Elise? Why have you denied it?"

"I wanted to tell you before you went away, when we were in the kitchen together, but I couldn't."

"Why not?" he asked.

"Because I'm scared, 'Arry. I'm scared of losing you. So many of your men have already died. You might be next. Losing Jean-Claude was bad enough, but he was only a friend. If I lost you, it would be too much to bear."

"Elise." Harry's voice was patient. "Look at me, please." She raised her eyes to his. "You can't deny how you feel, because you're afraid of it. Not saying that you love me doesn't make it any less true," he said. "It just means that I don't know about it. If I go away and something happens to me, you'll still feel the same. It won't hurt any less, just because you haven't said the words."

"At least I could pretend. I could fool myself into thinking it wasn't real."

"But, Elise, don't you understand? Love's always real." His eyes were still locked with hers, even in the near darkness. He held her face in his hands, wiping the tears from her cheeks with his thumbs. As he leant towards her, she closed her eyes and he held his breath. He looked down at her. She was so young, so innocent and he wanted so much to kiss her, but if he did, he wondered, would he be able to stop; would he even know how to? There was something about her that made him forget who he was, who he ought to be; something that made him lose himself. He closed his eyes for a second, then sighed and pulled away again.

"I think we should go in," he whispered. "It's getting late and I have to help Edward check that the men are all back." She opened her eyes and nodded, letting him take her hand. As they reached the edge of the tree, its still curtain hiding them from view, Harry stopped sharply.

"I want to ask you…" he said, turning back to her. "Why me?"

"What do you mean?" Elise asked.

"Many men pass through here, Elise. Evidently quite a few of them fall in love with you – or at least they say they do. So, why me? Why do you love me and none of them?"

"All sorts of reasons, but I think it's because you make me feel safe; you make me feel wanted for myself. I know that you'll look after me and… somehow, I feel that I belong to you."

"Of course I want you and I'll look after you, but please don't think that you belong to me Elise… I'd rather you belonged *with* me." He bent down and, placing a finger under her chin, he raised her face to his. Then he kissed her. He didn't care about stopping anymore. He didn't care about who he was or what he ought to do. He didn't care about losing himself, only about finding her. His hands stroked across her shoulders, down her back and around her hips, pulling her closer to him. Without breaking their kiss, he lowered her to the ground, feeling her arms reach up around his neck, her fingers pushing through his hair, drawing him in, further and further.

After a few minutes, Harry broke away first. He raised himself above her, staring down into her eyes.

"Am I doing it wrong?" she asked, looking up at him and biting her lip, her voice full of doubt.

"God, no," he replied. "You're doing everything right… a bit too right, if anything."

"Oh. I'm sorry."

"Don't be sorry, Elise," Harry laughed. "It was meant as a compliment. Doing things too right in these circumstances is a good thing."

She smiled up at him. "I've never done this before, 'Arry. I don't know what you expect."

"I don't expect anything," Harry said, "And, to be honest, I've never done anything quite like this either."

"But, surely, with your wife…?" Elise left the sentence unfinished.

"It wasn't like this, Elise," Harry whispered. "It's never been like this." He leant down and kissed her again, feeling her rise up to meet him, matching his every move. Again, he knew he had to stop. A voice in his head told him to stop. He wanted to ignore it but reluctantly he pulled away from her.

"I'm sorry," he said, kneeling up, his breathing heavy and uneven. "I probably shouldn't be doing this. I shouldn't take advantage of you. I've been trying not to, ever since we got here; ever since I first saw you, in fact."

"You don't have to be sorry," Elise said, sitting up and running her hands across his chest. "I'm not." Harry looked down at her sparkling eyes and tender smile, then stood and helped her to her feet.

"I really do think we'd better go in now," he said. He took her hand, kissed the palm and held back the branches of the willow tree to let her pass through before leading her across the road and into the farmhouse.

"So, everything worked out alright then?" Edward asked, as soon as Harry had closed the bedroom door.

"Sorry?" Harry turned, looking down at his friend, who was lying on his bed, one arm behind his head and a nonchalant smile on his face.

"How can I put this?" Edward said, his smile turning into a broad grin. "Let's just say that the willow tree doesn't hide quite as much as you might like to think."

"You saw us?"

"Yes. I saw you."

"Did anyone else?" Harry looked worried.

"No. Just me. I was on my way back from the barn. Oh, thanks for helping, by the way."

"I was otherwise occupied." Harry smiled.

"As I've already said, I did notice." He waited a moment, while Harry took off his boots. "Was it worth the wait?" Edward asked.

"Yes." Harry didn't look up.

"So, I presume that now we're hoping for a long rest, delayed reinforcements, and that we get sent back here as often as possible? Would that be about right?"

"Yes, something like that."

"I thought as much," Edward said, with a yawn, turning over onto his side.

Harry lay on his back staring at the ceiling, wondering at the difference twenty-four hours could make. Only last night he had hoped to be sent as far away from Elise as possible; now all he he wanted was to be able to stay near to her. He wanted more of her. He wanted all of her.

Reinforcements from the Middlesex Regiment started to arrive the next morning and, with them came Captain Pilcher. Luckily Quinnell and his men were in the process of getting ready to leave, so there was only a short-term problem with billeting the new men, who were quite happy to sit out in the field after their long march. Pilcher found Harry in the courtyard, in conversation with Sergeant Warner.

"Are you Belmont?" he asked.

"Yes, sir," Harry said, saluting smartly.

"This place is an absolute shambles," Pilcher said, looking around the farm. Harry and Warner exchanged a quick glance. "I can see my arrival here is well overdue," Pilcher continued. "Where are the other officers?"

"Lieutenant Wilson is in the farmhouse, sir," Harry replied.

"And the others?" Pilcher looked around.

"Wilson and myself are the only ones left, sir."

"Well, go and get this Lieutenant Wilson then, Sergeant," Pilcher ordered, turning to Warner, who strode quickly across the courtyard and disappeared into the house, returning a few minutes later with Edward behind him.

"Wilson?" Pilcher enquired.

"Yes, sir." Edward saluted. Pilcher looked him up and down.

"Well, I can see I need to lick things into shape around here." He paced up and down, his hands behind his back. He had a long thin face with a high forehead and a well-trimmed moustache. His perfect, spotless uniform with its shiny buttons and polished belt immediately told Harry and Edward that he'd not seen much, if any, real action. He turned to face both men, Sergeant Warner having moved to one side. "We're expecting further reinforcements later this afternoon, which will bring us just about up to strength. Then, my orders are that we're to leave tomorrow morning."

"Where are we going?" Harry asked.

"To the front lines, of course, where else? You've had a rest. Now it's time to get back into the thick of it."

"I assumed we'd be going back into the front lines, sir. What I meant was, whereabouts exactly?" Harry asked.

"You don't need to know the details, Belmont. You're not in charge anymore." Pilcher looked up at Harry, his eyes narrowing.

"No, sir," Harry replied.

"Now, once these Royal Fusiliers have moved off, I want you to get the new men into their billet. I'm going to have a word with the people in the farmhouse." He marched off towards the door.

Harry and Edward looked at each other, their eyebrows raised.

"Right-ho, Warner." Harry turned to the Sergeant. "Can you go and politely ask Lieutenant Quinnell what time he thinks they'll be going? We'll be outside with the new arrivals."

"Yes, sir." Warner turned and moved towards the barn where Quinnell and Ferguson were organising their men.

"Belmont! Wilson!" Pilcher called from the door of the farmhouse. "Do either of you speak French?"

"Yes, sir," Harry said, wearily.

"Over here, then. Where are you going, Wilson?"

"I'm just going to check on the new men, sir."

"Very good. Carry on." Harry arrived at the farmhouse door. "In here, Belmont. I can't get this girl to understand a word I'm saying."

They went into the kitchen. Harry looked across the table at Elise, hoping that his face showed how sorry and embarrassed he felt.

"What to you want to say, sir?" he asked.

"Tell her that I want to have a look round," Pilcher explained. "I need to see the sleeping accommodation for the officers."

"There's only the three of us, isn't there?"

"No, we've got two more coming this afternoon with the rest of the men, Belmont. Just ask the girl, will you?"

"I don't really need to, sir. I can show you around."

"Oh, very well. Tell her what we're doing, will you?"

Harry explained and then led the Captain up the stairs. Elise was intrigued and followed behind.

"This is the best room, here, sir." Harry said, opening the first door.

"I'll have that one, then," Pilcher announced, glancing inside.

Harry then revealed the second room, which he suggested would suit the two new officers. "Wilson and I are already sharing that room down there," he said.

"And that last door at the end?" Pilcher asked, pointing to Elise's bedroom.

"That room belongs to the young lady, sir."

"I don't think we should allow her to sleep up here, where there are officers," Pilcher said. "She'll have to sleep somewhere else." Harry fought to control his temper.

"It's her house, sir. If anyone should go, it should be us, not her. We just avoid going near that end of the corridor."

Pilcher backed down. "Well, it's not very satisfactory, but I suppose it will have to do. Now, I'm going into the village," he continued. "I'd like you to have everything organised by the time I get back."

"When will that be, sir?" Harry asked.

"I don't know, do I, Belmont? Just get on with things, will you?"

"Very good, sir," Harry said. Pilcher began to descend the stairs. Once he was out of earshot, Elise turned to Harry.

"He seems very unpleasant," she said.

"He's also very dangerous." They started down the stairs, where they found Edward sitting in the kitchen.

"Is everything alright out there?" Harry asked.

"It's fine. Warner's with them at the moment." Edward looked up at Harry. "What on earth did we do to deserve him?"

Elise picked up her basket, ready to start collecting the vegetables for dinner but, as she was about to leave, she placed a hand on Harry's arm.

"Why do you say this man is dangerous?" she asked in broken English for Edward's benefit.

"Because," Harry replied, speaking slowly, "once we're back in the trenches, he won't know what to do, but he's the one in charge."

"Oh." Her face fell.

Harry reverted to French. "Don't worry, my darling. I'll take care of him."

"I'm not worried about him."

"You don't understand, Elise. What I mean is that, after about five minutes in the front line, he'll probably be asking me what he should be doing, rather than telling me what I should do. He won't know which way to turn."

"Does this mean you'll be leaving soon?"

"Yes." They'd both almost forgotten that Edward was still there with them. "We'll talk later," he said. He kissed Elise on the forehead and she went out into the sunshine.

"Do you think he's ever even seen a trench?" Edward asked once she was gone.

"Maybe in training," Harry replied.

"You actually think he's done some training then?"

"We can hope."

"What were you just saying to Elise?"

"Which bit?"

"How do I know? I couldn't understand any of it?"

"I just told her that once Pilcher's in the front line, he'll be lost and then he'll hopefully turn to us for help."

"I give him ten minutes."

"You're optimistic. I said five."

Further reinforcements arrived during the afternoon from the Queen's Regiment, not long after Quinnell and Ferguson had departed with their men. Harry and Edward were sad to see Ferguson leave, but Quinnell certainly wouldn't be missed. With the new men, there also came two new officers, Second Lieutenants Canter and Mullion. They were both quite young and neither had been in action before, but they were keen to help. Once the second barn was clear of Royal Fusiliers, Harry suggested a division of the work.

"Lieutenant Wilson," he said to Edward. "Why don't you and Mullion make a start with the Middlesex men, while Canter comes with me and we'll deal with the men from the Queen's Regiment?"

"Sounds good to me," Edward replied.

"Once we've got the men settled, I'll show you to your own billets," Harry said to Mullion and Canter. "That's the first rule when you come out of the lines, by the way. You always make the sleeping arrangements for your men before yourselves."

"Really?" Mullion asked.

"Yes – always."

"Even if you've got no idea where you are or where you're going to sleep?"

"Well, you nearly always know where you are," Harry smiled. "Where you are going to sleep tends to take care of itself most of the time. Sometimes you have to improvise a bit, but you must always find somewhere for the men first. Then worry about yourself."

"What if you manage to settle the men and then can't find somewhere for yourself?" Canter asked.

"That doesn't normally happen," Harry replied. "But if it does, you make do."

"I see," Mullion said, nodding his head. They paired up and went to work.

Pilcher returned late in the afternoon. His breath told them that he'd spent most of the day in the estaminet. He found the four officers in the kitchen, sitting at the table.

"Is everyone settled in?" he asked.

"Yes, sir," Harry replied.

"Good." He looked around the room. "I'm going upstairs for a while. What time do we eat around here?"

"Usually around seven o'clock, sir," Harry said.

"Right."

"He doesn't like to do much, does he?" Mullion whispered once they'd heard the bedroom door close.

"That's what we're here for." Harry smiled across the table, then got up. "I'm just going outside for a minute."

"I'll join you," Canter said, getting to his feet. Edward noticed Harry's shoulders drop and the disappointed look on his face.

"I say, Canter?" Edward stopped the other man in his tracks. "I thought I might take a turn around the grounds before dinner. Do you feel like joining me?"

"Alright then," Canter replied. "Are you coming Mullion?"

"I don't mind if I do."

"What about you, Lieutenant Belmont?" Canter said, looking at Harry.

"No thanks. I'll just go and sit down outside, I think. Keep an eye on things here."

"I don't mind staying here with you, if you want," Canter offered.

"No. You go off and enjoy yourselves," Harry said. As he reached the door, he glanced back at Edward, mouthing a 'thank you', to which Edward just smiled.

Harry found Elise in the orchard, sitting with her back against one of the tree trunks, her legs drawn up to her chest. She was pulling at a loose thread on her skirt and didn't notice him until he cast a shadow across her.

"What's wrong?" Harry asked, dropping to his knees alongside her.

"I've heard that you're leaving in the morning," she replied, looking away to hide the tears in her eyes. "Which means we only have this evening to be together."

"We have all night to be together, Elise," Harry faltered. "If you want." He couldn't believe he'd actually said the words. She looked up at him and nodded her head. Harry leant down and kissed her.

"Are you sure?" he asked. "Really sure? I mean, we haven't known each other for very long."

"I feel as though I've always known you 'Arry."

"I know." He kissed her again.

At dinner, Pilcher reappeared and talked about the following day, explaining what he expected of them all. Harry thought that Pilcher's expectations of Canter and Mullion were a bit high, considering they'd got no experience themselves and he made a mental note to speak to both of them.

"We've got a full day's march ahead of us tomorrow," Pilcher announced at the end of the meal. "I'm going to turn in. Go and check on the men and then get some sleep. It'll be a busy day tomorrow." Without thanking Elise, he left the room.

"Come on, then," Edward said, sighing heavily as he got up from his chair. "We'd better do as we're told."

"I'll be along in just a minute," Harry said. Edward looked back at him and nodded, guiding Canter and Mullion out of the door while explaining what they had to do.

Harry turned to Elise, who was standing, leaning against the sink.

"Do you still want this?" he asked.

"Yes," she replied.

"Are you sure? You don't have to." He crossed the room, placing one hand on either side of her.

"Yes, I'm sure."

"Shall I come to your room later?" he whispered.

"Yes."

"It will have to be after everyone has gone to sleep. Will you wait?"

"Of course I'll wait." He smiled, kissed her and went outside to join the others.

The men didn't really need checking on, or taking care of. They knew what lay ahead of them and wanted only to sit together, writing letters, talking and thinking.

Canter and Mullion were nervous, so Harry went into their room with them to start with, trying to quell their anxieties, and answer their questions. Eventually, he joined Edward in their own room.

"We need to keep an eye on those two," he said as he closed the door. "Pilcher's asking far too much of them and they're not ready for it yet."

"I know," Edward looked up from his bed. "They have no idea what's in store for them."

"Hopefully they'll be able to follow our lead." Harry was pacing the floor.

"They'll be fine as long as they ignore everything Pilcher says." Edward smiled.

"I've been meaning to thank you, Eddie," Harry said.

"What for?"

"I should think you've had enough of helping out with my duties, walking around the farm, touring the grounds and generally showing off the sights."

"It's all in the line of duty, Harry. You'd do the same for me." Edward laid down, resting on his pillow. "Shouldn't you stop marching up and down and get into bed? God knows when we'll next get a decent night's sleep in a proper bed with real sheets."

Harry stopped and looked at the floor, his hands deep in his pockets.

"How drunk do you think Pilcher was tonight?" he asked.

"Very. Why? Are you worried he's got a problem?"

"Yes. But that's not why I asked."

"What is it then, Harry? You're behaving very strangely."

"Do you think he's drunk enough that he'll sleep soundly all night?"

"I should think so. He was staggering around all over the place when he came upstairs. Why do you ask?" Harry sat down at the end of Edward's bed.

"Eddie," he said, "I have another favour to ask."

"Ask away."

"Could you cover for me, if anybody asks where I am?"

"When?"

"Now. Well, tonight. All night." Harry knew he was mumbling.

"Why?" Edward sat up in bed.

"Because I'm asking you to, Eddie. I know it's a lot to expect, especially if his lordship wakes up. I don't want to get you in any trouble, but it's important."

"Where are you off to, then?"

"Where do you think?" Harry looked up at Edward.

"Oh," Edward smiled. "I see. Consider it done then."

"Even if he wakes up and wants to know where I am?"

"Even then. I'll think of something."

"Thanks, Eddie. I'll be back before dawn."

In the darkness of the corridor, Harry hesitated, leaning against the wall. The palms of his hands were damp with sweat. Could he do this, he wondered. More to the point, should he do this? She was so young and so innocent, but whenever he was with her, whenever he looked into those deep brown eyes, he felt himself falling into her and all sense of convention, all of his principles simply disappeared. He just ached for her with a longing he'd never felt before and yet he had no idea what he was going to do when he got inside her room. It had been over four years since he'd made love and, while he remembered perfectly well what to do, he also knew that making love to Elise was going to be very different to anything he'd ever done with Bella. He closed his eyes for a moment, remembering... He'd loved Bella very deeply, there was no denying it; she'd captivated and enthralled him. He'd wanted and needed her. Her death had numbed him. He'd felt nothing for so long afterwards, that he'd thought he'd forgotten how to feel... Until he'd met Elise. She'd brought him back to life and immersed him in desire. He felt no sense of guilt or betrayal: Bella was in the past and every instinct in his body was telling him that his future lay with Elise. He knew how much he yearned for her, but he also knew that there would be nothing chaste or restrained about their lovemaking. He wondered suddenly if he might be a disappointment. He knew, however, that there was no turning back now. Even if he could, he didn't want to and even if he wanted to, he couldn't. He would have to follow his intuition and hope for the best.

He took a deep breath, wiped the palms of his hands down his trousers and knocked quietly. He heard a faint 'Entré' from within and opened the door slowly, peering around it into the dim, candle-lit room. Elise was sitting on the large cast iron bed, her knees clutched up to her chin. Her long hair, now untied, was hanging down by her sides. Her naked white shoulders were exposed and, as she sat up to face him, Harry saw that the lace bodice of her thin cotton nightdress was tied only loosely with fine ribbon. He closed the door softly and crossed the room, sitting next to her on the bed, his arm touching hers.

"Elise," he murmured softly, "Are you really sure about this? You don't have to do anything you don't want to. I meant what I said earlier. We don't know each other very well. We can wait, if you want to." He stroked the outside of her bare calf with his fingers.

"I don't want to wait."

"Good. But please don't do this just because you think I might be dead tomorrow."

"Don't say that," Elise whispered. She reached across and placed one hand on his arm, feeling the heat of his body through the thick fabric of his shirt. Harry noticed that her fingers were shaking.

"Are you cold?" he asked, looking into her eyes. There it was: that look, pulling him in. She shook her head. "Are you nervous?" he whispered. She nodded. "Don't be," he murmured. Without hesitating, he knelt up next to her, leaning over to undo the ribbon.

In one move, he pulled the nightdress over her head and pushed her back, pressing her arms into the downy softness of the mattress, feeling the smoothness of her skin against his lips as he kissed his way down her body.

The night progressed too quickly and between small snatches of sated sleep, Harry instinctively explored every inch of Elise, beguiled by her welcoming anticipation of every new experience. She was arousing and intoxicating. When the new day was little more than a blink away and the first rays of dawn were just beginning to streak across the night sky, he made love to her again, very slowly, watching her intently, wanting to remember every moment, to absorb every movement, every taste, every sight, every sound.

Harry sat on the edge of the bed. Elise reached across to him, her fingertips just touching his thigh. He turned, smiling down at her full lips, her pink flushed cheeks and shining eyes. Looking at her hair, wild and tousled, spread across the pillow, he recalled burying his face in those dark curls during the night.

"Must you go already?" she asked.

"Yes," Harry replied, turning away again. "We have to leave at six; the men will be getting ready. I told Edward I'd be back by dawn."

"Stay for a little while longer." Elise urged, clambering across the bed on her knees and pulling him back onto the creased sheets. Harry turned over, pinning her to the bed. He kissed her neck, forcing an involuntary moan from her parted lips. He felt her relax beneath him, heard her inhale deeply, saw her eyes close.

"Oh God, Elise," he whispered, finding his way back to her again.

Luckily, it took him only a few minutes to get ready. He turned his back to her while he dressed. There was no embarrassment between them but he couldn't bear to see her naked body lying on the bed, not knowing how long it would be until he could see her, touch her, taste her again. Once dressed, he turned back and was surprised to see that she had put on her clothes and was standing by the door, her hair tied loosely behind her head.

"Why have you got up?" he asked as he walked to her and placed his hands on her hips.

"I can't lie in bed and just watch you leave me." She rested her head on his chest.

"I don't want to leave you." He wrapped his arms around her.

"We won't be able to say goodbye downstairs, in front of everyone." She took a deep breath. "Perhaps you should say goodbye to me here."

"I can't say goodbye to you anywhere, Elise."

"And yet," she pulled away from him, raising her voice. "You can walk away calmly and go back to fight and maybe…"

"Don't think I'm calm, Elise. I'm anything but calm."

"Then don't leave." Tears began to fall down her cheeks.

"I have to. I don't have a choice. I'm sorry."

"Sorry for what? For coming into my life? Making me love you? Going away and maybe never coming back again?" She moved forward, reaching for the door handle, desperate to escape the terrible atmosphere she was creating. Harry stood in her way. He took her wrists and pushed her back against the wall.

"No, Elise, not like this," he said. "You know I have to go. Please don't make it any harder." He held her arms tightly by her sides, crushing her against the wall with his body and kissing her, her lips wet with salty tears. He broke away, standing back. "I have to go now."

He stroked her cheek with his fingertips. "I will come back. I'll find a way. I promise." He turned, pulled the door open and walked out into the hallway.

Chapter Nine

Autumn 1916

"I'm glad we're back here," Edward said, descending the dugout steps behind Harry and Canter. "I didn't like being in those bloody woods. They gave me the creeps."

"It's still the same as when we left it," Harry said, looking around. "It hardly seems like a month since we were last here. Which bunk do you want, Canter?"

"Oh, I don't mind. I suppose we should let the Captain choose first, shouldn't we?"

"I couldn't care less," said Harry, putting his coat down on the bed nearest to him. They all ducked their heads at the same time as a shell landed nearby, loosening the mud above them. "Eddie?" Harry said, turning round. "You know you said you were glad to be back here? Would you care to revise that statement?"

"It's still better than being in those woods," Edward said, dusting himself down. "Who's on duty first?"

"I'll go," said Canter. "Mullion's already up there. When do you think the Captain will get here?"

"I've got no idea," said Harry. "It depends on how long it takes at H.Q."

"With any luck, they'll keep him for the duration," Edward said under his breath, lying down on his bunk. Canter went back up the steps, humming to himself. "He's turned out alright really, hasn't he?" Edward said, once Canter had disappeared.

"Yes," Harry replied, sitting at the table. "They both have. It makes up for Pilcher being so utterly bloody useless." They both looked up as another shell burst close to the trench, followed by another and another. The bombardment started in earnest.

"I think I'll go up as well," shouted Harry, standing up again. "Neither of them have been in anything quite like this yet."

"No." Edward got up, pulling on his helmet. "I'll come with you."

Harry led the way up the dugout steps. At the top, Canter was standing close to the front wall of the trench, his hands clasped over his ears and his eyes tight shut beneath his helmet. Harry ducked as he came though the dugout entrance, his helmet still in his hand.

He crossed to Canter and took hold of one of his arms, pulling it to his side.

"Are you alright?" Harry shouted. Canter kept his eyes shut. Harry shook him. "Canter!" he shouted.

"Yes, sir!" Canter opened his eyes.

"Are you alright?" Harry repeated.

"I think so, sir," Canter replied above the din, clods of earth falling around him.

"Where's Mullion?" Harry shouted.

"Down that way, I think," Canter said, pointing to his left.

"Go and have a look, will you?" Harry called to Edward, who nodded and walked off. "Warner!" Harry called.

"Yes sir!" Warner appeared at his elbow.

"How are the men?" Harry shouted.

"Oh, you know, sir," Warner replied, shrugging his shoulders.

"I'll go around myself, Warner," Harry said. "You stay here." Harry turned back to Canter. "We need to go along and check on the men. Come with me."

Canter nodded his head and followed Harry, who finally pulled his helmet on. They moved through the trench. Men were cowering in funk holes, their shoulders hunched over, their faces bowed. Some sat on the ground, their heads buried between their knees, their hands over their ears. Harry went along, placing a hand on their backs or shoulders, smiling or nodding as they looked up. Occasionally, one of them would smile in return. Every once in a while, they'd all stop, holding their breath as they heard the familiar whine of a shell coming close overhead, hoping it would land somewhere else. Then, as it crashed, hurling mud skyward, they'd heave a collective sigh of relief, until the next time. The sentries peered through loopholes, shrinking back at every eruption. As he rounded each traverse, Harry looked back, checking that Canter was still behind him. The young second-lieutenant was a few paces to the rear. His face was pale, but he looked up at the men as they turned round and tried to make eye contact with them. Finally, they reached the end of their section and turned to retrace their steps. Harry paused for a few moments.

"How do they do it, sir?" Canter asked.

"The men?" Harry said. "They do it, because they have to. They don't have a dugout to shelter in, so they do the best they can."

"They look so scared," Canter said.

"So do we," Harry replied. "Come on. Let's get back."

They started back along the trench, but had gone only a few feet when they heard a loud explosion just ahead of them. It was followed by a ghostly silence, and then screams: ear-piercing screams and cries.

"Come on!" Harry yelled to Canter, running down the trench. "Move!" he shouted at the men standing in his way, who quickly stood aside. Rounding the next traverse, Harry was met with a sickening sight. The back wall of the trench had taken a direct hit. The men who had been cowering there had disappeared. All that was left of them was skin, sinew, bone, flesh, and blood. Lots of blood. A few men were standing around. One of them, a youngster named Stubbs, his uniform splattered with blood, his horrified face distorted, his eyes bulging and mouth wide open, was screaming and screaming. Harry grabbed the man nearest to him, Private Acres, and dragged him towards Stubbs.

"Get him out of here!" he shouted to Acres, who took Stubbs by the arm and led him away. Within moments, Canter ran around the corner of the traverse, took in the sight before him and vomited.

"Canter," Harry said, turning to him and blocking his view. "Go on back to the dugout. Find Warner and tell him to come here. Tell him I need sandbags and lime. Don't look down. Don't look around you – just go." Canter stared at Harry, nodded his head and ran forward. Harry glanced around him. "Is anybody injured?" he shouted above the noise. No-one answered. Two men stepped forward with shovels. Harry took one and they began scraping down the sides of the trench, which were spattered with blood and loose pieces of flesh, dragging them onto the ground. A few minutes later, Warner arrived, carrying another shovel, the empty sandbags and a bag full of lime.

"Christ!" he hissed, through gritted teeth. He handed his shovel to one of the men and held open a sandbag which Harry started to fill with what was left of the four men who he had smiled at just a few minutes before. Suddenly, Edward came around the corner of the traverse, panting and out of breath.

"Harry!" he shouted.

"Yes!" Harry replied.

"Oh, you're alright. Thank God."

"I'm alright, yes."

"Let me help," Edward called.

"We're fine, Lieutenant Wilson," Harry shouted, looking up. "Can you go and find Canter, please. He was with me when it happened. And there was a Private Stubbs. You should find him with Acres. Deal with him, can you? He's in a state."

"Will do." Edward called. They looked at each other for a second or two, before Harry resumed his task.

It took Harry, Warner and three of the other men nearly an hour to clear up the trench, by which time the bombardment had died down. Afterwards, Harry stayed with the men for a while, and had a drink of tea. Then he went and found Stubbs, who was sitting on the floor of the trench, a few yards from the dugout entrance. Edward was standing above him and shook his head as Harry approached. Harry sat down next to Stubbs.

"How are you?" he asked. Stubbs nodded his head, although his expression remained glazed. "I know it doesn't help," Harry continued, "But they really wouldn't have known anything about it."

"It doesn't help, sir." Stubbs said.

"Hawks was a particular friend of yours, wasn't he?" Harry said, recalling one of the men who had died.

"Yes, sir," Stubbs replied. "We'd been together since the beginning."

"I'm truly sorry, Stubbs," Harry said, placing his hand on Stubbs's arm.

"Thank you, sir," Stubbs replied, looking at Harry and attempting a smile. Harry got up and went over to Warner who was standing a few feet away.

"Take care of him," he said.

"Yes, sir. I will," Warner replied, moving towards Stubbs who now held his head in his hands.

"Come on Eddie," Harry said, walking to the dugout. "We'd better get down and see if Canter's alright."

"I think Pilcher's back," Edward replied.

"Oh good! That's just what we need."

"Are you sure you're alright, Harry?" Edward asked, looking up from under his helmet.

"I'm fine," Harry replied, patting Edward's shoulder and ducking his head below the dugout entrance.

"Where have you been, Belmont?" Pilcher asked, as Harry descended the steps.

"I've been with the men, sir," Harry explained. "We took a direct hit. Four of the men were killed. One of the privates was upset, sir. His best friend was among the dead."

"I know about the shelling. Canter told me. I should have heard it from you, Belmont. You should have left the men to clear up the trench and come back here to report to me."

"I didn't know you were here, sir," Harry said and sat down on his bunk. Canter was sitting on the other side of the dugout staring at the floor. Edward went to sit at the table.

"Well, I'm here now," Pilcher said, eyeing Harry.

"And do you want me to report to you, sir?" Harry asked.

"No, not at the moment, Belmont. I've just got back from H.Q. We've got orders to make a raid tonight," Pilcher said, looking around the dugout.

"Tonight, sir?" Edward said.

"Yes, tonight, Wilson. We're to raid Spoon Trench, just opposite. Protective barrage starts at 19.45. The raid itself will begin at 20.00."

"Who's going?" asked Edward.

"I'm going to lead this one myself," said Pilcher, puffing out his chest. "The 9th Royal Fusiliers carried out a successful raid here a couple of weeks ago. They took nearly twenty prisoners evidently."

"You're going yourself, sir?" Harry asked.

"Yes, Belmont."

"Shouldn't you stay here, sir?" Harry suggested. "You are in charge, after all."

"No, Belmont. Don't question my orders."

"Who's going with you, sir?" Edward asked.

"I thought Canter and Mullion could come. I'll need a good sergeant as well. That man of yours, Belmont. Warner, isn't it? He'll do. Then I'll need about a dozen or so men. That should do."

"You want to take Warner as well as Canter and Mullion?" Harry said, standing up.

"Yes. It will be good experience for Canter and Mullion and Warner's an old hand at this sort of thing," Pilcher replied. "I've already made my decision, Belmont, so don't start arguing with me."

"Why not leave one of them behind, sir?" Harry suggested. "Leave Warner here and I'll come along instead." Edward glanced up sharply at Harry.

"No, Belmont." Pilcher's voice was becoming more agitated.

"I've got just as much experience as Warner, sir, and I'll be more able to help Canter and Mullion. They'll take orders from me," Harry said.

"They'll take their orders from me, Belmont. The decision is made," Pilcher replied, his anger rising.

"I really think I should come along, sir. Perhaps Canter could stay behind then. He's had rather a shock with the shelling, sir."

"Belmont!" Pilcher stepped forward. "I'm not going to tell you again!" Harry stood his ground.

"Canter and Mullion have never been on a raid, sir," he persisted. "You might be better off taking me along."

"If I wanted you there, Belmont, I'd have asked you. And how are Canter and Mullion going to learn, if I don't teach them?" Edward and Harry exchanged a look. "Both of you can go up now," he said to Harry and Edward. "Send Mullion and Warner down, will you? I need to brief them on the raid." He turned away from them, leant across to his bag and pulled out a bottle of whisky. As Harry went to climb the steps, he glanced back at Canter, who was still staring at the floor.

Up in the trench, Edward went in search of Mullion. Harry found Warner talking to a few of the men. Stubbs was standing up now, smoking a cigarette.

"Warner?" Harry called.

"Yes, sir," the sergeant replied, approaching him.

"I'm afraid the captain wants to see you," Harry said.

"Me, sir? What for?" Warner asked.

"There's going to be a raid tonight. He wants you to go."

"Oh. What's it in aid of?" Warner asked.

"Having a look at the trench opposite of us – the usual nonsense." Edward and Mullion came up behind Harry. "I did try to talk him out of it, Warner," Harry continued.

"He did," Edward said, joining the conversation. "He offered to go in your place. In fact, I think he offered to go in everyone's place. That was about the strength of it, wasn't it, Lieutenant Belmont?"

Warner looked up at Harry. "Who else is going then, sir?" he asked.

"Second Lieutenants Canter and Mullion, about a dozen men." Harry paused. "And the Captain."

"The Captain's going?"

"Yes, I'm afraid so."

"And you offered to go in my place, sir?"

"Yes, Warner," Harry said. "You'd better be getting down there."

"Thank you, sir," Warner said, looking up at Harry as he went down into the dugout.

At seven thirty, Canter and Mullion came out of the dugout. Both looked nervous. Harry and Edward were waiting for them.

"Has he briefed you?" Harry asked quietly.

"Yes." Mullion nodded his head.

"Remember," Harry said, "When you're out there, stick close together and stay quiet. If anything happens keep your head down. Other than you two and the captain, everyone else has done this plenty of times before, so do what they tell you. Follow Warner's lead. He'll know what to do." Harry patted them both on the shoulder and turned to Warner, who was standing close by with the other men. He waited for Warner to finish speaking to the men, then beckoned him over.

"Are you alright, sergeant?" Harry asked.

"Yes, thank you, sir," Warner replied. "How are they?" He nodded towards Canter and Mullion.

"Nervous. Keep an eye on them, will you?"

"I'll do my best, sir," Warner said.

"I know you will." Harry held out his hand and shook Warner's. "Take care of yourself, Warner," he said. "I'll see you when you get back."

"Yes sir," Warner replied.

Harry and Edward stood by the dugout entrance after they'd all gone.

"What a bloody awful day," Edward said.

"It's not over yet," Harry replied.

"Do we know who was killed earlier?" Edward asked.

"Sanders, Eliot, Hawks and Donovan," Harry said.

"I thought they'd got you," Edward said, looking down at the ground.

"I wondered why you appeared out of nowhere."

"I just heard the explosion. I knew you were down that end of the trench. I assumed the worst."

"Well, I'm still here."

"You won't be much for longer, if you keep offering to go out on raids with Pilcher. What the hell were you thinking of?" Edward asked.

"It was an instinct, I suppose," Harry replied. "He hasn't got a bloody clue what he's doing. I just thought someone should go, who has a vague idea what's going on. Warner knows what's what, but Pilcher won't listen to him."

"Canter and Mullion will," Edward said.

"They're not leading the raid, though. I was hoping he'd take me along and I could steer him in the right direction."

"Let's keep our fingers crossed. They might get back alright. The Germans might be asleep."

"Not after our artillery started firing at them, they won't," Harry said. "They'll be expecting something."

"We'll know, anyway, in an hour or two – one way or the other."

Harry went to check on the sentries. It was a little before ten o'clock by the time he returned to the dugout entrance, where he found Edward looking anxiously at his watch.

"I'd have thought they'd be back by now. We're not that far from the German lines. I thought I heard some firing a little while ago over to the right, but then it went quiet again."

"They won't be much longer, I'm sure." Harry was trying to sound reassuring. "What was that?" he said sharply.

"I didn't hear anything," Edward replied.

"Listen!" There was a faint noise coming from directly in front of them. Harry peered through the loophole in the parapet.

"Oh Christ!" he said. Moving along to the fire step, he climbed out of the trench, crouching as low as he could.

"Harry! What the hell are you doing?"

"Stay there!" Harry said quietly over his shoulder.

Edward looked up, waiting for something to happen. Then he saw activity on the parapet. A body was being rolled over the sandbags.

"Take him!" It was Harry's voice. "Take him, Eddie!" Edward did his best to lower the body into the trench. At the same time, a little further along, he saw the captain and three other men walk around the traverse. When Edward looked back up again, he saw Harry lying flat on the sandbags, peering into the trench.

"Get down there, Warner," Harry said, glancing over his shoulder.

"After you, sir." Edward heard Warner's voice.

"Stop bloody well arguing, Warner and do as you're told." Warner slid down next to Edward, followed by Harry.

They all stood together, looking down at the body lying by Edward's feet. It was Canter. Edward was bending down.

"He's still alive," he said, "But only just. He's got a nasty wound in his shoulder and another in the leg. I'll deal with him." Edward turned to his platoon sergeant, who was standing nearby, and instructed him to find some stretcher bearers.

"Are there any more out there, Warner?" Harry asked. "I can go back out."

"No, sir," Warner replied. Harry looked around.

"This is all of you?" Harry said.

"Yes, sir."

"Excuse me, sergeant," Pilcher approached them. "I don't need you to report to Lieutenant Belmont, thank you."

"Sorry, sir," Warner said, turning away. Harry stood in front of the entrance to the dugout as Pilcher went to pass him.

"What happened?" Harry said quietly.

"I don't have to answer to you, Belmont," Pilcher said through gritted teeth.

Harry fixed his eyes on Pilcher until the captain looked away, then Harry stepped aside and let him pass.

Harry found Warner sitting in a funk-hole drinking a cup of tea. He saw Harry approaching and began to get up.

"Stay there," Harry said, standing next to him. "What happened out there?"

"It was chaos, sir. I know I shouldn't say so, sir, but the captain didn't know what he was doing."

"Tell me about it," Harry said.

"We'd got to within about twenty yards of the German lines, sir. I honestly don't think they knew we were there. It seemed to be going alright. Then, there was a noise off to my right, from a little way in front. I don't know what it was, sir, but it definitely came from their trench. I put my head down, just in case. All of a sudden, the captain, sir, he starts yelling his head off, screaming at us to pull back. He gave away our position good and proper. All hell broke loose. Mr Mullion was hit in the head straight away. Killed outright he was. I didn't see them all go down, sir. I did see Mr Canter, though. He was quite close to me. I managed to get hold of him and held him down until the firing stopped. Then I checked around. The captain and a couple of the men seemed to have disappeared. Everyone else was dead, so I got myself back to Mr Canter and dragged him back. I didn't really know what had happened to the captain, or the other men, or I would have stayed out there longer and looked for them."

"From what I can gather, it would seem that they got a bit confused on the way back and fell into the trench a little further up," Harry said. "You did well, Warner. Thank you."

"Don't thank me, sir. It should never have happened."

"You did all you could, Warner." Harry turned and walked away. As he reached the dugout entrance, he looked back. Warner was staring into his cup of tea.

In the dugout, Pilcher was sitting at the table, a cup of whisky in front of him. The bottle next to it, which had been half full before the raid, was nearly empty.

"What is it, Belmont?" Pilcher asked, looking up. "Shouldn't you be on duty?"

"Wilson's up there," Harry replied.

"What do you want, then?" Pilcher asked, taking a gulp from his cup.

"I want to know what happened on the raid," Harry said.

"It's quite simple, Belmont. The Germans got wind of us and opened fire. I managed to get three of the men back here."

"And lost nine others, plus one officer dead and another wounded," Harry said, looking down at him.

"I can't help that. They didn't do as I said," Pilcher stood up, leaning across the table and staring at Harry. "Why? Has Warner been saying anything?"

"No," Harry said.

"Look, Belmont, I'm not responsible if people are going to start panicking," Pilcher said, still looking at Harry.

"We're the officers," Harry said, turning to go. "That means we're always responsible."

"Belmont!" Pilcher shouted. "Get back here!" Harry stopped, but didn't turn around. "You will kindly address me as 'sir', when you talk to me," Pilcher continued. Harry paused for a moment, stopped and looked back. He stared at Pilcher for a few moments, then walked slowly up the steps.

Chapter Ten

Winter 1917

7th Battalion, Royal Sussex Regiment, BEF
Wednesday, November 7th 1917

Dearest Mother and Father,
I am just writing very quickly to let you know that I have been granted a few days' leave, starting next Tuesday. I don't know exactly when I'll be home – it depends on transport – so expect me at anytime.
I look forward to seeing you all.
Your affectionate son, Harry

****

7th Battalion, Royal Sussex Regiment, BEF
Monday, November 12th 1917

My Darling Elise,
This is just a quick letter to let you know that I am going back to England tomorrow to see Rose. I have ten days' leave, but will come back to France early, probably arriving with you on the 20th or 21st.
I can't wait to see you again.
With all my love,
Harry

****

At least the train from London was running vaguely to time. Harry had been delayed for over three hours at Abbeville, and then for a further two hours at Boulogne. He looked out of the window into the darkness, seeing nothing but his own reflection looking back. It had been more than a year since he had been in England and everything seemed strange. In a way, he was pleased not to be able to see the landscape stretching out before him: it would only serve to remind him of the normality of this life. There had been very few civilians at the station, except the young women serving tea and coffee. The one who had approached Harry was pleasant enough, but her smile was somehow patronising and he'd declined her offer. At first, as the train had departed, it had been full of soldiers, all relieved to be granted a few days at home. Some were tired and slept wherever they could find enough space to sit down; others were excited and noisy, calming down only when they saw Harry, or another officer. As the train passed on through the countryside, their numbers dwindled; friends said goodbye, wished each other luck, and the train became quieter. Harry settled into the corner of his compartment. There were two other occupants: an elderly man, reading a newspaper; and a young woman, who smiled over in Harry's direction every so often. Harry closed his eyes, shutting them out and allowed his mind to drift.

He woke with a start. The woman was standing above him, shaking his arm.

"Excuse me," she said. "I don't like to wake you, but I think I heard you say to the guard that this was where you wanted to get off."

"Oh! Yes, thank you." Harry said, looking out at the station. He stood, taking his case and cap from the luggage rack. "I didn't realise how tired I was."

"You'll have to hurry," the woman said. "We'll soon be leaving again."

"Thank you," Harry repeated. He smiled, and opened the door of the compartment, jumping down onto the cold, unlit platform and closing the door behind him. The station was deserted. He sighed heavily and braced himself for the six mile walk home.

The lanes and paths were familiar, even in the darkness. He'd walked this route so many times, coming back late from university, or trips to London and nothing had changed in all the intervening years, except he now saw things differently. The mist that hung over the fields, reminded him of the gas that floated above No Man's Land, invading every hollow and recess. Bare trees loomed out of the darkness like skeletons, their branches beckoning. Bare hedgerows snaked like barbed wire along the roadside. He pulled up his collar, ignoring the sights and the reminders and focused on the empty, hollow sound of his own footsteps.

A little over two hours later, he walked up the driveway to his parents' house. It was in complete darkness and he wondered whether he should wait until the morning, rather than waking everyone. It was after one now and he knew that he could easily sit out the rest of the night on the doorstep: he'd certainly spent many nights in worse places during the last three years. Deciding that his mother would never forgive him, he rang the bell and waited. Initially nothing happened; he rang again and then, after a few minutes, a light appeared in the hallway. He heard the latch being pulled back and the door opened just a crack.

"Mr Harry!" Polly exclaimed, opening the door further to let him step inside.

"What is it, Polly?" Harry heard his father's voice from the top of the stairs.

"It's me, father," Harry called, removing his cap and coat and throwing them on the chair by the stairs.

"Good Lord!" Richard peered over the top of the banisters. "I'll just fetch your mother."

"Don't disturb her if she's asleep, Father."

"Nonsense, Harry. I'd never hear the end of it." He disappeared, returning a minute or two later and descended the stairs. "She's just coming." He shook Harry's hand warmly. "You look tired, son."

"I am. It's been a terrible journey." Both men looked up as they heard Margaret coming down the stairs, a warm dressing gown covering her thick winter nightdress.

"Harry, my dear!" she cried out, kissing him on his cheek. "We'd given up any hope of seeing you today,"

"He's had a rough journey, dear." Richard explained.

"Would you like something to eat or drink? Or perhaps you'd rather just go straight to bed?"

"A cup of tea would go down well, Mother, if it's not too much trouble."

Margaret turned to Polly, who'd been waiting in the shadows. "Polly dear, would you mind making us some tea?"

"No, ma'am. Of course not." The girl disappeared in the direction of the kitchen.

"Come into the sitting room." Richard went ahead, switching on the lights, while Margaret followed behind smiling and taking Harry by the hand. Once inside, Harry glanced around the familiar space. Nothing had changed; all the furniture was the same; the pictures still hung in their usual places; the curtains were closed, keeping out the cold November night. He sat in his old chair. The fire had gone out and the room felt a little chilly but Harry didn't care.

"How's Rose?" he asked.

"She's very well," Margaret replied. "You'll see her tomorrow. She'll be ever so excited." Harry wasn't so certain. She was five years old now and it had been such a long time since they'd seen each other. He wasn't sure if she'd even remember him.

"Would you like the fire lit?" Richard asked. "I can easily spark it back to life; it hasn't long gone out."

"No, Father. Don't worry, everything's fine. I'll just have a cup of tea and then I'll go up to bed."

Richard and Margaret sat opposite him on the sofa, unable to take their eyes from his face. He was beginning to feel a little self-conscious when Polly re-appeared, carrying a tea tray.

"Oh, thank you, Polly. Just leave it on the table and run along back to bed," Margaret said.

The girl smiled at Harry as she closed the door. Margaret poured the tea, handing Harry his cup, which he held awkwardly. Bone china felt strange, smooth, and unnatural in his hands. Putting it to his lips, he tasted clean tea for the first time in months; made with proper milk and fresh water that didn't taste of petrol. Did such things really still exist? His mother watched him keenly from over the top of her cup.

"How long can you stay?" she asked eventually.

"I have to go back on the 19th," he replied, not looking at her. He hated lying.

"Well, that's not so bad. We're grateful for anything. It's been so long." Her face radiated pleasure and Harry felt his guilt increasing.

"I think I'll head off to bed, if you don't mind. I'm exhausted. I'll take this with me." Harry stood up, his cup shaking on the saucer.

"Of course not, son." Richard got to his feet. "We'll have plenty of time to catch up tomorrow."

"Yes, Father."

"Goodnight, dear," his mother said. When Harry reached the door, he looked back. His parents were looking at each other, smiling. The domestic scene made him feel uncomfortable and he was glad to leave the room.

Upstairs, Harry undressed quickly. He crossed to the window and opened it. The chill November air invaded the room. Closing his eyes, he sighed.

"For God's sake. I've only been back here for ten minutes. Why can't I just bloody well breathe," he said aloud. He shut the window again and turned to lay down on the bed, not bothering to cover himself, not caring about the cold. He looked out of the window at the crescent moon, wondering if Edward would be on duty, checking the sentries, perhaps looking up into the sky at that same moment. He tried to take a deep breath, failed, turned over and went to sleep.

Harry wasn't used to more than a few hours' sleep at a time, so he woke just after dawn. He dressed quickly in old clothes and left the house quietly, walking down the garden. His mother's roses had been pruned back and tidied ready for the winter; the lawn had been raked of leaves. It had been months since he'd stood next to trees with branches; even longer since he'd seen shrubs and bushes or put his feet on proper grass, rather than mud. Mud overflowing with death. Turning back towards the house, he sat on the terrace steps, his elbows on his knees, hands clasped beneath his chin. The damp air reached and gnawed into his bones, but he enjoyed the feeling. It felt just the same here as it did in France. He thought about Edward and Sergeant Warner. They'd be doing the rounds about now, checking the sentries. He smiled. Edward would be getting excited. His leave was due to start today. Only six days, but that would still give him a clear three days with Isabel, so he'd spent their last night together in the dugout, telling Harry all his plans. Harry glanced at his watch. Seven-thirty. He got up, walking slowly back into the house, hands deep in his pockets and head down.

In the sitting room, Polly had already lit the fire and Harry sat beside it, watching the flames licking up the chimney and waiting. Another half an hour passed before he heard footsteps on the stairs. The door opened and his mother entered.

"Harry! When on earth did you get up. I expected you to sleep until lunchtime."

"I haven't been up for very long," he lied. "Where's Rose?"

"She's just coming. I haven't told her you're here yet. I was going to tell her over breakfast." As Margaret finished her sentence, the door opened and Rose entered.

"Grandmama," she said, not noticing Harry at first. "I can't find my blue hair ribbon, and neither can Susan. Have you seen it?"

"No dear," Margaret replied. The little girl turned to leave. "Rosie, come back a minute. Look who's here." Margaret stood to one side, revealing Harry. He leant forward, looking across the room at her. She'd changed. Her hair was longer than Harry remembered. Her face was not so rounded. She looked even more like Bella. Rose glanced uncertainly between the two of them. She didn't seem to know who he was and eventually turned her gaze to her grandmother, asking a silent question.

"It's Daddy," Margaret prompted. Rose looked at Harry for a long moment before crossing the room and holding her hand out to him formally. He took it in his. Still so small; so soft.

"Hello." She curtsied slightly, looking at him from beneath her long eyelashes

"Hello." It was all he could say. He longed to scrape her up in his arms, but the doubtful look in her eyes held him back.

Rose pulled her hand free of Harry's before returning to her grandmother's side.

"Is he staying for breakfast?" Rose asked, taking hold of Margaret's skirt.

"Of course, dear. He's staying for a few days." The little girl glanced over at her father, his eyes still captivated by her. "Run along now and find Grandpapa," Margaret continued. "Then we can all eat together." Rose turned and fled the room.

"Sorry, dear." Margaret closed the door quietly. "It would have been better if I'd been able to warn her first."

"Warn her?" Harry's voice betrayed his dismay. "Do you really need to 'warn her' that I'm home? Is it that bad?"

"I didn't mean it like that, Harry."

"Sorry, Mother. I know you didn't." Harry looked back into the fire. "It's not your fault. It's mine."

"No it isn't. You can't help the war."

"I should have come back here during my last leave. It's been too long since she last saw me."

"But you only had three days. You'd never have got back here. You were much better off going to Paris: at least you got some rest there." Harry couldn't look at her. 'Paris': that was what he'd written. He'd even given them details of restaurants, hotels, clean sheets, hot coffee with cream and thick, juicy steaks. He closed his eyes, just for a moment, remembering those few days at the farmhouse with Elise: the intensity of her kisses; the softness of her skin; the smell of her hair; her hands, touching him, caressing him; her warm body beneath his, surrendering to him. He opened his eyes. He'd never been to Paris in his entire life and now, here he was lying again: cutting short his time with them to go back to her. Only Edward knew all of it; knew all of his deceit. Only Edward knew the extent of his guilt. That didn't matter though, because Edward understood.

The door opened and Richard entered, holding Rose's hand.

"Good," Margaret announced. "We're all here. Now we can have some breakfast."

During the course of the day, Margaret continually encouraged Rose to spend some time with her father. At every suggestion or request, she would shy away, hiding her face, or disappearing upstairs to 'find' something. Harry talked to Susan and she tried explaining to Rose, but by mid-afternoon, everyone was beginning to despair. Rose had gone upstairs, yet again, in search of a particular doll, that her grandmother knew she rarely played with. Harry got up from his chair.

"Where are you going?" Margaret asked.

"I'm going to find Rose."

"Be careful with her, Harry."

"Of course I will."

He found Rose in the nursery, sitting quietly on the window seat looking down the garden. She sat with her knees bent up to her chin, her face resting on the folds of her skirt and, just for a moment, Harry thought of Elise. She didn't turn when he entered. Harry glanced around the room, but there was no doll in sight. He walked over and stood behind her.

"What are you looking at?" he enquired.

She didn't answer. He waited for a while and then turned. In one corner of the room was a small table, under which stood a familiar box. Harry went over, pulled out the box and removed its lid. He smiled. Inside were several sketch pads, boxes of pencils and tins of watercolour paints. Taking a pad, and pencil, he carried a chair over to the window, sitting down quietly. The view over the garden was not exactly inspiring, especially at this time of year, but it was holding her attention, so Harry began drawing. Neither of them spoke, but after half an hour or so, Rose climbed down from her seat and walked around behind Harry, looking just over his shoulder. A faint smile crossed his face.

"What about the squirrel?" she asked.

"What squirrel?" he enquired, sitting up and looking further down the garden. "I can't see one."

"There, on the fence, right at the end." She pointed, her face inching closer to his. He could just about feel her breath on his neck.

"Oh yes. I'd missed him." Harry quickly added the the the squirrel to his sketch. "How's that?" he said.

She nodded her head in approval.

"Would you like to keep it?" he asked.

"Yes please." He tore the page from the book, handing it to her. "Can you do another one?" she asked.

"What would you like next?"

"Can you draw people?"

"Yes. Who would you like me to draw?"

"Can you draw Grandmama?"

"Yes, if that's what you want."

"Shall I fetch her so you can see her face?" She turned to go.

"There's no need," Harry said. "I can draw Grandmama from memory." Rose came back and settled down onto the window seat again. She watched him, his pencil tracing over the page. Every so often he glanced up at her. She was no longer uncertain or afraid; just interested in what he was doing.

Before long, he'd finished and beckoned her across.

"Do you want to look?" He turned the pad, holding it up for her to see. She jumped excitedly, clapping her hands together.

"It looks just like her. Can we go downstairs and show Grandmama? Can we?" Harry allowed himself to be pulled from his chair and dragged towards the door, sketch pad in hand. Rose tugged him down the stairs and threw open the door to the sitting room.

"Grandmama! Grandmama!" she cried. "Look what Daddy's done."

Margaret looked up from her knitting; firstly at Rose and then at Harry, a smile spreading across her face. "What has he done, darling?" she asked.

"He's drawn a picture of you. Look!" Rose took the sketch pad from Harry and presented it to her grandmother.

"So he has. Well, isn't that lovely. Daddy's very clever isn't he?" She heard the front door open. "That will be your grandfather," she said.

"Why don't you run along and show him too." Once Rose had left the room, she turned to Harry.

"Whatever made you think of that?" she asked.

"I couldn't think of anything else."

Later that evening, when it was time for Rose to go to bed, she went across to her grandmother, and whispered in her ear. Margaret nodded and Rose crossed the room, standing before Harry, who was sitting in front of the fire, warming his toes, sleep beckoning.

"Would you come upstairs and read me a story, please?" she asked politely. Harry looked up, surprised.

"Of course," he said. He stood up and Rose took his hand, leading him from the room. "Goodnight, Grandmama. Goodnight, Grandpapa," she called behind her as she opened the door.

Half an hour later, Margaret peered round the door of Rose's room, to find both of them fast asleep. Rose's head was resting on her father's chest. The book he'd been reading had fallen to the floor and Harry was breathing deeply, his arms clasped tightly around his daughter.

The next morning, Harry got up early. He dressed and went outside. It was a fine winter's morning with a thick frost settled on the grass and around the edges of the leaves. He strolled down the garden, passing the greenhouse. A large cobweb was strung across the laurel bush, its gossamer strands laden with icy crystals. He pulled at the door of his studio. The handle was stiff with cold, but eventually it gave way. Passing inside, he closed the door. He opened a box of paints, removing them and holding the tubes in his hands. Powders were lined up along the back of the bench and he pulled them forward, imagining holding a brush in his hand, imagining mixing the colours. He found a couple of palettes, holding one in his hand. He missed painting. Sketching was one thing, but he longed to hold a brush, feel it becoming part of him, feel it taking over his mind and body. He searched out some sketch pads, leaving them on the bench and then discovered a new box of pencils and put them in his pocket. He could take them back with him. He left the bench as it was, turned and bent down, looking through the canvasses that were propped up against the wall. Finally, he found the one he was looking for. Rose stared back at him. He'd painted this when she was about eighteen months old and they'd been visiting his parents. He crouched down, holding the canvas in his hands. He'd captured her eyes, twinkling green; her hair, a beautiful rich auburn, hanging in ringlets around her face; her cheeks, soft and pale, with a hint of pink. *One day*, he thought to himself, as he replaced the canvas, *I'll paint her again*.

The day before Harry was due to leave, the Belmonts were supposed to visit William and Charlotte for lunch. William had arranged it with Margaret as soon as news had been received of Harry's visit. Just after breakfast, however, William arrived and asked to see Harry privately.

"I'm afraid we're going to have to cancel lunch today," he said.

"What is it William? What's happened?" Harry knew something was very wrong.

"Katherine got a letter this morning. Philip's been killed."

"Her fiancé?"

"Yes. The letter came from his commanding officer. She didn't believe it was true at first, so she telephoned to his parents. They'd had a similar letter. She's inconsolable. I don't know what to do."

"Would it help if I came over to see her?"

"I was hoping you'd say that, Harry. Would you mind?"

"Of course not. I'll just let Mother and Father know. Give me a minute." Harry left William alone and went to make brief explanations, rejoining him in the hall a few minutes later.

"You'll want a coat," William pointed out. "It's freezing out there."

"My jumper's quite thick enough. And anyway, I'm used to it." Harry didn't know how to tell William that the only coat that even vaguely fitted him was his army great coat, the sight of which might only upset Katherine further.

"How is it out there?" William asked after they'd been walking for a few minutes.

"Fairly bloody, to be honest." Harry wasn't sure if William really wanted to know.

"How do you cope, Harry?"

"We have each other." They walked on in silence.

"Katherine's in her bedroom," William announced as they entered the house. "Charlotte's up there trying to talk to her through the door."

"How's young George getting on?" Harry asked as they climbed the stairs. He'd only seen William's son three times since his birth.

"Oh, he's fine. Growing up fast. But then they do, don't they?" Harry felt like saying that he wouldn't know, that he'd missed out on most of Rose's growing up, that he'd missed too many birthdays, too many Christmases, too much that mattered. He felt like asking William whether he knew how lucky he was, but he didn't. On the landing, Charlotte greeted Harry, kissing him on the cheek.

"I can't get her to open the door," she said, looking worried. Harry glanced beyond Charlotte, to the closed door.

"Would you like me to try?" he asked. Charlotte nodded and Harry stepped forward, tapping gently on the oak panel. "Katherine?" he called. "It's me, Harry. Can I come in?" There was only silence. "We can talk, Katherine. I might be able to explain things for you, if you want." The room remained silent for a moment, but then Harry heard the sound of footsteps approaching the door. Charlotte stood back as the door was unlocked. Harry turned the handle and entered, closing the door behind him. Inside, the room was in semi-darkness, the curtains half closed. Katherine was sitting on the edge of the bed, clutching a piece of paper in one hand; a handkerchief in the other. Harry crossed the room and crouched in front of her.

"I'm so terribly sorry," he said quietly.

"He should never have gone," she replied, drying her tears.

"He did what he thought was right."

"Yes, and now he's dead. And I'm alone."

There's no arguing with that one, Harry thought.

She held the crumpled piece of paper out towards him. "His commanding officer wrote to me."

"He would do, yes. Your letters were probably amongst his belongings, or else the C.O. would have remembered censoring Philip's letters to you. What does he say? Do you mind me asking?"

"Read it for yourself." She handed Harry the piece of paper.

Harry took the letter and read it through. It was a standard issue letter of condolence. *Valued officer; greatly missed; died gallantly; served his country.* Just like all the rest.

"It's a lovely letter." He handed it back to her. "You should be very proud, Katherine. He was obviously very much respected. His commanding officer must have thought highly of him to write that."

"Really, Harry?" she asked.

"Yes, of course. He wouldn't have written it otherwise." The lies spilled forth, but he still managed to look into her eyes. "You miss him terribly, Katherine. You'll go on missing him. I'm not going to lie to you and tell you that it will all get better soon. It won't. But you have William and Charlotte and they'll help you." She nodded her head slowly. He sat next to her. "We'll all help you." She began to cry again and he waited silently until her sobs had subsided. "Shall I send Charlotte up with some tea for you?"

"Yes please," she whispered. He stood, crossing to the door.

"Katherine," he said. She looked up at him. "If you need anything – anything at all – please let me know. Write to me. I'll do whatever I can." He closed the door quietly behind him.

Outside, William and Charlotte were waiting.

"How is she?" William asked.

"She'll be fine – eventually." Harry replied quietly. "Just give her time. She'd like some tea if you don't mind."

"I'll go and see to it myself," Charlotte said. "Will she let us in now, do you think?"

"She hasn't locked her door," Harry answered. Charlotte turned, descending the stairs.

"What should we do?" William asked.

"Just be patient with her," Harry replied.

"Charlotte will know what to do." William looked at Harry. "Shall we go downstairs?" Harry nodded.

In the sitting room, the fire was ablaze and Harry sat down in one of the big armchairs.

"I really can't thank you enough, Harry," William said, his back to the fireplace. Harry smiled self-consciously, not answering. "Will you stay for some tea yourself?"

"I will, thank you." Harry wasn't keen to be away from Rose for too long, but one cup of tea couldn't hurt. William went out to the kitchen and, on his return sat opposite Harry.

"I've been reading about the fighting around Passchendaele," he said. "It's been going on for months. We've sustained very heavy losses, by the looks of things, but then I suppose we have to keep pushing them back, don't we?" Harry looked across the divide between them.

"Yes, I suppose we do."

"You haven't been anywhere near there, have you?"

"No."

"Oh good, so you're well away from the danger, then?"

"Yes, well away from it all," Harry said, recalling the previous months. They'd spent eighteen solid weeks in the trenches, either in reserve or in the front lines around Monchy. The Germans had attacked almost continuously and the order had been to hold the line. Over sixty men in the Company had been lost, including Canter, who had only returned to the Battalion two weeks earlier. He'd been been shot in the neck and bled to death. Warner and Edward had worked on him for ages, trying to staunch the flow of blood. *Yes*, he thought, *well away from it all – no danger whatsoever.*

"I expect they're going to throw you back into the thick of it, then?" William asked.

"Probably," Harry replied. The tea arrived and Harry began to wish he'd declined the offer. William handed him a cup.

"I don't suppose you're allowed to tell us where you're going?" William asked.

"No. I'm not actually entirely sure where the company will be when I get back."

"How will you find them, then?"

"I'll go to H.Q., and they'll tell me where to go. Usually they get it just about right."

"That all sounds a bit hit and miss to me," William laughed. "I always thought everything would be more organised than that."

"It's not that bad," Harry replied. *If only you knew*, he thought to himself. Charlotte came into the room.

"How's Katherine?" Harry asked, grateful to change the subject.

"She's a little better. I'll give her a while and go back up to see her. Thank you Harry. We were at our wit's end." She paused. "Has William told you our news?"

"No." Harry looked from one to the other. Charlotte smiled at him.

"We're going to have another baby," she announced.

Harry hesitated. "Oh." He tried to sound pleased. "Congratulations."

"We decided it was high time George had a brother or sister," William said.

"I see." Harry drained his cup. "I'm sorry to cut and run," he said. "I really do have a lot to do. I'm off early in the morning."

"Of course, old man." William got up. "We understand."

"You will take care of yourself, won't you?" Charlotte said, walking to the door.

"I always try to." He kissed Charlotte on the cheek and shook William's hand.

"Look after Katherine," he said. "She'll need you both."

Leaving this time was worse than ever. Just as before, there were tears. Rose sobbed; his father shook his hand; his mother kissed him, tears trickling down her cheeks. The difference was that this time he was lying. He was letting them believe he was heading back to imminent danger. He was walking away, knowing their nerves would be on edge from that minute onwards; knowing they would dread every telephone call, every knock on the door. Knowing that while they began to live in fear, he would be dashing across France, rushing back to Elise for a few precious days with her. If he really cared about them, he thought, surely he'd stay with them for those few extra hours. Surely he'd give up Elise, sacrifice her happiness and his own and spend every minute with them. Consumed by guilt, he walked away.

Chapter Eleven

Winter 1917

Harry arrived at Bethune early in the evening. The town was less busy than usual, with just a few officers sitting inside the cafés. At the base of the Belfry, Harry noticed a lone soldier standing talking to a local girl; she giggled suggestively and reached out, pulling the young soldier closer as Harry walked by. By the time he'd walked to Lapugnoy, it was late and the estaminet was closed. He was disappointed. He craved coffee, but the farmhouse wasn't far away now. He continued on through the village, picking up his pace. It was a cold night, the sky was clear and Harry pulled his collar up a little further. Edward was due back from leave today and Harry half wished that he could be there to greet him; that they could share their news. He'd been angry with William and knew Edward would understand, sympathise, and make Harry laugh again.

As Harry walked through the farm gates and into the courtyard, he was surprised to find the house in darkness. The curtain was open at the kitchen window, but there was no light to welcome him. Elise was expecting him, and he'd assumed she'd wait up. He was disappointed. There were no soldiers in the barn and the farm was deserted. He pushed on the door gently, half expecting it to be locked, but it opened easily. Elise was sitting at the kitchen table.

"What are you doing sitting in the dark?" he asked. He heard a sniff, dropped his bag and walked around the kitchen table. "What is it?" He crouched down next to her.

"It's Henri," she said. *Oh God*, thought Harry, *not another one. How many more?* "We've had a letter," she continued. "It came last week."

"What did it say?" Harry took her hands in his, looking up into her face. Her eyes shone and glistened with tears in the moonlight.

"It just says that he's missing."

"So, it doesn't say he's been killed."

"No."

"Well, missing isn't dead, Elise." Harry wondered how much longer he could keep on lying.

"I don't understand, 'Arry. Surely someone must know where he is? How can he just go missing?" Her face was streaked with tears, her eyes swollen. She was still beautiful.

"If he's wounded," Harry explained, "he might have been taken to hospital. Things get muddled." *Or he might be lying in No Man's Land with a hundred other corpses, all of them 'missing',* Harry thought to himself. "You can't give up," he said aloud. She smiled at him, but carried on crying. "Is there something else?" he asked, sensing that she hadn't told him everything.

"Yes."

"Tell me." His voice was gentle and calm.

Elise took a deep breath and turned away from him, looking out of the kitchen window into the courtyard. "It's been such a bad harvest, 'Arry." The words tumbled out. "There was too much rain. I've been worrying for weeks. I don't think we have enough food or money to get through the winter. I can't get my mother to understand. All she cares about is Henri. She's always expected this to happen, so now she sees losing the farm as inevitable anyway." She turned back to him. "I don't know what to do."

"Well, the first thing I'm going to do is take you to bed."

"Oh, 'Arry, I can't."

"I mean, to sleep, Elise." He bent down and lifted her from the chair. She put her arms around his neck and let him carry her up the stairs.

He kicked open the door to her bedroom and stood her down on the floor. She looked up at him.

"We'll deal with everything tomorrow," he said, undoing the buttons of her blouse. "You need to sleep."

"I haven't slept for days."

"You will tonight." Once she was naked, he lowered her into the bed, covering her with the sheets and pulling up the blankets. He sat down next to her, watching her breathe. She curled herself up and he leant over her. "I'll be back in a minute," he whispered.

"Don't leave me," she murmured, her voice thick with exhaustion. "Please don't leave me."

"I'm not. I won't be long."

Down in the kitchen, Harry poured himself a cup of coffee from the pot on the stove. It was nearly cold, and very bitter, but he didn't care. He stood by the window, looking out over the farm. He already knew what he was going to do, he just needed to think through the details, work out exactly how to arrange things, how to phrase the telegram. Once he'd drained the cup, he picked up his case and went back upstairs. Elise was asleep now, still curled up. He undressed quickly, climbing into bed behind her. He pulled her towards him and wrapped himself around her soft body. She sighed and nestled into him. He felt her breathing deepen, felt her shoulders relax. She slept soundly.

Harry woke before dawn, dressed in the darkness and went downstairs. He searched through the drawers in the kitchen, and eventually gave up trying to find a piece of paper. He went back upstairs and quietly opened his case, checking to see that he hadn't woken Elise. Inside, he found his sketch pad and a pencil and wrote a few words on a single leaf, which he tore from the pad and left on his pillow. Once downstairs again, he pulled on his coat and left as quietly as possible, heading back towards Lapugnoy.

The village was, once again, silent. No-one was awake yet. The dawn was just beginning to break on the horizon, but there was no sun. Grey clouds hung heavy and menacing. Harry continued on, in the direction of Bethune, arriving there in the middle of the morning. The shops were open and there were more civilians than the last time Harry had been there in March, when the town square had been bustling with soldiers. Women carried shopping baskets, a few children were playing with a ball. It had seemed strange to Harry that life in England could be so normal. It seemed even more strange that people here still carried on as usual, even though the war was going on only a few miles away. One of the boys threw the ball and it landed at Harry's feet. They called to him and he picked it up, throwing it back to a young blond boy, in a shabby red sweater, who thanked him with a gap-toothed grin. Harry smiled and turned towards the bank.

"I want to see the manager, please," he said to the cashier. There were no other customers in the bank, and the young man behind the counter looked bored.

"I can help you, sir." He looked at Harry through his thick glasses, which explained why he wasn't in uniform.

"I'm sure you can, but I'd like to see the manager anyway, please." Harry was persistent.

"Very well. Please wait here." The young man got up and walked through a door behind him, closing it briefly. Within a minute the door opened again and the youth came out, followed by an older man, with a large moustache, and a bulbous nose, which supported small pince-nez. His stomach bulged over his trousers, leaving a gap between them and his waistcoat. He sighed and looked Harry up and down indifferently, taking in the well-worn uniform.

"Yes, monsieur. What is it?"

"Can we talk privately?" Harry said, with a voice of authority that Elise would not have recognised. The manager hesitated, but moved to one side, letting Harry pass into his office.

Their business took a little over half an hour to conclude. When the bank manager opened the door to show Harry out, he beamed at him then offered his hand, which Harry took and held onto.

"I'm going back to the front tomorrow," he said. "But I'll be sending a telegram to my contact in England first. If there are any problems, I'm sure he'll notify me."

"Oh, you can rely on us, monsieur."

"I do hope so." Harry released the manager's hand.

"It's been a pleasure doing business with you, monsieur," he said, bowing slightly.

Harry glanced down at him, nodded and left the bank.

In the post office, Harry composed the longest telegram he'd ever written. He sent it to his father's office, rather than the house, knowing that the delivery of a telegram at home would terrify his mother. He also didn't really want his mother knowing about what he was doing. He closed the message with one simple phrase: 'No questions please Father and thank you.' He knew his father would do as he asked.

Outside, it had begun to rain. He buttoned up his great coat, hunching his shoulders against the driving downpour. It would take him hours to walk back to the farmhouse and he resigned himself to a soaking.

When he got back, it was already beginning to get dark. The lamp was lit in the kitchen and as he opened the door, Elise ran from the sink, where she was washing vegetables, and threw herself into his arms.

"I'm soaked through!" he said, bending to kiss her.

"I don't care," she replied.

"Well, let me take my coat off, at least." He peeled her arms from around his neck, taking off his dripping coat and laying it over the back of one of the chairs. He turned and picked her up, lifting her off the floor. He buried his face in her neck, kissing her.

"Where have you been?" she asked. "I thought you'd gone."

"I left you a note," he said in between kisses. "It was on the pillow."

"I know, but it's in English." She pulled it from her pocket and handed it to him. He put her down and smiled at her.

"I'm sorry," he said, taking the note from her. "I left very early this morning. I didn't realise. It says: 'I'll be back later this afternoon. I love you.'," he translated.

"Well, I didn't know, did I? I can't read English. I thought you'd gone," she repeated.

"Elise... I left my bag here. Of course I hadn't gone. I wouldn't just leave."

"So, where have you been all this time?" Harry pulled out a chair and sat her down, then did so himself, not letting go of her hand.

"I went into Bethune."

"Bethune?" She was surprised. "You walked all the way there, and back?"

"It's not that far."

"You wasted a whole day of your leave walking back to Bethune? Why on earth did you do that?" Elise asked. Harry looked down at her hand, so small in his.

"I had some business to attend to." Harry took his wallet from his pocket, emptying its contents onto the table. "On the way back, I got to thinking. This is all the money I have on me, Elise. But you can have it." He passed the notes across the table. "It's only a few Francs, I'm afraid."

"I can't take all your money. You might need some."

"I won't. I'll be fine. I get paid again soon." She looked away. "I checked before I left this morning," he continued. "You need feed for the horses, and the cows. If you don't feed them, you won't have any milk."

"Thank you. It's very generous." He placed a finger under her chin, turning her face back towards him. There were tears in her eyes.

"What is it?" he asked, leaning forward to kiss her.

"It's so kind of you, 'Arry. Really it is and I love you so much for trying to help, but it won't be enough. It will last us a little while, perhaps, but then what will I do?"

"Well, Elise," he said, "in a couple of weeks, you'll go into Bethune yourself."

"What for?"

"You'll need to go to the bank."

"What are you talking about 'Arry?" Her confused eyes looked directly into his. He gave in.

"I'm sorry, I've been teasing you." He paused. "I went into Bethune today to visit the bank. I've arranged to transfer some funds from my bank in England."

"What for?"

"For you, Elise." She still looked confused. "I went to see the bank manager," Harry continued. "I've arranged that you can go to see him in about two weeks or so. The money should be there by then."

"How did you manage all this? What did you do? Did you just walk into the bank and ask them for the money?"

"No. It's not quite that simple. I sent a telegram to my father. He will deal with my bank in England and they will send the money. I had to see the bank manager in Bethune to make sure that you can collect the money. I don't want there being any difficulties when I'm not here to deal with them."

"So you told your father about me? About us?"

"No. I just said I needed the money."

"And he'll do it? Just like that?"

"Yes, he'll do it. It's my money, Elise, not his." There was a moment of silence.

"I'm not taking your money, 'Arry. I've already decided that I'm going to sell the farm. We don't know whether Henri will come back. My mother's right. We can't cope without him."

"Elise, do please be quiet!" Harry got up, went to the stove and poured himself a cup of coffee. "You're not selling the farm. You belong here – all of you. Anyway, it's done now, so stop arguing."

"I don't think you understand how much money it takes to keep a farm going, 'Arry. You said yourself there's feed to buy, then we'll need seeds for next year's vegetable crops, and we'll need to buy food for the winter. We won't be able to grow or sell anything until next summer." Elise lowered her head onto her hands, a deep sigh shaking through her body.

"Will what I've given you out of my wallet be enough to last for the two weeks until the funds come through from England?" Harry asked.

"Yes, of course."

"Then you've nothing to worry about," Harry said, leaning back against the sink and sipping his coffee.

"Nothing to worry about? 'Arry… we'll have to survive for over six months. It will take too much money."

"Three hundred francs won't be enough, then?" Elise raised her head, turned and looked at him.

"How much?"

"Three hundred francs." He walked over to her, put his cup down on the table and sat down again. Tears pricked her eyes.

"How much?" she said again. He took her hand in his.

"I'm not going to keep saying it." He smiled at her, stroking the back of her hand with his thumb. "Will it be enough?" he asked. "Tell me. I can arrange for more, if it isn't."

"Enough?" She was incredulous. "It's far too much 'Arry! I can't take it. It's impossible."

"No it's not. I have enough money. And now so do you."

"But you don't have to give all your money to me. I don't want you to. You need it for your daughter, for after the war. "

"It's not all my money, Elise. Not by a long way. I can afford to do this."

"Really?"

"Yes, really."

"I still can't accept," she said after a moment's hesitation.

"You can and you will." Harry got up again. "I'm not taking no for an answer, Elise." He stood at the window, his back to her. "I'm going back tomorrow afternoon. I need to know that you're alright. I have enough to worry about out there without fretting over whether you've got food to eat and a roof over your head. I told you I'd look after you and keep you safe. This is the only way I can do that at the moment."

"You care about my family that much?"

"I care about you, and you care about them, so yes."

He heard her chair scrape across the floor, then felt her hands on his arms, her cheek resting against his back.

"How do I thank you?" she whispered.

"You don't." He turned, holding her head to his chest. She reached up, drawing him down to her and kissing him. "Actually," he said, pulling away and looking into her eyes. "There is one thing you can do."

"Yes?"

"Could we have something to eat, please? I'm absolutely starving."

Elise made soup and while it was cooking, Harry walked up behind her and put his arms around her. "I've been thinking," he said. "There must still be a few young men in the village who haven't enlisted. Or some older men, maybe? Will you use some of the money to hire someone to help around the farm, please?"

"I will," Elise replied. "If you want me to." Harry moved her hair to one side, kissing the back of her neck. She moaned and leant into him.

"Just don't hire anyone too handsome, or who's likely to start declaring their undying love for you."

Elise laughed, "There's no-one here between the ages of fifteen and fifty."

"Even so…"

"I think I can resist the temptation, 'Arry."

"Good."

"Thank you," Elise murmured, leaning her head back towards him.

"I thought I said you didn't have to thank me."

"I'm not thanking you for that."

"Oh, what are you thanking me for then?"

"For helping me to forget, just for a little while."

"About Henri?"

"Yes."

"You mustn't worry," Harry said.

"I don't when I'm with you."

"I'm glad," he turned her around, bending to kiss her.

"The soup will burn," she said.

"I really don't think I care."

"I thought you were hungry."

"I am." He kissed her again.

They ate the soup in bed, the sheets and blankets pulled up against the cold. When they'd finished, Elise curled up into Harry's arms, her head resting on his chest.

"Can you really afford to give us all that money, 'Arry?" she asked.

"Yes. Don't worry about it." He kissed the top of her head.

"I had no idea you were so wealthy."

"I don't talk about it very much."

"Why?"

"I just don't. It really doesn't matter to me."

"That's easy to say, when you've got money." She looked up at him. "Why didn't you tell me?"

"I don't tell anyone. It's not that I've singled you out. Nobody knows about it, except Edward."

"Why does he know and not me?"

"He knows everything."

"Does he?" Harry could sense her building resentment. "And do I know anything?" she continued, "Anything at all?"

"Yes."

"What do I know, 'Arry? What have you ever told me? You hardly ever talk about yourself."

"I told you about Bella, and Rose and that I paint... and that I love you."

"And that you still love your wife."

"Is that what this is about? My feelings for Bella?"

"No. It's about the fact that I know nothing about your life; your parents, the people you know, how you feel about them, what you do when you're with them. Who you really are."

"Well, for a start, I don't know that many people. I don't find it easy to talk to strangers."

"You talked to me. You must talk to other people."

"I only talked to you because Captain Johnstone had ordered me to, otherwise I couldn't have." He ran his fingers down her arm. "It would have been impossible... You'd taken my breath away."

They lay in silence for a while.

"'Arry?" Elise said.

"Yes, my love."

"Can I ask you something?"

"Yes, you can ask me anything you want."

"What will happen to us after the war?" Harry didn't reply immediately. He thought for a few moments, then sighed.

"I don't know. I don't want to tempt fate by talking about the future. None of us do."

"But every time you leave me, you tell me you'll come back. Isn't that tempting fate? Or are they just words, just something you say to make me feel better?" Harry turned over, pulling her closer and looking into her eyes.

"No, Elise," he said. "Every time I've said it, I've believed it. It's just that it's hard for me to make any definite plans for after the war. It's hard for any of us." Elise looked away.

"But I don't know where I stand," she whispered. "You've never mentioned me to your family. No-one knows that I exist. You've never told me what will happen to me. When it's all over, are you just going to leave me behind and go back to England, to your family and your daughter? Will I just be a memory – like your wife?"

"Of course not, Elise. What on earth would make you think that?" Harry said.

"Because you've never said anything, 'Arry. I don't feel as though I'm part of your life. Not your real life. Not your future. I'm just another part of the war... someone that you visit every few months, make love to and then leave again. And one day, when it's all over you'll be gone."

"What the hell are you talking about?" Harry leant up on his elbow, looking down at her. "Don't you have any idea how much you mean to me?"

"Three hundred Francs?"

"What?" Harry sat up.

"I'm sorry," she whispered. "That was unfair. You've been very kind to me, and very generous, and I know that you love me 'Arry, really I do. But that is about all that I know. And, in any case, what does that really mean? You loved your wife, and then you lost her, and you got over it. If you never saw me again after the war, you'd soon get over me too."

"Oh God, Elise. Is that what you really think?" She looked away. Harry laid down again, reached across and turned her face back towards his, noticing the look in her deep brown eyes that were, once again, pulling him in. "I'm sorry," he said. "You're right. I suppose I thought you knew. I've been thinking that making love to you and showing you how I feel is enough, but it's not, is it? There's more to it than that and I need to explain it to you now – properly – because I'm not here every day to tell you what you mean to me… if I was, you'd never doubt it." He looked beyond her, out of the window and into the night sky. He thought for a while before turning back to her. "I've never really spoken about this before, but I think it's the only way I can explain myself to you." He paused for a moment. "When I lost Bella," he said finally, "I didn't get over it like you think; I fell apart. For months – years even – all I did was exist. I looked after my daughter, I went to work. Then I gave that up and we moved away to my house by the sea. I took up painting, but I couldn't paint Bella. I couldn't cope with the memories. I couldn't even bring myself to look at a rose in bloom for years, because they reminded me of her and of the first time I saw her. I didn't live; I was too numb to live. It was all a pretence. That went on for over two years. Then the war started and, ironically, it made things better. I met Edward and he helped me and, very slowly, I started to rebuild my life."

"I didn't realise it was like that. You must have loved her very much."

"I did, but that's not the point." Harry ran his finger down her cheek. "The point is, Elise, that I found you, and you made me whole again; you made me who I am now. I've changed because of you." He hesitated. "And I know that if I lost you, if I had to live without you – however it happened, whatever took place between us – I know that it wouldn't be the same… not this time. I wouldn't fall apart again, not like that…" He felt her shoulders sink.

"Oh," She looked away again, tears filling her eyes. "So I don't mean that much to you… You don't love me as much as your wife."

"No! That's not true. That's not what I mean at all. Look at me, Elise." She turned back and blinked. A single tear spilled down her cheek and onto the pillow. Harry wiped it away with his thumb and held her gaze. "That's what I'm trying, so badly, to explain. You see, I know that if I couldn't be with you, if I lost you, it wouldn't be the same as it was with Bella. I thought there couldn't be anything worse than losing her, but now I know that's not true, because without you, Elise, I wouldn't fall apart… I would fracture. I would disintegrate. I would shatter into so many pieces that no-one would ever be able to find them all. And the pieces of me would be scattered so far and so wide, that nothing could ever bring them back together and no-one – no-one, Elise – could rebuild me. It would be impossible for anyone to save me and I'd never, ever be whole again." He waited. She stared at him. "Now, do you understand how much you mean to me?" he whispered and wiped the fresh tears from her cheeks. She nodded.

"I think so."

"I have no idea what will happen to us after the war," he sighed, pulling her closer to him. "I don't know how I'm going to explain you to Rose and my family or where we'll live, or what we'll do. I can't make any commitments about our future together, Elise. The only thing I can really say for certain is that, if I make it, I won't live without you, and I promise I'll never leave you again."

She turned over towards him and he wrapped them both in the blankets.

"I wish you could stay with me now," she said.

"I'll stay for as long as I can."

"It won't be long enough." She huddled into him. Then, slowly and reluctantly, they gave in to an exhausted sleep.

In the morning, Harry woke first and watched Elise sleeping for a while, then he roused her from her drowsiness with the softest kisses. She smiled up at him, her mouth opening to his and, although he didn't know why, he felt like they were starting from the beginning; he was losing himself and finding her for the first time, all over again. It was as though everything was new: he was steering her down a different path, patiently allowing each tender progression to take them deeper and deeper into each other. Her skin shivered to his touch. Her lips trembled when he kissed her. He waited, delayed, prolonged and then, when she was ready, he made love to her so gently that she wondered if he thought she might break.

Harry spent the rest of the morning clearing the kitchen garden of dead and decaying vegetables. He really didn't need this. His fingers pressed through the pulpy flesh of rotten stalks and leaves, mingled with sodden mud. The smell was putrid and made him retch. Elise was in the house, and didn't see him bent over, clutching his stomach, holding back the vomit as it rose up into his mouth. After lunch, for an hour or so, he chopped wood, stacking it in the barn. He soon built up a sweat, and worked in his shirt sleeves, despite the cold rain. Half an hour before leaving, he went upstairs, washed and changed into a clean shirt, packing his wet one into his case. He put his tunic and belt back on, and went downstairs into the kitchen. He laid his coat across the back of a chair, his cap on top and put his case on the floor. Elise was standing leaning against the sink, her cheeks already damp with tears.

"Is it time already?" she asked.

"Just about." His voice sounded distant, even to him. "I love you," he whispered, crossing to her, burying his face in her hair and kissing her neck.

"Promise?"

"I promise. Never ever doubt that. It's the only thing that matters." He paused. "I meant everything I said last night, Elise. Every single word of it: I can't lose you. I can't be without you. Not now. Not ever."

"And I won't lose you?" He looked at her and saw the doubt, the fear in her eyes.

"No," he said. He looked at his watch. "I'm sorry," he continued. "I really have to go now." He kissed her before turning and putting on his coat and hat.

"You will come back won't you?" Elise asked, moving towards him.

"Of course," Harry replied. He reached out, took her hand and drew her into him, kissing her, caressing her hair. "I miss you already," he whispered. He heard the cracks in his own voice and, breaking away from her, picked up his case and left, without looking back.

Elise was still standing alone in the middle of the room when the realisation hit her. He hadn't said the words. For the first time, he hadn't actually said the words. She ran out of the house, ignoring the icy drizzle that bit into her skin. His retreating figure was still visible on the road leading back towards the village.

Harry heard the footsteps running up behind him and turned, dropping his case as she threw herself into his arms.

"What is it?" he asked, catching her. "What's wrong?"

"You didn't say it," she cried. "You didn't say it."

He looked down into her eyes as he lowered her to the floor, then quickly undid his coat. "You'll freeze," he said, wrapping her into its folds. "What didn't I say?"

"You didn't say that you'll come back. You didn't say the actual words. You always say the words."

Harry smiled, running his fingers down her cheek, pushing the stray damp hairs from her face and staring into her eyes.

"I will come back, Elise." He pulled her in even closer, holding her tight in his arms. He caught his breath, trying not to choke, blinked quickly, and looked out across the blurring fields and into the distance.

Chapter Twelve

Harry dropped his case at the bottom of the dugout steps. Edward looked up from his bunk, delighted to see him.

"What sort of time do you call this?" he asked, swinging his legs round and sitting up.

"It's taken me bloody ages to find you."

"Well we've been having a rather exciting time in the last few days. Trust you to miss it all." Harry took off his coat, shook the rain from it and sat on the chair nearest to Edward. "You should have seen it, Harry," Edward continued. "The tanks were magnificent."

"Where the hell are we?" Harry asked.

"There's a village just ahead called Banteux. The 8th Royal Fusiliers are holding the front line. We've been here in reserve since the night of the attack."

"Tell me all about it then. I can see you're dying to."

"Well, we got the order to attack on the 20th. Just before dawn. The Bosch didn't stand a chance, Harry. They just took one look at the tanks and started climbing out of their trenches with their hands in the air. We were hard-pressed to know what to do with them all." Harry marvelled at Edward's excitement.

"Why have we stopped here, then?"

"Absolutely no bloody idea. We could have just carried on into Banteux and beyond, but they ordered us to halt here."

"And you've been here ever since?"

"Yes."

"No further orders?"

"No."

"How's Pilcher been?" Harry asked.

"Same as usual," Edward replied. "Either stone drunk, or twitchy and on edge, making everyone nervous. He was totally useless in the attack and got into a blind panic. You're the only one who seems to know how to control him."

"What condition is he in at the moment?"

Edward held up a bottle of whisky, three quarters gone, that was standing on the floor next to his bunk. "Well he drank most of this before going up, so I'd say verging on stone drunk."

"Christ!" Harry shook his head. "Who does that actually belong to?" he asked.

"Me. I brought it back with me."

"Give it to me," Harry said. Edward handed over the bottle and Harry went across to his case. Opening it, he placed the bottle inside. "Is there any more?" he asked.

"Not that I know of," Edward replied. Harry closed his case again, placing it on one of the empty bunks. "How are the new men?" he asked, sitting back down at the table. "I didn't really get to meet them properly before I left."

"They're alright, I suppose. Newby had a rough time during the attack, but that wasn't a bad thing, really. It calmed him down a bit. He was a bit too big for his own boots. He's easier to deal with now. Ferris is still very nervous, and I don't think Pilcher's helping with that. Didn't you see them on your way in?" Edward asked.

"Only briefly. I didn't see Pilcher though."

"He's probably staggering about the trench somewhere. We're due to relieve them at midnight."

"Oh, good. A whole hour's rest in the dry!" Harry smiled.

"Get some kip if you want. I'll wake you."

"I can't be bothered. How was your leave, by the way?" Harry asked.

"Wonderful," Edward replied. "Although so much has happened since I've been back, it seems like a lifetime ago."

"How was Isabel?"

"She was especially wonderful." Edward smiled across at Harry.

"And the vicar?"

"He was the same as usual."

"Have you broken the news to him yet?"

"No. It's still the best kept secret in England, I think." Edward coughed and looked embarrassed. "Something happened while I was there though…"

"What was that?"

Edward stared at the ground. "Well, we managed to spend most of Sunday afternoon together and…" He looked up again. "Do you remember Isabel's friend, Connie?"

"The one with the wounded fiancé?" Harry asked.

"Well, they're married now, but yes." Harry nodded. Edward continued, "She invited us round for tea on the Sunday."

"That was nice of her. And the vicar didn't object?"

"No. She's a perfectly respectable married woman now. Anyway, once we'd had tea, Connie had to go and visit her husband. He hasn't been well, evidently and he's back in the hospital again. I thought we'd have to leave, but she said we could stay on for a bit longer and show ourselves out. Then, once she'd gone, Isabel explained that they'd arranged the whole thing between them, so that she and I could have some time alone."

"How shocking!" Harry mocked.

"Be quiet!"

"At least you got to spend some time together, without the vicar, for once."

"Yes, I'm just not sure that Isabel intended things to go quite as far as they did…" Edward went bright red, lowered his head again, and turned away.

"Oh." Harry wasn't really that surprised. "It had to happen sooner or later," he said.

"Yes but most people wait until they're married," Edward mumbled.

"Do they, Eddie? Even now?"

"We should have waited though, shouldn't we?" Edward turned back to Harry.

"You're asking me?" Harry laughed. "You do know where I've just spent the last few days, don't you?"

"Yes, but that's different."

"Why?" Harry asked.

"Because it's you and Elise."

"And what's the difference between us and you? Except for the fact that we're not engaged and you are?"

"I want to know what you think, though, Harry. Do you think we should have waited?"

"No." Harry heard Edward's sigh of relief and smiled to himself, feeling more of a father-figure than ever. "You love her, don't you?" he said.

"Yes. More than anything."

"And was Isabel alright about it? She wasn't upset or anything?"

"No. She was fine. She was… happy."

"Well then. Nothing else matters really, as long as you take care of her."

"Of course I will."

"Then what are you worrying about?"

Edward paused for a few thoughtful moments, staring at his own hands. "How did you get on then, Harry?" he asked suddenly. "How was Rose?"

Harry looked at the map on the table. "She doesn't really know me anymore."

"Was it that bad?"

"It was to start with. She was afraid of me. She hid from me. Then she got used to me, and then I left. I felt really terrible lying to them, Eddie."

"You didn't have any choice though, did you?."

"Yes, I did," Harry reasoned. "I could have stayed."

"But then you wouldn't have been able to see Elise. How was she this time?"

"Not as well as I'd hoped. When I got there, they'd just found out that her brother's missing."

"Oh hell." Harry got up and went to sit on the bunk next to his case. "What happened?" Edward asked.

"Oh, I lied to her too. I told her that being missing doesn't mean you're dead."

"You're getting quite good at lying these days. Still it's kinder, I suppose. Better than telling her that the poor bugger is probably in several pieces out there." Edward nodded towards the dugout steps.

"I suppose so. I couldn't have told her the truth anyway. She'd already got enough to worry about as it was."

"Why, what else was wrong?"

"They'd run out of money. It's been a bad harvest. She was worried about losing the farm." Harry paused, leaning back and looking up at the ceiling. "Still, at least there was something I could do about that."

"What did you do?"

"I went into Bethune and saw the bank manager. I've arranged to have some money sent over from England for her."

"How on earth did you manage that from here?"

"I sent a telegram to my father. He'll deal with it."

"So, you've had to tell him about Elise?"

"No."

"What did you say then?" Edward asked.

"Just that I needed the money. It was quite a lot by most people's standards, so I don't know what he'll think about that."

"I do! He'll assume you've got some girl into trouble, that's what!"

"For this amount of money, Eddie, it would have to be considerably more than one girl!"

"It's bound to raise a few eyebrows, Harry."

"I'll worry about that when the time comes."

"Do you trust him to send the money, without knowing why?" Edward asked.

"Yes. It's my money and in any case, I have a habit of trusting the people I love." They looked at each other, their eyes locking, just for a moment.

"Why didn't you just explain the whole thing to your father?" Edward said at last.

"I don't want to tell them about Elise."

"Why not?"

"The same reason I don't like to talk to Elise about them."

"But you've already told her about Bella and Rose. What harm can it do to tell her about the rest?"

"I do talk to her about some things, but I don't tell her about my leave in England, or what I do with my family. I never talk to them about Elise and I don't talk to either of them about what we do here."

"Why, Harry?"

Harry thought for a moment. "It's just that I can't share the things from one place with the others. I have to keep them all separate."

"You tell me about all of them, though."

"You're different."

"I am?" Edward said, yawning.

"Yes, Eddie. I don't have to explain anything to you. You understand all of it."

"How on earth do you remember what to say? I mean, it must make it complicated when you're at home, or with Elise," Edward said.

"Not really. It actually helps me to make more sense of it all."

"You can make sense of all this?"

"I can if I keep my separate worlds apart, yes."

Edward thought for a little while. "I presume Elise was a little surprised to discover that you're a man of means?" he asked.

"You could put it that way, yes."

"How did she take it?"

"Alright, I suppose."

"What happened, Harry? Something clearly did."

"Oh, it was nothing to do with the money. It was to do with me keeping secrets, really. No, not even that. I suppose it was something to do with me having separate worlds – except she doesn't really know about me having them. So, from her perspective, it was about me not talking enough – not telling her about the things she needs to know and understand. I was thinking on the way back here – if you added up all the time Elise and I have spent together, it's less than three weeks in total. We've never celebrated a Christmas or birthday together. It's no wonder she was so confused – we hardly see each other."

"So what happened, then?"

"We talked. Well, actually I talked. She cried."

"Oh God, that sounds bloody awful."

"No. It wasn't. It really wasn't. Talking really helped, and afterwards... well, everything's even better than it was."

"I didn't think that was possible."

"Neither did I, but it is..."

"What is it? There's something else."

"Yes. There was one problem."

"Oh? What was that?"

"Elise wanted to talk about the future. She wanted to know about my plans for after the war."

"Didn't she understand that you can't make any?"

"No."

"That must have been a bit awkward."

"Yes and no. I explained why none of us make plans; I told her that I'd never leave her, but I still couldn't really promise her anything - not in the way she wanted. She was looking for something definite and I couldn't give her that. I wanted to, but I couldn't. I felt guilty for not giving her the answers she was looking for but I had to be honest. I didn't lie to her about any of that, Eddie. I couldn't make her promises with what I haven't got, could I?"

"What do you mean, 'what you haven't got', Harry?"

"I mean a future, Eddie."

At ten to twelve, they both put on their coats, pulling up their collars against the cold.

"Oh well, here goes," Edward said, climbing the steps. Harry followed close behind.

In the trench, they were met by Pilcher, who looked at his watch as they appeared.

"Just in time," he announced, slurring his words just a little. "Keep your eyes open, won't you?"

"Naturally, sir." Harry answered, turning to speak to Warner, who was standing a little way from the dugout entrance. Pilcher stared at the back of Harry's head then, accompanied by Newby and Ferris, descended the dugout steps.

"How have you been, Warner?" Harry asked.

"Not too bad, sir." Warner replied. "Although it would be lovely if this rain would stop." Harry looked down at his feet, already sinking in the mud.

"How long has it been going on for?"

"Days, sir. It looks like it might start snowing soon, too."

"That's it, Warner, look on the bright side." Harry patted Warner on the arm.

"Excuse me? Lieutenant?" Harry turned. Ferris stood behind him, coatless.

"What is it, Ferris?" Harry asked. "Why haven't you got a coat on? It's freezing cold and pouring with rain, in case you hadn't noticed."

"The captain sent me up – he said it was urgent."

"Does he want me down there?"

"Yes, sir. He asked me to come up for you. I think there's something wrong." Ferris looked nervously from Warner to Harry and back again, rain dripping from the end of his nose.

"Alright, Ferris, get back down there. I'll be along in a minute. Lieutenant Wilson!" Harry called to Edward, who walked over to him. "Eddie," he said quietly, "His lordship wants me. Hold the fort, will you?"

"Will do. What does he want?"

"No bloody idea." Harry went slowly down the steps, feeling the warmth coming up to meet him.

In the dugout, he found Captain Pilcher pacing the floor. Newby and Ferris sat together on a bunk in the far corner, both looking up nervously at Harry.

"What have you done with it, Belmont?" Pilcher demanded before Harry had even reached the bottom step.

"With what, sir?" Harry looked Pilcher directly in the eyes, his face a picture of innocence.

"You know perfectly well what." Patches of red had appeared on Pilcher's cheeks and his moustache was twitching.

"I'm sorry, sir. I'm afraid I don't." Pilcher walked forward, standing directly in front of Harry, their faces only inches apart. Harry looked at a spot above Pilcher's head.

"The bottle, Belmont," Pilcher whispered. "What have you done with it?"

"What bottle, sir?" Harry didn't lower his voice. "I'm afraid I don't know anything about a bottle."

"There was a bottle over by Wilson's bed. Perhaps I should ask him?"

"Oh, *that* bottle. That belongs to Lieutenant Wilson, sir." Harry stood up straight, making himself significantly taller than the captain.

"What?" Pilcher spluttered.

"The bottle that was by Wilson's bunk belongs to him, sir." Harry spoke slowly.

"That's not what I asked you, Belmont. I asked you where it is."

"We finished it, sir."

"But I've never seen you take a drink, Belmont. You're lying."

"I used to drink, sir, many years ago. I was soaking wet when I got back tonight, and I thought a quick drink would take the chill off. Lieutenant Wilson offered me some from his bottle."

"There was nearly a quarter of a bottle left." Pilcher's eyes narrowed.

"Was there, sir?" Harry asked. Both men stood still for a moment or two. "Will there be anything else, sir?" Harry continued. "I should really be getting back on duty."

Pilcher sat down heavily on one of the chairs, staring at the table. "Get along then," he murmured, waving Harry away.

As Harry began to climb the stairs, he looked back and noticed that Pilcher's fingers were shaking.

Back in the trench, he told his story to Edward.

"You'd better hang on to that bottle," Edward said. "If he finds it, he'll not only drink it, he'll probably have you up on a charge."

"Right now, I really couldn't care less what he does. At least he won't be drinking any more tonight."

"He'll get hold of some more tomorrow. You know that, don't you?"

"Well, that's tomorrow."

Harry looked back towards Warner. "Have you had any sleep yet, Sergeant?" he asked.

"No, sir."

"Well, go along now. We'll keep an eye on things." Warner hesitated. "What is it?" Harry asked, approaching him.

"Oh, nothing, sir," Warner replied.

"There's something wrong," Harry said.

Warner looked around him. "It's just a feeling, sir," he said. "No more than that."

"Not another one, Warner. I've told you about that before." Harry smiled. "Off you go and get some sleep. Try to find some shelter out of this rain."

"Yes, sir." Warner went along the trench and around the corner of the traverse, leaving Harry and Edward alone.

"Give it half an hour and we'll go for a quick inspection." Harry suggested, moving back to stand next to Edward, who nodded his head, vaguely.

"What's the matter?" Harry asked.

"I've been thinking."

"Oh God, not you too! Between Warner's feelings and you thinking, I don't stand a chance." Edward's face remained serious. "What is it that you've been thinking?" Harry asked.

"You know what you were saying earlier about not having a future?"

"Yes." Harry looked at the ground.

"Do you really believe that?"

"Oh, I don't know," Harry replied. "I didn't have the best leave, I suppose. It made me think, and I don't like to think. Not about the

186

future, anyway." Edward didn't say anything. "What is it, Eddie?" Harry asked. "What's bothering you?"

"Do you remember, I said earlier that I'd take care of Isabel?"

"Yes."

"Well, what's going to happen to her if I don't get back?"

"Nothing, Eddie, because you're going to get back." Harry looked away to his right, as though he'd heard something, which he hadn't.

"But I might not, Harry. Her father's a dreadful man. Really he is. She's terribly unhappy at home. She desperately wants to move out. She wanted to get married during my leave, especially after we… you know. But there wasn't time for me to sort out a licence or anything. And, in any case, I've got nowhere for her to live. I was living in halls at University and I always stay in hotels or with friends when I go home. She's thought about moving in with Connie, but there isn't really the space and things are difficult with her husband's injuries and everything. What's going to happen to her, Harry? There's no-one else to look after her."

"Eddie, calm down, for heaven's sake. Stop worrying about it. She'll be fine, because you'll go home and you'll take care of her."

Edward moved round and to stand directly in front of Harry. "We've both been out here too long," he said. "The law of averages says that one or other of us isn't going to make it back."

"That's just superstition. Anyway, if it's going to be one of us, it's more likely to be me. I'm a bigger target. Stop panicking, Eddie."

"Are you a complete bloody fool?" Edward shouted. There was a moment's shocked silence and then Edward cleared his throat. "Look, Harry." His voice was calmer. "I know you're probably going to tell me to bugger off, or something, but I want you to promise me that if anything happens to me, you'll look after Isabel."

"Bugger off."

"Please, Harry, will you just listen to me. Financially and all that, you know…" Edward was stumbling over his words. "… Well, things aren't that good for me, exactly." He faltered again. "I've still not completed my studies at university. I'm not even sure what I intended to do when

I finished. I hadn't really thought about it. I've never had a job in my life, except the army. And that's hardly a job, is it? I've got very little money and no prospects at the moment. In fact, I'm not entirely sure what I was doing asking Isabel to marry me."

"You fell in love, Eddie. That's what you were doing."

"Don't change the subject, Harry. I'm worried about her. I just want to know that she'll be alright."

"Of course she'll be alright, Eddie. You'll make sure of that. You'll go home, you'll finish university and get a job. You and Isabel will get married, you'll make a home together. If you ever need money, I'll help you out, you know that. You'll be happy. You'll see."

"Harry!" Edward spoke through gritted teeth. "What's the matter with you? For Christ's sake, wake up, will you? You might be lucky enough to live in three separate worlds, and be perfectly happy in all of them, with your daughter and your lover and all your money, but it's high time you realised that in one of your worlds, things aren't so bloody wonderful, actually. Men are getting blown to pieces, having their guts ripped out and their balls shot off, every minute of every day. I'm just asking for a promise from you that you'll take care of Isabel, if I don't make it back. Is that really too much to ask after all this time? After everything we've been through together? Can't I even trust you enough to do that for me?" He was breathing heavily, saliva gathered in the corners of his lips.

Harry looked at the ground. When he spoke, his voice was barely audible. "Of course you can," he murmured. "I promise, Eddie. Whatever it takes. Anything she needs, I'll do it. I'll look after her. Trust me."

Edward paused, allowing his breathing to slow. "Thank you," he said. He was feeling ashamed of himself. "I'm sorry, Harry. I shouldn't have said all that. I shouldn't have shouted at you."

"It's alright." Harry turned away to his right. "I'll go and inspect the men," he said. He stopped for a moment, keeping his head down, not looking back. "Eddie," he said quietly, staring at his feet, "I'm not really perfectly happy in all of my worlds, just one of them: this one. It doesn't matter how much I love Rose or need Elise – and I do need her… I need her so much it hurts – this is still the only place where I'm completely and honestly happy. And I'm not oblivious to all the blood and guts and balls. I just try not to think about them. Because in this world, Eddie, in this far from bloody wonderful world, the world that we share, I have too much to lose. I would have thought that you of all people would know that."

Edward went to speak, but Harry had already begun to move away, further down to the opposite end of the trench, rounding the traverse to inspect the sentries.

When Harry returned half an hour later, Edward still hadn't moved. "I really am sorry, Harry," he said, looking up into Harry's face.

"Don't worry, Eddie. Really, it's fine."

"No it isn't, Harry. I shouldn't have said those things to you. I know you care about all this shit just as much as the rest of us. You're just much better at hiding it."

"No I'm not. Well, not from you."

There was a moment's silence. "Harry?" It was Edward who spoke first.

"Yes?"

"I hope you didn't mind me asking. About Isabel I mean?"

"No."

"I didn't ask you because you're rich or anything. I asked because you're you. I don't expect you to provide for her for the rest of her life, or buy her a house, or anything ridiculous like that. Just check up on her. Make sure she's alright for me."

"Eddie." Harry placed a hand on Edward's arm, looking into his pale blue eyes. "I've already said, I'll do whatever it takes, and that's what I meant. I'll buy her a house, I'll support her indefinitely, I'll give her anything and everything she needs if you're not there. Whatever it takes." He paused. "But, in all honesty, it doesn't matter, about any of that, because you will be there. I promise." He looked down at the ground, his voice lowering to a whisper. "I'm going to make sure you get back. I'm not going to let anything happen to you."

The next morning, after breakfast, Pilcher came up out of the dugout. All the officers were in the trench, Harry being the nearest to the dugout entrance.

"Belmont!" Pilcher called.

"Yes, sir." Harry didn't move.

"I'm going to H.Q."

"Yes, sir." Pilcher stared at him, and Harry sensed he wanted to say something else, but thought better of it. The captain had soon gone around the traverse and out of sight. Harry moved along the trench a little way behind him, coming upon a small group of men.

"I hate that bastard!" Harry overheard one of them saying. "Shame there's never a sniper around when you need one." The man was looking into a small mirror, balanced in the wall of the trench and held a cut-throat razor in his hand. Harry stopped in his tracks.

"Travis!" he called.

"Yes, sir." The man stood up, dropping the razor. He had a worried expression on his reddening face.

"I presume, Travis," Harry said, looking him up and down, "That you were referring to one of our snipers and the possibility of taking out a few of the bastard Germans opposite?"

"Erm, yes, sir." Travis looked confused.

"Very good, Travis. Excellent idea." Harry smiled. "Carry on."

His inspection completed, Harry went back into the dugout, leaving Newby and Ferris on duty. Edward was sitting at the table, writing a letter. Harry laid down on his narrow bunk, looking up at the ceiling.

"We're back up in two hours," he said.

"Fine," Edward replied, continuing to write. "They seem to be doing alright, don't they?"

"Who?"

"Newby and Ferris."

"They're better when Pilcher isn't with them." Edward finished his letter, folding it in half and putting his pencil away in his pocket.

"Harry?"

"Yes."

"Are we alright?"

"We'd be better without Pilcher, but I'm sure we'll cope, even with him. He's a bit of a liability." Harry turned onto his side, propping himself up on his elbow. "The men are a bit restless, though. I don't think they like it here. And the bloody weather's not helping. Warner's right – it really does look like snow today."

"Harry, shut up."

"What? You asked if we were alright. I'm just answering you."

"I meant us, not everyone else."

"Oh, sorry. Of course we're alright. Why? Is something wrong?"

"God, Harry. You've got a short memory. I'm talking about last night."

"Oh, that."

"Yes, that. I feel terrible. I said such horrible things to you."

"Don't worry about it, Eddie."

"And you will take care of her?"

"Yes."

"Thank you." Edward got up and crossed the dugout, sitting down at the end of Harry's bunk. Harry bent his legs and moved his feet to make room. "You know what you were saying about having separate worlds?" Edward asked. "Does it really help?"

"Yes, it does."

"And did you mean what you said about being happiest here?"

"Yes," he said. "England isn't the same anymore. Home isn't the same. It's changed, or maybe I have. Maybe the war has made me different, and it's them that have stayed the same. Rose doesn't remember who I am, not once I've left. I'm gone from her for too long each time and I don't feel like her father anymore; she looks to my parents – not to me. When I was there, I spent some time with Bella's family. Her sister's fiancé has been killed so I went to the farm to see if I could help. It's the first time the war's really touched them. I realised that, until now, it's just been a series of stories told in newspaper articles. It's not even real to them. They have no understanding of our lives at all... and I'm not really sure they want to. They've enjoyed their ignorance, and they're still trying to protect it – even now."

"But surely, you're happy when you're with Elise?"

"Of course I am; especially now. But I'm always having to hold something back. She's incredibly young, Eddie. I think I'd forgotten how young she is. I can't tell her everything, so I have to pretend. Her brother's possibly still here, somewhere and she loves him so much. Even before he went missing, she'd have been devastated if she knew what it's really like here… she was always frightened of something happening to me, but now with what's happened to Henri, it's ten times worse. I keep lying to her about him and about this place… I do it to protect her, but I still despise myself for it." He paused. "That's why I'm happiest here, I suppose," he continued. "When I said I'm honestly happy here, I was being literal. I can be honest when I'm here. I know what I'm doing and who I am. I don't have to explain myself, or what I'm doing. I can just be myself. It's different for you, Eddie. You've got Isabel to worry about: she's miserable at home and you want to be there to help her. Rose and Elise don't really need me – not in the same way. I want to protect them and keep them safe but I know, deep down, that if anything happened to me, they'd be fine. They'd be upset; they'd grieve, but after a while, they'd be fine. They'd get over it. They have family and friends to help them and to love them. They don't need me in the same way that Isabel needs you. If they did, it would be impossible for me to be here… I couldn't bear it… I don't know how you do. But as it is…" Harry hesitated and looked over at Edward again. "You do understand, don't you?" he asked.

"Yes." Edward smiled up at Harry.

"I thought you would."

"I might understand what you're saying, Harry but, if I'm being completely honest myself, I think you're talking the biggest load of utter horse shit that I've ever heard. They do need you. We all do… and how you can fail to see that is beyond me."

Pilcher returned at around noon. Harry and Edward were on duty in the trench.

"Come down into the dugout, both of you," Pilcher commanded.

"Yes, sir." Harry turned to Warner. "Back in a minute," he said, before going down the steps.

Harry was the last one into the dugout, by which time, Pilcher had already opened the bottle of whisky that he'd brought back with him. He poured a large cupful and looked at Harry across the brim as he drank most of it down in one gulp.

"We've been given our orders," he said, wiping his sleeve across his mouth. "We're to move forward this evening into the front line trench to relieve the 8th Royal Fusiliers. We'll be attacking at 07.30 tomorrow. I want you to have the men ready to depart at 18.30 hours." He turned away, showing his dismissal and drained the cup of its contents. Edward moved towards the steps, but Harry stood still, motioning that Newby and Ferris should leave. They both put on their coats and went up after Edward.

"Are you still here, Belmont?" Pilcher said as he turned round. He picked up the bottle and refilled his cup.

"Yes, sir," Harry replied, knowing that he was about to take an enormous risk. "I was wondering, with respect, sir, whether it's wise for you to keep drinking so much." He waited. Pilcher put the bottle down heavily on the table.

"Who the hell do you think you are, Belmont?" he said, looking up, his eyes alive with anger.

"I know it's not my place to say…"

"No it's not, Belmont," Pilcher interrupted. "And I'll thank you to keep your opinions to yourself."

"Very good, sir," Harry said. "Perhaps, sir, you could give me the details of tomorrow's attack."

"What the hell for, Belmont? I'll tell you in the morning with the others."

"With respect, sir," Harry repeated, trying to remain calm, "I think it might be better if you told me now. My old C.O. always used to tell one of us the night before, just in case anything happened to him before the off," Harry lied. "It makes sense really, when you think about it."

"Yes, I suppose it does, Belmont." Pilcher sat down at the table, with the map in front of him. Harry moved forward.

"We're to cross No Man's Land here." Pilcher pointed to the map. "We only have to cover about fifty yards. Then we'll come to a sunken road. We cross that and on the other side is Pelican Trench. We're to move along to our right and after about 350 yards, we'll be met by B Company. Then we're to hold the trench." He looked up at Harry. "Happy now?" Harry was still looking at the map.

"It looks like a death-trap, sir. Surely the Germans have the advantage over us. They'll have the road covered. We're going to walk straight into their gunfire. Wouldn't we be better off going across a bit further over to the left?" Pilcher got to his feet again.

"It's not for you to question the orders, Belmont," he said.

"Very well, sir." Harry turned to go.

"I didn't give you permission to leave, Belmont," Pilcher cried, moving forward and tripping over the leg of the table. He fell to the floor.

Harry bent to help Pilcher to his feet. "I rest my case," he said under his breath.

Pilcher dusted down his uniform. "You would do well not to keep challenging me," he said, staring up at Harry. "As it happens, I'm going to need you during this attack, but once it's over, I'll be taking action against you. You need to remember that I'm your commanding officer." He sat down, pouring himself another cup of whisky. Harry walked over to the dugout steps, pulling up his collar. He looked back at Pilcher.

"Yes, I'm afraid you are," he whispered.

Chapter Thirteen

November 24th 1917

The rain had turned to sleet at about four o'clock that afternoon, just as it was becoming dark. Within two hours, the sleet became snow. The men were ready on time, but the mud under their feet was quickly turning to a quagmire and by the time they completed their journey to the front line, it was one thirty in the morning. Their feet were wet and freezing inside their boots. The 8th Royal Fusiliers moved off, grateful to be leaving the weather, the trenches and any thoughts of an impending attack behind them.

Newby, Ferris and Edward were left on duty, positioning the men, while Pilcher went down into the dugout, followed closely by Harry.

"What are you doing here, Belmont?" Pilcher asked, when they reached the bottom of the steps.

"I just thought I'd tag along, sir," Harry replied, looking at Pilcher, who stared hard at him.

"I'm Captain Dunstan." A tall thin, balding man stood up from the table and shook Pilcher's hand.

"Ready to hand over?" Pilcher asked.

"Yes." Dunstan looked at Harry, who glanced around the dugout. "The Germans have control of the sunken road ahead," Dunstan said. "You've got about two hundred yards of trench here. I understand that you're launching an attack in the morning. We were told to expect some supplies for you, but they haven't arrived yet. I should imagine they'll be here soon, though."

"Very well. I'll take over from here. You can go." Pilcher dismissed Dunstan.

"With pleasure," Dunstan said, putting on his cap and coat. "Is it still snowing?" he asked of Harry.

"Yes, sir. I'm afraid so," Harry replied.

"Good luck." Dunstan looked back towards Pilcher, who had sat down at the table and didn't respond. Harry followed Dunstan up the steps. At the top Dunstan turned to Harry, lowering his voice. "How drunk is he?" he asked.

"Very," Harry replied.

"It's not really my place to say, Lieutenant, but should he be here in that condition?"

"Probably not, sir."

"Well. There's not much I can do to help, I'm afraid, but in case you need to know, I think you'll find your Battalion H.Q. will be set up in one of the old German dugouts back in the communication trench. All the best, Lieutenant."

"Thank you, sir. You too." Harry saluted the captain, who returned his salute and walked away.

"He seemed a nice chap," Edward said, joining Harry.

"Yes, he was."

"Lucky bugger."

"Yes."

"I take it his lordship is down there?" Edward asked. Harry nodded in reply. "Did he have any whisky left, or has he drunk it all?"

"No," Harry replied. "He had two full bottles yesterday. He's still got about half of the second one left."

"Oh well. Look on the bright side," Edward whispered. "He's so far gone, he probably won't remember to court-martial you. In fact he probably won't even remember who you are."

"I'm not really sure I care."

"I do."

"Where are Newby and Ferris?" Harry asked.

"Newby's a bit further along there." Edward nodded to his left. "Ferris has gone off in the other direction."

"Right. You go and get some sleep. I'll send them down when they get back."

"What about you?"

"I'll be down soon."

At just before five in the morning the first group of bomb carriers arrived, laden with boxes of grenades. They left their crates and returned the way they had come. Edward came out of the dugout shortly afterwards.

"What the hell happened to you?" he asked of Harry. "You said you were coming down for some sleep."

"Are the other two still down there?"

"Yes, but you've been up here by yourself all this time."

"I'm getting worried," Harry said, ignoring him.

"Why?"

"The other companies haven't arrived yet."

"When were they supposed to get here?"

"I don't really know, but I imagine the same time as us. We're all part of this attack. We're supposed to link up with B company in Pelican Trench. C and D companies have different objectives, I presume, but it's all part of the same assault. If they're not even here, what the hell do we do? Do we still go ahead, or do we wait?"

"Should we tell him?" Edward nodded towards the dugout.

"No idea."

"Perhaps we should give it a bit longer."

"I'm going to explain to everyone what we're doing," Harry said, decisively.

"He doesn't normally bother until about ten minutes before the off and, even then he doesn't tell us anything useful."

"Yes well, I'm not him, am I? He's told me what we're going up against and I think it's best if the others knows what's going on. Can you gather them round?"

Edward went in search of the Newby and Ferris and also found Warner and the other sergeants. They stood huddled around Harry, the snow falling more heavily now. Harry explained their target and objectives, pointing out that the Germans, with the advantage of high ground, had control over No Man's Land and the sunken road.

"Once we're in the trench, it should be a bit easier. Tell your men to get across and in there as quickly as they can. Then we're to bomb our way up to our right. After about 350 yards, we should meet up with B Company, coming in the opposite direction."

"Where will the Germans be in all this?" Edward asked.

"I can't imagine they'll be waiting there with open arms," Harry said, looking around at the white, blank faces surrounding him. "This one's going to be difficult," he said.

"Where is B Company?" Newby asked. "Shouldn't they be on our right, if we're going to link up with them?"

"Yes, they should."

"But they're not here." Newby's voice had achieved a higher note.

"Don't worry. They'll turn up." Harry glanced at Edward. "So, you all know what to do. We're due off at 07.30. Our artillery will start at 07.00." Harry thought to himself that this should give the Germans just about enough notice of their arrival. He dismissed everyone and turned to Edward.

"I suppose it's far too late for me to suggest you getting any sleep?" Edward asked.

"Just a bit." They both looked up as Ferris came back around the traverse.

"It's B Company, Lieutenant Belmont. They're just arriving."

"Well, that's alright then." Harry's nonchalance disguised his own concern. "At least we should be able to complete our part of the operation. Well done Ferris." He watched the young Second Lieutenant disappear again then looked at his watch. "They're cutting it a bit fine. It's nearly six o'clock. Still, I suppose that's their problem."

The bombardment started at 7am on the dot.

"Is that it?" Edward asked as it began. "It's a bit feeble. I'd been expecting something a bit more earth-shattering, considering what we're going up against."

"Perhaps they know that his lordship's got a hangover," Harry laughed.

"Do you think we should go and get him?" Harry asked.

"No. He'll only make everyone nervous. It's bad enough as it is. I'm off to do the rounds. You should as well. Just to calm the men a bit."

"Yes. See you back here?" Harry nodded. They walked in opposite directions down the trench. Every so often Harry would stop, saying a few words of encouragement to one or two of the men, usually those who looked most worried. A couple of them were singled out because he knew their wives had recently had babies and he wanted to ask after them. A bit further along, Harry came across Travis.

"Seen any snipers lately?" he asked, smiling.

"No, sir." Travis looked round.

"Well, keep your eyes open, won't you?" He stopped and spoke to Warner. "How's it looking?" he asked. "How are they?"

"Nervous," Warner replied. "This doesn't look good, and they know it. It's not going to be easy getting across."

"I know." Harry turned to go. "See you over there," he called.

"Yes, sir." Warner gave the order for the men to mount the fire-steps.

Harry began to move back along the trench. When he reached the dugout entrance again, it was twenty past seven. Pilcher arrived at the top of the dugout steps just as Harry rounded the corner of the traverse.

"Where's Belmont?" Pilcher asked Edward, looking around suspiciously.

"Here, sir," Harry said.

Pilcher turned. "Where have you been? You should be here." He pointed to a space in front of him.

"I've just been talking to the men, sir," Harry said.

"Get them ready," Pilcher said, his words slurred.

"They already are," Harry said under his breath.

"Shouldn't you be further along the trench, Wilson?" Pilcher asked, swaying and steadying himself against the trench wall.

"No, sir," Edward said, looking at Harry. "Newby's down that way, and Ferris is covering the other end."

Looking at his watch, Pilcher raised the whistle to his mouth. Harry and Edward opened their holsters and removed their revolvers. Pilcher glanced up and down the trench. The artillery fire died away. Harry looked down at Edward, their eyes meeting. They didn't say anything. A few feet behind them, the whistle blew.

Harry was one of the first out of the trench, so he saw the three bullets slice into Travis's chest and saw him fall backwards into the trench. There was a tremendous noise of bullets swishing and whistling past to either side. Harry looked to his left and right. He couldn't see Edward. He quickly looked behind him. There was still no sign. *Move on, must move on.* His feet carried him forward. To his left, he saw Warner, waving men on, saw three men to either side of him fall away, the ground catching them. They all carried guns. He had his revolver, the men had their Lee Enfield rifles. None of them were of any use. There was no time to open fire. All anyone could do in this hail was to run and hope for the best. The ground was churned up by the rain and snow, making it hard work. Several men slid into shell-holes and didn't resurface. So many fell, picked themselves up and then fell again, cut down by the torrent of bullets. Just ahead lay the sunken road. Harry could make out the rise in the ground, which marked its boundary. Jumping over this, he landed on the firmer ground of the road. He'd hoped it would be a sanctuary from the noise and fury of No Man's Land, but instead it was even worse. The Germans had taken advantage of the high ground on either side and were sweeping the whole area with a constant barrage of machine gun fire. Feeling the bullets whistle past, Harry threw himself back against the side of the road, holding his breath. He looked left and right. The ground was already strewn with several bodies and he was completely alone. He waited, looking first one way and then the other. He couldn't make out Edward's body anywhere. A few minutes passed and then Pilcher jumped down beside him.

"What the hell are you doing standing here, Belmont?" he asked, taking a step forward.

"Sir!" Harry shouted. He tried to grab Pilcher, but was too late. The first bullet struck him in the neck. The second tore through the side of his chest. He fell back onto Harry, looking up into his face.

Harry lowered Pilcher to the ground, holding him in his arms. "Lie still, sir," Harry said. He could feel the blood seeping through his own tunic as he tried to staunch the flow from Pilcher's neck and he knew the captain had no more than a few minutes left, if that.

Harry heard Pilcher say, "I'm going to die, aren't I?" His voice sounded very weak, almost pitiful.

"No, sir," Harry lied. "Just hold on."

"I shouldn't be here."

"No, sir. You shouldn't," Harry said, honestly this time, as he felt Pilcher's body go limp and weighty in his arms. Harry was alone again, surrounded by blood and bodies, his clothes soaked. He looked across the road to his left and, through the snow saw Warner standing up on the bank on the other side, signalling to him. He looked harder and finally understood. Lifting Pilcher's body from his legs, he stood and, keeping his body pressed hard against the wall of the road, started moving along to his left. The road bent round slightly and afforded some shelter from the bullets. After waiting a few seconds to catch his breath, Harry ran headlong across and jumped up. Two pairs of hands pulled him up the muddy bank, where groups of men were sheltered in and around some bushes. He lay down flat on his back, breathing heavily, feeling the freezing cold ground beneath him and the snow falling on his soaking clothes and upturned face.

"Oh! Shit! No! Harry, you're wounded!" It was Edward's voice.

"No, I'm not, Eddie. It's not my blood," Harry said calmly, looking up at Edward, who was crouched next to him. "Thank God you're alright, Eddie," he whispered. "I couldn't find you."

"We knew you'd be around here somewhere," Edward said, relaxing and sitting down. "You always are. It was Warner who spotted you. Are you sure you're all in one piece?"

"Yes." Harry sat up, then knelt and finally stood, looking around him.

"Whose blood is it, by the way?" Edward asked, following Harry's lead and standing up.

"Pilcher's."

"Oh. He's dead I take it?"

"Very."

"I suppose you're in charge then."

"Edward," Harry looked down at his friend. "You're exactly the same rank as me. Why don't you take over? I'm exhausted – and freezing."

"You're better at it than me. Besides, I haven't got a clue what to do next."

"Fabulous." Harry looked around again. "The trench is supposed to be over in that direction." He pointed straight ahead.

"They don't seem to be defending this area so heavily," Edward said, looking at the few yards between themselves and the trench in front of them.

"That's because they think no-one will have made it through that lot. Come on, let's get everyone together." Harry moved forward, towards Warner.

"Thank you, sergeant," he said as he got nearer.

"It's nothing, sir."

"It's a lot more than nothing. You took one hell of a risk standing up there like that." Warner shrugged his shoulders and Harry cleared his throat. "We need to gather the men together," Harry continued. "Let's see if we can't still make something out of the day."

Newby and Ferris had both made it across, and although Newby had a wound to his arm, he was happy to carry on. They grouped the men together, and Harry led them into Pelican Trench. They rounded the first traverse without difficulty, but then, as Harry turned the next corner, he was faced with a wall of grey uniforms, about fifteen feet ahead of him. He threw a grenade, which was followed by three others from the men behind him. The first two rows of men fell, but behind them more moved forward. Harry threw another two grenades, and called out for more. A fierce battle followed as A Company fought their way down the trench, bomb for bomb against the grey men. After the first three traverses, Harry moved back. He and his men had run out of grenades and they allowed other armed men to move forward. At the rear, he stormed at Warner:

"Where the hell are the bloody grenades, Warner? We can't fight these bastards with our bare hands."

"Sorry, sir," Warner said. "I am trying. The bomb carriers are doing their best. They can't get across the road."

"Of course. I didn't think. I'm sorry, Warner."

"Sir."

"Just keep at it." Harry grabbed several more grenades and told his men to do the same. They turned and headed back down the trench. It took them over an hour to reach their objective, climbing over the grey bodies to reach the junction where B company should have been waiting for them. Edward moved forward to Harry.

"Where are they?" he asked.

"No bloody idea. They're supposed to be here. They're supposed to come from that direction." Harry pointed down the trench.

"Is this them? Edward asked. Harry looked at the approaching men, then frowned.

"What the hell?" he cried. Edward turned as the first shot rang out. "Get back!" Harry shouted, pushing Edward behind him.

They ran back the way they had come, with a hoard of Germans pursuing them.

"Get back!" Harry shouted again, pulling out his revolver and returning fire. Harry's men were falling over the scattered bodies in the trench, desperate to escape the flying bullets. "Grenades!" shouted Harry. Two men stepped forward and threw their bombs in the direction of the Germans. Several fell, but the remainder followed. Harry and his men soon reached the end of the trench again and clambered out into the open.

"Quickly! Get back to the road!" Harry ordered, waving them all away. The German troops were climbing out of the trench. He threw himself to the ground and opened fire.

"Get across!" Harry shouted over his shoulder, reloading his gun. As he fired his revolver into the advancing men, he became aware of volleys of gunfire coming from behind him. He turned and saw that Warner and Edward had lined up several of the men in the bushes.

They were firing and re-loading their rifles. Taking advantage of their covering fire, Harry clambered back to the sunken road.

"Off you go – all of you!" Harry ordered. The remaining men all jumped down, followed by Warner.

"Go on Eddie." Harry pushed Edward and jumped down after him. Climbing up the other side, Harry saw that most of the men were retreating across No Man's Land. The Germans halted their pursuit and the machine guns fell silent. Harry lagged behind, checking to left and right to make sure all the men got back. Finally, he fell into the trench, from which they'd left just a short while earlier.

Breathing heavily, and leaning against the trench wall, Harry looked around him.

"Alright?" he asked Edward.

"Hardly. You?"

"Not exactly. Warner? Where are you?" Harry called out, pulling himself upright.

"Here, sir!" Warner replied appearing from Harry's right.

"Well done, Warner. We couldn't have done that without you, yet again. I'm sorry to put you straight back to work, but can you see how many of us made it back?"

"Yes, sir." The sergeant walked away.

"I wonder what became of B Company?" Edward asked.

"Who knows? I suppose they came up against something similar to us and couldn't make it through."

"What happened to Pilcher?"

"He took a bullet to the neck and another to the chest."

"Did he die straight away?"

"No."

"Oh God, Harry."

"It's alright." Harry looked down at his uniform, still wet with Pilcher's blood. "I'll wait until Warner's reported back. Then I'd better get back to H.Q. and let them know what's happened."

"Perhaps they'll know what happened to B Company."

"Only if someone's made it back to tell them."

Warner came back along the trench. "I've only made a rough count at the moment, sir," he said. "Looks like we've got about 150 men left. I'll do a proper roll-call in a little while. I'll let them get settled first."

"A hundred and fifty?" Harry said. "So we've lost about seventy? What about officers?"

"Mr Ferris is not back, sir." Warner looked at the ground. "Mr Newby is wounded."

"Badly?"

"He says he can carry on."

"Can he?"

"I'll go and take another look, sir. We also lost countless bomb carriers, sir. I've got no idea how many of them, though."

"Thank you, Warner." Harry turned to Edward as Warner moved away. "Will you be alright, if I go to H.Q.?"

"Yes."

"I should't be more than half an hour, or so."

"I'll be fine. I've got Warner to look after me." Edward smiled. "Thank you, Harry," he said.

"What the hell for? That was a bloody disaster."

"For getting us back. That's what."

"Getting a hundred and fifty men back is hardly cause for congratulation, Eddie."

"I meant for getting us back, Harry."

Harry looked at him. "I said I would. I made you a promise, remember?" He turned and walked down the trench, rounded two traverses, took a turn to his left and entered the communication trench. Further along on his right he stopped by the entrance to a concrete dugout. Once part of the German front line, this dugout was well built and certainly protected enough for Battalion Headquarters. The sentry on duty saluted to Harry as he ducked his head to descend the stairs. Harry vaguely returned the salute.

In the dugout there was a large table, on the opposite side of which sat three officers. They were looking at a detailed map and didn't acknowledge Harry's arrival. Behind them, a sergeant hovered with a clipboard. He cleared his throat and one of the officers looked up. His face shone in the candlelight

"Oh. Who are you?" he said.

"Lieutenant Belmont, sir. A Company," Harry replied.

"Where's your captain?"

"He's dead, sir."

"Are you sure about that, Lieutenant? Did you actually see it happen?"

"Yes, sir." Harry looked down at his uniform. "He died in my arms. This is his blood."

"I see."

"What happened?" asked another of the officers, looking up from the map. "You were supposed to link up with B company."

"They weren't there, sir."

"So you made it to the junction in Pelican trench?"

"Yes, sir."

"Give us as much information as you can, please, Lieutenant."

Harry told them everything he knew.

"How many men have you got left?"

"About one hundred and fifty, sir."

"That's not too bad." Harry's mouth fell open. They all looked up as they heard someone else coming down the steps.

"Who are you?" the first officer asked again.

"Lieutenant Gibbons, sir." The newcomer glanced at Harry. "B Company." Harry returned the look.

"What happened to you?" the officer asked.

"We came up against heavy fire in the trench, sir. Our C.O. was killed. There was no way through. We were forced back. We had to retreat. The last I saw, the Germans had turned and were heading towards the junction."

"You didn't think to follow them?"

"We'd lost too many men, sir. I only hope they didn't make it as far as A Company."

"They did," Harry said, still facing forwards.

"Oh. Sorry."

"That will do!" the officer barked.

"Yes sir," Harry replied.

"We really do need to get control of Pelican trench. I want you to have another go at it."

"Sir?" Harry couldn't believe his ears.

"We're not going to ask you to do it in broad daylight. We'll go for it tonight." He consulted the other officers. "We can get artillery cover from 22.00. Start your advance at 22.50. Same objectives as this morning. I know it won't be easy, but this is an important attack. We really need to get control of this area." He looked around at his fellow officers, who both nodded. "Right, off you go then."

Harry and Gibbons were both dismissed, but Harry hesitated.

"What is it?" the officer asked.

"I'd like to ask, sir, how I go about recommending one of my men for a medal? It's not something I've ever done before."

"Oh, I see. What are the details?" Harry explained. "Well, when you get back, write it all down. Give his name, rank, number and exactly what happened. Send it all in." The officer looked back down at the map and Harry climbed up the steps. Gibbons was waiting for him.

"I'm truly sorry," he said. "We'd have got there if we could."

"I can't believe they're sending us back." Harry looked up at the sky; grey clouds were gathering overhead. "I'd better get back. I'm one of only three officers left."

"Lucky you. I'm the only one in our company."

"Good luck," Harry said. "Hopefully I'll see you later tonight."
Gibbons smiled and Harry walked away.

Chapter Fourteen

November 25th 1917

"Are they completely insane?" Edward asked. He'd just finished writing a quick letter to Isabel and he and Harry were sitting in the dugout.

"Yes, of course they are. We've always known they were mad." Harry was looking at the map.

"They're sending us back, through all that?"

"Yes. What I'd really like to know is how I'm supposed to tell the men. I mean, they've been through enough today. And now I have to tell them, that I'm really sorry but it wasn't good enough and would you mind awfully doing the whole thing all over again tonight, just to see if I can get the rest of you killed."

"You didn't get anyone killed, Harry." Edward moved from his bunk and sat next to Harry at the table. "It's not your fault. The fact that there are still a hundred and fifty of us left is mainly due to you."

"Rubbish, Eddie. Warner had an awful lot to do with it."

"Yes, he was rather extraordinary out there today, wasn't he?"

"Actually, he always is. Can you do me a favour?" Harry asked.

"Of course."

"I need to know Warner's full name and number."

"Do you want me to find out?" Edward seemed confused but Harry didn't elaborate.

"Yes, please, if you don't mind. I just want to take another look at this." Harry pointed to the map. "I'm going to see if I can work out a better way to get across." Edward went up the dugout steps, returning a few minutes later.

"First name, Thomas. No second name. Number, 18419," Edward announced, brushing the snow from his shoulders.

"It's snowing again, I see," Harry said.

"Even worse than yesterday. It's still not settling, thank goodness. The ground's too wet."

"Good."

"What do you need Warner's details for?" Edward asked.

Harry pulled forward a piece of paper and started writing. "Because I'm recommending him for a medal. He deserves it after this morning."

"I couldn't agree more. Who's going to recommend you for yours?" Edward asked. Harry continued writing, not looking up, so Edward waited. "Am I allowed to?" he asked eventually.

"No." Harry stopped and pointed to the map. "Look," he said, "I think if we cross further over to the left, we can go down into the sunken road on the bend, where I crossed earlier." He used his pencil to indicate the spot on the map. "It shouldn't be so bad there. What do you think?" He resumed writing while Edward studied the map.

"Sounds like a good idea. We'll know the lay of the land this time, too. And it will be dark." Harry finished his note and folded the paper.

"I have to get this back to H.Q., Eddie. Can you get one of the men to take it for me?"

"Yes. Give it to me." Edward took the paper from Harry. "I'll see to it."

"How is Newby, by the way?" Harry asked.

"Not too bad. Just a flesh wound to his arm. He won't hear of going back."

"Thank God for that," Harry said. "Can you send him and Warner down here? I want to see what they think of my idea."

"Will do," Edward called as he climbed up the steps.

The bombardment started exactly on time at ten o'clock.

"Well, at least they've put a bit more effort into it this time," Harry shouted above the noise. "We've got a whole forty-five minutes to endure."

"And it's finally stopped snowing," Edward said. Harry looked up.

"Bloody marvellous. A full moon and a clearing sky. Just what we need." He checked his watch. "Time to move," he shouted, looking at Edward. "Newby's got his end of the trench covered. You'd better be getting along now." They didn't have enough officers and NCOs left for Edward and Harry to stay anywhere close together, and they both knew it.

"See you over there, then." Edward attempted a smile.

"Stay on the left, remember? Keep as far over as you can, and keep your head down."

"Thanks Harry," Edward said.

"What for?"

"Everything."

"Thank me when it's over," Harry replied. Edward nodded and turned away, walking slowly down the trench. Harry watched his retreating back, until it turned around the corner of the traverse. He took a deep breath.

Just as he had earlier in the morning, Harry went along his section of the trench, checking on the men. They were more nervous and worried now. Their faces pallid, their eyes betraying their fear. He tried speaking to them, cheering them, but felt it wasn't really working. He didn't lie to them. If they asked how bad it would be, he told them that it would be just as bad as it had been in the morning. He saw them swallow hard, try to smile and then they'd thank him.

"How many will we still have by morning?" he asked Warner when he got back to the dugout entrance.

"As many as we can, sir." Warner replied. "How much longer?"

"Two minutes." Harry looked up and down the trench as Warner moved away. The bombardment had already stopped. The men were standing on the fire steps, waiting for the sound of his whistle. He put it to his dry lips, staring at the trench wall in front of him, then removed it again, licking his lips. He put the whistle back in his mouth, glanced at his watch, took a deep breath, and blew hard. All around him, men began to climb. To start with, it was quiet. The moonlight wasn't too bright and Harry assumed they were hidden from view. Looking to left and right, Harry motioned his men to move forward. The ground sucked at his feet, slowing him. Occasionally he would tread on something hard. Men he'd known by name formed a pathway across No Man's Land. Halfway across, a flare suddenly went up and the guns came to life. Machine gun and sniper fire rang out and everyone started running; shouts broke out. Harry heard screams as men were cut down. He picked up his pace, glancing around to his right. A hail of bullets tore through the five men next to him, felling them. Instinctively, he looked to his left. Edward was standing still on the lip of a shell-hole, looking back and waving his men forward. It seemed to Harry that there was a momentary silence. Everything was hushed and still. Harry heard a single shot ring out; saw his head jerk backwards, saw him spin, his helmet dropping from his blond head into the watery crater. Then Edward fell forward.

"No!" Harry heard the sound of his own voice above the renewed din. He forgot the attack and ran, dodging through the stream of advancing men. This time there was no silence and he didn't hear the shot. He just felt a thud, hammering into his left leg, then there was a burning pain in his knee, searing through the flesh. He felt himself falling, his arms flailing above his head. There was a second shot and then agony. So much pain, scorching into his hand. He crashed to the ground.

He could see the stars above his head. He looked to left and right trying to get his bearings. Rolling over onto his stomach, he screamed as the pain ripped through his knee. Raising his head, he could just see Edward in the distance, lying face down on the edge of the shell-hole about fifty yards away. Harry lifted himself onto his elbows, his hand in front of his face. In the light of the flare, he saw the fingers; three of them, hanging from the knuckle, bones shattered, threads of flesh and skin. He looked away, focused on Edward and began dragging himself forward. Each movement was agony, jolting his hand, tearing at his knee. Every few minutes, he stopped, breathing hard, then hauled himself on again. As he approached Edward, he heard something. It was muffled but sounded a bit like his own name. Was it in his head? It must be. Why would he be saying his own name aloud?

"Eddie!" He called. That was his own voice. He could hear it. He recognised it. One final effort brought Harry alongside Edward's body, their heads side by side.

"Har…" Edward was trying to say. Harry looked at him. He had almost no face. Even in the half light of another flare, Harry could make out the tear starting just below his eye, stretching down the whole of one side of his face and beyond to his neck, blood dribbling slowly and steadily. He could see Edward's tongue through the side of his mouth, his teeth visible, where his cheek should have been.

"Eddie! Oh God, no!" Harry dragged himself a little closer, crying out with every move. He finally managed to clasp Edward's fingers in his own.

"Is… it… bad?" Harry could just about make out Edward's slurred, broken words, spoken through his shattered jaw.

"Don't talk," Harry ordered.

"Is… it… bad?" Edward tried again.

"Yes."

"Knew… you… wouldn't… lie… to… me."

"No, I won't lie."

"Am I… going… to die?"

Harry swallowed hard and looked up at the sky.

"Tell… me."

"Yes." Harry looked back again, their eyes meeting. "I think so."

"How… long?"

"I don't know."

"Minutes…? Hours?"

"I'd say hours, rather than minutes, Eddie. You're bleeding badly, but I might be able to get you back. I'm wounded but I could try."

"Don't… want… to… get… back. Not… like… this. Isabel… pity… remember?" Harry didn't take his eyes from Edward's. "Please… Harry."

"What Eddie? What do you want?"

"Shoot… me."

"No, Eddie. You can't ask me to do that."

"I… can't… ask… anyone… else."

"No. There's no other bugger here." Harry tried to laugh. It didn't work.

"You're… the… only one… I… trust." Harry felt the light squeeze of his fingers.

"I won't do it, Eddie. I can't. Look at my hand." Harry fought the pain, holding up his right hand. He felt the bile rising in his throat. Then he lowered his hand to the ground again.

"Other… hand." Harry heard Edward's voice again.

"You want me to shoot you with my left hand?"

"You… can't… miss." Harry fell onto his back, staring up at the stars. "Please… Harry. Please… it hurts… so much." He heard the voice and felt Edward's fingers closing around his.

"I can't do it," Harry said, under his breath. "Not to him. Please God. Anyone else, but not him. Please. I'll do anything, but not this." The throbbing pain from his wounds started to engulf him. He took a deep, shuddering breath and closed his eyes. The stars went out.

Part Two

Chapter Fifteen

Someone was lifting his hand. They dropped it again. The pain roused him and brought him back to his senses. He felt the person move away. Then he heard a moan, a distant groan coming from his own mouth. His eyes opened, just a crack and he saw a face, peering down into his. Unshaven, flushed cheeks, greying hair, blue eyes. *Oh God, blue eyes.* He heard words he didn't understand. A question, perhaps. Then a hand behind his head and water to his lips. He swallowed. More voices. More meaningless words. He turned his head slowly, first right, then left. Lifeless ice blue eyes stared back at him. He felt strong hands lifting him, moving him away. He kept his fingers wrapped around the now-cold hand, until someone prized it free.

Pain seized him, tore through his knee, burned into his hand. Then it crushed his chest, engulfing him; suffocating him. He closed his eyes again.

****

The sun was shining in through the window beside his bed, the brightness reflecting off the white walls. Well, they were nearly white. It was the closest thing Harry had seen to white in a long time. The colour made his eyes hurt, so he closed them again. He saw a jagged tear; teeth bared, pleading blue eyes. Ice blue eyes. 'Shoot me.' He could still hear the words. Still feel the fingers entwined in his.

He sensed a shadow across his face.

"Lieutenant Belmont?" The man standing beside him spoke English well and with only a slight German accent. Harry opened his eyes. "You have returned to us, then?" Harry didn't answer. Blue screens had been pulled around, blocking the rest of the ward from sight. A nurse stood at the end of the bed. She was a portly woman, dressed in white, with heavy eyebrows and stern eyes above unsmiling lips. "I want to explain what has happened to you," the doctor continued. He wore thick-rimmed glasses in front of soft, grey eyes. His hair was white and his face kind. He looked down at Harry, "Do you know where you are?" he asked. Harry looked out of the window. The doctor waited, but when Harry didn't speak, he said, "You are in the officer's hospital at Thorn. You arrived here six days ago." Again he paused, anticipating a response. None came. "You were very sick, Lieutenant. You had lost a lot of blood." The doctor sat on the edge of the bed, folding his arms. "Dealing firstly with your knee injury," he continued. "The bullet had become lodged, but we were able to remove it in surgery. Lieutenant, I can only assume that you tried to drag yourself back to your own lines and, in doing so, I'm afraid to say that you have done some severe and permanent damage. It would have been better for you if you hadn't tried. Your leg would probably have been much better if you'd stayed still, but as it is, the leg will not bend properly again, and you will need to use a stick. You will always be in pain… quite severe pain, especially if you put your weight on it." He looked at Harry, who kept staring at the bare tree outside. The doctor breathed in deeply. "Now, for your hand. I understand that it was badly infected by the time you arrived at the field hospital. The doctors there tried to treat you, but I'm afraid they did a poor job." He paused. "By the time you arrived here, the infection had spread and I have had to remove your arm, back to the elbow." Harry didn't move. "Do you understand what I am telling you, Lieutenant?" There was an almost imperceptible nod of Harry's head. "Do you have any questions?" Harry shook his head. "Very well." The doctor stood up. "We will try to help you, Lieutenant, but how well you recover from now on is up to you." He touched Harry gently on the shoulder. "Try to sleep some more," he said.

He turned away and, moving to the end of the bed, he pulled the screen to one side, allowing the nurse to pass through. As they walked away, Harry heard them talking in German, their voices fading. The sun was beginning to set and shone through the branches of the tree outside the window, the reflection yellowing.

The nurse returned a little later to remove the screens. She said nothing and retreated from the room again.

"I'm Collins." Harry heard a voice coming from the opposite side of the room. He raised his head a little. A man smiled. His arm was in a sling and there was a bandage around his head. Harry lowered his head again. "We've all been rather worried about you, haven't we?" Collins continued. "This is Robertson," he continued, even though Harry was no longer paying attention. "And the fine upstanding gentleman next to me, is Captain Grainger." Two other voices sounded their greetings.

"You're with the 7th Sussex, aren't you?" Collins asked, but received no answer. "I heard about the debacle at Banteux. It must have been terrible. Was that where you were?" Still Harry said nothing. Collins looked across at Robertson, who shrugged his shoulders.

"Leave him be, Collins." It was Grainger who spoke. "The poor chap's only just come to. Let him rest."

"Yes, sir. Yes, of course. We'll have a proper chat later, shall we?" Harry turned onto his side, facing the window, ignoring the pain in his knee.

Darkness fell. The tree became a shadow against a deep purple sky. Dim lights were lit. An orderly arrived with hot soup, which he placed beside Harry's bed. Harry heard a slight cough and turned his head. It was Grainger, standing beside him, leaning on a walking stick.

"Do you want some help?" he asked. Harry shook his head. "You should try to eat something, Lieutenant," he said. "I'll help you, if you like."

"No, thank you." Harry heard his own voice for the first time in days. Weeks maybe. It sounded remote, disconnected. "I'm not hungry." Grainger sat down on his bed.

"How are you?" he asked. Harry didn't answer. "Alright," Grainger continued. "You don't have to talk, if you don't want to." Harry thought for moment.

"What's the date?" he asked.

"It's the tenth of December," Grainger replied. Harry nodded. "It will have taken you a few days to get here from the field hospital, and you've been here nearly a week already." He cleared his throat, looking at the heavily bandaged stump where Harry's arm used to be. "Are you right handed?" he asked. Harry nodded. "I can help you write to your family, if you want. We're allowed to write. The letter might get to them before Christmas, if you're lucky. It would help set their minds at rest." Harry shook his head, turning away again. "Another time, then," Grainger suggested, standing up again. "Let me know if there's anything you want."

Harry's whispered, "Thank you" was barely audible.

It was dark. 'Shoot me, Harry.' Edward's torn face flashed across his vision, followed by Warner's, a broad grin on his face and teeth bared. 'Shoot him, sir! Shoot him. Can't you hear him? It's what he wants.'

"I can't." He heard his own voice. "Not Eddie. I can't do it. Don't ask me, Warner."…. 'It's the only thing to do, sir. Can't you see, he's dying? You owe him that much.' There was a gun in his hand. 'Shoot him, sir!'

"Stop asking me!"

"Lieutenant! Wake up!" There was a voice, close at hand. It wasn't Warner. He knew Warner's voice. This was a stranger.

"I can't, I'm sorry, Eddie," Harry repeated. "Please don't ask me anymore."

"Lieutenant. Wake up." Harry felt a hand on his arm. "Lieutenant." The images faded. Harry opened his eyes, focusing on the face above him. Captain Grainger stood in the muted light. "It was a nightmare," he said. His voice was gentle and soothing. Turning, he took a glass from the table beside the bed and lifted Harry's head, helping him drink the cool water, then lowered his head again.

"That's better," he said and looked down the bed at the crumpled sheets. "I'll be back in a tick," he said. Harry felt cold. He tried to move, to shift his body, to pull up the sheet. His leg hurt. Then he felt the wetness around his groin and closed his eyes again. Oh God! He heard a whispered voice, then footsteps and a hand on his shoulder.

"Don't worry." Now it was a woman's voice. He heard the screen being pulled into place; felt strong arms on either side, lifting his limp, unresisting body. Between them, they changed him and the sheets. He kept his eyes closed; kept his mind closed. His leg really hurt now. The pain ground into him. He didn't care. As he was lowered back down onto the pillow, the nurse removed the screen. He opened his eyes. Grainger was standing next to him.

"Try to get some sleep," he whispered and walked away. Harry shook his head, looking out of the window again. The stars shone, twinkling through the ghostly, prowling clouds.

Grainger sat down next to him the following morning, a notepad and pencil in his hand. "How are you feeling now, Lieutenant? That was a rough night," he said quietly. Harry nodded. "Don't worry," Grainger continued. "We've all had them."

"Was that you, helping the nurse?" Harry asked, not turning his face away from the window.

"Yes," Grainger replied. "They don't have very many orderlies on duty at night."

"You shouldn't have had to do that."

"Why not? I've done far worse in the last three years, believe me. Anyway, she's a nice girl, Nurse Beck. Easily the best nurse here. I couldn't leave her to manage by herself. You're a big chap."

"What about your leg?" Harry turned, nodding down to Grainger's stick which was propped up against the bed.

"It's not as bad as it looks. The stick's just for show, really. Now, what about that letter?" Grainger asked. Harry shook his head. "You've got a family back home, haven't you?" Grainger continued. Harry nodded. "Well then, you should let them know that you're alright. Are you married?"

"No."

"Parents?" Harry nodded. "Well, let's write to them, shall we?" Harry shrugged. Grainger put the pad on the bed, holding the pencil poised. "What's the address?" he asked. Harry said nothing. "Lieutenant!" Grainger barked. Harry's head jerked upwards. "Your family will probably have been told that you're missing, believed killed. Until they hear differently, they're likely to think that you're dead. Now, you're going to bloody well write to them, and that's an order." Harry turned his head slowly and gave the address.

"That's better." Grainger's voice softened again and he started writing. "What do you want to say?" he asked. "We can start with 'Dear mother and father' if you like," he suggested.

"No," Harry said quietly. "Dear mother, father and Rose."

"Who's Rose?" Grainger asked. "Your sister?" He was writing as he spoke.

"She's my daughter."

"I thought you said you weren't married." The pencil was poised again.

"I'm not."

"Oh. I see." Grainger seemed embarrassed. "So," he continued, "we've got 'Dear mother, father and Rose'. What do you want to say next?"

"Just say that I'm in a German hospital. Tell them that I've been wounded, but it's not too bad."

"You want to lie, then?" Grainger looked up.

"I've become quite good at it."

"Do you want me to tell them that you'll be going to a P.O.W. camp."

"Will I?"

"I'm not sure. Certainly not for a while yet and they might decide your injuries are too bad. In that case you'll be interned, probably in Switzerland, for the duration."

"Do I get any say in where I'm sent?"

"You can request internment."

"Can I request that I'm sent to a P.O.W. camp?"

"Why would you?" Grainger asked. Harry didn't reply. "So, what do you want me to tell them?"

"Just say I'm a prisoner." Grainger wrote again.

"Anything else? Any messages?"

Harry thought. "No," he said.

"Very well." Grainger looked at him. "We ought to explain why the letter isn't in your own handwriting, otherwise they'll worry."

"I suppose so."

"What do you want me to tell them?"

"Just say that I've got a wound in my hand. Nothing more… absolutely nothing more." Grainger finished writing.

"All done," he said, folding the page in half. "I'll see that this gets off today, if possible. You never know, they might get it before Christmas. Is there anyone else you'd like to write to? We're allowed six letters a month."

"There's no-one else." He turned away. Grainger got up and began to move away. "Thank you," Harry said over his shoulder.

At lunchtime, the orderly brought a plate of thin stew, leaving it next to Harry. He looked at it, then looked away.

"Try some. It's really quite good." Grainger stood by his side again. "Let me help you to sit up a little." He put his arm under Harry's and pulled him up the bed, then sat beside him, the plate in his hand. He filled a spoon with a small amount of stew and held it out towards Harry, who leant forward, taking it into his mouth.

He felt himself retch. Grainger grabbed a bowl from the table and held it under Harry's chin while he vomited. When he'd finished, Grainger wiped his mouth with a towel, then helped him take a drink of water.

"Sorry," Harry whispered.

"Don't be. It happens," Grainger said, getting up. "We'll try again tomorrow."

The next day, Harry vomited again, but the day after, he managed to swallow a little soup, only gagging twice. When he'd finished, Grainger smiled.

"Perhaps we should stick to the soup for a while," he said. "It seems to go down better."

It started to snow on Christmas Eve. Harry watched the flakes falling, settling on the the window ledge and the branches of the tree. Christmas Eve. A snow-bear. Rose, touching its nose, her tiny hands clasped in his to warm them. Christmas Day. Rose in his arms, wrapped in his coat, sleeping next to his chest, his breathing timed with hers.

"Look on the bright side," Collins's voice interrupted his thoughts. "At least here we get better food, and there's more of it. In some of the camps, I hear they're just about starving."

"You hear an awful lot for someone who never leaves this hospital," Robertson said, laughing. They were sitting together at a small table in the middle of the room. A red-cross parcel had just arrived and they had interrupted their game of cards to unpack it. Grainger was sitting on his bed, reading a book.

"One of the orderlies was telling me about it," Collins said.

Despite their attempts to pretend that it was unusual or special, Christmas Day was really the same as every other day. The only difference was that, unlike most other days, they allowed themselves to focus on home and family and all the festive delights they were missing. So, by the end of the day, even Collins was sitting quietly on his bed, staring into the distance of memories and happier times.

Just before Harry went to sleep Nurse Beck came on duty to make her rounds.

"Happy Christmas, Lieutenant," she said when she reached his bed.

"Happy Christmas," he replied, not turning his head away from the window.

"You can look at me, you know," she said. He glanced round. Dark brown eyes shone in the dim light. "I haven't seen you for a few days. I've been working on another ward. How are you now?"

Harry shrugged.

"Well, try to get some sleep," she said, pulling the sheets up and tucking them in. She walked away to check on Collins.

Harry closed his eyes, overcome by tiredness. He tried to block the memories, but couldn't. Dark eyes, with highlights of brown, flecked and shining in candlelight. Almost black hair, curls untamed, lying loose across the pillow. *Elise*. Skin, soft to his touch. His fingers tracing about her waist, around her hips and down her thigh. His lips following, kissing across her stomach and downwards, tasting her. *Elise*. Her hips rising up to meet him. Her hands knotted in his hair, clutching him closer. Her mouth opening in a soft moan, her breathing heavy and erratic. *Elise*. Looking up at her face Harry could hear himself screaming. A tear, ripped from cheek to neck; her teeth exposed, tongue protruding. 'Shoot me, 'Arry.'

"Lieutenant!" Harry felt a hand on his arm. "Wake up!" A woman's voice.

"Elise?" He heard himself cry.

"No," she replied. "It's Nurse Beck." She held his hand in hers while he calmed. "Would you like some water?"

"Yes, please."

She raised his head from the bed, helping him to drink from the glass.

"Are you alright now?" she asked. Harry nodded. She went away.

The new year was two weeks old when Harry received his first letter. The orderly brought it in to him and for the whole day, he left it lying beside his bed. It was late in the afternoon when Grainger hobbled over to him and asked whether he needed help opening the envelope.

"No," he replied.

"Do you want me to open it anyway?" Grainger asked. Harry shrugged, then heard paper tearing. "Here you are." The letter was held in front of him. "Take it, Lieutenant Belmont," Grainger said firmly. Harry held the piece of paper and saw his mother's writing.

'Our dearest Harry,' he read, *'You cannot imagine our relief on receiving your letter. We've been thinking the worst since receiving the telegram, so to hear from you feels like a miracle. We have been truly blessed. Your letter arrived on Christmas Eve. It was the best Christmas present any of us could have hoped for. Once we had recovered, your father went straight round to William and Charlotte to give them the*

news. They were thrilled, naturally, and send their love. We're worried about your injuries and what care you are receiving and wish we could get you home, but we are sure that you will be bearing up well. You always do. Please thank the man who helped you write the letter. It was kind of him to do so, and thank you for taking the trouble to let us know that you're alright, Harry. Rose, of course, doesn't really understand, even though I've tried to explain...' The words blurred.

The page fell to the floor. *Of course Rose doesn't understand*, Harry thought, *she hasn't got the vaguest bloody idea who I am anymore. What does it matter to her whether I'm alive or dead, where I am, or what I've done – or not done?* He closed his eyes..

By late January, the snow was thick on the ground. Harry was awake long before everyone else, but then he hadn't been to sleep. He stared at the tree as the sun rose. It was a bright, clear winter's morning, so different to the one he was remembering. That had been a cold day as well, but foggy with a hoarfrost on the hedgerows... that was six years ago now. On this day last year, he'd been at Arras, where the Battalion had been digging new trenches each night. It had been cold, tiring work and he'd somehow managed to forget the date, until Edward had accidentally reminded him. Even then, just as the previous year, his friend had refused to let him dwell on it, had cheered him, reminded him of better times, and they'd worked together, helping the men get through the night's freezing work. Now, he had no such excuse; the date and its memories filled his mind.

Annabelle is dead. He could still hear the words, just about. He couldn't remember her face; not clearly; not anymore. There were just snippets, vague outlines. Rich auburn hair and emerald green eyes. Eyes... ice blue eyes... *Edward is dead.*

The others woke just before breakfast, which Harry didn't eat. He could manage most meals by himself now, provided his food was cut up for him, but today, he didn't bother. He didn't want to eat. He just lay on his bed, staring at the tree.

"What is it?" It was mid-morning and Grainger was standing by the bed. "Something's wrong. Something different." Harry didn't move. Grainger waited, then turned, moving away.

"It's my daughter's birthday." Harry's voice was little more than a whisper really. Grainger turned back again.

"Today?" he asked. Harry nodded. "Oh. That's hard."

Harry turned over.

"Do you have children?" he asked.

"No. I only got married a couple of months before the war started," Grainger explained. Harry looked at him properly for the first time, taking in his greying hair, neat moustache and gentle light brown eyes and realised that they were probably about the same age. "At least now," Grainger continued, "I should have a chance." He paused. "How old is your daughter?" he asked.

"Six," Harry replied.

"When did you last see her?"

"November, just before… just before this happened."

"I see. Well at least she knows you're alright now."

"She doesn't even know who I am. She was three when I came out here. I've only been home a handful of times. Each time it got worse and worse. By my last leave, she was actually scared of me."

"It will be easier when you get home, properly."

"What? With this?" Harry raised his stump. "She was frightened of me when I was whole. She'll be terrified of me now."

"What about your wife? Surely she can explain?" Grainger said and then paused. "Oh, sorry. I forgot. You said you're not married." He coughed, blushing.

"Not any more. My wife died." The words didn't hurt anymore.

"I'm very sorry. I didn't realise."

"Why should you?"

"When did it happen? If you don't mind me asking."

"No, I don't mind at all. She died six years ago, today."

"Oh, Christ." Neither man spoke for a while. Grainger thought it best to change the subject. "What did you do before the war?" he asked.

"I used to be a solicitor, years ago."

"Did you enjoy it?" Grainger asked.

"No. I gave it up." Harry replied.

"To do what?"

"My daughter and I moved to Cornwall. I became a painter."

Grainger looked down at Harry's stump, blinking back tears. "Oh dear God," he whispered.

The leaves were starting to bud on the trees, birds sang in the hedges beneath and the rain fell gently on the window pane, trickling down in slow rivulets which Harry traced with weary eyes. Occasionally, the sun shone, its golden rays, the hues of early spring, lighting the ward. Grainger and Collins were to be moved. They were well enough to be transported to the officers' camp at Breesen. On the day of their departure, Collins came over and shook Harry's left hand, wishing him luck, then went to sit with Robertson. Grainger pulled up a chair next to Harry's bed about an hour before the transport arrived.

"Well, Belmont," he said. "I hope everything works out for you."

"Thank you, sir."

"Do you know what, Lieutenant? That's the first time you've called me 'sir' since you arrived."

"Sorry, sir."

"I honestly couldn't care less, Belmont." Grainger paused, lowering his voice. "Can I ask you something?" Harry shrugged. "Who's Eddie?" Harry turned, looking at Grainger. "You call his name every night," he explained. Harry remained silent. "Is he one of your men?"

"He was a fr… a fellow officer."

"He died?" Grainger asked. Harry nodded. "You were close?"

"Yes."

"Were you with him when it happened?" Harry nodded again.

"Yes, sir. I was wounded on the same night."

"I'm sorry," Grainger said. Harry looked away. "Having to watch a friend die is the worst thing you can do," Grainger continued. Harry thought to himself that there were infinitely worse things, but said nothing. There was a pause.

"Sir?" Harry said, turning slowly back to face Grainger.

"Yes."

"I was just thinking. You remind me of someone I once knew."

"Who's that?"

"My Commanding Officer from the beginning, when I first got out here. Name of Johnstone."

"What happened to him?"

"The Somme," Harry said. Grainger nodded.

"What kind of C.O. was he?" Grainger asked.

"He was the best officer I ever knew, or heard of."

Grainger looked self-conscious. "Thank you, Belmont," he said. He recalled the letter he'd helped write. "Your first name's Harry, isn't it?"

"Yes, sir." Grainger reached into his tunic pocket and took out a folded piece of paper, handing it to Harry.

"When you get home. If you need anything – any help or just someone to talk to, perhaps. That's my address. Look me up."

"Sir?" Harry raised his head. "You've been so kind to me since I got here. I don't understand."

"Don't understand what?" Grainger asked.

"You don't know anything about me."

"I know enough," Grainger said, standing up. "Take care of yourself, Harry," he said.

"Thank you, sir."

Chapter Sixteen

Harry stood on the veranda, leaning on his stick. He looked out over the lake, towards the hills and fields stretching into the distance. The sun was hot on his face. Several men were walking in the grounds beneath him, some smoking pipes or cigarettes. Further along the veranda, Major Atkins sat, looking at Harry.

"I still don't understand what you're doing here," he said.

"Sir?" Harry turned awkwardly.

"By rights, you should have been interned. Sent to Switzerland. Men with injuries like yours shouldn't be sent to places like this."

"There's nothing wrong with this, sir," Harry said, looking around the converted hotel. It offered clean sheets, warm water, reasonable food and some freedom; a great many more creature comforts than Harry had found anywhere in almost four years of war, except during his leave at home, and in Elise's bed.

"Nonetheless," the Major continued. "It's not right. We don't have the proper medical facilities here. Didn't the Control Commission come to see you?" The Major was certainly persistent.

"Yes, sir."

"And they didn't accept you for internment?"

"The doctor who interviewed me said that our forces were advancing, and by the time they'd processed my paperwork and transported me, the war would probably be over."

"They should still have made the effort. This isn't really the place for you."

Harry cleared his throat. "I also requested not to be interned, sir."

"You did what?" Atkins stood up, walking across to Harry and looking up at him. "Why on earth would you do that?"

"I asked to be sent to the camp at Breesen. Unfortunately, they sent me here instead."

"What's at Breesen, then?" Atkins asked.

"Just someone I know."

Atkins looked at Harry, with a hint of suspicion in his eyes, then went to sit down again. "You'd better go and see the Colonel," he said, folding his arms across his chest. "He said that he wanted to talk to you."

"Do you know where he is, sir?" Harry asked.

"In the lounge, I believe," Atkins replied, closing his eyes.

Harry struggled down the stairs, taking them one at a time, his body twisting as he took every step. In the hallway, a group of men gathered around a noticeboard.

"What time does the concert start?" one of them asked.

"Eight o'clock. Straight after dinner," came the reply.

"Are you going?"

"Might as well. The last one was pretty good. There's bugger all else to do around here in the evenings. With any luck they've persuaded that chap from the Buffs to play the piano again. He was excellent."

The piano. Harry pictured his blond head bowed over the keys; his hands moving swiftly back and forth, the men singing along to the tunes, applauding each one as he finished. His eyes looking up, searching for Harry's, seeking approval. His eyes. Blue eyes. Ice blue eyes.

Harry turned away, passing through the wide door into the lounge. A layer of smoke hung above the heads of the men sitting in the armchairs scattered around the large room. The windows were all fastened tight shut. Harry coughed, feeling his lungs tighten.

"Ah, Lieutenant!" Colonel Hendy looked up from his seat. "Come in, come in. Sit down. We don't stand on ceremony in here." He motioned to a chair near the empty fireplace. "Cigarette?" He offered a silver case.

"No thank you, sir." Harry replied. The other men in the room, all senior officers, looked on.

"I've been meaning to have a word with you," Hendy said, taking a cigarette from the case and tapping it on the back of his hand. "How long have you been here now?" he asked, striking a match.

"About two weeks, sir."

"Yes, I thought so. Finding your way about alright?" Hendy asked.

"Yes, thank you, sir."

"Good, good." Hendy hesitated. "I've been thinking, Lieutenant," he continued. "I've been wondering what we can find you to do. There's talk of sending you to Switzerland. You shouldn't be here, you see. But if we can find you something useful to do, they'll let you stay."

"What do you want me to do, sir?" Harry asked.

"Well, that's the problem. I don't see what you *can* do, in your condition. What was your occupation before the war?"

"I was an artist, sir." A silence descended.

"Oh dear. I'm sorry." The colonel spoke first.

"It doesn't matter," Harry said, staring out of the window.

"I still don't see what you can do." Hendy's compassion was short-lived.

"Could he teach?" The voice came from the far corner of the room. Harry looked up. A red haired captain peered over the top of his book. "We could do with someone to teach art classes. We've already got music classes. Why not art?"

"Could you?" Hendy asked. Harry thought for a few moments, sensing that every eye in the room was focused on him.

"I suppose so, in theory," he said. He felt a strange ache in his hand, which confused him momentarily, because it was in his right hand.

Hendy paused. "Well," he said, "I'll have a word with the Kommandant. We'll need some supplies, I presume?" he asked.

"Just some paper and pencils, really."

"Yes, I don't imagine that we've got any budding Turners in our midst." The colonel laughed at his own joke and looked around the room. A few of the others joined in. Harry wasn't one of them.

Harry held the first class outside. Several of the other officers carried chairs outside and Harry asked for them to be set up facing the lake. He cast his eye over the scene before him. The still lake was in the foreground, bordered by trees on one side. In the background, the fields stretched toward the green hills, above which a few white clouds scudded across the sky. The class was a large one. A notice had been put up a few days before and a great many men had added their names to the list, eager to try something new to relieve the boredom. Harry asked them all to sit down.

"Thank you for coming, gentlemen." He felt self-conscious, leaning on his stick, his stump hanging limp, his sleeve sewn short, back to the elbow. "Firstly, I need to explain a few basics." He cleared his throat. "Drawing and painting isn't just about looking at what's in front of you," he said. Several of the men glanced around them, their eyebrows raised. "What I mean is, you don't have to try to paint every blade of grass, every leaf, every ripple on the lake. That's not how it works." They looked at the scene behind him. There was a man in the back row, with brown hair, a thin moustache and glasses perched on the end of his nose. He looked on avidly, his eyes piercing Harry's, who waited until he'd got everyone's full attention again. "You should focus on what you see, not what you're looking at. Think about how you feel," he continued. Again they looked at each other, except the man at the back, whose gaze remained fixed on Harry. He took a breath. "Of course you can just paint the trees, the hills, the meadow and the lake, if that's what you want. But it should make you *feel* something." Still more blank expressions looked back at him. He wasn't making a very good job of explaining this. To him it was instinctive, rather like breathing, except that, when he thought about it, he couldn't remember when he'd last breathed – not properly. They were all staring at him now. "Why don't you make a start," he said. "Try to get something down on the page. I'll come round and see how you're getting on."

They each stared down at the paper in front of them, then at the scene which Harry had just vacated. Some started tracing their pencils across the page straight away, others looked more thoughtful, squinting into the afternoon sunshine. Harry stood and watched them for a while. Then he began walking around, looking over their shoulders as they sketched. Occasionally, he would lean forward, offering words of encouragement, even where there was no hope of improvement. As he walked along the back row, he stopped, standing still and watching. The man with the brown hair, a captain, was a little younger than Harry. He sat, hunched over the page, so Harry could only just see what he was doing. It wasn't in Harry's style, admittedly. It was too disciplined, too controlled for Harry, but the man had talent, there was no denying that. Harry approached, looking over the man's shoulder.

"Try relaxing your grip a little, sir," he said. The captain jumped and turned his head. He said nothing, but blushed to the roots of his hair. "It will help," Harry continued. "The pencil will flow better. Try it." It was difficult to start with. The captain kept turning the pencil and clasping it tighter.

"Relax, sir," said Harry again. "Work with it, not against it." Harry longed to take the pencil, to show the captain what he meant. He felt a shrinking in his chest and moved away.

At the end of the lesson, the captain stood, picked up his drawing and moved away quickly, saying nothing to any of the other men. Harry looked after his retreating figure and began to collect up the unused paper and pencils, a few at a time.

The classes continued twice a week throughout the waning summer weeks and into the autumn. The captain gained in confidence, while they carried on with landscapes, but when they moved indoors and concentrated on still life drawings, he struggled again. Harry took a little more time with him, motivating him to use his flair. His drawing improved, but he still didn't speak, leaving each class quickly as soon as it was finished. Then one late October afternoon after the lesson had finished, Harry was standing on the veranda looking over the lake. The leaves were falling from the trees. It was turning cold, but he didn't care. He breathed in, trying to inhale fully, to fill his lungs.

"Excuse m-m-me," a voice said from behind him.

Harry turned with difficulty, seeing the captain with the brown hair closing the door. "Yes, sir," he said.

"I just w-w-wanted to thank you, away f-f-from the others," the captain stammered.

"What for?" Harry asked.

"All your h-h-elp. It's b-b-been v-v-very k-k-kind of you."

"It's nothing, sir. You're very good. You should carry on with it when you get home."

"I think it's helped. I c-c-couldn't t-t-talk at all b-b-before." Harry didn't answer. "C-C-Can't b-b-be easy f-f-for you, though." The captain nodded towards Harry's stump.

"It doesn't matter."

"D-D-Don't b-b-believe you."

"It doesn't. Nothing does. Excuse me, sir." Harry walked past the captain, opened the door and went inside.

It was a week later that the rumours started to whisper round the camp. Harry finished the lesson early. None of the men were concentrating. Even the captain was distracted. They left the room quickly, wanting to see if any more news had been heard. Harry stayed behind on his own, collecting the discarded papers and pencils a few at a time and putting them away in the corner cupboard.

"Have you heard?" a voice said. Harry turned. He recognised the red haired captain, who had first suggested that he might teach the men how to draw.

"Heard what, sir?" he asked, continuing with his task.

"The rumour is that the war will be over within a week or so." Harry didn't say anything, just collected a few more pencils and limped across to the cupboard, placing them inside.

"Aren't you pleased?" the captain asked. "It means we'll be going home." There was still no reaction. Harry piled up the papers, looking at a few of them.

"Lieutenant!" Harry automatically stood upright, staring straight ahead. "I'm talking to you. I'd like an answer."

"Yes, sir."

"Well, it's an answer, I suppose." The captain began moving the chairs to the edge of the room, where they belonged. "I've been watching you, Lieutenant, ever since you arrived here."

"Yes, sir."

"You do rather stand out."

"Yes, sir."

"Apart from the odd occasion in these classes, and your interview with Colonel Hendy, I'm not sure I've ever seen you talk to anyone in the three months since you arrived."

"Yes, sir."

"Could we try a different answer, Lieutenant?"

"No, sir."

"Very well." The captain smiled. "Have it your way, Lieutenant."

"May I go, sir?" Harry asked.

"Yes." The captain watched Harry limping slowly up the stairs. Colonel Hendy came out of the lounge and joined him.

"He doesn't change, does he?" Hendy said.

"No, sir. I was just trying to talk to him. He just doesn't seem interested."

"Did you know, he's not written home since he arrived here?"

"Well, he can't write can he, sir?" the captain pointed out.

"Someone would help him, though, wouldn't they? He'd only have to ask. I know for a fact that a couple of the chaps in his art class have offered."

"I still don't think he's that well, you know," the captain said.

"The problem is, I'm not sure he cares," Hendy replied, walking away.

Harry was sitting in the library reading a book. It was a bitterly cold and he felt it gnawing into his knee. Several other men were playing cards in the far corner of the room. Suddenly the door burst open and a man named Henderson, came running in. He was one of Harry's students.

"It's over!" he cried. "It's bloody well over!" Harry looked up. "Do you hear me?" The card players leapt up. Henderson continued, "The war! It's over." Harry nodded, watching the others run from the room. He looked back at his book and turned the page.

****

The train arrived in London on a raw, misty Monday morning. Harry opened the door and began to climb down onto the platform. Someone held their hand out to help him.

"This way, sir." A corporal in the RAMC had stepped forward.

"I can manage," Harry said.

"Very good, sir," the corporal said, moving back. "You need to go to that ambulance over there, sir. The one on the left." He pointed towards the vehicle at the station entrance.

"Ambulance?" Harry turned to look at the man.

"Yes, sir."

"I'm not going to hospital," Harry said. The corporal could hardly argue with him.

"I've just been told to direct you to the ambulance, sir," he said. Harry moved forward, the corporal walking a few steps behind him. Harry turned.

"Are you going to follow me all the way down there, Corporal?"

"I'm supposed to help you, sir."

"I see." Harry carried on walking, leaning heavily on his stick. "Corporal," he said after a few paces.

"Yes, sir." The corporal ran forward.

"What day is it?"

"Monday, sir."

"Yes, but what date?"

"November 25th, sir." Harry stopped. November 25th. A year ago to the day. The two men stood still, the corporal waiting for Harry to react or move, or say something. Other men passed, some on stretchers carried thigh high, others, like Harry with sticks or on crutches. Harry felt himself spinning, felt as though his body was rising above the crowded station, whirling in mid-air. A cloud descended over his body, blackness covered him. Then there was blood; so much blood, seeping slowly from the wound. Harry could feel the wet earth beneath his back, feel it sucking him down. Bared teeth, sinews and torn flesh. The softness of his fingers. Blue eyes, pleading, staring. Lifeless, ice blue eyes… and darkness.

"Lieutenant?" He heard a voice. It was a woman.

"Sir?" Another voice. A man this time. He was so cold. "Should I sit him up, miss?"

"No, corporal, leave him where he is. Just put this under his head, will you?" Harry felt his head being lifted, felt something soft placed beneath it. He opened his eyes. Indistinct figures leant across him, blurred and foggy. "Lieutenant? Can you hear me?" The woman spoke again. Harry tried to nod his head. "Don't move," she said. "Where's that stretcher, corporal?"

"I'll go and find out, miss."

Harry blinked, the fog cleared a little. He saw a face, a blue cape, a red cross. He moved his lips.

"Not hospital," he heard himself speak.

"Don't try to talk," she said. Harry's head hurt, but not nearly as much as his knee. "You've had a fall. You've cut your head open. Just lie still."

"No."

"Lieutenant. You must lie still. Wait for the stretcher."

"No," Harry repeated, then lifted his head. "Where's my stick?" His mouth was working properly, now that his head was back in focus.

"It's beside you, but you must lie still."

"No. Help me get up, please."

"No, Lieutenant."

"Then I'll do it by myself." Harry began to lift himself on his left arm.

"Oh, for heaven's sake!" Her voice was impatient, exasperated.

Harry looked around "You two!" he called out to a couple of privates who were walking past. "Come here, please. Can you help me to get up?" Harry felt hands under his arms, lifting him up.

"Thank you," he said, turning to the privates.

"That's alright, sir," one of them said. "Anything else we can do, sir?"

"Could you just pass me my stick, please?" Harry pointed to where it lay on the ground. It was put into his hand. "Thank you," he said. The two men departed. Harry turned. The nurse was standing, her arms folded, looking at him impatiently.

"Happy now?" she said. Just at that moment, the corporal arrived with two stretcher bearers. "Where have you been?" she snapped.

"We are a bit busy, in case you haven't noticed," the closer of the two men said to her. "Can I take it you don't need us anymore?" he continued, with a hint of irritation in his voice.

"It would seem not," she replied. The man rolled his eyes upwards and they walked away again. She turned back to Harry. "Exactly what do you plan to do now?" she asked.

"I think I'm expected on that ambulance." He nodded forward in the direction of the vehicle, its doors still wide open.

"And I suppose you're just going to walk over there yourself, are you?"

"That's the general idea, yes."

"Lieutenant," she began. "You've just had a very bad fall. You may not be aware of it, but you have a nasty gash above your right eye and on top of that your leg was badly twisted when you fell. You don't have to try to impress me with your bravery and strength. I'm not that easily impressed anymore. Let me get the stretcher bearers back."

Harry began to step forward. His leg took his weight, despite the pain that wracked through him.

"Don't listen to me then," the nurse said.

Harry looked straight ahead and replied, "I wasn't."

The doctor's office had frosted glass panels on two walls and a large mahogany desk against a third. A window on the fourth, overlooked the busy London street. He sat writing notes, while Harry did up his shirt buttons.

"Need some help with that?" the doctor asked.

"I can manage." Harry slowly threaded each button through its hole. He leant back on the doctor's couch and bent down, then pulled on his braces, hoisting them over his shoulders. They kept his trousers in place while he prepared to do battle with his fly buttons.

"I know you can," the doctor replied. "Trouser buttons must be the most difficult," he observed, watching Harry struggle.

"Yes, sir." Harry finally shrugged his way into his tunic, but didn't do it up. He was tired of buttons.

"Come and sit down," the doctor suggested. Harry picked up his stick and limped across the room, trying to control his breathing as he lowered himself onto the chair next to the captain's desk. "Alright?" the doctor asked.

"Yes, sir."

"That looked like it hurt."

"Only because I had to balance, sir. It's tiring."

"Drop the 'sir', please, Lieutenant Belmont. The war's over."

"You're still a captain, sir."

"I'm also a doctor," he smiled. "You're in a pretty bad way, Belmont. You were even before you took that tumble."

"I don't feel too bad," Harry said.

"Of course you don't. I believe you. And, in return, I expect you to believe that my name is really Sarah Bernhardt," the doctor said. "You're exhausted. You're underweight and neither of your wounds has really healed properly. Now you've added a head injury to your list of ailments. All in all, I think I'd really like to keep you here for a while."

"I'd rather not, sir. I spent over six months in hospital in Germany."

"Not that it did you much good. I suppose you'd rather go home would you? Enjoy your wife's care and attention, a bit of home cooking, build yourself back up again?"

Harry paused, looking at the floor.

"Not exactly," he said, his voice little more than a whisper.

"That's good then." The doctor's voice was resolutely cheerful. "How about a half-way house? A compromise? There's a convalescent home, run by nurses, in Shropshire. A bit of a long way away, I know. But it's very good. I think you're up to the journey, as long as you don't go throwing yourself around any station platforms again. It's ideal for you. You need a good long rest and plenty of fresh air."

"If you think so, sir."

"Well, I can't let you go home, yet. You're not ready; nowhere near. You will have to stay here for a couple of days while I sort out the formalities and while we just make sure that head wound hasn't done any lasting damage. If everything is alright, you should be away by the end of the week."

"Very good, sir."

"The nurse outside will take you to a ward. You can make yourself comfortable and I'll be round later to check on you."

"Thank you, sir." Harry got up, moving to the door.

"You're not very good with instructions, are you, Belmont?" the doctor said, returning to his notes.

"Sorry, sir?"

"Drop the 'sir', Belmont."

Chapter Seventeen

Winter 1918

"How long do you think he'll be here?" Richard Belmont rubbed his temples, looking across the wide table. Margaret sat by his side. Her face was pale. They'd had a long train journey, including several changes, which had taken almost the whole day. The station had been deserted and they'd had to wait for nearly an hour while the station master found them a taxi. A half-hour journey had brought them to Waschurch Convalescent Home, a large sandstone Victorian house on the corner of a street at the edge of a quiet village of the same name. Surrounded on two sides by gardens that overlooked the countryside, it was in an ideal situation for its residents. They now sat in the office of Miss Goodwood, the matron of the home and had just finished a welcome cup of hot tea. Miss Goodwood was a stout woman with grey hair and a kind, slightly weather-beaten face. Her light brown eyes looked at them from across the desk. Behind her, the wall was lined with shelves of books, untidily stacked. The room was well lit and the curtains closed, protecting them from the rain that beat against the windows.

"It's difficult to say, Mr Belmont," she answered. Her voice was gentle and sympathetic. "It very much depends on your son."

"What do you mean?" Margaret asked.

"Physically, his wounds are beginning to heal now, but he's still got some way to go yet." Miss Goodwood began, choosing her words very carefully.

"Weren't his wounds healed already? It's been over a year now since he was injured and captured," Margaret said.

"There were complications."

"What sort of complications?" It was Richard who spoke.

"He's very weak, but that's not uncommon with wounds like his. He's only been here for a short while and we haven't seen very much improvement yet, but it's still early days. He injured his head on the way back to London as well, and that hasn't helped."

"How did he manage that?" Richard asked.

"I understand that he had some sort of shock at the railway station and fainted. At least, that's how it was reported to me."

"Harry? Fainted? He's never fainted in his life. What sort of shock was it?" Margaret enquired.

"I don't know the details, I'm afraid."

"Has he been in a lot of pain?" Richard asked.

"Oh yes. His time in Germany at the beginning must have been very difficult, I imagine."

"Is he still in pain now?"

"Yes he is. We offer him treatment for his pain, but so far he has refused."

"Can't you make him take something?" Margaret asked.

"We can't force him to, no."

"How is he, in himself?" Richard asked.

"He's very tired and has lost a lot of weight."

"We can soon fix that once we get him back home," Richard said. Miss Goodwood looked down at her hands. "So, when can he leave?" Richard asked.

"Perhaps sometime in the New Year. I can't make any promises."

"In the New Year? Not until then?" Margaret looked at Richard. "I didn't think it would be so long. I thought he'd be here for a few days and then come home and recover there, with us. We can look after him, you know. We're his parents."

Miss Goodwood sighed. "Mr and Mrs Belmont," she said, patiently. "You are aware of the extent of your son's injuries, aren't you?"

"Well, he didn't write to us very often, while he was in Germany," Margaret said. "We received two letters while he was in hospital. But then nothing after he'd gone to the camp, except a postcard saying that he'd been moved. That would have been because they wouldn't let him write, though, wouldn't it? We know there was something wrong with his hand. He said so in his first letter and a nice captain had to write for him. Other than that, he didn't mention anything to do with any wounds."

"Can I get you some more tea?" Miss Goodwood asked.

"No thank you," Richard said. "What is it that you're not telling us?"

Miss Goodwood looked from one of them to the other. "I think you'd better prepare yourselves for a shock," she said. Richard didn't avert his gaze from Miss Goodwood, but reached across and took Margaret's hand in his. He felt her fingers shaking and tightened his grip a little. Miss Goodwood looked at the blotter on her desk. "Your son sustained a serious injury to his knee as the result of a gunshot wound," she began. "The doctors in London believe he must have attempted to drag himself back to the British lines. He must have tried desperately hard to get back, because there was considerable damage done to the knee joint itself, consistent with dragging the leg for some distance. The pain he suffered must have been extraordinary at the time. I'm surprised he was able to remain conscious, let alone move. The bullet was lodged in the knee for several days, I understand. The doctors in the German hospital removed it." She breathed in. "Perhaps... if he hadn't tried so hard to get back, things would be different... but we'll never know now."

"Can he walk?" Richard asked, surprised that he could speak.

"He has no movement in the knee, but yes, he can walk, with the aid of a stick. He manages quite well in fact, despite the pain, which is very severe, especially when he stands. That's the main problem really. He will always be in pain and will always need the stick. We really don't think there will be any improvement." Richard finally looked away from Miss Goodwood and turned to Margaret. Her eyes were brimming with tears.

"My poor boy," she whispered. Richard glanced back at Miss Goodwood.

"There's more, isn't there?" he asked. "There's something else?"

"Yes, I'm afraid there is," she said.

"More?" Margaret looked up.

"Tell us," Richard said.

"Your son received a second wound, to his hand."

"Oh we already know about that one," Margaret interrupted, sighing with relief. "That was the wound he told us about in his letter."

"Wait, Margaret," Richard said. "Let Miss Goodwood finish."

"The wound was very serious, I'm afraid. I understand that his hand was shattered and an infection set in. By the time Lieutenant Belmont arrived at the hospital in Germany, the infection had spread." She looked up. Their faces were frozen in anticipation. "I'm so terribly sorry to have to tell you this," she said. "I'm afraid that they had no choice. They had to amputate his arm at the elbow. It was the only thing they could do."

"Oh, good God, no." Richard cried, holding Margaret's hand still tighter. The tears finally overflowed down her cheeks.

"I'm so very, very sorry," Miss Goodwood said, her voice calm and sympathetic. "This must have come as such a shock to you both."

Richard blinked, swallowing hard. "We thought it was just a minor wound," he said. "Harry didn't say anything in his letters. We were so relieved to hear from him, so glad that he was still alive…"

"So you should be."

"But all this?" Richard continued. "All this pain. The shock of it all. He's gone through all of it alone? Without telling anyone?"

"He has a friend," Margaret said. "Edward, was his name. They served together. Perhaps Harry has been able to talk to him. Has he been in touch?"

"Not since he's been here. One of the nurses told me yesterday that she'd heard him calling out for 'Eddie' in his sleep. I suppose that might be the same person?"

"Yes, we don't know anyone else with that name."

"Perhaps you can try to find him?" Miss Goodwood suggested. "It sometimes helps."

"My poor boy," Margaret repeated, taking a handkerchief from her handbag and dabbing her eyes.

"Which hand?" Richard said, suddenly, looking up at Miss Goodwood.

"I'm sorry, Mr Belmont?" she asked, confused.

"Which hand? I mean which arm? Which one has he lost?"

"Oh, I do apologise. I didn't understand what you meant. It's his right arm."

Richard blinked again, releasing his own tears. Miss Goodwood looked away.

It took Richard a few minutes to compose himself. "I'm sorry," he said.

"Don't worry, Mr Belmont. This has been a tremendous shock for you both."

"It's not that. It's so unfair, you see."

"Do you mean the fact that he was right handed?" Miss Goodwood asked. "Well, you needn't worry, Mr Belmont. He's doing quite well with his left, you know. He can dress and feed himself with very little help. I understand from Lieutenant Belmont that one of his fellow officers in the German hospital helped him at first."

"No, Miss Goodwood. You don't understand," Richard said. "He is… He *was* a painter – an artist. That's what he did. It was all he ever wanted to do."

Miss Goodwood nodded her head slowly, recalling her question to Harry on the day of his arrival. She'd asked what he'd done before the war. His answer had been very simple, his voice distant, his eyes remote. "It doesn't matter," was all he'd said.

"Can we see him?" Margaret asked, her voice trembling.

Miss Goodwood hesitated, thinking, watching their faces. "It's rather late." She looked at the clock on the mantlepiece. "I understand that you intend staying at the hotel in the village?"

"Yes," Richard confirmed.

"Well, might I suggest that you return in the morning? You can see Lieutenant Belmont then. I think it would better for all of you. He tires very easily and the mornings are his best time of day."

"Can't we see him now, just for a few minutes?" Margaret persevered.

"No, Margaret. Miss Goodwood is right," Richard said. "Harry needs to rest and so do we. We can't go and see him now. We're in no fit state. He can't see us like this." Margaret nodded slowly.

Miss Goodwood got up from her seat. "I can't tell you how sorry I am," she said.

"We're very grateful to you, Miss Goodwood," Richard said. "For everything you're doing." He and Margaret rose and shook hands with Miss Goodwood, then slowly left the room. Their heads were bowed, but tilted towards one another in mutual distress.

The next morning, Richard and Margaret arrived not long after breakfast.

"Are they here already?" Nurse Stewart asked, seeing them walking up the driveway.

"Yes – it would seem so. But it's not their fault. They haven't seen him for over a year, nurse." Miss Goodwood went to the door before they could ring the bell.

"Good morning, Mr and Mrs Belmont," she said. "I'm afraid you're a little early. Would you like to come into my office. We could have a cup of coffee before you go in to see Lieutenant Belmont. The nurses are still doing their rounds at the moment."

"I'm sorry. We didn't realise," Richard said.

"Don't worry." She opened the door to her office, ushering them inside and showing them to seats.

"There's one thing I still don't understand," Richard said, once seated.

"Yes, Mr Belmont?"

"Well, I thought that amputees were interned, or repatriated. Not sent to Prisoner of War camps."

"That was the usual practice, I believe, yes." There was a knock on the door and nurse Stewart entered with their coffee. "Thank you, nurse. Just leave it on the table."

"Why wasn't Harry interned then? Or repatriated?" Richard asked, taking a cup from Miss Goodwood.

She stirred her coffee. "I understand from Lieutenant Belmont that it was partly because, by the time he was well enough to leave the hospital, it was quite close to the end of the war." She replaced the spoon in her saucer, but didn't look up. "And he told me that he'd asked not to be interned."

"He did what?" Richard asked, incredulous.

"He was given the choice, evidently, and chose to go to the camp," Miss Goodwood explained.

"But the conditions would have been better in Switzerland, surely?" Margaret enquired.

"I understand so, yes," Miss Goodwood replied.

"Why would he do that? It doesn't make sense," Richard said.

"Perhaps Edward was in the camp too," Margaret suggested. "Maybe Harry wanted them to stay together. That might be why Harry hasn't heard from him. He might be ill too."

"I did ask him for an explanation," Miss Goodwood said quietly. "All he would say to me was that he didn't want to go. He said he wasn't entitled."

"Of course he was," Richard exclaimed. "He's an amputee."

"I don't think he meant it like that." Miss Goodwood got up from her chair. "Shall we go along now?" They both put their cups back on the desk and stood up. Richard straightened his tie and Margaret brushed down her coat, then they followed Miss Goodwood from the room.

The corridor was lined with etchings of stately homes and churches, hanging from the oak panels. Chairs had been placed beside occasional tables, on which there stood plants and ornate arrangements of silk flowers. Harry's room was the last one they came to. Miss Goodwood paused outside, her hand resting on the handle.

"He knows you're coming," she said, turning back to face them. "But please don't expect too much. He's very quiet. He won't be as you remember him." Richard took Margaret's hand and they both nodded their heads. Miss Goodwood opened the door.

He was sitting in a high-backed armchair directly opposite, with his back to them, looking out of the French doors which led onto the terrace and the garden beyond. It was still raining and droplets of water were tumbling down the glass. They could only see the back of his head and noticed at once the specks of greying hair.

"Lieutenant Belmont," Miss Goodwood said. "Your parents have arrived." He didn't move. "Would you like me to help you turn around?"

"I'll do it," Richard offered, stepping forward.

"Yes, let your father help you," Margaret said.

"I can manage." Harry spoke quietly, not turning his head. Richard moved back again. Slowly, inch by inch, using his left hand and bent leg, Harry dragged the chair away from the window, turning it into the room. Margaret gasped, her hand moving instinctively to her mouth. Miss Goodwood frowned at her.

"I'll fetch you some chairs," she offered.

"Let me help," Richard said. They returned moments later, carrying two chairs from the hallway, which were placed beside the single bed that stood behind the door. Miss Goodwood left.

Margaret sat and removed her gloves before looking around her. In the furthest corner of the room was a large chest of drawers, topped with a lace runner and a vase of red silk roses. Next to this was a small fireplace, alight, the flames flickering gently. As her eyes circled the room, they finally came to rest on Harry again. His haggard, blank expression looked back at her. His eyes were hollow and empty. The hair at his temples was grey. His skin, once bronzed, was pale and drawn. He stared at her for an instant, then looked away. Richard removed his coat and, laying it on the bed, undid his jacket buttons and moved forward to Harry, extending his right hand.

"It's good to see you, son," he said, expectantly, his arm hanging in mid-air. Harry looked up, waiting. He held his father's gaze, until Richard finally coughed and lowered his hand, embarrassed. Harry raised his left arm and they shook hands awkwardly.

"How are you?" Margaret asked.

"Fine." Harry looked at her.

"We've been so worried about you," she said. He didn't take his eyes from hers. "We heard so little from you." Harry said nothing. "William and Charlotte send their love," she continued. "They have a little girl, now. They called her Anne." Harry nodded. "And young George is thriving." She was running out of things to say, but feared a silence. Harry looked away.

"How's it been, son?" Richard asked, filling the gap.

"Fine," Harry answered, not looking back.

"Do you want to talk about it?"

"No."

"What was it like in the camp?" Richard enquired.

"Fine."

"Did they give you enough to eat? Margaret asked, looking at his thin frame. He turned his gaze back to her.

"Yes."

"What did you do there?"

"Drawing."

"Sorry?" Richard exclaimed, looking at Harry's stump, lying at his side. "You did what?"

"I taught drawing."

"Taught them? Taught who, the Germans?" Margaret said.

"No, I taught the other officers."

"Why did you do that?"

"They asked me to."

"That's just cruel," Richard said under his breath. Harry heard and looked at him for a moment.

"Is it?" he said, turning his gaze back to his mother.

"Have you heard from your friend since you've been back?" Richard asked. Still Harry stared at his mother, but said nothing. "You know, your friend, Edward," Richard continued. Margaret noticed Harry's eyes glaze and then darken. "Was he in the camp with you?" Richard enquired. Harry didn't speak.

"I'm surprised he hasn't contacted you," Margaret said. "You were so close."

"I expect he's not home yet. That'll be it," Richard said, looking at his wife. "Harry only got back so quickly because he was injured. Most of the soldiers are still out there. That's right, isn't it Harry?" He looked across at Harry, who had closed his eyes.

Margaret nodded her head. "Of course, I didn't think. Oh well, Harry dear. He'll be home soon. I'm sure he'll come and visit you…"

"He's dead." Harry wondered if he'd said the words aloud, or if they were just in his own head. He really didn't know.

"I'm sorry dear? I didn't hear what you said?" Margaret leant forward. Harry opened his eyes.

"He's dead." It was definitely aloud this time, perhaps a little too loud. He looked at their faces. His father's eyes were sad, his mouth slightly open. Tears filled his mother's eyes, but she fought them back. It was obvious that neither of them knew what to say. Harry sighed, then leaning on his left arm, he sat up, turning to his father. When he spoke his voice was suddenly stronger, more purposeful.

"I may need to have access to some money – possibly quite a lot. I don't know how much yet, or when I'll need it. I won't know until I get out of here. Can you arrange it?"

"Yes. I can get to the bank by the end of the week," Richard said. "We can transfer the control of your funds back to you as soon as possible, if you want. You'll have to sign some forms."

"Fine. Send them through to me. If it can't be done in time, you'll just have to arrange it for me."

"What do you need the money for, Harry?" Margaret asked.

"It's personal." Harry said. He sat back again. "I'm tired," he murmured.

"Yes, of course you are, son." Richard got up. "We'll leave you to rest."

"We'll come back next week, shall we?" Margaret suggested. Harry said nothing. "What is it, Harry?" she asked. "Why do you keep looking at me?"

"Rose," he said. Margaret turned her head away, pulling on her gloves.

"Don't you worry about Rose," she said. "She's absolutely fine."

Richard pulled on his coat. "Yes, Harry. Rose is doing well. There's nothing for you to worry about. You just concentrate on getting better."

"Does she remember me?" Harry asked.

"She will," Margaret came and stood next to him, bending to kiss his forehead, "When you get home."

"How did it go?" Miss Goodwood was waiting for them outside her office.

"He's changed so much," Richard said.

"The first visit is always the worst."

"Yes, I'm sure it will be easier next week."

"You're coming back next week, then?"

"Yes," Richard said.

"Miss Goodwood," Margaret said, "Excuse me for saying so, but do you think you could remove the roses from Harry's room?"

"They're not real, Mrs Belmont. We find the smell of real flowers upsets the men. It reminds them of the smells out there, you see."

"It's not that," Margaret said. "It's the fact that they're roses. He's always been affected by the sight of roses. It's to do with his wife. She died, you see."

"But Mrs Belmont, he asked to have them put in his room. They used to sit on the table outside his door and he asked if I would move them inside."

"He did?"

"Yes." Miss Goodwood moved towards the front door. "Did you manage to ask him about his friend?" she asked.

"Yes," Richard sighed. "He's dead, unfortunately."

"Oh dear. I hope Lieutenant Belmont didn't find that too upsetting."

"He didn't seem to react at all, actually. It's strange really. They were so close at one time."

"I see. I'll talk to him later. Well, Mr and Mrs Belmont, what day do you think you'll be coming next week?"

"Shall we say Wednesday again?" Margaret suggested.

"Very well. We'll see you again next Wednesday." As they walked back down the driveway, their umbrella fighting the strong wind, Miss Goodwood closed the door, shaking her head.

Harry felt the rain soaking through his shirt, dripping from his hair and down his neck. It was cold and by rights, it should have made him shiver, except he was too numb. He stood on the footpath, leaning on his stick and looked up at the sky. There were grey clouds overhead and clear drops of rain falling onto his upturned face. He closed his eyes and felt mud, thick clogging mud, sucking him down. Then there was darkness all around him, surrounding him. It consumed him, pulling him further downwards, so far downwards that he knew there was no way back. He tried to breathe but there was a pain somewhere. He opened his eyes, trying to locate it, but nothing was clear anymore: there was just a haze of mingled colours and shapes. He wanted it to go away. He wanted it all to go away… for there to be an end to everything.

Then he felt something warm around his shoulders, hands, an arm, a coat, or was it a blanket? He couldn't be sure. He felt himself being turned and guided back towards the house.

"Come back inside, Lieutenant." He heard the voice, soft and gentle. It was Miss Goodwood. "You're soaked through," she said. "Nurse, go on ahead, please. Make a hot water bottle and a cup of tea with lots of sugar." Harry was aware of someone running away. He moved forward. Every step made the pain in his knee sear through his entire body.

"Mind the steps, Lieutenant. Lean on me."

"I can manage." The words came from his own mouth.

"You don't have to. Lean on me." He leant on his stick, but felt her take some of his weight. A few more steps, then suddenly the rain stopped. Now he felt cold. He heard doors being closed behind him. His teeth started to chatter, his limbs to shake. "Can you stand Lieutenant, just for a few minutes longer?" He nodded his head. "Let's get you undressed." He felt his braces being released, the buttons of his trousers being undone. His shirt was unfastened. His underwear was pulled off.

"Ah nurse, good." Someone else had entered the room. "Put the bottle in the bed." He felt a rough towel being rubbed over his legs and across his chest. Then he was in warm pyjamas. Hands held him, lowering him into the bed. Sheets were pulled up. "Nurse, fetch some extra blankets, please." The door opened and closed again. A chair was pulled up to the bed, beside him. His head was raised. A cup held to his lips. Hot sweet liquid. He swallowed. His head was lowered again. The door opened. He felt a weight added to the bed.

"Shall I put some more wood on the fire, Miss Goodwood?" It was a different voice.

"Yes, please. Then you can go back to your other duties. I'll stay with him. Thank you, nurse."

Harry opened his eyes. It was dark and the curtains were closed but there was a dim light from the fire. He felt warm right through to his bones. He turned his head, gazing around the room. He could see more clearly now and Miss Goodwood was sitting in the chair by his bed, looking at him.

"Lieutenant," she said. "It's very late. Try to go back to sleep."

"Why are you here?" he asked.

"I just wanted to keep an eye on you for a while."

"Was I outside?"

"Yes."

"Was it raining?"

"Yes."

"Sorry. You don't need to stay with me now. I'll be fine. I won't go out again." Standing up, Miss Goodwood stretched and rubbed her aching back. She walked to the door.

"You were calling someone's name in your sleep," she said as she turned the handle.

"Whose?" Harry asked.

"It sounded like 'Rose'."

"Oh."

"Who is Rose?"

"It doesn't matter."

Miss Goodwood closed the door behind her. "It does to me," she said quietly, as she walked down the corridor.

"I don't want them to come again." Harry was sitting up in bed, the day was overcast, but it had stopped raining. Miss Goodwood had refused to let him get up and dressed. She was sitting on the chair next to him again.

"Why?" she asked. Harry didn't answer. He looked at the wall above the fireplace. "You have to give me a reason, Lieutenant."

"Can you stop calling me Lieutenant?" Harry did not turn his head.

"Not really. You are still in the army, Lieutenant. If you weren't you couldn't stay here."

"Can't you call me something else?"

"Such as?"

"Mr Belmont, or just Belmont, or Harry: anything but Lieutenant?"

"Mr Belmont, then."

"Thank you."

"Now, why don't you want to see your parents again?" Miss Goodwood asked.

"Because I don't."

"That's a child's answer, Mr Belmont." He turned to look at her.

"Because they don't understand."

"None of us do. Not really. How can we?"

"At least you don't pretend you do. Can you write to them? Ask them not to come?"

"And what am I supposed to say? They're planning to come again next week."

"Tell them anything you like. I don't care. Just make sure they don't come again."

"You want me to lie to them?"

"Why not? I did."

Miss Goodwood sighed. "I could tell them you're not well enough. That wouldn't be a lie," she said. Harry nodded. Miss Goodwood got up. At the door, she turned around. "You won't be here forever, you know, Mr Belmont. At some stage, you will be well enough to go home. Then you'll have to face them."

Harry didn't look at her. "I'll worry about that when I get there."

Chapter Eighteen

Winter 1919

The taxi pulled up at the end of the driveway. Harry sat still looking out of the window.

"Here we are, sir." The driver turned, then climbed down and opened the door. "Would you like me to help you inside, sir?" he asked. Harry paid him.

"No, thank you." He shuffled across the seat, slowly putting his weight on his legs and standing upright, using the door for support. The driver handed him his stick. "Thank you," Harry said again. He looked at the house. Nothing had really changed.

"What about your case, sir? I'll take that for you, shall I?"

"Oh, yes. Thank you." They started up the driveway, the driver walking ahead of Harry. "Just leave it on the doorstep, thank you," Harry said. The man put the case down and turned. Harry climbed the steps, balanced his stick against the wall and reached into his pocket, feeling for some loose change, which he held out to the driver.

"No, sir. I won't hear of it." He took off his cap, bowing his head slightly. "I lost one of my sons, sir... at Gallipoli."

"I'm sorry," Harry said.

"The other two boys came back in one piece though, sir. We've been lucky, really, compared to some," he said. Harry lowered his hand. 'In one piece'. The words stuck in his mind.

"Thanks for your help," he said.

"It's my pleasure, sir." The driver went back down the steps, placing his cap back on his head.

Harry put the change back in his pocket and stood for a while looking at the door. Taking the weight on his right leg, he leant forward and rang the bell, then picked up his stick. The door opened after a few moments. Polly was standing inside, her eyes wide open.

"Mr Harry, sir." Her voice was a whisper.

"Would you mind taking my case, please?" Harry said, glancing down.

"Yes, sir. Of course." Polly reached down and picked up his case. She turned and walked back into the house. Harry followed her and stood in the hallway. There were fresh flowers on the hall table that must have come out of his mother's greenhouse. He felt sick.

"Mrs Belmont is in the sitting room, sir," Polly said. "Would you like me to show you in."

"I think I can find my own way," Harry replied, limping across the hall.

He opened the door. His mother looked up and leapt to her feet, crossing the room to him. "Harry!" she exclaimed, reaching up to kiss his cheek. "We weren't expecting you until later. We only got Miss Goodwood's letter, saying that you were coming home, in yesterday's post."

"Can I sit down please, mother," Harry said.

"Yes, of course dear." She guided him across the room.

"I can manage, Mother," he said. She pulled back.

"Yes, I know you can."

Harry sat down in the chair nearest the fire, placing his stick by his side. Margaret resumed her seat on the sofa. There were more flowers on the sideboard and on the table by the window. Harry felt the smell filling his nostrils and fought against the urge to retch.

"How are you, Harry?" Margaret asked.

"Fine," he managed to say.

"Your father will be home any minute now. He planned to come home at five to be here in time. We didn't expect you until at least six."

"I caught an earlier train."

"Well it's certainly a lovely surprise. We've waited so long for this day."

"Yes, Mother." Harry said.

"How was the journey?" she asked.

"Fine."

"You must be tired."

"Yes." The key turned in the door.

"That will be your father," Margaret said. "Richard!" she called, "Come in here!" The sitting room door opened and Richard entered, carrying his briefcase. Harry struggled to his feet again.

"What is it?" Richard said. He stopped in his tracks. "Why, Harry! We weren't expecting you yet."

"So I gather," Harry said. Richard walked across the room, hesitated, and offered his left hand to Harry. "How are you, son?"

"Fine," Harry said. Richard crossed to the sideboard.

"This calls for a celebration. Would you like a sherry, Margaret?"

"Yes please, dear."

"Do you want anything, Harry, just this once."

"I'll have a whisky, please."

"So, army life has given you a taste for it, at last, has it?" Richard smiled. Harry wondered briefly if he should tell his father that this was the first drink he'd had in seven years, almost to the day, but he said nothing. Richard poured the drinks, handing them out.

"Welcome home, Harry!" He and Margaret raised their glasses. Harry sat down again and drank his whisky in one mouthful. It had no effect at all. "You're looking much better, son," Richard said, sitting opposite Harry. "We got Miss Goodwood's letter explaining that you weren't well enough for visitors. We were disappointed obviously, but we understood."

"Yes," Margaret said, "but now that we've got you home again, we'll soon get you better, won't we Richard?" Harry stared at her.

"Yes, dear," Richard replied. "A good rest and plenty of home cooking and you'll be as right as rain." Harry didn't take his eyes from his mother.

"Where's Rose?" he asked. Margaret glanced at Richard, then back at Harry. He noticed their exchanged look.

"She's at William and Charlotte's for the afternoon. It's George's birthday today."

"Oh."

"She's coming back before dinner. You can see her then."

"Can I?" Harry silently acknowledged the bitterness in his voice.

"I spoke to her this morning, Harry. She knows you're coming home. We're all going to eat together tonight."

"Does she know about this?" He looked down at his stump.

"I have tried to explain, Harry. So has Susan. It's not easy."

"No, it isn't."

"You must be tired, Harry," Richard said. "Why don't you go upstairs? You can change out of your uniform. It might be easier for Rose if you're not wearing it," he suggested.

"I can't change," Harry said.

"Oh, do you need some help?" Margaret offered.

"No I don't. I have nothing to change into. Nothing will fit anymore."

"Oh yes, I didn't think, dear. I'm sorry. Well, we can go out and get some new clothes."

"I'll go by myself." Harry clambered to his feet and crossed to the door.

"We want to help, Harry," Richard said.

"Then there's one thing you can do."

"What's that Harry?" Richard asked. Harry opened the door.

"Get those bloody flowers out of here."

At seven o'clock, Harry opened the door to the sitting room and peered around. Rose was sitting on the sofa next to Margaret. Her auburn hair had grown and was tied in a plait down the back of her neck, with a blue bow at the end. She wore a pretty floral party dress that Harry had never seen. He closed the door quietly and stood completely still, watching her.

"It was so lovely, Grandmama," she was saying. "George had the most enormous cake. Aunt Charlotte had it made in the village. He had ever so many presents too. I hope my birthday is that exciting. There's only two more days to go now."

"It sounds wonderful, Rose. I'm sure you'll have a lovely day too. We've been arranging it for weeks," Margaret said. She looked up, noticing Harry for the first time. "Rose, darling. Look who's here." She nodded towards the door. Rose turned and looked at him. It was the look he'd dreaded most. In his parents' eyes he'd seen pity, concern, confusion, sadness. This was fear. She noticed his stick first, then her eyes moved up to the stump and, dwelling on it for a few moments, her lip started to tremble. Then she looked upwards still further to his face. There was no sign of recognition, just fear.

"You remember Daddy, don't you?" Margaret asked.

"Of course she does," Richard said. She didn't take her eyes from Harry's face. "Come and sit down, son," Richard said. Harry limped across the room. Rose watched his every step until he sat down, self-conscious under her gaze.

"Would you like a drink, Harry?" Richard offered.

"Whisky, please," Harry replied. Richard went to the sideboard. The flowers were gone. He handed Harry a tumbler of whisky, which he held for a while.

"Can you draw?" Rose's voice was very quiet.

"Sorry?" Harry turned to face her. She was still staring at him.

"My daddy can draw," she said. "He used to draw pictures for me. He drew all sorts of things. He drew Grandmama once. Can you draw?" Harry took a large mouthful of whisky, swallowing it down quickly.

"No, not any more," he replied.

"Then you can't be my daddy," she cried, burying her face in her grandmother's lap.

"I'll go," Harry said quietly. Putting the glass down on the table, he picked up his stick and slowly stood up. Richard followed him from the room.

"Come back in, Harry. Give her some time. She'll get used to you."

"No." Harry began climbing the stairs. "I frighten her."

"I'll speak to her again," Richard said.

"No."

"Harry don't give up. She's only young."

"I know she is… And she shouldn't be frightened. Not by me."

"She didn't mean anything by it," Richard said, talking to Harry's retreating back. He vaguely heard Harry's whispered reply:

"It doesn't matter."

"Happy birthday!" William boomed as he walked through the sitting room door. Harry jumped, unable to help himself, then climbed out of his chair. "Seven already," William continued. "A proper young lady!" He bent down to kiss Rose, then stood and shook Richard by the hand. Charlotte had quietly followed him into the room, the baby, Anne, on one hip and George, now four years old himself, holding her hand. She looked around apprehensively, her eyes settling on Harry. Charlotte stopped suddenly, the colour at once draining from her face.

"Oh, Harry!" she cried. She released George's hand, and burst into tears. Harry looked at the floor. William turned, looking from his wife, to Harry, then to Margaret, who quickly stepped forward.

"Let me take Anne, my dear," she said taking the baby from Charlotte, while William put his arm around his wife.

"There now, dearest. Come and sit down. You mustn't upset yourself," he said, his voice calm and soothing. He guided her to the sofa. Harry sat back down again while Rose opened her present from William and Charlotte. It was a doll with red hair.

"It's lovely, Aunt Charlotte." She ran across the room to the sofa. "What's wrong?" she asked, noticing Charlotte's tears.

"Nothing, Rose. Aunt Charlotte just had a bit of a shock, that's all," William said. "Why don't you go and play with your new doll for a little while."

"Yes, Rose," Margaret said "It's not long until tea."

"Would you like George and I to come and play with you?" Richard offered.

"I don't like dolls," George sulked.

"Well I'm sure you can make an exception, just this once," Richard said, taking the boy by the hand.

"I don't want to play with silly dolls," George pulled his hand away and walked over to Harry, standing in front of him, his eyes wide.

"George," William called, "come away!"

"You've only got one arm," George said to Harry, who looked up to find the boy's inquisitive face staring at him. He gazed from the stump and into Harry's eyes, then back again. "Where did it go?" There was a collective silence, a collective holding of breath and everyone looked at Harry.

"I lost it," Harry replied, his voice quiet.

"How did you manage to lose it?" George asked. "I lost one of my trains once. I can't imagine losing a whole arm, though."

"It's only really half an arm, technically," Harry said.

"I suppose it is, yes."

"Did you find your train?" Harry asked.

"Oh yes. It was under the bed. I don't know how it got there. I can't remember putting it there." He turned his head to one side. "Have you tried looking under the bed for your arm? You'd be surprised what I found under my bed, when I looked."

"No. I haven't thought of that. Perhaps I'll try later," Harry said.

"So, how did you lose it?" George persisted.

Harry coughed. "It was an accident," he replied.

"Oh dear. I fell down the terrace steps last summer and cut my head open. That was an accident, but Mummy was very cross with me and told me to be more careful."

"Well, Mummy was right. Did your head get better?"

"Oh yes. I had a bandage and everything. Will your arm get better."

"I don't think so, no."

"Is your mummy cross with you?"

"George!" William called. "Leave Uncle Harry alone." He got up and walked over, taking George by the hand and leading him back to the sofa with him.

"I don't mind," Harry said under his breath. "He's fine."

"Let's have tea," Margaret said. They all went into the dining room, where Mrs Cox and Polly had laid out a special birthday tea for Rose. She was especially pleased with the large cake which Mrs Cox had baked herself, with a filling of raspberry jam. Harry stood by the window while they ate. Once everyone was settled, William joined him.

"I'm sorry about all that earlier, Harry," he said. "George doesn't understand."

"George was alright," Harry replied. "I enjoyed talking to him."

"Really?"

"Yes."

"So, how are you?" William asked.

"Fine."

"Why don't you come and sit down with us and have some tea?"

"Eating is a bit tricky. It's probably best if I don't – not in front of everyone and especially not at Rose's birthday party." Harry raised his stump a little.

"Yes, I didn't think," William said. "How do you manage?"

"I get by."

"Of course you do." William looked down the garden. "You're still in uniform, then? I'd have thought they'd have discharged you by now."

"They have. I just don't have anything else that fits at the moment. Even this isn't very good, but it's better than anything else I have here."

"Oh, I see. I'd better go and help Charlotte with the little one. We'll chat more later, shall we?"

"Fine." Harry looked out of the window again.

Once tea was finished and 'Happy Birthday' had been sung, everyone filed back into the sitting room. Harry trailed behind, watching them. Once they were all inside and the door was closed, he turned and started to climb the stairs, his head bowed.

"Where are you going?" Margaret asked from below him.

"Upstairs."

"I can see that, but it's Rose's birthday, Harry."

"Yes, I know it is, Mother."

"Then you should be downstairs with her. You've missed too many of her birthdays." Harry turned.

"Do you think I don't know that?"

"Then come down again, Harry."

"I'm embarrassing everyone. Me being here is creating an atmosphere and I don't want to spoil her special day. It's not fair on her."

"You should still be with her, Harry. She's your daughter."

"Really? She doesn't seem to think so. She's seven years old and it's not just the birthdays I've missed – it's Christmases, Easters, holidays, new shoes, new dresses... For God's sake, I've already missed out on half her life."

"Give her time, Harry," Margaret pleaded.

"She could have all the time in the world, I wouldn't mind. I'd wait forever for her. But no amount of time is going to alter the fact that she's scared of me and no matter how hard I try, I'll never be the same father to her that I was before." He resumed his climb.

It was dark outside. The knock on the door was soft.

"Come in," Harry said. His father entered the room, but Harry didn't turn round. He was leaning against the window frame, looking down the garden.

"I wasn't sure if you were still awake," Richard said. "But I saw the light under the door and thought you might be."

"Has everyone gone?" Harry asked.

"Oh, yes. Ages ago. It's gone ten o'clock."

"Did Rose have a nice birthday?"

"Yes."

"Good."

"What are you doing up here?

"Just thinking."

"What about?"

"The same thing I usually think about on Rose's birthday, when I'm not with Rose."

"Yes, of course. I should have realised." There was a pause.

Richard cleared his throat. "I'm glad I've caught you on your own, Harry," he began. "I wanted to ask you something."

"What about, Father?"

"That telegram you sent, Harry."

"Yes?"

"It did rather take me by surprise, to be honest."

Harry turned sharply to look at his father. "You did manage to arrange it, didn't you?"

"Yes, of course. It seemed as though it was important. I made the arrangements the same day and then I went back into the bank a week or so later to make sure the money had gone through alright."

"Had it?" Harry asked.

"Yes." Richard heard the gentle sigh of relief as Harry resumed his gaze down the moonlit garden.

"Thank you," Harry said.

"That was a lot of money, Harry," Richard pointed out.

"No it wasn't. Not really."

"Well, it was a lot more than you could possibly have needed at one time."

"Yes it was."

"So it wasn't you that needed it?"

"I said 'no questions', Father."

"I know you did, Harry. But when you got back to England, when we visited you at Waschurch, you said you would need to withdraw another significant amount at some point in the near future. You need to be careful."

"No I don't. It's my money, Father and I'll spend it how I choose. Rose's future is taken care of. What I do with the rest of my money is up to me."

Richard was shocked. "I know it is, Harry, but surely you're not suggesting that you're going to spend all of it on this matter – whatever, or whoever it is?"

"I'm not suggesting anything yet. I don't know how much money I'll need – I can't honestly imagine it will be very much at all, considering how much I'm worth."

"Good," Richard sighed.

"But, Father," Harry continued, slowly turning back into the room, "there is something very important that I have to take care of and doing so may mean that I have to lay out a considerable sum of money. Please understand that I don't really care what you think. I don't want your opinion and I don't need your approval. If I have to spend the whole of my fortune to take care of this matter, then I will. If I have to borrow more, I will. If I have to sell everything I own, including Watersmeet and Holly Cottage and the shirt off my back, then I will do it, without a second thought and I won't regret it for an instant."

"Harry! You can't be serious."

"I've never been more serious in my life, Father... about anything."

"But why are you doing this, Harry?"

"Because I have to."

"I don't understand. I think you should tell me what this is about. We can talk it through. I might be able to help. We don't have to tell your mother. We can keep it between ourselves."

"I said 'no questions', Father."

Harry missed breakfast the next morning. When he came downstairs, he was wearing his greatcoat over his uniform. Margaret came out of the sitting room.

"Are you going out, Harry?" she asked. "If you want to go and buy your clothes, I can come with you. Rose is at school today."

"I'm not going to buy clothes, Mother. That can wait." Margaret noticed the knapsack on his shoulder.

"You're leaving?" she asked.

"I'm going away, yes."

"But you're still not well."

"I'm well enough."

"Where are you going to, Harry?"

"Not far."

"Why do you need to take a bag, then?" she asked.

"Because I don't know how long I'll be gone," he replied.

"But you've only been back a couple of days."

"This is important. I have to go."

"Rose is important, Harry," Margaret said.

"Rose doesn't need me. She has you. I have to go."

"Right now?" she asked.

"Yes, right now."

"I don't understand, Harry."

"You don't need to understand. I made a promise. I intend to keep it."

Chapter Nineteen

Winter 1919

The front garden was immaculate. Even in the depths of winter, the lawn was perfectly trimmed; the flower borders were free of weeds, anticipating the crocuses and daffodils that would appear in a month or two. A bare, woody wisteria hung around the black painted door, beside which was a small slate sign with white lettering, bearing the word, 'Vicarage'. Harry rang the bell and stood back a little, waiting. The door opened suddenly.

"Yes?" The dog collar was high and stiff. "What do you want?" His voice was gruff and abrupt. His hair was grey and swept back from his face. He wore glasses on the end of his nose and his lips were thin and pressed together tightly. He looked Harry in the face, ignoring the rest of his body. Behind him, Harry saw a small slender, grey haired woman appear from a door at the end of the hall, her hands clasped in front of her and a worried expression on her face.

Harry managed to speak with a voice of authority, finding his officer's demeanour from somewhere. "I have come to see your daughter, sir," he said.

"Who are you?"

"A friend. Well a friend of a friend," Harry said.

"She's not here." The door began to close. Harry balanced himself quickly but carefully, taking the weight onto his right leg and pushing his stick forward to block the doorway.

"When will she be back?" he said firmly, locking eyes with the vicar's.

"She won't be. She doesn't live here anymore. I'd like you to leave now." Harry removed his stick, and the door was closed in his face. He stood for a moment, then turned, limping back down the path. He was almost at the gate when he heard the door opening behind him again. He looked around and saw the small thin woman scurrying down the path. She held out a piece of paper. Harry balanced himself again, taking it from her. He opened it.

"It's the address of her friend, Constance," she said. "That's where Isabel went when… when she left. As far as I know she's still there. It's across the other side of the town, I'm afraid. Quite a long walk…" She glanced down at Harry's stick.

"Don't worry. I'll find it," he said. "Thank you."

"I must go." She turned back to the house, hastening back up the path and closing the door quietly. Harry looked at the piece of paper, read the address and shook his head. He opened the gate and looked first left and then right. He had no idea which way to go. On the opposite side of the street, a man was walking a dog.

"Excuse me," Harry called. "Could you give me directions?" he asked and started to cross the road.

"Stay where you are," the man said. "I'll come to you." Harry showed him the piece of paper.

"Can you tell me how to get to that address?" he asked. The man studied the address for a moment, then nodded his head.

"It's quite a walk," he said.

"So I gather," Harry replied. The man turned, facing into the road, and gave Harry directions.

"Do you want me to write it down?" the man offered when he'd finished. "I don't live far away. We could go back to my house and I could draw you a map if you want."

"That's very kind, but no, thank you," Harry said. "I'll be fine with the directions. Thank you for your help." He crossed the road and turned to his left, as instructed, hobbling down the street.

It took him nearly two hours to reach Constance's house by which time, the cold and the pain in his knee had begun to wear him down. A small terraced property stood before him. It was neat and tidy, the step was polished and the windows were clean, although the paint around them was flaking. Harry waited for a moment, catching his breath, then knocked on the door. It took a minute or so before it was answered. A well-built man stood before him.

"Yes, sir?" he said, taking in Harry's uniform and injuries at the same time. His expression didn't change, but Harry noticed that he stood erect.

"I'm looking for Constance?" Harry enquired.

"That's my wife, sir," the man said, relaxing just a little.

"Is she here?" Harry asked.

"No, sir. She's gone to the shops. You're welcome to come in and wait for her, sir, if you want to."

Harry was longing to sit down and was so thirsty his mouth felt like dry sand.

"Would you mind?" he said.

"Not at all, sir. Please, come in." Harry was shown into a sitting room, formally arranged with a small unlit fireplace. There was a sofa against one wall and a chair next to the fireplace, with a table in between the two and, by the window, a cupboard, on top of which stood a potted plant, its leaves wilting a little.

"We don't tend to light the fire in here, sir. Not unless we're expecting visitors. Just give me a minute and I'll get it lit."

"Don't go to any trouble," Harry said.

"Well, we could go through to the kitchen, sir?" The man looked doubtful.

"The kitchen's fine," Harry said. The man opened another door and they went through to a tidy kitchen, with a range along one wall, in front of which was a clothes horse, loaded with towels and undergarments. In the middle of the room was an oak table. The man moved the clothes horse, folding it closed and standing it against the wall.

"Excuse me, sir," he said. "Take a seat." He pulled forward a chair. Harry sat down, leaning his stick against the table.

"Would you like some tea, sir?" the man asked.

"Yes please, if you don't mind," Harry replied. The man turned, picking up the kettle from on top of the range, using a cloth to protect his hand. As he crossed to the sink, Harry noticed that he walked with a slight limp himself.

"I'm really looking for Isabel," Harry said, feeling an explanation was overdue. "Isabel Murdoch."

"Yes, sir?"

"I understand she lives here?"

"No, sir."

"Oh." Harry's disappointment was obvious. "Has she moved on?"

"No, sir. She never lived here – not really. She stayed here for a couple of nights, that's all. Connie has her address, though. She'll be able to give it to you, when she gets back, sir." The kettle began to whistle.

"You don't need to keep calling me 'sir'," Harry said, watching the man pouring water into a teapot.

"But you're a lieutenant, sir."

"I was. I'm not anymore." The man looked at Harry's uniform. "I'm only wearing this because none of my clothes fit," Harry explained. "I haven't had time to get anything new yet."

"You're still a lieutenant, sir."

"What were you then?"

"Lance-Corporal, sir."

"Lance-Corporal what?"

"Prentice, sir." He put a cup in front of Harry and poured a hot, straw-coloured liquid into it, offering Harry milk from a china jug. Harry took the jug adding a small amount of milk, declining sugar and sipping from the cup.

"Thank you, Lance-Corporal Prentice," he said, looking up. The man smiled. "I understand you were wounded? A leg wound, wasn't it?" Harry asked.

"Hip, actually, sir. Right back at the beginning. It was a short war for me. I was in the army before. Joined in 1912, you see, sir. Went over with the first lot at the beginning of August."

"I see," Harry said.

"It was a shrapnel wound... Battle of Ypres, it was, sir. The first one, that is. I was never well enough to go back. Once they'd finally fixed me up I was sent to Aldershot – helping to train the new recruits."

"I see," Harry repeated.

The back door opened suddenly and a woman entered. She was shrouded in a coat, hat and thick scarf.

"Good Heavens, Bob," she said. He got to his feet, taking her shopping basket and putting it on the table. "It's freezing out there. I wouldn't be surprised if it started to snow soon." She turned, removing her scarf and noticed Harry for the first time.

"Oh. I didn't realise we had company. Is this one of your old army friends?"

"No dear," Prentice said, helping her with her coat. "This is Lieutenant..."

"Belmont," Harry supplied, getting to his feet.

"Harry?" Constance said, looking him up and down, her eyes resting on his stump.

"Yes, Harry. How did you know?"

"Edward used to talk about you all the time," she said.

Harry sat down again. His name. Edward's name. It was going to be mentioned a lot in the next few days and Harry would have to get used to it – he must find a way to get used to it. Prentice looked at Harry's face and sensed something was wrong.

"The lieutenant has come to find Isabel," he said, filling the silence.

"Oh, well, she's not here," Connie said, starting to unpack her shopping basket.

"I explained that already, dear. I said you could give him her address."

"Of course – as it's you. It's in my address book, in the other room. I'll fetch it." She went through to the sitting room, returning a few minutes later with a small black book, a pencil and a piece of paper. She sat at the table and scribbled a few lines, handing the paper to Harry.

"Do you know where it is, sir?" Prentice asked as Harry got to his feet.

"No, but I'll find it," Harry replied, looking at the scrap of paper he'd just been handed.

"I'll take you there, sir." Prentice said.

"No, Prentice. I wouldn't dream of it."

"It's no trouble, sir." He'd already started to pull on his coat. "I'll be back in about an hour, Connie," he said to his wife, doing up the buttons.

"Alright, Bob," she said, then turned to Harry. "It was nice to meet you, Lieutenant."

"You too, Mrs Prentice, and thank you for your help." He and Prentice went out of the back door, through a small back yard and out of a gate. An alleyway at the back of the house took them onto a narrow street and Prentice turned to his right.

"This way, sir," he said.

They walked in silence to begin with, turning this way and that, down several streets which all looked the same. Harry struggled with pain and breathlessness. As they got further and further from the centre of the town, the houses became smaller and grubbier.

"Where does she live?" Harry asked, becoming concerned.

"It's not good, sir, if I'm being honest."

"Why didn't she stay with you?" Harry asked.

"It was difficult, sir," Prentice said. "We haven't got a great deal of space, you see. My wounds were still bad on and off, at the time and I was sleeping in the spare bedroom some nights, so that Connie could get some rest. I'm sure we'd have managed, somehow, if we'd had to, but there was a falling out with her father. She didn't want him to know where she was, so she moved on."

"Did he come looking for her?"

"No, actually, he didn't. We've never heard a word from him." They stopped outside a building. It was grey: completely grey. Even the windows were grey, with torn curtains and bare woodwork.

"She lives here?" Harry's mouth fell open and he looked up and down the tall building, three floors high.

"Yes, she's down there, sir." Prentice nodded to the basement. "Do you want me to wait, sir."

"No, thank you, Prentice. I can't thank you enough for your help."

"It was a pleasure, sir."

Harry balanced on his right leg, laid his stick up against the railing and held out his left hand, which Prentice shook.

"Goodbye, sir," he said. "And good luck to you."

"Thank you." Harry watched Prentice walk away, and turned. He slowly descended the basement steps. At the bottom there was a smell of rotting food coming from an open dustbin. Harry retched and swallowed hard. The door, which had once been white was now a yellowing grey. He knocked, keen to escape the smell. The door was opened by a petite woman, with an apron tied around her waist. Her hands were red and wet. Her hair was tied up, and looked dried out.

"Isabel?" Harry asked.

"Yes," she replied. She looked him up and down, recognition dawning. "You're Harry," she said.

"Yes, I am. Can I come in?" She stood to one side to let him enter. Harry lowered his head, ducking through the doorway. The room was filled with the smell of laundry. In the middle was a table, stacked with folded clothing and sheets. The sink in the back corner of the room was full of grimy water, a pile of crumpled linen lying next to it. Isabel closed the door. "How do you know who I am?" Harry asked, looking down at her, taking in the high cheekbones, the pale face and the red-rimmed eyes.

"Edward described you in his letters. They were full of you. When he was here, he spoke of very little else. I think I'd know you anywhere," she replied.

"Even like this?" Harry looked down at himself.

Isabel nodded. "Yes," she said quietly. "Your face… your eyes… they're exactly how I imagined them."

Behind him, Harry heard a faint sound; a vaguely familiar whimper. He turned round, slightly unsteady on his feet after so much walking. In the corner at the front of the room was a small single bed and next to it, alongside the wall, was a crib. Harry stared, hearing the sound again, a little louder this time. He turned back to Isabel, raising an eyebrow. She nodded her head in answer to his unasked question.

"I had no idea," he whispered. "Neither did he. He'd have told me."

"No. He didn't know," she said, lowering her eyes. "He was killed several weeks before I found out I was expecting."

"Yes, of course," Harry replied. The whimper became a cry. She went to the crib and lifted out the baby, turning back to Harry.

"This is Edward," she said, the boy cradled in her arms. Harry looked at them both. "Edward Harry," she continued. "I thought… I thought he'd like that." Tears pricked Harry's eyes. He fought them and turned his head away. After a few minutes he turned back again.

"Not Harold?" he asked.

"No. Edward only ever called you Harry." She looked at her baby. "Is Harry alright? I didn't realise your name was Harold. Do you mind him being called Harry?"

"Of course not." He moved forward, touching the baby's hand. "I'm honoured," he murmured.

"Would you like a cup of tea?" she asked. Harry looked at the corner of the room that passed for a kitchen. It didn't look as though she had any food, let alone tea or milk.

"I've just had one, thank you," he said. "I've come from Connie's house. She told me where you live"

"Oh, I see. How did you find Connie?"

"Your mother gave me the address."

"She did?"

"Yes."

"And my father?"

"He slammed the door in my face."

"I'm sorry."

"Don't be." Harry looked around the room. "What happened?" he asked.

"You mean how did I end up here?"

"Well, yes."

"My father threw me out, when I found out I was carrying Edward's child."

"He did what?" Harry felt his fist clench around his walking stick.

"It was late at night, so I went to Connie's. I had no-one else to turn to. But I couldn't stay there. I didn't want him to find me. I wasn't sure what he'd do, or what he'd try to make me do. I thought he might try to force me into having the baby adopted. I found this place and moved here a few days later. Connie didn't want me to, but she agreed to keep my address a secret."

"And you've been here ever since?" Harry asked. The baby started to cry loudly.

"Yes." Isabel paused, looking uncomfortable. "I'm ever so sorry," she said. "I need to feed him."

"Oh, yes." Harry said. "I should have realised. I'll make myself scarce." Isabel followed him to the door. "I'll come back in a little while," he said, taking another look around the room before going outside into the cold again.

Over two hours later, Harry stood in the doorway for the second time. It was already dark.

"Sorry I've been so long," he said, turning around and looking up the steps. "Bring those things down here," he called. A teenage boy started to descend to the basement, a basket under one arm and the other piled high with strung packages.

"What's all that?" Isabel asked, standing to one side. Harry followed the boy into the room.

"Put everything on the table," Harry instructed. He balanced himself, resting his stick against one of the two chairs and reached into his pocket. He found some loose change and handed it to the boy. "Thank you," he said. Isabel, still standing with her mouth open, closed the door as the boy passed through.

"What is going on?" she asked.

"It's just a few bits and pieces," Harry said, moving his stick and sitting down on the chair. "Just some fruit, vegetables, bread, tea. Nothing much."

Isabel looked embarrassed. "Nothing much?" she said. "I don't know what to say."

"You don't have to say anything," Harry replied. Isabel walked over to him, looking at the provisions.

"Thank you," she said.

"You especially don't have to say that," Harry muttered, turning his head away.

"Let me make you some tea, now." She began unpacking the basket.

"That would be nice," Harry said, undoing the buttons of his coat. The room was cold and damp. "Do you want me to add some more wood to the range?" he offered, although he wasn't sure if he could.

"I don't have very much wood left," Isabel explained, not looking at him.

"Isabel?" Harry asked, "When did you last eat a proper hot meal?"

"We get by."

Harry pulled out his wallet and removed a piece of folded white paper. "Take this," he said, pushing it across the table. "I wish I'd thought about it earlier. Tomorrow morning, I want you to buy some wood, or coal, if you prefer."

"I can't take your money," she replied.

"You can, and you will, Isabel. Either that, or I'll order it myself and have it delivered. It's up to you."

"Thank you," she said.

"I have a proposition," Harry said, watching her fill the kettle.

"Yes?" She sounded uncertain but didn't turn around.

"I have a house…"

"I may be poor, Harry," she interrupted, putting the kettle down and turning to face him. "But I'm not coming to live with you, if that's what you're thinking. You may have been Edward's closest friend, his only real friend, but he wouldn't have liked that. I don't even know you. It wouldn't be right…"

"I'm not suggesting that you come to live with me, Isabel," Harry cut in. "Come and sit down."

She did as he said, looking at him doubtfully.

"I have a house," Harry repeated. "I don't use it. It's empty. I want you to live there. You and the baby." He couldn't say the name.

"Is this your house in Cornwall? I wouldn't want to live so far away from here. At least I have Connie here."

"How do you know about my house in Cornwall?" Harry asked.

"Edward told me in one of his letters. He said you'd shown him drawings of it. He said it looked lovely..." She glanced at Harry's stump, her voice fading.

"I'm not talking about my house in Cornwall," he explained. "This is a house not too far from here. Just a short train ride away, in the village where I grew up. Connie can come to visit. She can come to stay, if you like – the house is big enough. At least you'd be away from here. You'd both be safe." He looked around him.

"I couldn't take your house, Harry. It's too much," she said.

"No. It's not enough," he replied.

She thought for a few minutes. "Even if I could agree, what would I do? Here, I can work. There are plenty of people who need their laundry done. It wouldn't be the same in a village. I couldn't make enough money."

"I'll give you money to live on."

"No," she said firmly. "I won't accept that."

"Very well. I'll find you work in the village."

"I'm not at all sure about this," Isabel said. "Where are you going to get the money from? You can't get yourself into debt for me."

"Didn't he tell you about that?"

"Tell me about what?"

"Nothing," Harry said, pausing briefly. "The money isn't a problem. I have more than enough to do this," he continued. "Don't worry about it." He thought for a few moments. "Just out of interest, Isabel, did he ever mention a farm that we stayed at in the summer of 1916?"

"Yes," she said, thoughtfully. "I think so. The one with the mother and daughter living there?" Harry nodded.

"What did he tell you?" he asked.

"Oh, goodness me. It was a long time ago now. I know he wrote me quite a few letters while you were staying there. I think he said it was a nice place. Yes, that's right. He described it to me. He said there was an enormous willow tree and a big orchard at the back of the house. There was a stream where he used to doze in the afternoons sometimes. Oh yes, I remember he told me all about a very rude officer that you met. And he told me that the daughter was very kind. She picked vegetables and cooked for you all and looked after you. He said she was pretty. I remember that bit because I was quite jealous at the time and wrote to tell him so, but he wrote back and said I was being silly and, in any case, she was spoken for, so I had no need to worry. You might not have known this, Harry, but she was in love with one of the soldiers, in your Company. I think he might have been one of the other officers, from what Edward said. He knew about it, but I'm not sure it was common knowledge. He said that the girl and this officer were trying to keep it a secret from the other men. They were very, very happy together, evidently. I can't remember her name now…"

"Elise," Harry said quietly, lowering his head and closing his eyes.

"That's it, Elise. It's a lovely name, isn't it?"

"Was that all he told you? He didn't tell you who the officer was?" Harry asked.

"No he didn't. Why? Does it matter?"

"No," Harry replied, opening his eyes and looking at the floor. So, Edward hadn't told her about his money, or that Harry had been Elise's officer. He'd kept Harry's separate worlds apart for him, right to the end. He'd never betrayed Harry's trust, even to Isabel.

"About this house of yours," she said suddenly, interrupting his thoughts. "Villages can be funny places, sometimes. What would the people there think about me having a baby but not having been married to the father?"

"They don't need to know. If it worries you, we'll tell them you were married. Look, Isabel," he continued, finally looking up. "If you really want to stay in the town, I'll buy you a house here."

"You'll buy me a house?"

"Yes, if necessary. But I think you could do with a fresh start, somewhere else and the village is a good place to bring up a child."

"I'll have to think about it," Isabel said. "I've always lived in the town. I can't just decide on the spur of the moment."

Harry said, "I understand. It's getting late. I'll leave you for now. I'll wait at the inn on the other side of town, near your parents' house – The King's Head."

"Edward used to stay there."

"I know."

"I won't be able to decide tonight."

"I came prepared to stay, Isabel. I left my bag at the inn when I got here. I didn't know how long this would take. I'm happy to wait there until you're ready."

"It might take me a little while to think about all of this. It's a big step."

"I know it is. I'm not going anywhere. You're not under any pressure, Isabel. Take as long as you need. Just contact me at the hotel when you've decided what you want to do. The choice is yours: the cottage in the village; or a house here in town. Either way, I'm not letting you stay here." Harry got up. "I'm going to go now," he said.

"But you haven't had your tea."

"I'm tired," he said. "My leg's quite painful."

"I'm sorry," she replied. "I should have thought." He went to leave. "Harry?" she said.

"Yes?" He turned as he reached the door.

"Why are you doing this?" she asked.

"Because he asked me to take care of you if… he… if he couldn't."

"And did he ask you to give me a house and provide for me?" she asked.

Harry managed a half-laugh. "Actually, he specifically asked me not to give you a house, or provide for you."

"But you're offering to do it anyway?"

"Yes."

"Why?" she asked.

"Because I said I would."

On the third day, just as Harry was finishing lunch, the landlord of the inn approached him.

"There's a young lady here to see you, sir," he said.

"Show her in," Harry said.

"She has a baby with her, sir."

"And what of it?" Harry looked up at the man, who turned away compliantly.

Isabel was shown into the dining room, clutching her infant and looking around her, a timid expression on her face. Harry stood, ignoring the meaningful expressions of his fellow diners. He leant over and pulled out a chair for her, with some difficulty.

"Please sit down," he said. "Have you eaten?"

"No, but it doesn't matter."

"Yes it does," Harry said, sitting down again. He raised his hand. "Waiter!" A young man with a spotty chin came to the table. "Lay another place please, and bring a menu for my friend." The waiter looked around him and hastened away, bringing back cutlery and a menu, which he placed before Isabel. The baby was asleep in her arms.

"Give him to me," Harry said.

"I'm fine," she said. "I'm used to eating with one hand."

"So am I."

Isabel's face fell. "Oh, God. I'm sorry," she said,

"Don't be. I've finished anyway. I can hold him, if you come round here and give him to me. Then you can eat in peace."

"Are you sure?"

"Yes." She did as he suggested, placing the infant into his arm. Harry adjusted his position slightly and the baby soon settled down, his head on Harry's shoulder. Edward's baby, snuggling into his neck; he could feel the hint of breath on his skin. Harry closed his eyes.

"Are you alright?" she asked.

"Yes." He opened his eyes again, looking at her. She seemed tired. "Have you reached a decision?" he asked.

"Yes. I'd like to accept your offer," she said quietly.

"Which one?"

"Oh. The cottage. Your cottage in the village. I think you're right. A fresh start would be good for both of us. I've been going over it in my mind and I think it's what Edward would have wanted… and in any case, I really couldn't let you buy me a house. It doesn't seem so bad living in a cottage that you already own. Once I get back on my feet, I could pay you rent."

"No. You're not paying me anything," Harry said firmly. The waiter returned, a notepad in his hand and pencil poised. Isabel ordered a bowl of soup and he disappeared again. "How soon can you be ready to leave?" Harry asked, changing the subject.

"A couple of days," she replied.

"Can you give me a fortnight?" he asked.

"Yes."

"I'm really sorry to delay you," Harry said. "But the house has been empty for six years. It's going to need some work."

"Will a fortnight be long enough? I can wait longer, if necessary."

"No a fortnight will be fine. I can arrange it."

"I don't have any furniture," Isabel said.

"The house is already furnished," he replied. "But if you don't like any pieces, I'll replace them."

"Really, Harry, I'm sure it will be perfectly alright." Isabel's soup arrived and she began to eat. "If you don't mind me asking," she said, "Why do you have a completely furnished house that's been empty for six years?"

"Did Ed.... Did he ever tell you about my wife?"

"Yes, I think he may have done once. He said that you had a daughter. Rose, isn't it?" Harry nodded. "I asked him about your wife and he mentioned that she had died."

"Well, the house was ours. When we were married, that's where we lived."

"And you haven't sold it, or rented it out? It's just stood there empty, all this time?"

"Yes."

"Why?" Isabel asked.

"I didn't know what to do with it."

Isabel had eaten quickly. She pushed away her empty soup bowl.

"Do you want something else?" Harry asked.

"No, thank you," she replied.

"You can have anything you want," Harry said. "I can get the waiter back."

"No, Harry. People are looking. I'd rather just go."

"Isabel," Harry said, "I couldn't give a damn if people are looking. Let them look. If you're hungry, have something else to eat."

"I'm not hungry, thank you. The soup was enough." The baby stirred. "I'll take him back now, shall I?"

"It might be best," Harry said. She got up and took the infant from him. Harry stood, taking his stick.

"I'll be going," Isabel said. Harry took his wallet from his tunic pocket. A hushed silence descended on the room. Harry looked around slowly, allowing the other diners to absorb his glare and then turned back to Isabel. Removing several notes from his wallet, he held them out to her.

"No," she whispered. "I still have some left over from the money you gave me the other day."

"Please don't argue with me, Isabel. This will tide you over for now. Do you need any more to cover the rent or anything?"

"No. I don't need any more money. We have enough."

"In that case, buy the baby some clothes. Treat yourself. Do whatever you want with it." The other diners were starting to whisper. She took the notes from him.

"Thank you," she said.

"Don't. Don't say that. I'll come back to fetch you in two weeks."

"We'll be ready."

Chapter Twenty

Winter 1919

"You want it done by the seventeenth at the latest, sir?" The builder was standing in the middle of the sitting room at Holly Cottage. Harry, who was stood alongside, had given him a long list of work to be carried out. "That won't be cheap."

"I didn't ask how much it would cost. I asked if you could complete the work in time. If you can't, I'll find someone who can." Harry was abrupt.

"I can get it done, sir. I'll just need to take on some extra labourers. Not that there's any shortage at the moment."

"You understand what I want?"

"Sand back and re-varnish all the floors. Redecorate throughout with plain colours. Clean up the kitchen and replace the sink, replace the flooring. Fix the roof. Replace the broken windows at the back and mend the back door."

"I also want the garden cleared."

"Yes, sir."

"Can you start right away?"

"Don't you want an estimate of the costs first?"

"No. I want the work done."

"Very good, sir. We'll be here first thing in the morning." He left with a broad grin on his face.

Alone in the cottage, Harry looked around. All the furniture was covered with white dust sheets, as it had been left when he'd closed up the house six years ago. He limped out into the hallway and slowly up the stairs. He knew exactly where he wanted to go, just for one last look before they painted over it. Opening the door, his heart sank. The roses had faded, their colours no longer vibrant. In the corner, the dressing table was covered. He sat on the stool and pulled off the sheet. It had been stripped of its contents before Harry had left. All the pots, creams, brushes and mirrors, packed into a box and disposed of. He didn't know where. He got up again. The bed, unmade, the mattress bare, still stood in the middle of the room. Carefully he sat on the edge, then lowered himself down, lying back and looking up at the ceiling. He closed his eyes, remembering. The night they'd returned from their honeymoon, he'd carried her up the stairs, her arms around his neck, her head on his chest. They'd undressed together and, with her nightdress on, she'd curled up next to him, nestling in his arms. He'd listened to her breathing, his fingers caressing her neck. Lying there on the mattress, he could still smell her hair, even after all this time. Opening his eyes, he pulled himself up. Sitting again, he looked down at himself, thankful that at least she hadn't survived to see him like this. At the door, he turned around, taking one last look at the room.

"Goodbye, Bella," he whispered.

Harry supervised the work himself, visiting every day to ensure everything was progressing to plan. On the Saturday before Harry was due to collect Isabel he asked his mother and father to accompany him to the cottage.

"I want to explain where I've been going for the last week or so," he said as they got to the gate.

"You've been coming here?" Margaret asked. The builders had finished, but their work was evident. "Are you going to sell it?" she continued.

"No," Harry replied.

"Are you moving back in here, then?" Richard said.

"No. Let's go inside and talk."

In the sitting room, the floor was varnished and shining. The walls were painted pale yellow and all the furniture had been uncovered. An upright piano had replaced the sideboard, which had been moved into the dining room.

"I've had one of Susan's sisters, Mary, coming in to help with some of the cleaning," Harry explained. "As well as the decorators and the builders, obviously."

"I don't really understand why," Richard said. "If you're not selling and you're not going to live here. Are you going to take on tenants?"

"No. Sit down." They perched on the edge of the sofa. "Do you remember me writing to you about Isabel during the war?"

Margaret looked confused for a minute, then said, "Do you mean Edward's fiancée?"

"Yes."

"What about her?"

"She's going to be moving in here next week. I'm going to fetch her on Monday."

"I thought she lived with her parents. Isn't her father a vicar, or something?" Margaret enquired.

"They've fallen out. But that's not really the point. That's not why I asked you here. We need to talk and I wanted to do it away from everyone else. I don't want anyone overhearing our conversation."

They both looked at him.

"She has a baby," Harry waited for a reaction. "It's Edward's baby." He noticed his father's eyebrows rise. "I'm telling you this, because I know that you're aware that Isabel and Edward weren't married. However, no-one else in the village will know that and I want it kept that way. I don't want either of you to reveal the truth. I've purchased a wedding ring, which Isabel will wear and the story is that she and Edward were married on his last leave and that's when the child was conceived. She's his widow. She'll be known as Mrs Wilson and I'm trusting you to keep her secret."

"Very well, Harry. If that's what you want," Richard said.

"It is."

"Did Edward know?" Margaret asked.

"Know what?"

"About the baby?" She looked at him.

"No. She only found out after… after he died."

"What about her family? Can't they help her?" Richard asked.

"Her father threw her out."

"The poor girl," Margaret said.

"Is this what you wanted all the money for?" Richard asked.

Harry looked at his father.

"Yes, partly," he said quietly. "There's one other thing," he continued. "There are some papers I need you to draw up for me."

"Yes?"

Harry explained what he wanted, going through all the details very carefully. His parents were surprised.

"Are you sure about this, Harry?" Richard asked.

"Yes. I want Isabel and Edward to be secure."

"Edward?" Margaret was bewildered.

"Isabel's son. He's called Edward. Will you be able to deal with all this, father? I need it done by Monday."

"Yes, Harry. I can arrange it, if that's what you really want."

"It is."

It was late on Monday afternoon by the time Harry and Isabel got to the cottage. Their journey had been difficult. Harry had struggled to find a porter to help them at the station and then they couldn't locate a taxi. The baby was tired and grisly by the time they arrived. The driver had deposited the cases on the doorstep and Harry managed to open the door, with a little difficulty. His knee was causing him a lot of pain.

"Mary?" he called from the threshold. The girl appeared from the kitchen, her plain uniform just covering her round figure.

"Yes, Mr Belmont." Harry had managed to get Mary to dispense with the title of 'sir' much quicker than Susan. "Oh, let me help," she said, rushing forward to pick up the cases at Harry's feet. They all moved into the hallway and Isabel closed the door behind them. "I'll take these along upstairs, shall I?" she said. Isabel didn't seem to know what to say.

"Yes thank you, Mary," Harry said. "The smaller case can go in the nursery. The larger one belongs to Mrs Wilson. Put it in the room opposite." The girl went up the stairs.

"Who's she?" Isabel whispered. Harry directed Isabel into the sitting room.

"She's your maid." Harry said, taking off his coat and throwing it over the back of the sofa. He sat down. "Give me the baby for a minute and take your coat off." Isabel did as he said.

"I don't need a maid," she said.

"You do if you're going to work. She'll look after the baby while you're working. If you don't want Mary here, then you can't work, and I'll have to support you, which you say you don't want." Mary came back into the room.

"Mary," Harry said. "Can you take the baby upstairs. Mrs Wilson will be up in a few minutes. We just have a few things to discuss."

"Yes, Mr Belmont," she said, taking the baby from him and leaving the room again.

Isabel waited for the door to close then went to sit near the fire.

"Who pays for the maid?" she asked.

"I do."

"So you're still supporting me, then."

"The maid comes with the house, Isabel," Harry said firmly.

"I can't argue with you, can I?"

"No."

"I've never had a maid though, Harry. I won't know what to do, or how to talk to her."

"She's never actually been a maid before, either. You can learn together." He was so tired, but he wanted to get through everything in one night, if possible. Then he could stop. Then everything could stop and it would all be over. "I've been thinking about what you can do by way of a job," he continued.

"Yes?"

"Ed… Edward told me once that you were a very good pianist. He said that you'd taught him how to play."

"Well, not exactly. He was being generous. He could already play a little. I just helped him to play better."

"I wondered if you'd want to give piano lessons? There are plenty of children in the village, but there's no-one here to teach any sort of music. I did wonder about approaching the school to see if you could work there, but while the baby is young, it might be easier if you worked here, I suppose?"

"Yes."

"What do you think?"

"I suppose I could do it. I've never taught other people before, but I could try. Would I be able to earn enough money though?"

"I'm not sure. Possibly not to start with." Harry paused. His head was pounding. "Look Isabel, I know you don't want me to give you any money, but I have to know that you're both safe. That's what he wanted, so that's what I have to do. I've decided to make you a monthly allowance to supplement your income."

"But we agreed that I would work, Harry. You said."

"I know, Isabel." He was getting really tired now and was finding it harder to disguise. "You can still have your job and earn your own money. The allowance isn't a lot, but it's enough to cover the basics. I'm not going to argue with you. I've already made the arrangements." Harry got up. "It's been a long day," he said, leaning against the sofa and picking up his coat. "Before I go, though, I have something I want to give you."

"You've done enough, Harry. No more, please." He handed her a brown envelope, which he'd taken from his inside pocket. "What is it?" Isabel asked.

"It's just some documents. You can look at them later – or tomorrow."

"What are they about?"

"The house."

"Which house?"

"This one."

"I don't understand," Isabel said. The envelope hung from her hand.

"It's yours."

"What is?"

"The house."

"What are you talking about, Harry?"

"I've signed the house over to you. It belongs to you now. The papers in that envelope confirm it."

"You can't do that, Harry." He could see her tears, even in the dim light of the sitting room.

"I already have."

"No, Harry. I agreed to live here; I was willing to pay you rent. I didn't agree to take the house from you."

"You're not taking it. I'm giving it to you." He decided to get it all over with in one go. "I've also put some money in trust, for the baby."

"I don't understand what you mean, Harry. This is all too much."

"You're tired, Isabel. We both are. All you need to know at the moment is that this house is yours forever; you need have no worries about money and the baby's future is secure. The paperwork for everything is in that envelope and I'll explain it all properly another time." He pulled on his coat. As he did up the buttons, he looked at her. "There's one other thing," he said. "If you ever need anything… anything at all – it doesn't matter what it is – you must ask me. If I'm not available, or you can't find me for some reason, you're to go to my father. Will you promise me?"

"I can't keep taking things from you, Harry," she said.

"Isabel," he said, his voice betraying his exhaustion, "please, will you just promise me that you'll come to me or my father if you need anything?"

"Very well, Harry. I promise."

"Good. I'm very tired, Isabel. Do you have everything you need for now?" he asked.

"Yes, thank you, Harry," she replied.

"Then, if you don't mind, I'll be leaving." He walked towards the door.

"Harry!" she cried. He stopped, leaning heavily on his stick, but didn't turn around.

"Yes Isabel," he sighed.

"You've done so much for us, but only three weeks ago, you'd never even met us. Why are you doing this?"

"Because I promised him that I'd take care of you," Harry said. "He asked me to and I promised." He looked up at the ceiling, moving slowly forward. She followed him into the hallway. He opened the front door.

As Harry crossed the threshold, Isabel spoke again. "Edward wrote me a letter the day he died," she said softly, "Although I only got it much later, of course. He told me that you'd all been in a raid that day, or an attack, or something. He didn't give me any details but he said you'd saved his life. In fact, he said you'd saved everyone's life."

"Not everyone's," Harry mumbled.

"Either way, Harry, he thought you were a hero."

"He was wrong."

"No he wasn't, Harry. He said in that letter, that you were the only man in the world that he'd ever completely trusted. I didn't understand what he meant at the time, but I think I do now. And I also think he was right." Harry didn't turn round. He couldn't. He felt the tears prick his eyes. He felt fingers close around his; saw a torn cheek, a shattered jaw and ice blue eyes. As the door closed behind him, he felt himself beginning to break and finally let the tears flood out of him.

****

Harry didn't visit the next day. He sent a note round to Isabel explaining that he was very tired and that his leg hurt. He said he would try to get round before the end of the week.

It was on Friday morning that he finally knocked on the door. Mary took his coat and showed him into the sitting room, where Isabel was sitting by the fire with Edward on her lap.

"Hello, Harry," she said, getting up. "Are you feeling better?"

"Yes, thank you. How are you?"

"We're very well, thank you. Come and sit down." Mary was hovering by the door.

"Would you like coffee, Mrs Wilson?" she asked.

"Yes please, Mary," Isabel said. When the door had closed, she turned to Harry. "We're getting along just fine, Mary and I," she said, "Now that we've both got over our nerves. She's very good, you know."

"I'm glad," Harry replied, his voice monotone.

"You look tired, Harry."

"Do I?" He stared at the fire. "Is there anything you need?"

"No. We're fine. Are you sure that you're feeling alright?"

"Yes."

"I was hoping you'd visit," Isabel said. "There's something I wanted to ask you. I've been wanting to ask you since you first came to see me."

"What is it?" Harry asked.

She spoke very quietly. "Can you tell me how he died?"

Harry looked at her. "Do you really want to know?"

"Yes I do. I keep imagining all sorts of terrible things. I need to know the truth. Please tell me."

"If you insist." Harry sighed. He got up, picked up his stick and walked to the window, looking out over the front garden. The trees on the other side of the road were bare, the lawn was neatly cut, the roses trimmed back. He thought of the mud, the shell holes, the trees like poles pointing to the sky, the bodies lying where they'd fallen, some weeks before, rotting black. He closed his eyes and tried to breathe. "We were…," he started, his voice vague and emotionless. "We were attacking a trench. Pelican trench, it was called. We had to cross a stretch of ground first. It was dark, just before eleven o'clock at night. The Germans set off a flare, then they started firing." He paused. "Edward was shot."

"Where was he shot?"

"Are you sure you want to know all of this, Isabel?" he asked.

"Yes."

Harry sighed again. "He was shot… in the head." He heard the sob behind him and waited.

"Did he suffer? Was he in pain?" she asked eventually.

Another pause. "No."

"Did he say anything?"

An even longer pause. "No."

"Were you with him?"

"Yes."

"I'm sure that was a great relief for him." Harry didn't answer. The door opened and Mary came in with the coffee. She put the tray down in front of Isabel.

"Would you like me to pour, Mrs Wilson?" she asked.

"No thank you," Isabel sniffed. "We'll manage." Mary left.

"I have to go," Harry said, turning round, but not looking at Isabel.

"But you haven't had your coffee."

"No."

"Did you mind? Telling me about Edward, I mean?"

"No," he lied… again.

Chapter Twenty-one

Spring 1919

"He still calls Edward's name, you know?" Margaret said to Richard as they sat together after dinner.

"I know. I heard him last night."

"It's every night, Richard and it has been for months now. Do you think it will ever stop?"

"I'm sure it will, one day. He's been through a lot," Richard said.

"He needs to move forward. He needs to get on with his life, but all he does is stay up in his room, or wander around the garden and sit under the apple tree."

"Perhaps I can find him something to do. He was much better when he was helping Isabel. He had a purpose. He spent a lot of time and money sorting that out, didn't he?"

"He told me," Margaret said, "that he'd made a promise – I presume that was to Edward, before he died. That's just the sort of thing Harry would have done."

"I know. He said to me that Isabel is his responsibility," Richard added. "But now, it's as though he doesn't care any more."

"That's what worries me – he doesn't care about anything. And that's not like Harry." Margaret paused for a moment. "And then there's Rose," she continued, sounding desperate. "We're going to have to do something about that. I don't think she's quite so scared of him now, she's just a bit uncertain. Susan says that Rose talks about him a bit more these days, but Harry needs to spend more time with her. He's got to make more of an effort. She's never going to get used to him again, if he doesn't."

"I know, dear. I tell you what, I'll have a word with him later. I'll see if I can find out what's behind it all."

In the garden, Harry had wandered down beyond his mother's greenhouse. He was sitting in the dark beneath the apple tree, picking at the damp grass. Was it really three years ago today that he'd first seen her? Could it be that long? Did it even matter now? He could still picture her coming out of the near darkness behind him, her milking bucket in her hand, her sparkling eyes and beautiful face, looking up at him. Those eyes, deep with intense passion. Had it really been there? Had there really been a longing, a desire, that had mirrored his own? Or had he imagined that? He laughed at himself. What did it matter? She probably didn't even remember him. Even if she did, she wouldn't want him anymore. He leant back against the tree, closing his eyes. He'd changed now. Everything had changed now. Never again would he watch his own fingers caress her delicate skin, or see hers stroke and arouse him. He'd never look down at her lying beneath him, feel her hands trail up his arms and around his neck as he raised himself above her. He'd never be able to feel her legs encircle his hips, pulling him inwards, downwards, matching his rhythm. He'd never see her head tilt backwards, her hands reach up to clasp the spindles of the wrought iron bed, feel her trembling body rise up to meet his, clamp his mouth over hers to muffle the sounds of her moans; or hear her whisper his name as he released her, letting calm descend over them. He wondered, even now, even after all this time, even after everything that had happened, if he could still lose himself and then find himself in her, but realised of course, that he couldn't; not now. He'd lost her long ago and he was too far beyond finding. He was broken; he was shattered into more pieces than even he had thought possible. Nothing could ever bring him back from where he was and no-one could make him whole again.

He shook his eyes open and struggled awkwardly to his feet, gripping his stick, shaking it, hating it and himself for who and what he had become. With an almighty roar, a raging howl that came from the pit of his stomach, he threw his stick away, as far as he could, hearing the sound of breaking glass. He stood, feeling the pain in his leg and the pounding of his heart in his own head. He wished it would stop; wished his heart would stop and it would all just go away. He saw the curtains being pulled back, the light flooding the terrace, and the French doors being opened.

"Harry?" his father called. "Are you alright?" Harry didn't answer. Richard looked down the garden, searching into the gloom for Harry's figure. Margaret joined him.

"Where is he?" she asked.

"I'm not sure. He must be down by the greenhouse," Richard said. "I'll go and have a look."

"Shall I come too?"

"No, you stay here. It's probably best if I go by myself."

Richard went down the steps and across the garden, treading carefully, unsure of his footing. As he neared the greenhouse, he saw Harry, standing by the apple tree.

"What is it?" Richard asked. Harry didn't answer. Richard went to him. "Why are you standing here?" he asked. "Where's your stick?" Harry did nothing. Richard looked around on the ground near them. "I can't see it, Harry."

"It's over there," Harry whispered, nodding towards the greenhouse.

"Oh. I'll go and have a look." Richard went to the side of the greenhouse, searching the long grass.

"It's too dark," he called. "There's too much broken glass." He walked back to Harry. "We'll find it in the morning. Come on, let's get you back into the house. Lean on me." Harry stood still for a minute or two, then leant on his father. It took them a while to get back up the garden. Harry stumbled twice in the darkness. Margaret stood by the doors and ushered them into the lounge.

"What happened?" she asked.

"Nothing," Richard said. "Harry's misplaced his stick, that's all." He deposited Harry in a chair. "I can't find it in the dark. We'll have to look for it in the morning."

"Are you alright, Harry?" Margaret asked. He didn't respond. "Would you like some tea?" she offered.

"No. I'll go to bed."

Richard moved forward. "I'll help you." He went to lift Harry.

"No."

"Harry," Richard said patiently. "You can't do it by yourself, not without your stick." Harry ignored his father. Placing his left hand on the arm of the chair, he tried to lift himself up. His left leg slipped forward and Harry slid down onto the floor. Margaret leapt forward.

"Leave me!" Harry shouted. She knelt down beside him.

"We can help you Harry," she said gently.

"I said leave me!"

"Harry," said his father.

"Get out!" Harry bellowed. Richard glanced at Margaret and nodded towards the door. She got to her feet and left the room.

"Let me get you to your room, son," Richard said calmly. "Then I'll leave you alone."

Richard bent down and Harry allowed his father to start to lift him. Once he'd got his right leg underneath him, Harry used it to stand properly and take his weight.

"Now, lean on me again," Richard said. They got to the door, which Richard opened. In the hallway, Margaret was sitting on a high-backed chair near the door to the kitchen. She was sniffing into a handkerchief. Richard gave her a sympathetic look as he and Harry passed by towards the stairs. Harry didn't seem to notice her. The stairs took some time to climb. Harry became short of breath and they had to stop frequently. Richard was relieved to finally deposit Harry on his bed. He sat, staring out of the window.

"Let me help you undress, son," Richard offered.

"No."

"You're exhausted."

"No."

"Harry, we only want to help."

"I don't want help."

"Let me just get you into your pyjamas."

"Leave me alone."

"Very well." Richard backed away, closing the door and returning to the hallway.

He bent down and kissed Margaret on the forehead, his hand on her shoulder.

"It's not going to be as easy as having a word with him, is it?" she asked, looking up at Richard through her tears.

"No my dear, I'm afraid it isn't."

Harry didn't come downstairs until lunchtime the next day. He'd found his stick beside his bed when he'd woken up. Richard had taken the day off work and he, Margaret and Rose were sitting at the dining table when Harry entered the room. Harry's hair was ruffled, he was unshaven, wearing corduroy trousers and a creased shirt.

"Come and sit down, Harry," Margaret said. "We've only just started."

Harry limped to the table and sat opposite his mother. Polly placed a bowl of steaming mushroom soup in front of him. He pushed it away, looking at Rose, who kept her eyes fixed on her dish.

"What are you going to do this afternoon?" Margaret asked. Harry didn't react.

"Why don't we all go for a walk?" Richard suggested. "We could just go around the village. Nothing too strenuous."

"Yes," Margaret hesitated. "Or, you could just take Rose, if you'd prefer, Harry." Rose looked up at her grandmother and Harry caught the glance.

"No." he said.

"Very well," Margaret said. "We'll all go."

"No." He got up and left the room, his soup untouched.

"Was it too much, do you think?" Margaret asked Richard.

"He has to do it in his own time, dear." Richard replied.

"Yes, I know, but he still has to do it."

They heard the front door close. Richard got up and went to the window.

"He's gone out," he said, leaning on the window sill.

It was nearly midnight. They'd long-since eaten dinner and Rose had gone to bed hours ago. Richard stood by the fireplace watching the hands turn on the clock.

"What do you think we should do?" Margaret asked. She was sitting in a chair by the window, looking out over the moonlit garden.

"I don't know," Richard replied

Margaret looked up to the sky. "It's a clear night," she said. "It will be cold and he didn't take a coat, did he?"

"No. He didn't even take a sweater. He was just in his shirtsleeves," Richard replied. "Perhaps I should go and look for him."

"Where would you look?" Margaret asked and Richard knew she had a point.

"I don't know," he said. "Why don't you go to bed, my dear. I'll wait up for him."

"I couldn't sleep."

"I know, but at least you'll be more comfortable in bed and there's no point in both of us sitting here."

"What if he doesn't come back?" Margaret asked, starting to sniff. Richard crossed the room and took her hands in his.

"He will. Now, you go along, up to bed."

"Very well. Please come up and tell me the minute he comes back," she urged. Margaret got up, kissed Richard on the cheek and left the room. He stood for a while, looking out into the darkness, feeling powerless and inadequate.

In Downley Woods, Harry sat sheltered beneath the trees. Looking up between the branches, he could see the moon and the twinkling stars peeping through the silhouettes of new leaves, just starting to sprout. He breathed in, but still couldn't fill his lungs. He felt a hand on his shoulder and turned. Edward was smiling down at him, handing him a cup of scalding coffee.

"Thanks," Harry said, taking the cup from him. They were in their billet at Wanquetin. It was April 1917. Edward sat down opposite him.

"What's the matter?" Harry asked, looking at his worried expression.

"Can I ask you something?"

"Yes," Harry replied. "You know you can ask me anything."

"Do you trust Elise?"

"Of course; absolutely. I tease her sometimes about the soldiers who stay at the farm, but I do trust her. Love and trust go together. You know that, Eddie."

"Yes, I suppose so." Edward paused, looking directly at Harry. "Oh ignore me. I'm just being stupid," he said.

"What's new?"

"Oh, do be quiet!" Edward smiled.

"Edward," Harry said, taking a gulp of coffee and grimacing. "I know exactly what you're thinking. It's been a while since you've been home and you're imagining all sorts of things. But you shouldn't… Isabel isn't going to fall in love with the next handsome young man she meets. She loves you. Stop worrying. You can trust her."

"That's not what I was thinking," Edward replied. "Well, not really, although it does cross my mind occasionally."

"What were you thinking then?" Harry asked.

"Just that it's not the same, is it?" Edward said.

"Not the same as what?" Harry asked.

"Oh, nothing," Edward said, looking down at the table. "It doesn't matter."

"You mean it's not the same as us, don't you, Eddie?"

Edward looked up again. "Yes," he said. "That's exactly what I mean."

"Well, you're right. It isn't the same. I trust Elise with my love; with my heart." Harry hesitated, looking into his cup. "But there are things about me that I'll never be able to share with her; never be able to tell her. You know everything there is to know about me and I trust you completely, Eddie… with my life. So yes, it's very different."

"It is, isn't it?" Edward said. "It's not just me, is it?"

"No, it's not," Harry replied quietly, raising his eyes and looking into Edward's face. "Now, stop worrying about it will you? We've got enough to think about as it is. We're moving forward again tomorrow…" The soft blue eyes faded.

A breeze blew across Harry's face, catching his hair. He heard the voice again; broken through the butchered face, "You're… the… only one… I… trust."

"Oh God! I should have told you then, that evening over coffee, when I had the chance," Harry said aloud, staring at the night sky. "I wish I'd said it properly. Did you know? Did you really understand what I meant, Eddie? Why didn't I tell you?"

"Harry!" He heard his name.

"Edward!" he called back.

"Harry!" It wasn't Edward's voice. Harry opened his eyes. The sunlight was shining down through the trees. He was cold; so very cold. He heard the voice again.

"Over here!" it called. He heard footsteps, then looked up. A blurred face was looking down at him. "Richard!" it shouted. Harry focused properly. It was William's face. "Over here!" William repeated, crouching down next to Harry. "Come on, old chap," he said, "Let's get you up." William leant forward, put his hands under Harry's arms, and began to lift him. Harry heard more footsteps and sensed another person by his side.

"Oh, Harry!" It was his father's voice. He felt another pair of hands. Felt them take his weight, supporting him. Then someone else arrived.

"Oh, Joe, it's you. Good." It was William's voice again, sounding authoritative. "Run back to the road. Bring the cart up to the edge of the woods. We'll take him back to the farmhouse; it's nearer."

His legs were cold. He couldn't move them.

"Don't try to walk, Harry. We'll carry you." That was his father again. They lifted him, carrying him through the trees until they came out into the early morning sunshine. The cart was approaching.

"Help us put him in the back, Joe," William said. Harry felt his legs being lifted. He cried out in pain.

"Mind his leg," Richard said.

"Sorry, sir."

He was laid down on the floor of the cart, which was lined with soft hay and a blanket was wrapped around him. William sat beside him. The cart started to move. With every jolt, pain seared through his knee, wracking his body.

"Hold on, Harry," William said. "We'll soon get you back."

The bed was warm and soft. William and Richard had undressed him, putting him into borrowed pyjamas, several sizes too big. Harry felt himself drifting. He heard voices, felt hands touching him, something in his mouth, under his tongue. He gagged.

"He'll be alright" It was Dr Price's voice. He recognised it, remembered it... *Annabelle is dead*. "I'm surprised he's not sicker than he is, to be honest. Just give him a couple of days in bed, to rest."

"Are you sure, Doctor?" It was his mother. Her voice was very quiet.

"Yes, Mrs Belmont. By rights he should have pneumonia, but he hasn't even got a temperature. Why did he do it? Do you know?"

"He hasn't been himself." His father spoke.

"No, Mr Belmont. Well it's been a difficult time for him." The voices were fading. The door closed. The sun was shining across the bed.

"Do you want some help?" Harry shook his head, his eyes still closed. "You should try to eat something." Grainger! It was Grainger. Oh, thank God. Harry opened his eyes. Richard was sitting on the edge of the bed, a bowl of soup in his hand. His mother stood beyond him, a worried expression on her face. Harry shook his head again, looking out of the window. "Alright son, we'll leave it for now. We'll try again later, shall we?" Richard got up. The door was closed behind them. Harry shut his eyes.

The next day, Harry woke early. He got out of the bed, took his stick and went to the window. The fields were alive with new crops, just starting to grow. In the garden beneath him, there were red and yellow tulips, their heads bobbing in the light breeze. In the distance, the trees of Downley Woods were bathed in the brightest green of newly formed leaves. He turned back into the room, feeling sick and weak. His leg ached and he sat back on the edge of the bed.

A little while later, there was a knock on the door. Harry didn't answer, but the door opened anyway and William's head appeared.

"Oh good. You're awake," he said, entering the room. Harry sat, motionless on the bed. "How are you feeling?" William asked. Harry said nothing. William crossed the room and leant against the window sill in front of Harry. "You had us all worried sick, Harry," he said. Harry looked up at William, but remained silent. "Still," he continued, "We can start to get you better now, can't we? Now that we've got you back here?" Harry stared straight ahead. They sat in silence for a while. "Why don't you talk to me, Harry?" William said at last, "I want to help. We've known each other a long time. Something's clearly wrong. Why don't you tell me what it is. I might be able to help if I can understand."

"Understand?" Harry spat out the word. "You want to understand, do you, Bill?" He got to his feet, leaning on his stick. "You want to know what it was like out there, do you? Do you really? You want to know what it felt like watching men you knew, men you liked, getting blown apart and then having to shovel their remains into sandbags. Just bits and pieces of them, mind you, just blood and flesh – nothing big enough to recognise, trying so hard not to puke your guts up, so the men didn't see you show any sign of weakness. You want to know what it felt like to sit under a bombardment for hours on end, wondering if the next shell was going to land on top of you, or worse still, land on someone else… a friend… someone that you lov…" Harry hesitated. "Someone that you'd known for years. Someone that you cared about," he said. "And all the while having to pretend you weren't completely bloody terrified, just so the men didn't feel afraid themselves. You want to know how it felt to take those men into battle, to lead them into a wall of bullets and watch them die all around you, some of them not even old enough to be there in the first place? You really want to know all this do you? You want to know what it was like to lie in a shell hole in the dark, waiting for the guns to stop, with a wounded man beside you and then use all your strength to drag him back to the trenches, only to find he'd died along the way? You want to know how it felt to have men die in your arms; to have them look into your eyes and beg for help, to hear them crying for their mothers and feel their blood seeping through your clothes and onto your skin, but holding on to them anyway, until they stopped breathing and the light went out of their eyes? Done that lately, have you, Bill? You want to know what it felt like to run across No Man's Land, with bullets flying everywhere, grazing past your head, treading on the bodies of men who'd died the day before, or the week before, or the month before? Men whose names you knew… whose faces you knew… when they had faces. Feeling your boots sinking into their flesh, and having to keep going. You want to know about that, do you, Bill? Do you really? Somehow I doubt it."

"I had no idea," William said quietly, his face pale. "I didn't understand."

"Of course you bloody well didn't," Harry said, breathing heavily. "None of you do. You never will. You weren't there. I was just a normal man, Bill. I had a daughter and I painted and I swam in the sea and slept in a bed and walked on the cliffs and I dreamed of a better life. And then I went to war and since then I've seen things that would make you vomit right here and now if I even began to describe them. I've done things to other men that you don't want to imagine. I've killed more men, in more ways that I can remember. I can still see their faces. I don't dream anymore because I can't close my eyes without seeing it all. And that's not even the half of it." Harry paused, choking, catching his breath. "It wasn't about making a 'big push' or holding the line, or any of that shit they were feeding you back here. It was about men getting blown to pieces, having their guts ripped out and their balls shot off and…" Harry stopped, remembering.

"I'm sorry," William said, looking at the floor. "I only wanted to help."

"Well, you can't."

"No. I'm sorry," William repeated.

"Don't be sorry," Harry said, turning away. "I don't want your pity and I don't want any of you to be sorry." William stared at Harry's back for a while, then left the room.

On the fourth day, the doctor said Harry was well enough to go home. Richard got a taxi to take them the two miles from the farm to their house. He helped Harry into the car, then went back to the front door. He shook William's hand; Margaret kissed Charlotte on both cheeks.

"We can't thank you enough for everything you've both done," she said.

"I'm not sure we've done anything," William said. "I'm not sure any of us can. He's very troubled."

"I know," Richard said.

"Do you?" William asked. "Do you really? I don't think any of us has the vaguest idea what he's been through. I don't think we've even scratched the surface."

"Has he spoken to you?" Richard asked.

"Yes. He told me some of the things he'd seen and done, and it shocked me to the core, but even then I'm sure he was holding something back."

"We're going to have to be patient with him. He'll come out of this eventually," Richard said.

"Of course he will," Margaret added.

"Just look after him," William said, looking over Richard's shoulder to the waiting taxi.

"Of course we will. If he'll let us."

Later that afternoon, Harry went to the French doors. He'd sat by the fire since returning. Margaret had been unable to persuade him to go to bed.

"Where are you going?" she asked, looking up from her knitting.

"Outside," he replied.

"Harry, you're not well enough. Come and sit back down again."

"I won't go far."

"Rose is playing out there," Margaret said.

"I'm not going to disturb her."

Harry went through the doors, closing them behind him. Margaret got up and stood at the window, watching him. He climbed down the steps, unsteadily. He didn't even glance at Rose, who was sitting on the swing. He limped down the garden towards the apple tree, now laden with blossom. Underneath it, he stood and looked up, turning around slowly on the spot. Margaret saw him, sighed and sat down on the chair by the window.

Harry looked at the apple blossom. Some of the petals had begun to tumble, lying on the grass at his feet. Once more, he felt arms winding around his neck, fingers through his hair, lips on his, soft skin pressed against his bare chest. He could still see her; still taste her. He shook his head, erasing the pointless memory. Glancing back up the garden, he watched Rose. She had her back to him, her auburn hair tied in a ponytail behind her head. She held the ropes of the swing in her hands, swaying gently back and forth. He turned away. He walked over to his studio, pulling on the handle. It was stiff. He put his stick against the door frame, balancing carefully and pulled harder. The door gave way eventually and a smell of turpentine filled his nostrils. Picking up his stick again, he stepped inside. It was warm and musty. The air was stale. He looked around. Canvases were stacked against the far wall. He went over, bent down and pulled them forward. The harbour, the cliffs, the beach. They were all there. Then Rose looked back at him, her babyish eyes full of love and laughter, with no trace of fear and uncertainty. Standing up, he let her fall back against the wall. The surface of the bench was covered with tubes of paint, powders, palettes, dried out pots of water, pencils. It was just as he'd left it. A sketch pad lay open. Harry balanced his stick against the bench and picked up a pencil in his left hand, running it over the page. The line was uneven, misshapen. He laid the pencil down. For a while, he didn't move, just looked down at the line on the page. It looked like something Rose had drawn when he'd first put a pencil in her hand. He felt the room start to spin, blood filling his head. Everything became hazy, out of focus. There was a pounding in his ears. He took the pencil in his hand and started to scratch at the page, harder and harder, wearing a hole through its surface, then through the next page, then a third. He turned to his side, dropped the pencil and swept his arm along the surface of the bench, scattering everything to the floor or into the sink. Glass shattered and coloured powder flew up, dusting the room. As it started to descend and settle, Harry's eyes fell on the canvasses. Picking up his stick, he turned, hurling it at them, tossing them across the floor. One landed at his feet. Rose gazed up at him again, her eyes looking directly into his. He bent and picked up the canvas. He looked at it, then began to smash it against the bench, splintering the frame, tearing the fabric across her cheek and down into her neck. He dropped it to the ground and leant on the bench, breathing heavily.

He heard a sniff, then a stifled sob and, turning his head towards the door, he saw Rose looking at him, her wide eyes staring directly into his. She stood still for a few moments, their eyes locked, her lip trembling, tears rolling down her cheeks. Then she turned, running up the garden towards the house.

Margaret found him sitting on the floor, glass shards, paint and splintered canvasses strewn around him.

"Oh, Harry. What have you done?" she kicked aside the broken glass and knelt down next to him.

He looked at her. She was a stranger.

"We need to get you into the house," she said. "Your father's not here, Harry. I can't lift you by myself. You're going to have to do it. I can help but I can't lift you." She stood up again, her skirt stained with paint. She picked up his stick and held it out to him. He took it from her. He seemed to be in a trance. "I don't know how we're going to do this," she said. "I'll go and get Polly." She went to leave.

"I can manage," he said, pulling himself up on the stick. He let his left leg take his weight for a moment, screaming in pain, while he bent his right leg, getting it underneath him and standing up. He walked out of the studio and began to limp up the garden. Margaret walked beside him.

Halfway up the garden, they passed Rose, who was standing with her tiny arms clasped around Susan's waist. Both of them were crying, and Susan stroked Rose's hair, but Harry noticed none of it.

"Come and sit down," Margaret said as they reached the terrace.

"No."

"Harry, you need to sit for a while." They went through the French doors.

"No I don't." He walked across to the sideboard and poured himself a large whisky which he drank in one gulp. Then he walked through to the hall, leaving her staring after him.

Up in his room, Harry stood by the window. He stood there for a long time. There was no hope, no peace, no light. There was just darkness. There was so much darkness. It was everywhere, surrounding him, consuming him. He didn't want to fight it: he wanted to float in it, fall into it, let it swallow him, devour him. Turning, he walked over to the wardrobe, leant his stick up against the wall and opened the door. He began to feel along the top shelf, reaching to the back, behind his uniform which had been stored up there. His hand soon found it. Hard and cold, he took it down. It seemed heavier than he remembered. He hadn't held it properly for years. He turned it over in his hand, then put it in his pocket. It was nearly dark outside now. Harry moved across to the bed, sitting down and switching on the lamp. He opened the drawer of the bedside table and felt around inside. He knew the box should be in here somewhere, but he couldn't find it. He stood up, wincing with pain and leant over the drawer, searching, pulling out the contents, strewing them over the bed. There it was. At last. He sighed with relief, taking it in his hand and opening it. It was nearly empty, but that didn't matter. His eye was caught by a small piece of paper by his foot. Harry put the box down on the table and bent down to pick it up. He unfolded it.

'Capt. John Grainger.' he read. There was an address underneath. He felt his head start to spin and just managed to sit down on the edge of the bed.

His mother knocked on the door. "It's nearly time for dinner, Harry," she called. "Are you coming down?"

"No," he managed to say.

"Do you want something on a tray?"

"No."

There was silence, then he heard her footsteps retreating.

'Capt. John Grainger.' He looked at the name again, not taking his eyes from it for what seemed like hours. Then he looked up, staring at the ceiling. He sighed and took the revolver out of his pocket, putting it on the table, next to the box of bullets. Picking up his stick, he went across to the window and leant against the frame. The garden was veiled in moonlight, shadows of the trees cast across the lawn. He looked beyond the greenhouse, where he could just about make out his studio. Rose, her face torn ragged down her soft cheek, still lay on the floor. He heard a voice: 'If you need any help; just a talk; look me up.' Harry turned and hobbled back across to his wardrobe. Reaching into the back, he found his knapsack.

He sat on the bed, with his coat already on and waited for everyone to go to bed. He'd cleared up his room, replacing the revolver in his wardrobe at the back of the top shelf, out of harm's way. The bullets were hidden away now in the back of his chest of drawers. He'd packed some clothes into his rucksack. There was a knock on his door, but he ignored it. His room was in darkness now, so whoever it was obviously assumed he was asleep and went away again. He waited a bit longer until silence had descended and he could be certain that everyone was asleep. He pulled his knapsack over his shoulder, took his stick and went down the stairs. He closed the front door behind him as quietly as he could and limped down the driveway.

Chapter Twenty-two

Spring 1919

It was mid-morning in the Oxfordshire village by the time Harry arrived. He'd caught the milk-train, having sat at the cold station for nearly five hours. He stopped in the busy market square, at the greengrocers, and asked for directions. The man looked him up and down, glanced at the piece of paper and pointed out the house, on the edge of the village green. Harry nodded and limped away. The greengrocer watched him go, shook his head and turned to his next customer.

A picket fence surrounded the pretty garden, its borders blooming, pots of peonies, pansies and primroses stood either side of the door. Harry stood at the gate, uncertain, then opened it and hobbled up the path. His knock was timid, but the door soon opened, revealing a tall, pretty, dark haired woman, probably in her late-twenties or early thirties, wearing a floral dress.

"Can I help?" she asked, her face compassionate.

"Captain Grainger?" Harry said, his voice almost indiscernible. "I'm looking for Captain Grainger. Does he live here?"

"Yes. Would you like to see him?" Harry nodded. "Come in," she said, stepping to one side. "He's in the garden. I'll fetch him for you." Harry waited in the hallway, feeling unsteady on his feet, while she went towards the back of the house. A few minutes later, Harry heard the familiar voice.

"What's his name?" Grainger asked.

"I don't know, John. He didn't say. He's in the hall."

"Alright, my dear." Harry raised his head. Grainger looked different. He'd gained a little weight and had shaved off his moustache. He looked at Harry.

"Good Lord!" he said. "Lieutenant Belmont. Harry!"

"You remember me?" Harry asked.

"Of course I do. Come in, come in." Grainger motioned to Harry to move further down the hallway and into the sitting room, but he stood still. "What is it, Harry?" Grainger walked towards him. "What's wrong?" He took in the dark shadows under the eyes, the greyed hair, the thin drawn face.

"I can't do this, sir," Harry muttered.

"Can't do what, Harry?"

"Any of it, sir. I can't do it anymore." Harry looked him in the eyes. "Can you help me?" he whispered, falling forwards. Grainger caught him, holding him up.

"Lillian!" he called over his shoulder. His wife appeared behind him. "Take his bag, will you?" he said. "I need to get him into the sitting room." Lillian removed Harry's knapsack from his shoulder, while Grainger took his weight. Then she opened the door to the sitting room. Grainger put his arm around Harry's waist, supported him and guided him into a chair.

"Shall I make some tea?" Lillian suggested.

"Yes," Grainger said. "With lots of sugar," he called to her retreating figure. There was a footstool in front of Harry and Grainger sat down on it.

"I'm sorry, sir." Harry said, his words slightly slurred.

"Don't be silly, Harry." Grainger said. "You look exhausted. We'll get you some tea and then you can go upstairs and have a rest. We can talk later."

"Can we, sir?"

"Of course we can."

Lillian came in with a cup of tea, which Harry drank, barely noticing its sickly sweetness. Once he'd finished, she took the cup from him and left the room. Grainger got up.

"Come on, Harry. Let's get you upstairs. A bit of rest will do you good."

"I don't want you to go to any trouble, sir."

"It's no trouble, Harry. Come on." He lifted Harry from the chair and helped him up the stairs.

The bedroom looked out over the back garden. Grainger opened the window. Harry could hear birds singing and, in the distance, a dog barked.

"Lie down, Harry," he said. "Get some sleep." Harry did as he was told.

As Grainger reached the door, Harry looked up at him. "Sir?" he said, "Can you help me?"

"I'll try, Harry."

"Thank you, sir."

"Who is he?" Harry heard Lillian's voice. They were in the garden just below his window. They were talking quietly, but he could still hear their voices. "Was he one of your men, John?"

"Not exactly. I met him in Germany."

"In the camp?"

"No. In the hospital."

"He looks in a bad way." Lillian said.

"He is. Very bad. I think it might be best if he stayed here for a while. Do you mind?"

"Of course not, dear."

"He needs my help," Grainger said.

"Is there anything you can do for him?"

"I have no idea, but I'll certainly do whatever I can."

Harry relaxed and closed his eyes.

It was dusk. Grainger had closed the curtains and was sitting on the edge of the bed. Harry had been awake for a couple of hours and Grainger had already helped him to have a bath and change into clean pyjamas. Harry had just eaten half a bowl of soup, which Grainger had removed and put on the bedside table.

"Do you want to tell me about it?" Grainger asked.

"I don't know where to start, sir," Harry replied.

"How have things been at home?" Grainger enquired.

"Bad. My daughter's terrified of me."

"It's early days, Harry, but children are resilient. She'll come round. You just have to be patient. How's it been with your parents?"

"They don't understand, sir."

"They can't, Harry. They weren't there. It's not their fault."

"They keep saying that they're sorry all the time, but I don't think they even know what they're sorry for. They're trying to make it all better. But that's impossible. It's not going to get better, is it, sir?"

"Have you tried talking to them?"

"Not really, sir." Harry said.

"Don't you think you should try? They might surprise you."

"I've never spoken to them about any of it, sir."

"Not even during the war?"

"No, sir. I didn't tell them anything."

"Why not?" Grainger asked.

"At first it was because my mother asked me not to, but after a while, I found it easier not to bother them," Harry replied.

"Who did you talk to, Harry? You must have had someone you could share it with."

"I had Edward."

"Your friend? The one who died?"

"Yes, sir."

"Well, Harry," Grainger said, getting to his feet. "I think the first thing you need to do, is learn to trust people."

"Trust?" Harry said, his voice suddenly very distant.

"Yes, trust."

"I did once, sir. I'm not sure I can anymore."

"You'll have to try. Now, you need some more sleep, Harry. We'll talk again tomorrow."

The next morning, Harry woke late. Downstairs, he found Grainger and Lillian sitting in the kitchen, drinking coffee.

"There you are!" Grainger said. "Come and sit down." Lillian got up from the table and fetched another cup from the dresser that lined the furthest wall of the kitchen. She poured Harry a cup of coffee and passed him a jug of milk.

"How are you?" she asked.

"Better, thank you," he replied. "I don't want to put you out at all."

"You're not putting us out," she said kindly.

"I can find a hotel, or an inn. There must be one nearby."

"You'll stay here," Grainger said.

"If you're sure, sir."

"I'm sure."

"Thank you, sir."

"You don't have to call me 'sir' anymore, Harry. My name is John."

"If you don't mind, I'd rather call you 'sir', or 'Captain'."

"Very well, if that's what you want. But I'm going to call you Harry, not Lieutenant Belmont." Grainger smiled.

"Would it be alright if I have a walk around your garden, sir?" Harry asked, getting up from the table.

"Yes, of course. Just be careful of the footpath. It's a bit uneven." Harry took his stick and went out of the back door.

"Why did he say that?" Lillian asked, once Harry was out of earshot.

"What?"

"About wanting to call you 'sir', or 'captain'? The war's over. I'd have thought that he'd want to forget all about it."

"I don't know," Grainger smiled. "Familiarity, I suppose. It's strange though. When we were in the hospital, he hardly ever called me 'sir'. Not until the day I left, actually."

"Are you going to be alright with him doing that? It will remind you of everything. I don't want you upset again, John."

"I'll be fine, Lillian. It's him I'm worried about."

Harry ate in the dining room that evening. Once they'd finished dessert, Lillian poured coffee and Grainger leant back in his chair, turning to Harry.

"Do your family know where you are?" he asked. Harry shook his head. "Why not?"

"I didn't tell them I was leaving," Harry admitted. Lillian looked from one man to the other, noticing the expression of annoyance on her husband's face.

"So you just walked out? In the middle of the night, I suppose? And they have no idea where you've gone?" Harry shook his head again, looking at his coffee cup. "Lieutenant!" Lillian jumped, dropping her spoon into her saucer. Harry's head jerked upright. "We must contact them and tell them where you are."

"I can't." Harry's voice was a whisper. "I don't know how."

"Well, I do." Grainger's voice softened again. "We'll write to them." He got up and went to the sideboard, taking out a notepad and pen. Sitting down next to Harry, he said, "Let's start with the address, shall we?" Harry gave him the details. Between them, with Lillian's help, they composed a letter to Harry's parents. It didn't offer an explanation of his actions; Harry didn't really have one yet, but it gave details of where he was, that he was well, and would be in touch again soon.

A little later, they sat together in the sitting room.

"What happened to you, Harry?" Grainger asked. "When you left the hospital, I mean."

"They sent me to a camp, sir, at Fürstenberg. It wasn't bad. It was a converted hotel."

"Why weren't you interned?"

"I asked them not to."

"Why on earth did you do that?"

"I didn't want any special treatment, sir."

Grainger looked at Harry, his eyes full of bewilderment. "Harry," he said, "you were badly wounded. You were entitled to special treatment."

"No I wasn't, sir. I didn't want it. I wasn't entitled to anything." Lillian looked at her husband. He raised his eyebrows and she shrugged her shoulders. They all sat in silence for a while.

"I never thought to ask you, sir?" Harry asked eventually. "What do you do? I mean, what did you do before the war?"

"I'm a teacher, Harry," Grainger replied. "There's a boys' school nearby. I'm very fortunate; they've kept my job open."

"What do you teach?" Harry asked.

"English," Grainger said. "I haven't been back yet. Not since getting home. I'm due to start again after half term." He looked closely at Harry. "What will you do?" he asked. "When you're better?"

"I won't do anything, sir," Harry said, honestly.

"Why not? You'll need to earn a living, Harry."

"No I won't, sir."

Grainger was confused. "What do you mean?" he asked.

"I have my own money, sir," Harry said. "I inherited it a few years ago – before the war."

"I see," Grainger said. "Well, that's one less thing to worry about, I suppose."

"Yes, sir. Rose's future is taken care of and there's…" Harry hesitated.

"And there's what, Harry?" Grainger asked.

"Edward's… wife," Harry said.

"What about his wife?" Lillian asked, picking up her knitting from a bag on the floor. Harry looked at Grainger.

"I've told Lillian who Edward is," he explained. "You cry his name during the night."

"Sorry, sir," Harry said.

"It doesn't matter," Grainger said. "Tell us about Edward's wife."

"Well, sir," Harry said, looking out of the window, "she's my responsibility now."

"She is?" Grainger said.

"Yes, sir. Edward asked me to take care of her."

"I'm sure he only meant check up on her, Harry, not take responsibility for her for the rest of her life – there's a difference, you know." Grainger pointed out.

"She's my responsibility, sir," Harry repeated.

"How is she getting along?" Lillian asked. "Since his death, I mean? I can't imagine how awful that must be." She glanced across at her husband.

"She had a baby," Harry replied. "Last August. He didn't even know about it. He died... before she even knew herself."

"How dreadful for her," Lillian said, lowering her head.

"How does she cope on her own?" Grainger asked.

"She was in a very bad way when I found her but she's better now, sir, I think," Harry replied. "I had a house, you see..."

"You had a house?" Grainger repeated, obviously confused.

"Yes, sir. She lives there now. Her and the baby."

"Oh, so you've rented her the house?" Grainger asked.

"No, sir. I gave it to her," Harry said. "She owns it now."

"You gave her a house?" Lillian said.

"Yes."

"Why?" Lillian asked.

"Because I made him a promise to look after her," Harry said simply. Grainger and Lillian looked at each other. Lillian shrugged again, but Grainger nodded his head and smiled.

Two days later, Harry received a reply to his letter, with an enclosure.

'Dearest Harry,' the letter read, *'We were so pleased and relieved to hear from you. Please don't worry about anything. We only want you to get well and come home again, whenever you are ready. Take as much time as you need. We will all be here when you get back. With fondest love, Mother and Father.'*

The enclosure was addressed to Captain Grainger.

'Dear Captain Grainger,' it read, *'Although we do not know you, my wife and I would like to express our heartfelt thanks to you for everything that you are doing for Harry. We were so worried when he disappeared and are very relieved to know that he is safe. All we want is for Harry to get well again, but we now appreciate that it will not be easy for him. We are only just beginning to realise that, despite our good intentions, we have not been acting in Harry's best interests, quite simply because we have no understanding of what he has gone through, and the fact that he has turned for help to you – a stranger to us – simply confirms our thoughts. We should have*

understood this sooner and, perhaps, sought assistance for him from other quarters, and for that, we blame ourselves entirely. Our only hope is that, one day, Harry will feel able to trust us enough to come home again. We thought that he already had, but now we can see that this was never the case; he has been lost to us for some time. Perhaps, with your help, he can find a way back through his difficulties. My wife has, intentionally, only written a short letter to Harry, as we don't want him to worry about anything at home, but only to concentrate on getting better. I am sure that you will appreciate that this has not been an easy letter for me to write, but I feel it is important that you should understand the full situation at home and and the strains that Harry has faced since his return from Germany. I know I am asking a lot from someone that I don't know, but please take care of him for us and, if there is anything that you need – anything at all – please write. Once again, sir, you have our eternal thanks. Sincerely yours, Richard Belmont.'

Grainger finished reading the letter and folded it in half.

"Harry?" he said. "Are you sure your parents don't understand?" Harry nodded. "Well, I have a letter here from your father," Grainger continued. "He didn't intend that you should see it, but I think you should read what he has to say. I think it will help." He passed his letter across the breakfast table. When Harry had read it, he looked up at Grainger and his eyes were filled with tears.

"Oh God, sir," he whispered. "How could I? What have I done to them?"

"Nothing you can't undo, Harry. But surely, even you can see that you're going to have to start trusting people again." He got up and left the room, placing a hand on Harry's shoulder as he passed behind him.

As the days passed, Harry still didn't talk very much. His nightmares continued and most nights he would wake in the early hours, the bedclothes soaked in sweat. He would lie awake until dawn, too frightened to go back to sleep. One day, about three weeks after his arrival, Grainger came downstairs early before setting off for work and found Harry sitting in the kitchen.

He saw Harry's face and sat down. "Was it a bad one?" he asked. Harry nodded. "I'll make some tea," Grainger said. They sat together in silence. "Do you want to tell me about it, Harry?"

"I can't."

"Was it to do with Edward?" Grainger prompted. Harry nodded, looking down at the table. "You keep saying 'sorry'," Grainger said. "It sounds to me as though you were trying to help him?" Harry didn't look up.

"Yes, sir," he said eventually.

"I'm sure you did your best, Harry."

"I don't know if I did the right thing, sir," Harry said, looking up.

"I'm sure you did, Harry. You're a decent, honourable man."

"Am I?"

"Yes, Harry, you are." Grainger's voice was soothing. "Whatever it was, Harry. Whatever it is that's troubling you about Edward, however you feel you failed him, you need to tell someone, otherwise you're never going to begin to get better."

"I can't, sir," Harry said. Grainger spread his fingers out on the table and took a deep breath.

"Do you remember, in the hospital, I told you that the hardest thing you could do was to watch a friend die?"

"Yes, sir," Harry replied.

"Well, I did it too, or something similar." Grainger got up and went to stand by the sink, his back to Harry. "In my case, the man was my sergeant, Harry. He was my responsibility. Knighton was his name. He came to me in the summer of 1915, just before Loos. He was the best man I ever served with. You know the type?"

Harry thought of Warner. "Yes, sir, I do."

"Anyway, we were near Ypres in the spring of 1917. We went out on a patrol one night. I don't know what happened, but they got wind of us somehow and opened fire. Knighton was hit. He was right next to me. They got him in the chest. Then another man, a youngster called Perry was hit too, in the leg and I knew he wouldn't be able to get back without help. There was no-one else nearby. Just me and the two of them." Grainger turned back to Harry. "I had a choice, Harry," he said. "I could only take one of them. Knighton looked at me and told me to get Perry back. I promised Knighton I'd go back for him. I grabbed Perry by the collar and dragged him across No Man's Land

and threw him into the trench. Then the Germans started shelling us. I couldn't go back, Harry. They were dropping everything on us. I got down into the trench and waited. It lasted about two hours, I suppose, by which time it was getting light. I didn't dare go out in daylight. I took a couple of men out to find him as soon as it was dark. Amazingly, Knighton was still alive and we got him back, but he died later in the hospital."

"There was nothing more you could have done, sir," Harry said. "You had to make the decision. You don't know that he wouldn't have died anyway, even if you'd brought him back first. We all had to make choices like that, didn't we?"

"Yes, Harry. That's what I'm trying to say to you. We all did it and whatever happened between you and Edward, you will have done the right thing, I'm sure of that."

"Don't be, sir." Harry hesitated. "He asked me to shoot him."

"Christ, Harry!"

"He was dying, sir. He'd been shot in the face and he was dying... slowly. He asked me to shoot him."

"This man was your best friend?" Grainger asked, sitting down again, his face pale.

"Yes, sir," Harry replied.

"Harry, that's impossible. You couldn't possibly shoot your best friend. No-one could. It's too much to ask."

"Yes, sir." Harry sighed, then whispered, "I know it is. I know it's too much."

"Look, Harry. There's no use feeling guilty about it. You couldn't do it. This happened when you were wounded, didn't it?" Harry nodded. "Well then," Grainger continued, looking at Harry's stump "You have nothing to reproach yourself for. You weren't even capable, were you?"

Harry paused. "I could have tried to get him back, sir."

"In your condition? You'd never have done it, and you'd probably have killed yourself in the process." Grainger noticed the look on Harry's face. "Harry?" he asked. "If things had been the other way round and you'd been dying, could he have shot you?"

"No sir, he couldn't," Harry replied.

"Well then," Grainger said.

"But, the difference is that I'd never have asked him to in the first place, sir," Harry said. He didn't want to talk about Edward anymore. "Your situation with Knighton, sir," he asked eventually. "How did you get through it?"

"I had a big advantage over you, Harry. I was still there. I had my men around me. They got me through it. I couldn't have done it without them." Grainger looked at Harry. "Can I ask you something?" he said.

"Yes, sir," Harry replied.

"Who is Elise?"

"How do you know that name?" Harry asked, looking up.

"A couple of nights ago, you were sobbing in your sleep. It was much worse than usual, so I came in to see you. You didn't say Edward's name this time, you said 'Elise'. You kept saying it over and over again."

"I don't remember that," Harry said.

"You didn't wake up. Eventually, you turned over and settled down again, so I left you."

"I'm sorry to have disturbed you, sir."

"That's not important Harry," Grainger said. "So, who is Elise?"

"She's a girl."

"Yes, I gathered that much."

"I met her in France." Harry sat in silence and Grainger watched him, waiting.

"I think there was a lot more to it than that," he said.

"Yes, there was, sir." Harry looked away. "We were lovers," he murmured.

"When did you meet her?"

"April 1916, sir."

"And when did you last see her."

"I spent part of my last leave with her, in November 1917. A few days before all this happened." Harry looked down at himself.

"Does she know about you — about what happened to you?" Grainger asked. Harry shook his head. "Does she even know you're still alive?" Harry shook his head again. "Good God, Harry. Do you ever tell anyone anything?"

"I don't want her to know," Harry said.

"Why not?"

"Look at me, sir. What use am I to her now?"

"Did she love you?" Grainger asked candidly.

"Yes, sir," Harry replied.

"Did she love you just because of how you looked?"

"No, sir, I don't think so."

"Did you love her?" Grainger asked, looking directly at Harry.

"Yes, sir," he replied.

"And you told her that, did you?"

"Of course, sir."

"And when you last saw her, how did you leave things with her? What did you tell her?" Harry looked away, feeling embarrassed. "Harry… I know you well enough to know that you wouldn't just have walked away from this girl. Not if you loved her… You're not that sort of man. What did you say to Elise the last time you saw her, the last time she saw you?" Grainger asked again, hoping he'd correctly guessed the answer before it was given.

"I told her I'd go back to her, sir. I promised that if I made it through the war, I'd never leave her again."

Grainger smiled inwardly. "So you've broken your promise then, haven't you?" Harry looked up, a contrite expression on his face. "That's not like you. You owe her an explanation, Harry. She at least deserves to know that you're alive. She deserves to know why you haven't been in touch."

"I haven't been in touch because she won't want me anymore."

"That's for her to say, Harry, but I think if we were to ask Lillian, she'd say that she'd rather have me back in pieces than not have me back at all. Has it even dawned on you that your Elise might feel the same way?"

"It's different, sir. Elise is very young, sir. She'd only be twenty-two, even now. She's probably found someone else already."

"I doubt it. Not if she loved you as much as you obviously loved her."

"I don't want her to be burdened with me. She has her whole life ahead of her."

"Yes, and she might just want to spend it with you, Harry."

"And if she doesn't?"

"Wouldn't you rather know?"

"I'm not sure."

"It might be one less nightmare, Harry, one way or the other. Surely one less nightmare is a good thing. At the moment, you're torturing yourself, because you don't know."

Harry stared into space for a while, remembering her long, curled hair; dark brown eyes; soft skin; her smile; the touch, sound, scent, taste of her.

"I'm no good to her any more," he said. "It wouldn't be the same."

"Of course it wouldn't be the same, Harry. You've changed. She might have changed too – who knows? Nothing's the same. But are you just going to give up; walk away and not even try to see her again?"

"I think it might be easier, sir, yes," Harry replied.

"Easier for whom?"

"Her, sir."

"Then you're a fool, Harry," Grainger said. "That's her choice, not yours. She has the right to know about you and to decide what she wants to do. And I'll bet she'll surprise you... everyone else has."

"What should I do, sir? Should I write to her?" Harry asked.

"I think you should go," Grainger said.

Harry sat in silence, wondering if he could face her, bear to look at her, talk to her.

"You think I should go back to France?"

"Yes."

"I don't know if I can do that, sir."

"Take some time. Think about it. It might help. It might help in all sorts of ways."

"Do you think so?" Harry asked.

"It might. Give it some thought."

The next day, in the early evening, Harry found Grainger in the garden. He was bent over, planting out seedlings in his vegetable patch behind the shed.

"I've decided, sir," Harry said. "I'm going to go."

"To France?" Grainger stood up straight, arching his back.

"Yes, sir. I thought I'd catch the train tomorrow morning."

"I didn't mean for you to leave right away, Harry. You've put on a bit of weight and you're looking a little better now, but are you sure you're well enough yet?"

"Not really, sir, but I'll manage."

"Why not give it a few more days, build up your strength a bit more? " Grainger suggested.

"If I don't go now, I might change my mind again. I might never go."

Grainger hesitated. "Harry," he said, "Would you like me to come with you?"

"Thank you, sir. But how could you? There's your wife and your job. You can't just disappear to France at a moment's notice."

"I could find a way, Harry, if you need me to."

"Thank you, sir. But I think I should do this by myself."

"You do realise, don't you, that when you get over there, you might have to travel close to some of the battlefields. It will be difficult."

"I know, sir. But I think you're right. I think I have to do this. I think it might help."

Harry got up early the next morning. He'd said his goodbyes to Lillian the previous night, but Grainger was waiting for him in the kitchen.

"Ready? he asked.

"I think so, sir," Harry replied.

"I really hope everything works out, Harry," Grainger said. "If it does, bring her for a visit."

"And if it doesn't?"

"Then you know where I am."

"I can't thank you enough, sir, for everything you've done for me." Harry said, shaking Grainger's hand.

"You don't have to, Harry. You'd do the same for me. We both know that."

"Yes, sir. I would."

"Has he gone?" Lillian asked when she came down to breakfast.

"Yes," Grainger replied.

"Do you think he'll be alright?"

"I have no idea. I hope so. If everything works out, I think it could really help him."

"And if it doesn't work out?"

"Then I don't see how he can be any worse off than he is now."

"He's going to find it difficult, being in France again. How did you persuade him to go back?"

"That wasn't too hard: he'd made a promise to someone and I knew he was too honourable to let them down. Harry's like that – hadn't you noticed?"

"I suppose so, yes. Who did he make the promise to?"

"A girl that he happened to fall in love with." Grainger took Lillian's hand in his and kissed it.

"John?," she said. "There's something I don't understand."

"What's that?" Grainger asked.

"You said that he wasn't one of your men?"

"No he wasn't."

"And you only met him briefly in the hospital?"

"Yes."

"He's a lovely man, John, he seems very kind and thoughtful, despite all his problems and I feel terribly sorry for him, but I don't understand why you're doing so much for a man you barely know."

Grainger paused, then got up. He took the cups down from the dresser then turned back to her. "That's easy, my dear," he said, "I'm helping him, because, in slightly different circumstances, it could so easily be me in his shoes, and he and I both know that. We were all in the same situation and I suppose it was just luck as to who survived and who didn't."

"But you both survived… you both came home."

"Did we?"

Chapter Twenty-three

Late Spring 1919

The train journeyed quickly through the French countryside. Harry sat in the compartment, reading a book and avoiding the scenery. After a while, though, he couldn't help but look. The green fields stretched into the distance. There were leaves on the tress, the flowers bloomed and hedgerows flourished. Then, out of nowhere, on the horizon, a glimpse of brown grew into a sweeping panorama of mud, pocked, furrowed and pitted. Harry turned quickly back to his book, but couldn't block the sounds. Shells fell all around him; bullets whistled past his ears; screams and cries filled his head. Harry felt his chest becoming tighter. He needed air. He needed to breathe. He put down his book and took up his stick. In the corridor, he opened the small window and put his face up close to the gap, sucking in the whistling air. He stayed there for the remainder of the journey.

Leaving the railway station and passing through Bethune, Harry felt the breath catch in his throat as his chest tightened. The ruins were unrecognisable. The bank was gone, as was the post office, from where he'd sent that telegram. The belfry had been beheaded and looked forlorn in the centre of the square: a fitting monument to all the slaughter. Harry had seen ruins before, but never of somewhere that he'd actually known. He began to feel his palm sweat and his heart race. His mouth became dry. If Bethune had been this damaged, what about Lapugnoy; what about the farmhouse? He leant forward and tapped the taxi driver on the shoulder.

"Could we hurry, please?" he urged. The man shrugged, barely speeding up at all. Looking out of the window, Harry hoped for distractions, but didn't even notice the fields, planted with new corn, swaying in the breeze.

Lapugnoy was the same as Harry remembered. There was little or no damage visible, just a few broken windows and Harry felt himself relax as the taxi pulled up outside the estaminet, once the favourite haunt of the men. The driver climbed down and helped Harry, passing him his knapsack and lifting it onto his back. Inside, the estaminet had changed very little, except there were fewer tables, and less customers. Harry's arrival attracted the attention of the few who were present, and every pair of eyes turned in his direction as he closed the door behind him.

"Hello, monsieur. What can I do for you?" said the owner, a small thin man, standing behind the bar.

"Do you have any rooms?" Harry enquired.

"Yes, monsieur," the man answered, looking closely at Harry. "Can I offer you a drink? A glass of wine, perhaps?"

"No, thank you. If you could just show me to a room," Harry said.

"Very well, monsieur." The owner came around the bar and took Harry's knapsack, directing him towards the back of the café. Passing through a door they ascended a narrow staircase, which led to a short corridor.

"This is your room, monsieur," the owner said, opening the door at the top of the stairs. Inside there was a large double bed, a chest of drawers and a wardrobe. A worn rug lay on the floor in front of the unlit fire. "Will this do, monsieur?" the man asked, nervously.

"Yes," Harry said.

"The bathroom is the next door along, on your right," the owner said. "If you need anything, just ask."

"Thank you," Harry said, as the door closed.

He glanced at his watch. It was nearly three o'clock. He wanted to go there now, but his nerves were beginning to get the better of him. He quickly unpacked his knapsack while he thought. It might take him an hour; he'd be much slower than before, but he could make it there in a hour, he was sure. He had to know; he had to be sure that she was still there. Even if she didn't want him anymore – he had to know that she was alright. The thought of any alternative made it harder to breathe. He finished unpacking and closed the drawers. He had to know. He limped across the room and opened the door.

The road was still uneven, Harry trod carefully, avoiding the pot-holes. It took him just under an hour, and he was hot by the time he came over the brow of the hill. He stopped for a moment, looking around at the scene before him. It was so different. The fields were no longer fallow. Fresh crops grew all around, as far as the eye could see. He kept walking. Approaching the gate, there was no-one to be seen. Harry moved across the road and passed under the draping branches of the willow tree. He leant against its bark, hidden from view, and looked at the farm. The kitchen garden was full of vegetables. The courtyard was swept clean and a tub of flowers stood outside the door. The window at the side of the house had been freshly painted. Through the archway, he could make out the orchard, the last of the blossom still hanging onto its branches. He heard the latch of the door and felt his skin bristle. A figure shrouded in black came outside, carrying two bowls. It was Madame Martin. She walked around the side of the house and sat on the old bench, facing Harry. Placing one bowl on the bench beside her, she put the other on her lap and started shelling peas. She looked around her, as she worked. A blackbird landed on the fence and she smiled at it, dropping the empty pods into one bowl, the peas into another. She held Harry's attention, so he didn't notice the second figure approaching, until he sat down next to her. A handsome young man, with short dark hair, maybe twenty-five years old, he wore brown trousers and a green shirt, open at the neck. They talked together, but Harry couldn't hear what they said. The young man pointed in the vague direction of the fields and then down towards the stream and Madame Martin nodded her head. They both looked round at the same time and Harry caught his breath. He felt the relief wash over him, followed by the familiar stirring in his chest that travelled down to the pit of his stomach. It was Elise. She looked exactly as he remembered. Her hair was tied up, but a little more loosely, perhaps; her skin was bronzed. She was wearing the same cream coloured dress with small blue flowers that she'd worn on the day he'd left in April 1916. The day he'd told her that he loved her; the day she'd said she wanted to be his friend. She'd come from the back of the house, carrying a small bundle of laundry in her arms. The young man stood, and walked towards her. They smiled at each other, then he laughed as she said something. She laughed too, throwing her head back. Harry felt suddenly uneasy, watching them. They looked briefly into each other's eyes and she placed the bundle in his arms. Harry felt a sharp spasm in his chest as his heart separated from the rest of his body and splintered. The pain was so intense, so severe, it was worse than any wound. There was no familiar numbness to this. It hurt. It hurt more than anything he'd ever felt before and he wanted to cry out, to shout and scream, to howl in agony. A baby. Her baby. Their baby. He tried to breathe, but his heart was no longer working; it had broken into too many pieces. The view became a haze, the house, the garden, the figures, all blurred together. He turned away, eager to escape, to be anywhere else, desperate to flee from this scene. He moved his foot forward, caught his stick on the tree trunk and fell to the ground. As he crashed down, he cried out. His stick fell away from him. His arm was trapped beneath him and his leg took the full brunt of the fall. He struggled to free his arm and turn onto his back. It took all his strength, but he managed it and sat up, feeling around for his stick, which was behind him. Leaning on it, he pulled himself up, welcoming the excruciating pain in his knee. For a brief moment, it silenced the other torture. Once he was standing again, he breathed heavily, regained his balance and turned around. Elise stood just a few feet away, looking at him. He saw her glance at the stick, her eyes moving up to the stump of his arm, up further to his face, the hair grey at the temples, the cheekbones still prominent. Then her eyes settled on his.

She ran to him, tears already streaming down her cheeks. He felt her arms around his neck, her soft body pressed against his.

"You're here," she sobbed. "How can you be here? I thought you were dead." Her fingers entwined in his hair. He pulled back, leaning away from her and removing her from him. "What is it?" she asked, looking into his eyes. "What's wrong?"

"What do you think?" Harry didn't bother to disguise the bitterness in his voice.

"I have absolutely no idea, 'Arry." She took a pace backwards. Harry looked towards the farmhouse, where Madame Martin still sat on the bench, looking in their direction. The young man, holding the baby, had moved to the gate and was watching them.

"That," Harry said.

"What?" She turned around, following the direction of his gaze.

"You didn't wait very long, did you?" he asked. He did a quick calculation. "Six months or so? Maybe a little more, but probably a great deal less. Did I really mean that much to you?"

"What the hell are you talking about, 'Arry?" she said, raising her voice, and placing her hands on her hips.

"The baby, Elise. Isn't it obvious, for Christ's sake? Your baby, your husband, or lover, or whatever he is. You wanted promises from me about our future? You wanted to know how I felt about you – about how much you meant to me? Well, I told you… And then, all that rubbish about how scared you were of losing me; about what would become of you if I got killed. Well this is what became of you, Elise. You jumped into bed with the next able-bodied man who turned up on your doorstep, and promptly had his child. Was he even the next man? Or were there others in between?" Elise stepped forward and slapped him hard across the face. Harry didn't even flinch.

"How dare you, 'Arry. I thought you were dead," she shouted.

"Was it wishful thinking?"

"'Arry! How can you say that to me? I didn't hear from you. What was I supposed to think? I waited and waited. I heard nothing. You didn't contact me. The war ended. Still I waited. Still I heard nothing. You've been alive all this time, but you let me think you were dead. Did I really mean that much to you?" She spat his words back at him.

"You know…" His voice cracked and he turned away, unable to look at her. "You know exactly what you meant to me, Elise," he whispered. "I opened my heart to you. I explained everything. I told you what would happen to me without you. Don't tell me now that you didn't understand. I refuse to believe that you don't know how much you meant to me."

"I thought I did, but judging from your behaviour, your opinion of me, I'm not so sure. You said you couldn't live without me. Did it ever occur to you that I might feel the same? And yet, in all these months, not once have you bothered to contact me. You've left me waiting."

"But you didn't wait, though, did you?" he thundered at her, his eyes dark with anger.

"Yes, 'Arry. I waited."

"Not for very long, Elise."

She calmed down very suddenly, tears filling her eyes again. "I'm still waiting," she whispered. "The baby isn't mine, 'Arry. The man isn't my husband, or my lover. He's Henri. The baby is his."

"That's Henri?" Harry murmured, looking back at the man, who had handed the baby to his mother and was leaning on the gate post with his arms folded.

"Yes. He came back last spring." Elise replied. "You were right. He was wounded. He wasn't dead."

Harry looked at the ground, his shame engulfing him. "I'm so sorry, Elise," he said, glancing up. They stood in silence for a while. She kept her eyes fixed on his. The intensity was still there, tempting him, pulling him in. Her mouth opened slightly. She was so beautiful and Harry knew at once that he couldn't stay. He couldn't look at that face, that body, then look at his own and know what she could have had; what they could have been. He knew that all he would bring her was sorrow and pain if he stayed.

"I should go," he said, turning away from her.

"What?" she said. "You're going?"

"Yes." He started to limp away.

"Why are you leaving?" she asked, following him.

"Because I don't want to stay," he replied, looking straight ahead. "I was wrong to come here. This was a mistake."

"But you've only just arrived. You can't go." She walked beside him, beginning to cry. "'Arry!" she sobbed. He kept walking, passing through the branches of the willow tree and onto the road. She ran in front of him, blocking his path. "Stop, 'Arry!" she cried. He stopped and sighed.

"What? What do you want, Elise?"

"I want you to stay. You can't leave," she begged. "Not like this… please. We'll forget about what just happened. Forget about all of it. I'm sorry for all the things I said. None of it matters. Stay with me, please." Harry was about to speak when he heard footsteps running up behind him.

"Elise?" It was a man's voice. Henri appeared in front of him and stood next to Elise, looking at her. "What is it?" he said to her. "Are you alright?"

"No, Henri, I'm not." Henri pulled his sister towards him, put an arm around her and comforted her, stroking her hair.

He looked up at Harry. "Who are you?" he asked.

"This is 'Arry," Elise explained, her voice muffled.

"It is?" Henri said. Elise nodded her head, pulling away from her brother and wiping her eyes on the cuffs of her dress. Henri looked Harry up and down. "I don't know what to say to you," he continued. "How do I ever thank you?"

"Thank me?" Harry said, surprised.

"Yes. My sister has told me everything."

"Everything?" Harry looked at Elise.

"Well, she's told me enough," Henri continued. "I know that it is you who looked after my family while I wasn't here. I owe you so much."

Harry let his head fall. "You owe me nothing, monsieur," he said.

"On the contrary, 'Arry. I can never repay you for what you did."

"You don't have to."

"Come inside," Henri said. "Have some coffee with us. Stay for dinner."

"I can't," Harry replied. "I have to go."

"We insist," Henri said, starting to walk back towards the house. He stopped and waited for Harry to move. Harry hesitated, but eventually turned and began limping after Henri with Elise following closely behind.

Inside the kitchen, they found Madame Martin sitting on a chair by the range, cradling the baby in her arms.

"My wife is not well," Henri explained. "She has a cold and the doctor says she must rest for a few days. Otherwise she'd like to meet you too."

"They can meet another day," Elise said, looking at Harry's expressionless face.

"Sit down," Henri urged, pulling out a chair for Harry. "I'll get you some coffee."

Harry lowered himself into the chair and balanced his stick up against the table. Elise sat opposite him, her eyes fixed on his.

"I can't believe you're sitting here again," she said, "Just like you used to." Harry looked at her, then looked away, out of the window over the courtyard. Henri put a cup of coffee in front of him.

"Thank you," Harry said.

"What happened to you?" Elise asked.

Harry looked back at her again, his face impassive.

"Elise," Henri said, "let him be."

"I was wounded," Harry said quietly.

"Where?" she persisted, not listening to her brother.

"In the hand and leg," he replied.

"No, I mean where were you."

"Near a village called Banteux."

"What happened?"

"I was captured by the Germans." Harry fell silent.

"Where's your friend?" Elise continued, "Edward?"

Harry said nothing.

"Elise," Henri said, "Leave it."

"He's dead." Harry stood, his chair scraping across the floor. He took his stick and walked to the door, opening it and going out into the courtyard. Elise got up to follow him.

"Leave him alone," Henri snapped. "You shouldn't have kept on at him."

"I just want to know what happened to him."

"You should give him time, Elise. He's only just arrived. Remember what I was like when I first got back?"

"I'll go and speak to him."

"Leave him, Elise."

"I don't understand, Henri," she said.

"No, you don't.

Elise sat impatiently at the table, looking out of the window.

"What if he's gone?"

Henri didn't answer.

"I'm going to look for him," she said, getting up. Henri realised it was useless to argue with her.

"Take care, Elise," he warned as she ran from the kitchen.

She rounded the corner of the house. He wasn't on the bench. Maybe he'd left already; gone back to the village. She looked down the road, craning to see. There was no sign of him. He couldn't have got that far. She ran to the back of the house, peering through the archway. In the furthest corner of the orchard, under an apple tree, Harry was sitting on the ground, staring up into the sky through the branches. She walked up to him. He didn't notice her until she spoke.

"I'm sorry," she said. "I shouldn't have kept asking questions."

"It doesn't matter, Elise."

She sat down next to him. "I'm sorry about Edward," she said. Harry didn't reply. A pall of silence fell between them. The wind blew petals of blossom onto her skirt. "Why didn't you write to me?" She asked after a few minutes. Harry looked across at her, then down at the stump of his arm. "You could have got someone to write for you," she said.

"To say what, Elise?"

"To tell me you were still alive."

"And then what?"

"I don't know. To tell me that you still love me. You do still love me, don't you?" Harry looked at her.

"How the hell was I supposed to get someone else to write that... to write what I really wanted to say?" he murmured.

"Then you could have told me yourself. You could have come back before now, 'Arry. You promised you would."

"I couldn't. I couldn't have come before now. It was impossible." He paused. "In any case, look what a mess I've made of being back here... I'm sorry, Elise. I shouldn't have jumped to conclusions and I certainly shouldn't have said those things to you. It was stupid and childish and I had no right. If I hurt you... If I offended you, I'm truly sorry."

"Don't be sorry. I don't care about that now. I'm so happy you're here. So happy to have you back." Elise waited for a moment. "You haven't answered my question. Do you still love me? I still love you. I've never stopped loving you."

"You love me, even now?" He looked down at himself.

"Yes. I don't care about that. It's not important."

Harry managed a half-laugh. "That's just pity, not love."

"It's not pity, 'Arry."

"Elise, I can only just about dress myself and, even then, it takes me ages and exhausts me. I can only feed myself if my food is cut up first. I'm like a child. You're young and you're beautiful. You should be living your life with a man."

"Yes... you."

"I don't want you to spend your life looking after me."

"But I want to look after you," she said, leaning towards him. He pulled away from her. "'Arry, I've never forgotten what you said. You told me that you'd fracture, that you'd break if we couldn't be together."

"I know. Don't I look broken enough to you then?"

"That's not because of me, though, is it? That's because of the war."

Harry paused. "Everything's changed now, Elise. I've changed."

"I don't care."

"No, because you don't understand," he said. "I'm different."

"How? How are you different?"

"I'm no good to anyone anymore."

"'Arry, that's just on the outside," she said softly. "You've always been good in here." She touched his chest and he let her hand rest on him.

"Not any more I'm not."

"Look around you, 'Arry," she said kneeling up and gesturing around her. "Everything you can see is because of you. You did all this."

"No I didn't. You did. You and Henri."

"No, 'Arry. You made it possible."

"All I did was give you some money, Elise."

"No you didn't. You gave us hope, about the farm, about Henri and about the future. You saved us."

"Think that if you want to, but it's not true and, in any case, that was then… before."

"You're still the same man, 'Arry. Nothing has changed, not really."

"Yes it has. You're seeing things in me that aren't there. Not anymore."

"Yes they are. I know you."

Elise reached forward, resting her hand on his cheek and turning his face towards her.

"'Arry," she said, "none of it matters to me." She leant forward, lowering her face to kiss him. He closed his eyes, welcomed her lips on his. He felt the familiar softness of her tongue and met it with his own. He reached up and touched her cheek, ran his hand down her neck. He felt her fingers worming into his shirt, between the buttons and opened his eyes. He took her arm and pushed her away.

"What is it?" she asked.

"I can't…" Harry hesitated, looking down. "Don't you see? I can't touch you like I did; I can't hold you like I did… I'm not able to… I'm not able to make love to you any more, Elise. At least, not in the same way. " His voice faded.

"Is that all?"

"All? It wouldn't be the same, Elise. It can never be the same as it was."

"No, it can't. I know that." She eyed him suspiciously. "You still haven't answered my question. Do you still love me? Or is this your way of telling me that you don't?"

"Of course I still love you. That's why we can't be together."

"We have to be together. I don't care what you say. I want to be with you."

"Even if I believed you, Elise, it wouldn't work"

"Why not?" she asked, sitting back on her heels.

Harry paused, looking up into the branches above him.

"Because there's more to it than that. I've…" He paused. He wanted to tell her. He needed to tell her. She looked at him expectantly, her eyes wide. She still had that look of trusting innocence and he couldn't take that from her. "Oh, it's no good," he said. He pulled up his stick, leant on it and struggled to his feet. She stood and helped him and, for once, he didn't argue. "I'm going," he announced.

"Going where?" she asked.

"To England."

"You're going home?"

"I can't really call it home anymore, but I'm going back to England, yes."

"Why?"

"Because I shouldn't be here. I don't belong."

"But I'm here, 'Arry." He looked down at her and started to walk away. "You promised me," she called after him. "You promised that when the war was over, you'd never leave me again."

"That was then. I can't honour that promise, Elise. Not any more. I'm sorry."

"So, you lied to me."

Harry stopped, turning back. "No," he said. "I meant it when I said it. I meant all of it — every single word of it — when I said it."

"Then stay."

"I can't," he murmured.

"But I've waited so long for you," she pleaded, moving towards him.

"I can't stay. I'm sorry." He walked away again.

"So you think you can just leave me again?"

"Yes." He called over his shoulder.

"'Arry!" Elise cried, catching him up. "You can't go, it's not fair." She pulled on his sleeve. He shook himself free.

"Nothing's fair, Elise. It's about time you understood that." She stopped. He walked on. She watched him go.

The sun was setting. Harry only stumbled a few times on the way back to Lapugnoy, but that was because the road was a blur. Everything was a blur. The visit had been a failure. He hadn't been able to explain. He'd thought that he'd be able to tell her, if he saw her again. All he'd wanted to do was tell someone all of it, to describe how it had felt; what Edward's death had really meant to him. He'd believed that she'd be the right person to tell, that if he shared it all with her, she could rebuild him, just like she had before. But he couldn't do it. He couldn't take that look from her face, which he now knew would be gone forever if he told her. He couldn't risk it. He still loved her too much: he always would.

The café owner offered him a glass of wine when he got back. Harry accepted and asked the owner to take the glass up to his room, then once inside and alone, he sat on the bed. He didn't think there was a train that night but decided he would leave as soon as he was packed and stay somewhere in Bethune, if possible. If necessary, he'd sleep on the station platform, so he could catch the first train in the morning. He drank the wine.

There was still just about enough light in the room for him to pack, but he turned on the bedside lamp anyway. He put his knapsack on the bed, carrying his clothes over from the chest of drawers and fitting them in. It was a laborious process, leaving him wondering why he'd bothered to unpack in the first place. He could only manage one item at a time and he'd nearly finished when there was a knock at the door. Harry limped over and opened it. Elise looked up at him.

"Can I come in?" she asked.

Harry said nothing, but turned and walked back into the room, leaving the door open. Elise followed him and closed the door behind her. He continued with his packing.

"'Arry," she said. "I'm not going to let you leave."

She sat on the bed, right next to his bag, trying to get his attention. He ignored her.

"'Arry," she persevered. "During the war, you used to come into my life every few months. You'd make me happy; you'd make me complete; you'd make love to me and then you'd leave and I'd live in fear until you came back again. And then, that last time, everything changed. You felt it too. I know you did. When you didn't come back, I thought you were dead and it was as though I'd died too, 'Arry, because I'd lost the other half of myself. Then, today, you returned to me. I'm not giving you up again. Not without at least understanding why."

He limped back to the bed, rested his stick against it and put the last shirt into his knapsack. She took it out again, putting it on the bed.

"I'm not letting you go," she said. He looked at her, picked up the shirt and put it back into the bag. "It's not that easy," she said, removing the shirt again.

"Easy?" he shouted. "Easy?" He picked up the knapsack and hurled it across the room. "You think this has been easy?"

"No, of course not," she said, standing and running her hand up his arm. "'Arry," she continued calmly, "something is very wrong with you. What is it? Please tell me."

"I can't, Elise."

"'Arry," she whispered. "You have to tell me. Because if you don't... if you leave me again, I think we'll both break. And you can't do that to me; not again. You helped me once, 'Arry. You saved me. Can't you do it again? Can't you save us? Don't you want to?"

"I don't save people anymore, Elise." He paused, lowering his voice to a whisper. "I kill them."

"Are you talking about the war? Is this about what you did in the war? Is that it?" He didn't say anything. "Henri has told me something about the war, 'Arry. But that wasn't you, not really." He stood in silence. "You once said that loving me was the only thing that mattered. Whatever you tell me now, nothing will change." She looked up at him. "I'll still love you."

He stared down at her. Could he tell her? If he was going to, now was the time. He either had to tell her everything or leave her... right now. Telling her all of it was the only way back to her; the only way back to himself. He knew he risked losing her forever and he knew what that would do to him, what that would do to both of them; but if he didn't tell her, he was going to have to walk away and lose her anyway. He sat down on the bed, leaning forward, his elbow on his knee, his forehead resting on his hand, his eyes fixed on the floor. Could he tell her? If he did, how would she feel about him? Would she hate him? What would it do to her? She came and sat next to him. He could feel the heat of her and he longed to touch her.

"Elise," he said quietly. "You say that you love me, but you wouldn't if you really knew me. Not if you knew what I've done."

"What have you done? Tell me."

"If I do... you'll never be able to think of me in the same way again, and I'm scared, Elise. I'm scared that if I tell you, I'll lose you."

"You won't. You'll never lose me. Tell me what it is."

Harry paused. He took a deep breath. It was now, or never.

"I killed him." His voice was a whisper.

"Who did you kill?"

Now or never. If he was ever going to say it, it had to be now.

"Edward." He'd said it.

"No, you didn't kill him, 'Arry. That was the war. It wasn't your fault."

"Yes it was. It wasn't the war, Elise. It wasn't that simple. It was me."

"I don't understand," she said.

Now or never. Harry took a deep breath and the words started to tumble out incoherently: "It all happened so suddenly. We were crossing No Man's Land. I saw him get shot."

"Were you near to him?" she asked.

"No, not when he was hit. I was a little way off. I was wounded too and I fell. I dragged myself through the mud, but when I got to him, he was just lying there." Harry breathed again and felt himself calming down. "Half his face was gone. The bullet had ripped a hole in his cheek and neck. He was bleeding... not gushing blood, but it was enough to kill him… eventually." He heard her sob. "He was saying my name, over and over. Just my name, nothing else."

"He could talk?"

"Yes. His jaw was shattered, but he managed it… just. It was hard to understand him. He… he asked me if he was going to die."

"What did you say?"

"I said 'yes'. I couldn't lie to him, Elise. I could never lie to him. I told him I'd try to get him back, but he said he didn't want me to. He'd always feared being maimed or scarred and going home to face the pity and the fear." Harry stopped, thinking for a moment about Rose. He sighed. "He was bleeding to death. I held his hand. He wasn't afraid. He was quite calm. He didn't want to live like that and he didn't want to die slowly. I'd always known that. He asked me… he asked me to shoot him. He begged me to shoot him."

"Oh 'Arry! No!"

"And, I couldn't do it, Elise," Harry said, turning to look at her at last.

"Of course you couldn't, my darling." She ran her fingers down his cheek.

"I tried to make excuses. I showed him my right hand," Harry continued, gazing back down at the floor. "It was badly damaged. I said I couldn't shoot him. He told me to use my left hand. He begged me again and again. He said he tr… He said he trusted me. I couldn't do it. I knew I should – he was in so much pain and I knew it was what he wanted, but I couldn't do it. I mean, how could I? He was my best friend! If it had been anyone else, I could have done it, but not him."

"You could have killed one of your own men?" Elise asked.

"Yes, if they'd asked me to, if it was what they really wanted, to put them out of their misery. I'm sorry if that shocks you, Elise, but that's how it was. I couldn't have let any of them suffer, not like that. But Eddie was different."

There was a long silence.

"What happened next?" she asked, her voice shaking.

"I couldn't do it," Harry repeated. "It was too hard, so I turned away from him, onto my back. I felt terrible. I felt guilty, but I wanted to pretend he wasn't there. I tried to. I closed my eyes and prayed that he would die, quickly and quietly. Then I think I must have blacked out for a while."

"And was he dead when you came to?"

"No, he was still alive."

"And now you feel guilty for letting him bleed to death slowly?" She turned to him. "You feel that you should have tried harder to get him back, don't you? Even if it wasn't really what he wanted. But how could you? Your injuries, 'Arry... they're too bad." Elise paused. "Or is it that you think you should have done for him what you would have done for one of your other men? Well don't. It was too much 'Arry. No-one could have done that – not to a friend. It's inhuman. You mustn't feel guilty. Watching him die like that doesn't mean you killed him." She paused. "How long did you have to wait? Did it take a long time?"

"No." Harry said, not taking his eyes from the floor.

"Did he say anything else to you before he died?" Elise asked.

"Yes he did. A little while later, I heard him say something. It was only five words but they were the clearest words I'd heard him say. He just said, 'Do it for us, Harry.' Then he squeezed my hand. I turned onto my side again and looked at him. He was watching me," Harry whispered. "I pulled him to me. I had to use my wounded hand and it hurt so much, but I didn't care. I wanted to hold onto him, you see. I couldn't let him die alone, without holding him. He wouldn't take his eyes from mine. He wasn't afraid. I'm sure he wasn't. He just looked at me the whole time. I cried and cried, but he didn't. He just kept looking at me. I let go of his fingers and I found my gun with my left hand. I put it to his chest, Elise, right next to his heart. I told him... I told him I was sorry... and then I pulled the trigger." Harry sat still. The silence between them was so enormous, it drifted out and filled the room. "I felt him die. I felt the life drain from him, saw his eyes turn cold. I turned over onto my back and held his hand again. I wanted to die. I needed to die, right there with him. It was me, you see. Not the war. I killed him, Elise," he said. He lifted his head slowly and looked at her. He saw the expression on her face. She stared at him, her eyes filled with fear. "And now," he said, "I've killed us."

He got up and limped to the window.

"Please go," he said.

"No, 'Arry."

"Just go."

"No."

"Get out!" He yelled. He looked outside. The darkness was descending again.

"You loved him, didn't you?" Her voice seemed very small and far away.

He hesitated, staring into the distance. "Yes, I did. I think he was the only man in the world I've ever really loved, and I never told him. I lectured you about saying the words, but I never said them to him and I should have done. I would have died for him, Elise. I would have given my life for his gladly, without hesitation and I wouldn't have regretted it. I'd give my life now, right this minute, if I thought it would bring him back. I promised to protect him. I promised I'd get him home again, and I failed him."

"'Arry," she said through her tears, "You don't understand love at all. You freed him."

"No, I killed him. I'm responsible." He still didn't turn around.

"But 'Arry, you saved him, just like you've always saved everyone. You did what he asked you to do. You did what he wanted: what he needed."

"I didn't do what I'd promised though, did I? I didn't get him home."

"No, maybe not. But you didn't get yourself home either, did you? You knew that you'd always have to live with this." She wiped the tears from her cheeks. "You knew that you'd be miserable without him, that you'd feel guilty, that you'd be haunted by what you'd done to him for the rest of your life. You knew all that, and you did it anyway, because you loved him… and I think he knew knew that, 'Arry. I think that's why he asked you."

"He asked me, Elise, because I was the only person there."

"No, 'Arry, I don't think that's how it was at all. He knew you were the only one who loved him enough to do it." Harry said nothing. "Don't you see?" she said, weeping. "That's the purest love there is."

343

Finally, she broke down and in between great heaving breaths, she wept with an abandon which possessed her, took control of her and shook her whole body. Harry stood, unmoved, at the window, leaning against the frame, with his back to her. The street below was deserted. He looked up into the night sky. The moon was nearly full and the stars beamed and sparkled. There were no clouds at all.

He closed his eyes for a moment. He'd so wanted to share his secret with Elise, to tell her what he'd done, to unburden himself. He'd risked everything to tell her, but he'd risked too much. He was going to lose her. From now on he would always be haunted by two pairs of eyes: one brown, no longer innocent, no longer trusting him; one blue, ice blue... both of them killed by him. Until they could look on him with love and trust, he'd never be able to forgive himself. He breathed in and opened his eyes again. He focused on the reflection in the window pane. His hair was greying; his own eyes no longer shone; they were dull and tired. His face was pale and he looked old beyond his years. He closed his eyes again and thought of Rose, recalling the fear and uncertainty on her face. Perhaps he should go back to Cornwall, leave her with his parents, or William and Charlotte. She'd be happier with them. It might be kinder, better, even safer for her. He opened his eyes again and looked back at the reflection in the window. Then suddenly, for the first time in months, he smiled. Looking back at him, he saw a mop of wavy blond hair, a wide, nonchalant, carefree grin, and a pair of eyes. They were blue eyes. They were bright, shining, laughing blue eyes.

As the image slowly faded, Harry took a deep breath, then turned, looking across the room. Her eyes, watching him, were still drowning in tears. He walked to the bed, put his stick down and sat next to her.

"Don't cry," he said gently, caressing her hair. She caught her breath, trying to contain her sobs. He turned and, placing his arm around her, he pulled her down onto the bed. He held her close to him, feeling the familiar warmth of her body. "Don't cry, Elise," he murmured, "Everything will be alright."

She looked up at him. "How can it be? How can anything ever be alright again?"

"It will be, you'll see."

"No it won't," she said.

"Yes it will," he whispered, kissing her. "I'm here."

Epilogue

24 Woodside Terrace
Hove
Sussex

Sunday, May 20th 1923

Dear Mr Belmont,

I can't tell you how surprised I was to get your letter and I was so pleased to hear the news that you are married now, and especially that you are married to the young lady from the farm in France.

In answer to your question, I'm happy to report that I can give you a little bit more information about what happened on the night that you were captured. We succeeded in taking Pelican Trench, and we held it for a few hours. Then, the Germans pushed us back again to our original starting position, where the 9th Royal Fusiliers came up in support, and we managed to stand our ground. We had a couple of quiet days after that which gave me the chance to send out search parties during the night. They found Lieutenant Wilson's body quite quickly. They brought him back in and we had a funeral for him. The padré said a few words. The men were all very downhearted, but it was a lovely service, really, all things considered. I sent out two more search parties the next night and then went out myself, trying to find you, but with no success. We didn't know at the time what had happened to you. We only found out about it, a week or so later, when we had been relieved and were sent back behind the lines. Mr Newby announced it to the men. You should have heard the cheer that went up. Everyone brightened up a lot after that.

I don't really think that there is anything more I can tell you about that time, but if you want to write again with any questions, I will gladly try to answer them, if I can.

I didn't realise on that day, that you had recommended me for my medal, and only got notified a few weeks after you were taken prisoner. I'm not sure that I deserved it, really. Without you, Mr Belmont, we'd never even have got back that morning. And as for how you came out and helped me in that raid, sir. You risked your life for me and Mr Canter that night, and I've never forgotten that. If anything, it should have been you getting a medal, not me.

Your offer of help is very generous, Mr Belmont. However, I am getting along very well now, thank you. I was very fortunate and was able to go back to my old job and I have recently been promoted. It's nice to have a bit of responsibility again, I must say.

I really am very pleased to know that you came through it safe and well and all in one piece and will always remember my time with you very fondly, sir.

I remain very sincerely yours,

Thomas Warner.

****

Harry put the letter down on the kitchen table, next to one from John Grainger. He glanced up. Susan was standing at the sink, washing up the breakfast china.

"I think I'll go and find Rosie. I said I'd help her with her drawing," he said, picking up his stick.

"Would you like me to bring you out some coffee, Mr Belmont?" she asked.

"No thank you, Susan. Don't go to any trouble. We'll come back in shortly." He picked up his stick and went outside. Rose saw him approaching and jumped up, running across the grassy bank.

"Daddy!" she cried, holding out her sketch pad. "I've done the sea and the sky. The cliffs are alright, I think. But I can't do the boats. They keep moving."

"Alright, Rosie. Let's go and sit down and I'll help you." She turned around and walked back with him to the rug where Elise was sitting.

She looked up towards them. Harry was able to walk a little better now. His hair was still flecked with grey, but he'd regained the weight that he'd lost and looked fit and well again. She stood as they approached and helped to lower him down to the ground, then he took her hand while she settled next to him. He kissed her fingers, then looked out at the scene as Rose was trying to draw it.

"You see," she said. "Every time I start, they move again."

"Well, don't keep looking at them all the time," he told her. "Here's an idea. Watch them for a while, study them hard." She picked up the pencil again. "Wait a minute," he said. "Don't draw anything yet. Just keep looking." Harry paused. "Now," he continued, "Shut your eyes, and imagine them." He waited for a minute or two. "Have you got the image in your head?" She nodded. "Now, open your eyes and draw them." Rose took up her pencil and started to sweep it across the page, tracing the lines of the boats. "There," Harry said, looking at the page and kissing the top of her head, "That's it."

He turned to Elise, who was watching them.

"Thank you," he whispered.

"What for?" she answered, her English now much improved.

"Helping me get her back."

"You did that yourself, 'Arry."

"I couldn't have done it without you." Elise reached over and kissed his bronzed cheek. He took a deep breath, filling his lungs with air. She turned slightly and leant into him, relishing the the strength of his body against hers.

"I need you to help me again," he said, placing his arm around her shoulders.

"What do you want me to do?" she asked.

"Can you write three more letters for me?"

"Of course. Do you want to do them now?"

"No. Just some time today will be fine."

"Who are we writing to?"

"Firstly, to John Grainger."

"Oh! Has he written then?"

"Yes. He's invited us to stay for a few days," Harry replied.

"That will be nice," Elise said. "We haven't seen Lillian or little Peter for months. And the other letters? Who are they to?" she asked.

"I want to reply to Sergeant Warner," Harry replied.

"Have you received an answer to your enquiries then?"

"Yes. He's told me what happened after that night."

"Oh. And do you feel alright about it?"

"Yes, I think so."

"I still don't understand why you didn't tell him about your injuries. That makes no sense to me."

Harry turned to look at her. "I'd rather he remembered me as I was, Elise."

"Why? He wouldn't think any differently of you."

"That's just the point. I am different."

"I see," she replied, but Harry knew she didn't. "Who's the last letter to?" she enquired.

Harry stared back out to sea. "The Imperial War Graves Commission," he replied.

It was a few weeks before Harry received a reply to his letter. He read it carefully, then put it beside his plate at the breakfast table. Elise was sitting opposite him and noticed his face.

"What is it?" she asked.

"It's a reply to our letter," Harry said. "I know where Edward is buried." His voice was subdued.

"Oh." Elise came and sat next to him. "Where?"

"The Cambrai East Cemetery." He took her hand in his. "I want to go there, Elise. Will you come with me?"

"Of course."

"I want to invite Isabel as well."

"Do you think she'll come?" Elise asked.

"I don't know, but I'm going to invite her anyway."

"What about Rose?"

"I think we'll leave her with mother and father, don't you? Susan can go with her."

"Yes, I think she's too young to come with us." Elise paused. "What do you think it will be like?"

"I don't know, but I'd rather Rose didn't see it at her age. I can take her another time, when she's older."

"Come on then," said Elise, getting up. "Let's go and write to Isabel and your parents."

By the beginning of July, the weather had turned much warmer and more humid. A letter arrived from Isabel accepting Harry's invitation to visit Edward's grave and he spent several days making arrangements for the trip, which he planned for the end August. One evening after supper, with all the planning completed, he and Elise were sitting together on the sofa. A storm had been brewing and Harry was becoming anxious.

"Shall we go to bed?" Elise asked, looking at the clock.

"Not yet," Harry replied.

"Do you want to wait up until the storm has passed?"

"Would you mind?" he asked.

"Of course not." She laid down next to him, curling herself up and placing her head in his lap. With the first rumble of thunder, she felt his grip on her tighten. She turned onto her back and looked up at him. "It's alright," she said. He nodded, staring straight ahead. He jumped, as a second roll of thunder sounded overhead. She put her arms around his neck and pulled herself up to him. "Look at me," she said, reverting to French and trying to make contact with his eyes. "You're at home, 'Arry. You're with me. Rose is safely in bed. We're all here together." He nodded again, looking at her now. Despite his tan, his face had turned pale; there were small beads of sweat on his forehead and his eyes were alive with fear. She held onto him, feeling his breathing intensify, his muscles tremble and his arm tighten around her with every flash of lightening, every crack of thunder. Suddenly, with no warning, there was an enormous thunderclap. Harry screamed, buried his face in Elise's shoulder and began to shake.

"Help me," he cried. "Please help me. Make the noise stop, for God's sake. I can't bear it!"

Elise held onto him. "Hush," she soothed. "It's only thunder. It won't hurt you. I'm here and I won't let anything hurt you, my darling." Her voice was gentle and calming. She put her hands over his ears, trying to muffle the sound.

"Please make it stop," Harry muttered, looking up at her again, panic filling his eyes. "Please make it stop. No more. No more," he mouthed.

"I know, I know," she whispered, lifting one hand slightly and placing her mouth close to his ear. "Just keep looking at me. It will be over soon, I promise. Just keep looking at me." They sat staring at each other and slowly the noise abated, then vibrated into a distant echo as it passed by.

"Better?" Elise said, removing her hands from Harry's ears. He nodded, his breathing slowly calming.

"I'm sorry," he said. "I'm so sorry."

"Don't be." She paused. "You still won't tell me about it, will you?" She lowered herself back down onto his lap, looking up at him. Harry rested his arm across her waist.

"No," he replied. "I can't."

"If only Edward was still here," she said, with a note of sadness in her voice. "You could have told him."

"I wouldn't have needed to, Elise. He was there with me. He would have known and understood without me having to tell him."

"I wish you would tell me, 'Arry. It might help you," she said.

Harry leant down and kissed her. "Yes, it might, my darling. But it wouldn't help you," he whispered. "And, in any case, I love you far too much to ever tell you."

"But, no-one else knows the truth about what happened with Edward do they?" she asked.

"No. You're the only person I've ever told about that."

"Then why won't you share the rest with me? It can't be any worse than that, surely?"

"Not worse, no… just different. Elise, I nearly lost you when I told you about Eddie. I'm not going to take that chance again by telling you any more of the things I've done."

"But it was you and your love that brought me back, 'Arry."

"Yes, and it took me many painful months to do it."

"They weren't that painful... you were with me."

"They were painful for me, Elise. It hurt seeing you like that, and knowing that I was the cause."

"It can't happen again... not if you're with me. And it's hurting you now, keeping it to yourself."

"I won't risk it, Elise; never. I won't take that chance with your happiness, no matter how many times you ask me." He changed position slightly, leaning over and holding her a little closer. "Anyway," he said, "you haven't told me yet, either."

"Told you what?" Elise asked.

"About this," Harry said, running his hand across her stomach.

"You know?"

"Of course I know, Elise," he said, with a smile.

"How?"

"Because you went to the doctors weeks ago, but you weren't ill; and because I've heard you being sick quite a few times... and, in any case, I'd have to be blind, Elise. It's starting to show."

"Why haven't you said something before now?"

"Because I was waiting for you to tell me," Harry said, still smiling. "How much longer were you going to wait and why have you waited so long?"

"You've been having a lot more nightmares lately – since you found out about Edward's grave. I didn't want to trouble you."

Harry's face fell. "Trouble me?" he said. "Elise, I don't want you to ever think that you can't talk to me. Please, please don't keep things from me. I know it's all been much worse over the last few weeks, but that's to do with the war and my memories and has nothing to do with you or us. I know I sometimes seem fragile but, when it comes to you, I can cope with anything... as long as you're here with me." Harry smiled. "You should have told me before now. This is good news... and I like good news."

"Is it? I wasn't sure if you'd think so, after what happened to Bella and I didn't know how you'd feel about a baby... with all of the noise and the upheaval."

"I'm apprehensive," Harry said, quietly. "But only about you. I'm not worried about the noise or the upheaval. I've done all of that before and Susan's here to help. She'll like having a baby in the house again... and so will Rosie." He pulled Elise in closer. "And as for you... Nothing's going to happen to you because I'm not going to let you out of my sight for a single minute."

"So, it's alright then? You're pleased?" She looked up at him expectantly, her eyes glistening in the lamplight; the look he loved so much captured his heart once more and he felt himself falling into her all over again.

"I'm thrilled, my love. I don't think I've ever felt this happy." He thought for a moment. "Well, maybe once or twice..."

"Such as?"

"Such as when you first told me you loved me, under the willow tree. And then there was that morning..."

"Which morning?"

"You know which morning. The one before I left the last time. I've never forgotten that." He kissed her gently, delighting in the softness of her tongue on his. "When will she be born?" he asked eventually.

"Early in December," Elise replied and sat up. "But who said he will be a she?"

"I really don't mind either way, as long as you're both alright, but I think I'd like another daughter," Harry said. "I missed out on so much when Rosie was little."

Elise smiled, then stood up and held out her hand to him.

"Come to bed," she said, helping Harry to his feet and handing him his stick.

Elise closed the bedroom door behind them and turned to find Harry standing in front of her. He pushed her gently back against the oak panels, taking the final pace to bring his feet either side of hers. Letting his stick drop to the floor, he placed his hand behind her head and leant down.

"I love you," he murmured, but didn't give her a chance to respond, quickly covering her mouth with his. She reached out and pulled his body hard against hers; their breathing ragged. Eventually, Harry broke free and leant back.

"You invited me to bed, I seem to recall," he smiled.

"Yes. Lean on me," Elise offered and helped him towards the bed where he balanced and started to undo his shirt buttons.

"Let me do that for you," she said, standing in front of him. As she undid each button, she kissed her way down his chest and then across his stomach. She stood and helped him to turn, then sat him down on the bed. Kneeling on the floor she pulled off his socks before helping him out of the rest of his clothes. Once he was naked, she stood before him and slowly removed her own clothing, not once taking her eyes from his.

Harry took her hand and, lying back on the bed, carefully pulled her down next to him, kissing her and twisting her hair between his fingers. After an age, Elise pushed him onto his back and knelt above him.

"You're so beautiful," Harry whispered, looking up at her flushed face as he touched and caressed her with his fingertips. He felt her slow, steady descent as she surrendered to him, heard her inhale, saw her eyes close, her lips part and her head tilt backwards. She was breathing heavily now, murmuring his name as he held onto her hip, their gentle rhythm matched. He sat up, clasping her to him, drawing her downwards, closer still. He felt her legs wrap tightly around him, her hands clutching at his shoulders, clinging to him. She threw her head back, but he pulled her towards him again, kissing her and stifling their cries.

"Thank you," he breathed as she collapsed onto him, her head on his shoulder.

"No. Thank you," she whispered.

"I'm not thanking you for that," he smiled. "Although it was wonderful."

"What are you thanking me for, then?"

"For everything." Harry lay back on the bed, dragging her with him and wrapping his arm around her. "For giving me a reason to come back from the darkness. For persevering at the farm and the café all those years ago when I wanted to leave. For making me stay. For being here with me. For helping me when it all gets too much. For having my child… the list is endless, really." He looked at the ceiling and sighed. "I'm sorry, Elise. I'm so sorry you didn't feel you could tell me your news," he said, kissing her cheek. "I hope I haven't spoilt it for you."

"Of course you haven't," she replied. "'Arry," she breathed, nuzzling into him, "you never ever have to thank me, or say sorry to me."

He looked across at her, kissed her again, and murmured softly, "Yes I do… and I always will."

****

"There are so many graves," Isabel said, looking around her, tears welling in her eyes. "How can there be so many?"

"Because there were so many," Harry replied.

"I didn't realise. How will we ever find him."

"Don't worry," Harry said, remembering the references on the letter. "I'll find him." They walked forward together, Harry leaning heavily on his stick. Elise and Isabel both carried flowers and Isabel looked at the newly erected headstones, reading the names to herself. Many of them had died not long before the Armistice, some within just days.

Finally, Harry stopped. They all looked down and read:

'Lieutenant
E. S. Wilson
Royal Sussex Regiment
25th November 1917'

Harry felt a lump rising in his throat, then he heard Isabel stifle a sob, saw her raise a hand to her mouth. He moved forward and handed his stick to Elise. He put his arm around Isabel and held her to him. She cried into his chest for several minutes and he could feel her shoulders heaving and trembling beneath him. Finally, her tears subsided and she stood back, nodding her head.

"I'm alright now," she said, wiping her eyes with a small lace-fringed handkerchief. She turned and knelt on the ground, placing her flowers at the foot of the gravestone. Harry and Elise stood and watched her. She kissed the palm of her own hand and rubbed it along the lettering of his name. Then she stood and walked away, back to the car, her head bowed. Harry watched her go, then turned back. Elise sniffed and he looked down at her.

"Are you alright?" he asked.

She nodded. "I hadn't expected it to be like this."

"Neither had I." Elise handed him the flowers she had been carrying. Red roses, just coming into bloom. She supported him while he leant forward awkwardly, placing them next to Isabel's. Elise helped him straighten again then handed him his stick and they stood together. After a while, she turned around, looking at the rest of the cemetery.

"Why are those graves different?" she asked, pointing.

"I think they're German," Harry said.

"German? Why are they here?"

"I believe this was their cemetery first."

"Oh. That seems strange."

"Not really. The front lines did move occasionally, even if it didn't feel like it. Would you like to go and look?" he asked.

"Do you want to?"

"Yes, I think I do."

They walked over to the other side of the cemetery and passed along the rows of crosses. Harry read some of the names.

"Do you still hate them?" Elise asked, stopping.

"No. I never did."

"This man here?" Elise asked, looking down at the grave nearest her. "Franz Werner," she read. "He might have been the man who shot you, the man who shot Edward. If that was so, you wouldn't hate him?"

Harry turned to her. "No. It wasn't like that, Elise. We were all doing the same thing: just trying to survive. In any case, how can I hate him? I didn't know him. I never met him and he never met me. To hate someone, you have to at least know them."

As they walked back past Edward's grave, Harry stopped and turned to her.

"Would you mind if I had a few moments alone with him?" he asked.

"Of course not. I'll go and wait by the gate."

He placed his walking stick between them and touched her swollen stomach with the back of his hand. "Will you be alright by yourself?" he asked.

"Yes, I'll be fine. Take as long as you need," she said, looking up at him and stroking his chin with her fingertips. "And then come back to me."

"Of course I will. I'm not going anywhere."

She gazed into his eyes. "You know what I mean, 'Arry."

"Yes, I do. Don't worry… I mean it… I'm not going anywhere. Stay where I can see you," he said, kissing her on the forehead. "I won't be long."

"I love you," she murmured.

"I love you too… and thank you, Elise."

He waited for her to leave, then turned to look down at the gravestone. He hesitated for a moment.

"I wish you could have seen him, Eddie," he said, lowering his voice to a whisper. "He's a beautiful boy. He's got your hair and your smile… and your eyes, especially when he laughs." Harry paused. "They're both safe and well, and I'll look after them, always. I promise. Whatever happens. Whatever it takes, remember?" He paused again, looking around, trying to compose himself. "I'm sorry, Eddie" he muttered. "I'm so sorry. It shouldn't have come to this. I should have got you back. I'd have given anything… everything… to get you back; to have you here now." He bent down and placed his stick on the ground, then leant forward and picked up a handful of soil from the foot of the grave. Standing again, he put it into his pocket, closed his eyes and took a deep breath. He felt that he had a small piece of Edward to take home with him.

Harry opened his eyes again and looked around the cemetery one last time. There were too many graves, too many men, too many friends. He saw their faces clearly before him: Johnstone, Hamilton,

Ferris, Warren, Dunlop, Travis, Pilcher, Mullion, Canter… and so many more… too many more…. "We all need you." That's what Eddie had said. And what had he done? He'd abandoned them. He'd gone home and left them all behind

Then Harry looked down at Edward's grave again, nodded his head and slowly smiled, because he knew he hadn't really abandoned them at all. He knew there was a part of him that he'd left here all along to watch over them, a part that would always be with them and could never leave. He knew he'd left them with the best part of himself. He'd left them with his love… he'd left them with Edward.

Author's Note

Being as this story has its basis in historical events, I always felt it was important that, where possible, the factual elements of the story should be as accurate as possible. As such, I have endeavoured to adhere to reality as far as is reasonable - allowing for a degree of artistic licence. So, for the best part, I have used genuine locations where the 7th Battalion of the Royal Sussex Regiment actually fought during the First World War, although I have occasionally changed the dates of the battles to fit into the plot. While the story itself is fiction and I have not used real names, many of the situations are true and are based on first hand accounts, letters or diaries of those who participated. My sources and literary inspirations for this novel include:

The History of the Seventh (Service) Battalion, The Royal Sussex Regiment - An invaluable book which provided everything I needed to know about the locations in which the Battalion fought, those who participated and those who died.

The Somme by Peter Hart - An excellent book in its own right, but one to which I referred for first-hand accounts of the experiences of soldiers in the First World War. This enabled me to put my characters in real-life situations wherever possible.

Somme by Lyn MacDonald - As with all of Lyn MacDonald's books Somme provides detailed background information, interspersed with accounts of those who served. Another book which enabled me to create a sense of reality within the war scenes.

Journey's End by R C Sherriff - A play, written in 1928 about the lives of officers serving on the Western Front in 1918, based on the real-life experiences of its author. This piece, together with my knowledge of Sherriff, allowed me to glimpse the personalities and atmosphere of front-line service, especially within the dugout environment where the play is set.

Barbed Wire Disease - British and German Prisoners of War 1914-1919 by John Yarnall and Prisoners of the Kaiser by Richard Van Emden - Two books which proved useful in researching the hospital and prisoner of war elements of this story.

The War Diaries of Siegfried Sassoon, *Memoirs of a Fox Hunting Man* and *Memoirs of an Infantry Officer* by Siegfried Sassoon - Essential reading for anyone interested in the First World War. These prose accounts of Sassoon's war, while useful for their factual content, were really of more benefit for the beauty of their prose to which I, for one, can only dream of aspiring.

In addition, I have always been fascinated by the war poets whose influence can be seen, on occasion, in my writing.

Light and Darkness

The title of this novel is a reflection of Harry's journey from Light into Darkness and, to a certain extent, back again. However, it is also the title of a poem by an often overlooked poet named Edward Wyndham Tennant, written in October 1915, whose own story is more than worth mentioning.

Known to his family as "Bim", Edward Tennant was the son of Edward Priaulx Tennant and his wife Pamela (née Wyndham). He had a happy and privileged childhood and was much beloved by his mother. When the war broke out, Bim was only 17 years old, but immediately enlisted in the 4th Battalion of the Grenadier Guards and, despite her natural concern for her son, Pamela would later describe these early months of the war as being made for Bim, allowing him "freedom and self-expression, and joy". When Bim's Battalion received orders to sail for France, he required special permission to embark, as he was still underage for overseas service.

During his first month in France, Bim faced the harsh realities of war when his Captain was wounded, leaving Bim in charge of the company, at the age of eighteen. He was shocked by what he witnessed and wrote to his mother that he considered the deaths that he had witnessed to be "murder". In his letters to his mother, Bim rarely gave her any details of the war, preferring to refer to cheerful anecdotes about his comrades or childhood memories. Although he had been keen to enlist, Bim saw this as a necessity and a duty, and was by no means bloodthirsty, writing: "I think I shot a German the other day: if I did, God rest his soul." Bim served in the Battle of the Somme, the first day of which was his 19th birthday and for the next few weeks, he was in and out of the front line on a regular basis, often enduring heavy shellfire. His letters home remained stoic and full of love, but he revealed more of his own sadness, recounting the names of friends he had lost, including the Prime Minister's son, Raymond Asquith.

On 22nd September 1916, Bim was shot and killed by sniper fire. Two days later, his Commanding Officer, Lieutenant-Colonel Henry Seymour wrote to his parents explaining the circumstances of his death and the location of his grave. Seymour revealed that, despite the fact that the Battalion was due to launch another attack the following day, the men had decided to erect a cross and fence around Bim's grave prior to going back into the lines. Pamela received many letters of condolence from Bim's fellow officers and the men who served under him, all of which report him to have been an excellent and gallant officer, in spite of his extreme youth. His platoon sergeant recounted an episode that was "typical" of Bim, in which the men had been marching and, noticing that a soldier was close to collapse due to exhaustion, Bim had approached him, relieved him of his rifle and pack and had carried them for him, helping and encouraging him to continue. After Bim's death, his mother gathered together all of his letters and poems and published them in a volume simply entitled Edward Wyndham Tennant, 4th Grenadier Guards. In her dedication, she sums up her own feelings about the loss of her son, while acknowledging that she was by no means alone in her grief:

'Emboldened by the thought of Bim's spirit of good-fellowship, and recalling that his first thought is ever to share his own, I would dedicate this Memoir to all those Mothers who have suffered the same loss. They will forgive the imperfections, and all I have found good to tell of my son here, they will feel to be most true of theirs. May the Light of Comfort shine on them.'

Printed in Great Britain
by Amazon

39081171R00212